A SAGA FILLED WITH
ALL THE TRIUMPH AND TEARS,
LOVE AND HEARTACHE,
COURAGE AND HONOR
OF A PASSIONATE PEOPLE

SARA AND AVREMEL. He was to keep all his promises
to her but one—the one that said he'd never leave her. She
lost hope, and in betraying herself betrayed them all . . .

EZRA AND SONIA. The battle-scarred veteran and the
American doctor. They would find each other, then find
that love alone was not enough . . .

THIS PROMISED LAND
by GLORIA GOLDREICH

author of *LEAH'S JOURNEY* and winner of
THE NATIONAL JEWISH BOOK AWARD

Also by Gloria Goldreich

LEAH'S JOURNEY
FOUR DAYS

THIS
GLORIA GOLDREICH
PROMISED LAND

BERKLEY BOOKS, NEW YORK

THIS PROMISED LAND

A Berkley Book / published by arrangement with
the author

PRINTING HISTORY
Berkley edition / July 1982

ISBN: 0-425-05464-0

A BERKLEY BOOK ® TM 757,375

Berkley Books are published by Berkley Publishing Corporation,
200 Madison Avenue, New York, New York 10016. The name
''BERKLEY'' and the stylized ''B'' with design are trademarks
belonging to Berkley Publishing Corporation.

PRINTED IN THE UNITED STATES OF AMERICA

For the fallen sons
and daughters of my people

PART ONE

Arrival

1888

Chapter 1

It was the sudden stillness, the swift, almost imperceptible cessation of motion and sound that wakened the sleeping boy. Ezra sat up on the narrow plank bunk and looked across the deckside cabin to the porthole. The salt-streaked, smudged oval of isinglass framed streaks of coralline light threaded with delicate strands of gold. Morning was tentatively inching its way across the Mediterranean, flecking the rolling waters with dancing gemstones of aurelian brightness. The sound of the ship moving steadily forward, thrusting itself determinedly against the rushing waves of a resistant sea, had been stilled. Instead, the boy heard the whisper of the vessel at rest. He was briefly soothed as he swayed to its rhythm. The old ship was cradled gently by the rise and fall of shorebound breakers. The *Vittoria* rocked stoically from side to side like a weary, aged creature seeking respite after a long and strenuous effort. Along the deck sailors moved softly and swiftly in their rope-soled shoes. Brief expletives exploded; curt directions were shouted.

"To the left! Son of a dog!"

"*A destra.* Idiot! Pig!"

The prow was thrust violently forward and Ezra clutched

his blanket. The words of the *Sh'ma* fluttered involuntarily to his lips.

"Hear O Israel," Ezra began as the ship foundered sadly, desperately and then, in graceful resignation, regained balance. The anchor had been dropped

A new and febrile excitement seized Ezra, banishing both the prayer and the sleepy confusion he had felt on waking. They had arrived. Their journey was over. They were in Jaffa harbor.

"It is the beginning," he whispered into the half-light. "We are here and it is beginning."

He turned to his brothers, stretched out together on the wider bunk opposite him, but the twins slept on. Saul clutched the blanket with both his hands, tenacious even in sleep. David stretched his hand upward, as though reaching through his dream for a soaring ball.

"I'll catch it," he growled and Ezra smiled.

Saul and David had spent the voyage from Constantinople tossing a hand ball to each other and occasionally enticing the younger sailors or deck boys into a game of catch. Gray-bearded sages, on their way to the holy land to die, had scowled irritably at the copper-haired brothers. A thin-lipped monk in a long brown cassock glared and swept his skirts indignantly out of their path as he passed them. The two portly German businessmen who spent their days at sea leaning against the deck rails as they pored over their leatherbound business prospectuses watched them absently and smiled. They too had sons and understood the need to chase after a ball as it neatly sliced the air. The women who strolled the deck smiled at the youngsters with secret knowledge, and moved their parasols to shield their faces. At fifteen the twins stood almost six feet tall and their bodies were lithe and muscular. Their faces glowed with health and joy as they sprinted through the Mediterranean sunlight.

But Rivka Wasserman stalked her sons with maternal fury. Lines of disappointment had etched their way indelibly into the corners of her mouth. Her pale skin blossomed with mottled petals of annoyance. The twins would not listen to her. They had never listened to her. Grimly she persevered, but the boys were skillful at avoiding her. They ducked gracefully beneath the tarpaulin-covered longboats while the sailors grinned in happy complicity and the three small daughters of the French chargé d'affaires in Jaffa giggled merrily behind their lace-trimmed handkerchiefs.

Rivka Wasserman had come on board with a supply of Hebrew primers, notebooks and pencils. Her embroidered portmanteau, across which laboriously stitched purple ostriches strutted, contained novels by Mapu and Smolenskin as well as a privately printed slender volume of poems by Yosef Ben Ami. The poet had once shared a meal with the Wasserman family in their Kharkov home, and that evening had been a highlight in Rivka's life. She had thought of it as a beginning. Other writers and poets would gather around her table and sit on the low-backed velvet chairs of her living room. Books and poems would be dedicated to her. She would have a salon. But the poet's first visit had been his last, although he wrote to them occasionally.

"My dear friend Ben Ami," she called him ever afterward, on the basis of those letters, and she would display the book with his spidery signature and confide her menu—on that memorable night—sweetened meat rolled in the thinnest of cabbage leaves, golden-hearted potato pancakes, apple strudel marbled with nuts, and candied citrus rind from golden fruits grown by Jewish farmers in the holy land. Rivka had sent Ezra to the kitchen to bring out an orange so that the poet might see the miracle for himself. But in truth, Ben Ami had eaten very little. He had a weak, undersized stomach, he told them, because he had been malnourished as a boy. He patted his abdomen from time to time during the meal, as though to reassure himself that it had not vanished completely. Ezra remembered always the poet's moist and sad eyes and the way the crumbs of his soft white roll dropped from his fingers into a snowy heap as he absently shredded the soft dough.

"Israel Belkind is right," he had told Yehuda Wasserman. "Russia is a graveyard for Jews. If we stay here we shall all become corpses. Alive or dead, we shall be corpses without the breath of Jewish life."

The poet's words made the boy Ezra shiver, and sour bilious phlegm rose in his throat.

"What are corpses?" he asked his sister, Sara, that night as she covered him with the down-filled comforter.

Fearless, dark-haired Sara knew everything. She and her

friend Chaim studied thick, leather-covered books and read the closely printed journals that arrived at infrequent intervals, encased in heavy brown paper envelopes plastered with wonderfully colored stamps. The stamps were given to Ezra, and the journals were hidden beneath Sara's mattress and tucked amidst a pile of fringed ritual garments in her brothers' cupboard.

"Corpses are dead bodies," Sara said.

Her voice was steady and matter-of-fact. She would never deceive him. His mother offered him whimsical stories or attempted to divert him. Babies, Rivka had told him, grew beneath toadstools in the czar's woodlands. Itzik, his classmate who had, as every boy in the class knew, died of pneumonia, had, according to his mother, left Kharkov to play in a land of eternal sunshine. No, he could not rely on his mother. It was to Sara he came for the truth.

"I don't want to die," he said then. Fear swept over him in an engulfing wave. He clutched the counterpane and swam upstream against it, steadfastly, desperately. He did not want to cry. He did not want to vomit. The twins would taunt him with the careless cruelty of elder siblings and his mother would stand in the narrow doorway twisting her long silken handkerchief into elaborate knots.

"He's so sensitive," Rivka would say sadly, proudly.

But Sara only laughed and patted him lightly.

"Of course you won't die, silly boy. Poets just talk that way. Besides, Russia is changing. Chaim says that all this hatred of the Jews and the pogroms come from the czar and the aristocracy. The poor peasant needs someone to blame for his poverty and ignorance. When we live in a better society, when everything is shared, they won't need a scapegoat and the Jews will be safe here. The Jews will work with the Russian proletariat to build a wonderful new society. Chaim knows. He knows everything." She smiled into the darkness, and a gemlike glint ignited her green eyes.

Ezra had watched his sister that night and felt a sharp, an almost angry jealousy for the tall, bespectacled Chaim whom the twins called Sara's shadow. ("Did you ever see a shadow with glasses, David?" "Only the one called Chaim, Saul.") But even the irrepressible twins had not teased Sara the morning of their departure from Kharkov. Their sister's green eyes were glazed like sea glass and brimmed with tears that spilled down her rose-gold cheeks.

"I don't want to go without Chaim," she had intoned piteously again and again.

Yehuda Wasserman, who was lashing together a straw hamper bulging with the family's linens, had paused in his work, the long rope lank in his hands.

"Let him come with us then. I'll pay for his passage," he said.

"You'll pay. Money. You think everything can be solved with money." Sara's voice burned with bitterness. "Chaim doesn't want to come. He doesn't think Palestine is the answer. He sees problems that go beyond the Jewish problem. Human problems. He believes that the future is here in Russia. We must care about others besides ourselves."

"Good luck to him then."

Yehuda turned back to his work. His fingers formed intricate knots, elaborate loops, and he observed them wonderingly, as though he had discovered a secret talent, unearthed a dormant legacy. Perhaps his ancestors in Egypt had formed such knots before their exodus. Or his grandfather, who had packed his belongings to come to Russia from Lithuania. Or his great-grandfather, who had traveled eastward from Germany. No. It was time that the generational odysseys were completed. He, at least, was packing to go home—to a Jewish homeland, the Jewish homeland. Soon it would happen and he would be there. He turned back to his daughter.

"Let Chaim do as he pleases. You are not his wife. You are my daughter. You come with me."

Dutifully Sara had come, and after the second day at sea she no longer wept but sat on deck in a canvas-covered chair, never facing the prow, but staring always into the winding path of foam which the *Vittoria* ruthlessly left in its wake. No matter how early Ezra reached the deck, Sara was always there, her dark braids neatly twisted into a shining coronet, staring backward, huddled into the scarlet wool shawl which she did not remove, even when the sun beat down on them at high noon. The shawl had been a gift from Chaim, a last gift, a leaving gift.

Surely Sara would be on deck now, Ezra thought, and he slipped quickly out of his bunk and plunged his feet into the black pumps his mother had bought him the day before they left. "In the wilderness there are no shoe stores," she had muttered, and it was the first time he realized that his mother had hesitations about the new land to which they were migrating. He was glad now that Rivka had insisted that her children sleep fully clothed during the journey. She feared nocturnal disaster, a fierce storm that would send them rushing for the longboats, pirates who would force them to eat pork and work on the Sabbath. But no matter, her children would be ready, and so each night of the voyage they dressed for the next day. Their sleep-wrinkled clothing was clean and still smelled of the early blooming lilacs that rimmed the Kharkov garden where they had last been laundered.

Ezra tiptoed out of the cabin but his sleeping brothers did not stir. Hurrying now, he rushed onto the deck. He and his sister would see their new land for the first time together. And if Sara cried, if the memory of lanky Chaim caused her to moan and finger the fringes of her shawl, he would put his arm around her and coax her to gaze toward shore where surely oranges and lemons dangled in golden roundness from branches thick with leaf and blossom.

"Sara!" he called into the rosy light of dawn, but there was no one on deck except a group of sailors who squatted on the newly scrubbed boards and ate flat round pieces of bread.

"Here boy. Eat some. Still hot. Good. Very good." Giorgio, a tall mustachioed sailor with whom Ezra had once played a secret game of quoits while his mother slept, held out the bread and pointed to the side rail.

An ancient skiff drifted alongside the *Vittoria* and an aged Arab, toothless, wearing an oversized western suit and a checked red and white *kaffiyeh,* smiled obsequiously, bowed, and brandished a basket of the flat bread. Its newly baked fragrance mingled with the sea air, and to demonstrate its softness, the old man popped a piece into his mouth and showed Ezra how the white flesh of the bread clung to his soft pink gums.

"Buy from me. Cheapest here," he pleaded and pointed to the laden gray sacks of *pita* in his boat as though Ezra was his only hope of a sale that day.

Ezra turned away and lifted his eyes to the shoreline, keeping them half-closed as he often did in synagogue when the ark was opened and just before the Torah in its crimson velvet covering and its shining silver ornaments was revealed to him. It was as though he feared that the holy radiance would blind him. A visitor, newly returned from a pilgrimage to Palestine, had shared their Sabbath meal once and spoken of oranges that burned bright upon graceful trees. Like tiny balls of sun they were, warm to the touch, sweet upon the tongue. The leaves of the olive tree, he had continued, were like slender flakes of silver. It was a luminescent land that had been promised them, burning with God's own brightness. Ezra did not want to be stunned by its blazing beauty.

But when he opened his eyes, it was a blackened reef that he first saw. Huge, oddly sculptured rocks, great clumsy boulders, and coal-colored crags guarded the shoals. Any large ship that veered too close to the death-stained barrier would be pierced by their hidden foundations. Concealed ore in their black surfaces shimmered in the bright light of dawn, and silvery micaceous veins glinted in teasing promise. The waters between the rock barrier and the beach were a pool of clear emerald green and the boy, who had lived always on the edge of Russia's dark woodlands, gasped with pleasure at the color. He had thought to see fruits of burning gold and had found, instead, a waterway of cool green. Laughter stirred within him and sudden, unfamiliar joy. He had never seen anything as beautiful as the stretch of sea that ended at the pebbled beach. The port waters of his new land were a magic grotto, beckoning him, welcoming him.

Courageous now, he lifted his eyes to the coast. Jaffa rose before him in graceful incline. Low-bowed boats, their brightly colored sails billowing against the gentle wind, drifted about the harbor. A scarlet-spinnakered dinghy flirted with an ancient ketch. He saw a row of buildings and even in the distance noted their graceful arched doorways and the gray pallor of their stony surfaces. In the distance, above them, a steepled building stood, and from its tower a bright light glimmered briefly. As the boy watched, it was extinguished. The priest had neglected his matutinal duties and allowed the church beacon to compete with the brightness of the rapidly rising sun.

Along the hillside ancient evergreens, thick with piny growth, cast long shadows, but where no trees grew the earth was brutally barren. He turned to the huddle of low-roofed buildings which surely was the city itself, nestled along a tier of uneven streets and ending again in a vast emptiness that stretched upward to a walled enclave over which the scarlet and gold banner of the Ottoman Empire fluttered. Along the slope of the low mount, isolated houses stood, low-built stone structures that crouched in the skinny shadow of a single tree. The surrounding hillsides were rock-encrusted buttresses, covered with dry patches of earth that changed color abruptly in descent, assuming a new dark richness. Groves of olive trees bent their silvery crowns low, as though seeking their shadows in the barren earth, but here and there, where the hill soil had been cultivated, it was dark and fertile.

Even from the distance, Ezra saw the dark fecundity of the earth's promise. He wanted his sister, Sara, to stand beside him and tell him why his heart felt so full and why tears burned behind his eyes. They were not, he knew, tears of sadness. They were like the tears that seared his eyes with the first brilliant flash of starlight as the Day of Atonement drew to a close, or the tears he felt sometimes on a Sabbath evening when he arrived home from the synagogue with his father and brothers and saw his mother and Sara seated at the festive table, the candlelight dancing in their eyes. Prayers fluttered to his lips at such times, prayers that glorified the sadness. "Blessed art Thou, O Lord our God, who hath sanctified us and sustained us and led us forth unto this happy day."

But no prayer came now as he stood on the deck of the *Vittoria* and looked across the bay at Jaffa harbor. He saw now that the leaves of the olive trees did shimmer like thin petals of silver in the sunlight. A poem leapt at him, half-remembered.

> "I have not yet sung to you, my land
> Nor have I known your beauty . . ."

It was a poem written by a woman pioneer, and he knew the words in Yiddish, Russian, and Hebrew. Softly, he recited it in all three languages and then felt in his pocket for a kopeck, which he threw down to the Arab who tossed him a pita in return. The dough was still warm, and he ate it slowly, rolling the warm pellets around in his mouth. Then he ran off to find his sister.

"Sara," he called. "We're here. It's beginning."

Chapter 2

Yehuda Wasserman wakened as the anchor dropped. He felt the *Vittoria* lurch uneasily and heard the splash as the huge metal weight struck the struggling waters and sank toward the ocean floor. Slowly, careful as always not to disturb Rivka, he slid down from his bunk and struggled into his boots, always damp and clammy in the seabound morning. The water in the bowl on the metal washstand was ice cold but he washed carefully, passing the cloth across his face and neck. He held Sara's small hand mirror and combed his hair, pausing before he pulled the comb through his beard. Two white hairs straggled within the soft mass of facial hair, and he plucked them out as though angry at their effrontery. He was not yet forty and too young for gray hairs. His father's beard was still dark in places. They were a long-lived family whose hair grew thick and dark through their middle years. His mother had given birth to his youngest brother on her forty-second birthday, and at the circumcision party his father had danced a wild hora, balancing an empty wine bottle on his head. Even now his father, although plagued by illness and disappointment, still took his turn drawing the water for the men's ritual bath each Friday. His father, the pious and righteous Reb Shimon.

Yehuda slammed the mirror down and Rivka stirred uneasily at the sound but did not awaken. He was relieved. She was tired, and he was glad to see her sleep. The voyage had been difficult for her and the leave-taking in Russia painfully wrenching. Rivka's father had wept openly, piteously. Her mother had swayed dangerously, and Rivka herself had moaned and rocked her aged parents in her arms. In the end Yehuda had had to pry his wife away from her parents. Poor Mother-in-law. Poor Father-in-law. Poor, poor Rivka. His heart turned for them but there had been no choice. Rivka lay curled up in her bunk like a small child. Her hands were clasped in sleep, and a trickle of saliva formed a foamy tear at the corner of her mouth.

She was an only child, born when her parents were resigned to thinking of themselves as childless. They had coddled and cosseted their pretty little girl, their wondrous gift. Her father, a prosperous grain merchant, had added a new wing onto his house, already the largest home in the town, when his daughter was born. Rivka's first birthday had been celebrated with a musicale. The church organist gave a concert on the newly installed Bechstein, and when the little girl was older he came each week to the Glauberman house to give her piano lessons. The rabbi and the Talmud scholars muttered darkly into their beards. No good came of consorting with *goyim* like that.

When she was five a tutor was brought to the house, and the little girl learned to read and write and do sums. She was a pretty child with pale delicate skin and thin fair hair that curled around her shoulders. The other girls wore their hair in neatly braided plaits but Rivka's hair flowed loose, and in the spring her mother crowned her with wreaths woven of wild flowers in the Russian fashion. She learned Hebrew too, and not only the prayer-book Hebrew which would be useful in the women's section of the synagogue, but the modern Hebrew of the newly enlightened Hebraists whom the rabbis scornfully dismissed as atheistic *maskilim*, intellectuals who pursued secular studies. Her tutor was a tall, handsome youth who had studied in Odessa. He had been hired not only to teach Rivka but to engage in Zionist dialogue with her father, the grain broker.

"And what do you think of Zvi Hirsch Kalisher?" her

father would ask, leaning back on his full-cushioned easy chair. Nuggets of barley nestled beneath his fingernails, and his daughter sat at his feet. Sometimes he passed his hands across her silken hair or stroked the pale flesh of her thin arm.

"He has a point."

The student was cautious. He liked his job. He liked reading Mapu to pretty, credulous Rivka. "In the land of Israel, sun-bronzed farmers carry a hoe in one hand and a rifle in the other. They toast life with wine grown from the grapes of their vineyards. Men and women dance barefoot in the harvest season and listen to nightingales in the citrus groves." Rivka listened with moist lips and wide eyes. Her small breasts swelled within the delicate bodices that were hand-embroidered by a Kharkov seamstress. The turquoise-blue thread matched her eyes.

The grain broker listened with furrowed brow and pondered the problems of the agricultural collectives as though he alone were responsible for Jewish settlement in the holy land. One day he came to the schoolroom to ask the tutor for further clarification of a question and found the tall, handsome youth whispering verses from "The Song of Songs" into Rivka's ear, his hand tucked inside her pale blue blouse. "Come with me from Lebanon, my sister, my bride." Rivka's eyes glowed and her breath came in short gasps. Within days the tutor was in Constantinople awaiting passage to Palestine, and the grain merchant was in the study hall asking the rabbi for the names of the most promising among the marriageable boys in the town. Who were the brightest and the quickest, with the greatest affinity for talmudic study? It had not escaped the grain merchant's notice that the best Talmud students made the best businessmen.

It was Yehuda Wasserman's name that was reluctantly offered. Yehuda, the rabbi acknowledged, was the brightest of his students but he had, alas, fallen from the path of the righteous. How fallen? Rivka's father, the enlightened man who held concerts in his parlor, was intrigued. Did the boy profane the Sabbath, eat pork, consort with goyim? The rabbi shuddered in horror. Thank God, no. After all, Yehuda was the son of the learned and devout Reb Shimon. But he had abandoned the study of the sacred books and aspired to enter a school of medicine. He was enrolled now in the Kharkov gymnasium.

The grain merchant asked about other students but immediately forgot their names. Rivka, his treasure, was young yet. Fifteen. A child. A baby. And so fragile and delicate. Sometimes when she spoke, her voice was so low her father had to strain to hear it. He listened as she moved through his large house. Her light footsteps fell like flower petals across the thick carpets. She sang, and he trembled at the sweetness of her voice. There was time.

On her sixteenth birthday he sent her to visit his brother in Odessa and there, at a meeting of the Chovevei Zion—the Lovers of Zion—to which her young cousin took her, she met a boy from Kharkov, a neighbor whom she had never known. Tall Yehuda Wasserman, whose soft, dark beard was flecked with flaming lights and whose green eyes were the color of quiet forest pools, touched her fingers and told her that he had often seen her walk through the Kharkov streets with her mother and he knew exactly where she sat in the women's section of the synagogue.

"In the middle of the third row," he said. "On the second day of Passover you wore a lemon-colored ribbon that almost matched your hair."

They traveled back to Kharkov together, and that night she visited her father in his study. She ran her fingers through his thinning hair, kissed his ear, and translated the passage of Rabbi Har Alkilai in "The Redemption of Zion" with which he was struggling. And then, as the candle burned low and sputtered, she took his hand in hers and told him that she wanted to marry Yehuda Wasserman.

"The medical student?" He had not forgotten the name.

"He is still studying. He has not yet been admitted to the school of medicine."

"Let us wait. It is always best to wait."

A year passed. Yehuda won a gold medal at the gymnasium but he was not admitted to the university. Too many Jewish students had applied that year. The son of a man who tipped the Russian examiner took the Jewish place.

"Come with me to America, to New York," Yehuda's brother, Mendel, urged while in the next room, Reb Shimon, their father, chanted a talmudic tractate and their mother wept softly.

"Why? To go from being a Jew in Russia to being a Jew in

America? There is no point. I want to go to a land that will be mine—my own.''

"Rivka's been reading too much Smolenskin to you," Mendel laughed harshly. He did not like the pale girl, the rich man's daughter, who trailed after his brother. One had to strain to hear her voice, and when she talked her thin hands fanned the air like aimless butterflies.

"Rivka's ideas on Zionism and mine are completely different," Yehuda had replied curtly.

It was true that the two of them shared the love of the Hebrew language so newly revived and molded to their diurnal needs. Daily they committed new words to memory. Avidly they read copies of the *Havatzelet*, the Hebrew-language newspaper passed from hand to hand among the Zionists and Hebraists of Kharkov. And it was true too that both of them talked of living in Palestine and building a Jewish homeland. But for Rivka, Palestine was the land of the Bible, the legendary heritage of Abraham, flowing with milk and honey. She dreamed of tall, swaying palm trees and a sapphire-blue Mediterranean. Her imagined desert was pearly white, and if she grew thirsty crossing it, handsome dragomen would find her streams of flowing waters and lead her to the shade of an oasis bowered by date palms. She fondled the oranges and the lemons that sold for astronomic prices in the Kharkov market and envisioned them growing in profusion, tended by sunbronzed warrior farmers. The tutor who had softly whispered romanticized Zionist tales while his long fingers fondled her breasts had done his work well. She was the poet's Zionist maiden, longing to move through the coolness of Galilean vineyards and to feel the sweet desert sun on her bare arms. She embraced shadowy figures as she thought of Zion. Sometimes Yehuda Wasserman danced into her arms, and sometimes it was the tall young tutor whose face she could not clearly remember.

But Yehuda Wasserman knew that the heat of the desert would be fierce and burning and that the promised land was bounded by unyielding rock and sand. He did not expect sweet waters. He anticipated foul-smelling swamps where mosquitoes bred disease. Twice he had traveled to Odessa for the funerals of young pioneers newly returned from Rivka's golden land. Skeletal, empty-eyed, they had come home to die of malaria. Yehuda Wasserman did not read the Hebrew novelists and poets. He read Pinsker and Hess and Ben Yehuda.

When he married Rivka, a copy of Pinsker's *Auto-Emancipation* rested in his pocket next to the slender book of marriage prayers his mother had given him. The marriage prayers included pleas for fertility. Yehuda Wasserman prayed fervently. He wanted a large family, sons and daughters. He wanted them to grow up as Jews in a Jewish homeland. He did not want them denied admission to university because of an accident of birth. He was resigned to the fact that he himself would not be a doctor. He would be, for the time being, a grain merchant.

Rivka's father welcomed him into the business and built the young couple a house. Yehuda worked hard and studied and thought deep into the night. Sara was born and then the twins. Rivka recited poetry over their cribs, played sonatas on the Bechstein for them as they crawled and toddled across the living room floor. Her children would grow up to love culture, to know music and poetry. She read the Bible to them in Hebrew, carefully enunciating each word. Sara listened wide-eyed. The twins chortled joyously and played hide-and-seek with each other.

Yehuda sometimes traveled to meetings of Chovevei Zion and returned thin-lipped and frowning. There was too much talk of self-sacrifice and a new social order, but no real planning. He subscribed to agronomy journals and ordered textbooks from California on the cultivation of citrus crops. His brother, Mendel, forwarded publications from the School of Agriculture at Cornell University. Gradually, Yehuda stopped going to Zionist meetings although Zionist leaders and visitors from Palestine were always welcome in his home.

Rivka taught a class in conversational Hebrew to a group of young girls. After Ezra's birth she was mildly depressed, and her father took her to the curative waters in Germany and then to Paris. He bought damask cloths for her table and cut glass decanters for her sideboard. She covered her volumes of Smolenskin in maroon-tooled leather.

"We are Zionists," she told her friends, "dedicated to the idea of a Jewish homeland."

Yehuda wrote checks to Chovevei Zion and made donations to the Bilu pioneers. Rivka bought oranges from Palestine when they appeared in the market and sent parcels of clothing to a yeshiva in Hebron.

Their floors were covered with deep carpets and an ornate *mizrach* hung on the eastern wall of their dining room, a framed petit point sampler showing two doves bearing an olive branch. The mizrach was a pictorial reminder of Jerusalem. Each Friday evening when Yehuda recited the *Kiddush*, the family faced Zion and looked at it. Rivka saw the sundrenched land of her dreams, where blood-red anemones ran wild through grassy meadowlands. Yehuda saw the parched unyielding soil which, with proper planning and agonizing work, a Jew might make his own.

Sara passed mysteriously through girlhood and talked for hours with her friend Chaim, walking the same forest pathways Yehuda and Rivka had trod. The twins ran barefoot through springtime fields, played truant from their yeshiva studies, and laughed when their mother scolded them. Small Ezra told himself stories and read until the Sabbath candles burned in a gutted blue flame of defeat. Rivka's parents grew old and frail. And then one afternoon, when the white cloth on the polished wood dining room table was bathed in the violet light of the dying sun, Yehuda Wasserman sat down opposite his wife, who was reading a slender French novel.

"The time is right," he said. "There is enough money now to do it the right way. There is a farm in Rishon LeZion I have heard about, and I know enough to make it a success. We must plan carefully, Rivka. We are going to Palestine."

She had not protested. How could she? After all, she had for years sung Zionist verses, accompanying herself on the piano. She had sung of the dew sparkling on Mount Hermon and of the irridescence of the river Jordan. Now at last, she would see the dew falling like pearls on Mount Hermon and trail her fingers through the Jordan's shining waters. She did not protest.

She moved very slowly through the spacious rooms of her Kharkov home deciding what they would take and what they would sell. She packed her linens carefully in large cases and straw hampers, calked against moisture and mildew. She folded her pillow slips and was startled to see that their embroidered edges were damp. She was crying. Her fears and unhappiness surprised her. This was what she wanted, what she had wanted since the handsome young tutor had sung

softly to her of the vale of Sharon and the narrow roads that
lead to Jerusalem. She remembered now how his hair fell in
copper-colored ringlets and how his breath had always smelled
sweetly of the parsley which he crunched between startlingly
white, small teeth. He had left for Palestine almost eighteen
years ago. Would she see him there? Had he changed? Had
she changed?

Abruptly she rose and drew the heavy bedroom draperies.
She undressed quickly and studied herself in the long bedroom mirror. Thin lines streaked her abdomen, which had
been stretched by her pregnancies. But her thighs were firm
and her breasts were full and as gently molded as they had
been when Ephraim, the tutor, had touched them, oh so
gently, as they walked through the apple orchard. She was
glad now that she had not nursed the children. She was a
young woman still, a young woman about to start a new life.
Slowly she turned before the mirror and passed her hands
across her body in a reassuring caress, and then quickly she
dressed again and returned to her packing. That night, for the
first time since Yehuda had announced his decision, she
played the piano and sang in her high sweet voice.

> "Come with me from Lebanon
> Oh my sister, Oh my bride."

Still, the leave-taking had been difficult. Her parents had
traveled with them to Odessa, and twice during the train
journey the grain merchant had leaned forward to trace his
daughter's features with his fingers. Her mother clutched her
hand and whispered urgent admonitions. The children must
be kept safe from missionaries. It was known that Jewish
children in the holy land were often the victims of missionaries.
And Rivka must never stay alone in a room with an Arab; the
men had strange desires. This her mother whispered furtively
and then blushed deeply, her withered skin turning the color
of a wounded pomegranate. A husband must be found for
Sara. The girl was mature for her age, capable of deep
feeling. Then the advice stopped and tears began.

At quayside Yehuda himself had clutched the grain merchant's frail shoulders. The old man was ill. Cataracts veiled
his vision. His fingers were twisted into arthritic knots. He
was selling his business.

"Come with us, Father-in-law," Yehuda pleaded. "Or at least plan to visit us soon."

The old man shook his head wearily. He moved with the lassitude of the old and the ill. But he did not complain. He was a shrewd businessman. He knew how to judge his profits and how to compensate for his losses. He had thought himself doomed to childlessness and he had fathered a child. He had thought to leave his large business to charity and he had four grandchildren who would be his heirs. All his life he had dreamed of Zion and one day a descendant born there would carry his name. He had, against all odds, come out ahead, and Yehuda, his son-in-law, a prudent man of business, would also succeed. He did not regret the match. He did not regret this journey.

Still, as the ship's horn blared its urgent summons, sorrow suffocated him. His breath came in shallow gasps and his chest heaved with sobs he could not contain. She was leaving him, his darling, his baby. She was sailing away from him to a land where strong men died of malaria and women were raped by marauding Arabs. His Rivka. He wept. His tears stained one handkerchief and then another. Rivka's mother trembled, and she swayed from side to side as though lost in prayer.

"God who has mercy on travelers and wayfarers, protect them," she said and leaned toward her daughter, her hand extended like the tenacious claw of a bird who will not release a fledgling. Spittle rimmed her lips and tears streaked her mottled cheeks.

Rivka cupped her mother's small lined face in her hands. She drew both her parents to her in a soothing embrace, rocking them against the strength of her body. She enveloped them, the frail, aged man and woman she might never see again, in the folds of her dark traveling cape.

"Mama. Papa," she moaned.

Again the imperious horn sounded. The captain shouted harshly, impatiently, and an officer spoke to Yehuda Wasserman in an urgent tone. One by one, Sara, the twins, and finally Ezra kissed the old couple who now seemed like bewildered children in their grief and loss. Finally Yehuda Wasserman firmly loosened his wife's grip and wrenched her away from her parents.

"Come, Rivka," he said, and his fingers were strong and tight about her arm. He pulled her forward and held her in the strength of his grasp while he himself turned to the grain merchant and his wife, mouthing a farewell, pleading forgiveness.

"Go in peace," Rivka's father had said at last through his tears, but her mother had looked at him with the startled, uncomprehending gaze of the newly bereft.

Rivka was not a good traveler. She had been ill during most of the journey to Constantinople, and during the first two days on the *Vittoria* she had gone on deck only to pursue the twins. Yehuda smiled ruefully as he thought of his elder sons. Rivka persisted in her efforts to imbue the boys with a love for poetry and music,

"You must listen to this," she would command them and proceed to read a long epic poem from a literary journal, never noticing that the twins had furtively left the room or disappeared from beside her deck chair.

Yehuda himself had few illusions about his sons. Still, they were good boys and he had no doubt that they would love the life in Palestine. They loved the outdoors and would be much happier in orchard and field than they had ever been in the study hall. And one thing was certain. Saul and David were strong enough. It was Ezra's health that worried him. The boy was always getting colds and coughs. In the summer he ran mysterious fevers, and often he lost his appetite and reclined weakly on his bed. Rivka cooked special food for him and brewed herb teas. She urged him to sit in the sun or near the warmth of the stove. Sara sat with her brother and read to him. She brought him extra covering and warm socks. Still a weakness pursued him, and his blue veins shone translucently through pale skin. But the boy's mind was strong, Yehuda knew. Ezra read omnivorously and questioned everything he read. The head of the yeshiva had shaken his head ruefully when he spoke of the boy.

"He's a brilliant student, Yehuda. But he studies like you. He questions, he doubts, he wants to understand that which cannot be understood. You're getting paid back, Yehuda Wasserman. Ezra will do to you what you did to your father, Reb Shimon."

"So be it."

Yehuda had not been disturbed. He was not Reb Shimon. If Ezra wanted to study medicine he would not oppose it. The boy could study law or even literature. He could go to

university in Europe or even in the United States. In the city
of New York, his brother Mendel had written, there was a
university which did not demand tuition fees and which admitted Jews without question. Or perhaps by the time Ezra was
ready for university there would be such an institution in
Palestine, in Jerusalem. Yehuda had heard it proposed at a
meeting in Israel Belkind's flat, a Zionist meeting at which
words and ideas hung as heavy in the air as the thick smoke
of cigars and pipes and the cigarettes rolled in thin strips of
brown paper.

"A Hebrew University," Belkind had said. "In Jerusalem,
where all courses will be taught in Hebrew."

Someone had laughed harshly then but Yehuda Wasserman
had not turned around. He saw no absurdity in the concept.
All things were possible in the land that they would build if
there was proper planning, proper organization. All things.
He included in his accounting death and disease, bankruptcy
and despair. Like his father-in-law, the grain merchant, he
was a businessman who faced realistic forecasts and kept
proper accounts. It was not improbable that Ezra might one
day study at a university not yet built in a land Yehuda had
not yet seen.

The *Vittoria*, held at anchor, swayed gently from side to
side. Seagulls screeched and the faint sound of ringing church
bells reminded him of Kharkov on a Sunday morning. Asleep
on the narrow bunk, Rivka smiled as though a pleasant
memory had wafted toward her in a dream. Perhaps in her
sleep, she too heard the bells and imagined herself home in
their high-ceilinged bedroom, waiting for the back door to
slam as their serving girl left for early matins. Her lips moved
and she spoke softly.

"Yes, Papa, I'm coming," his sleeping wife, the grain
merchant's only daughter, said.

Yehuda Wasserman drew the blanket up around her shoulders and walked softly out of the cabin. In the narrow below-
deck passage he saw the bright circlet of sunlight glinting
down from the hatch, and he ran to climb the rope ladder. His
heart pounded wildly as he hoisted himself up on deck and
looked past the red-streaked black rocks to the shoreline,
ablaze now with the first strong light of full morning.

Facing the shore at last, he saw the thick green arms of the
evergreens soar upward in the mild breeze; he saw the dried

earth of the parched hillsides; he saw the pebbled beach glinting with raddled secrets. Tears seared his eyes, and he squeezed them shut and opened them again to the blinding brightness of the sunswept harbor.

"I am here," he said to himself and was surprised at the huskiness of his voice. He thought to say a prayer. He was, after all, Reb Shimon's son. He fixed his gaze on a single cypress, concentrating on the distant tree just as his father often concentrated in prayer on a single flickering flame or a lone flower in the cut glass vase that adorned the Sabbath table.

"Blessed art Thou, O Lord our God," he said, "Who has guided us and preserved us and brought us to this happy day."

That at least would have pleased his father, he thought as he walked the sunstreaked deck, remembering the day he had told Reb Shimon that he would soon be leaving for Palestine, he and Rivka and the children.

He had delayed telling his father of his decision until the steamship tickets were purchased and concealed beneath the embroidered tea towels in Rivka's linen drawer and until he had packed the first barrel of kitchen utensils. Even then he had chosen a late afternoon hour, knowing that the call to evening worship would bring their conversation to a swift conclusion. Always, Yehuda Wasserman had dealt in such a way with his father. He had already applied and received assurance of his admission to the Kharkov gymnasium when he told his father of his decision to withdraw from the yeshiva. He and Rivka had already agreed on a marriage date when he informed Reb Shimon of their betrothal.

He knew himself to be no match for his father's zeal, for the deep religious conviction that governed the old man's life and actions. He had ideas and ideals, but his father had faith and belief, against which his son's intellectual weapons were frangible and ineffectual. Yehuda had learned early that it was pointless to argue with his father. He presented him always with a *fait accompli,* and he would not be dissuaded either by love or by fear. Yet he was nervous as he approached the study house at the end of a hidden lane where his father spent his days and nights. A small angry welt formed at his neck and his palms were damp and cold.

Dusk hovered over the narrow room and draped the seated

men in gossamer shadows. The bearded scholars in their frayed black caftans swayed from side to side in the half darkness. Only after evening prayers would the paraffin lamps be lit. Now they peered at the words in the columns of their open tomes with the intense gaze of lovers who spy upon each other in a shadowed dawn. A dozen dissonant chants created an odd harmony as they intoned the text on the pages of the heavy volumes.

"If two men find a single goat—to whom does it belong?" Reb Shimon sang the legal query as though it were a prayer, a song of faith. "To whom does it belong?" he repeated, and Yehuda approached his bench and noticed that a white thread wept across the shoulder of Reb Shimon's robe. He thought to pluck it off but instead he sat down opposite his father, who reluctantly looked up from the text and met the gaze of his son. The men around them continued to chant, to offer explanations and commentaries to each other. "Rashi says . . ." "Maimonides maintains . . ."

"I've come to say goodbye," Yehuda said. "At least to tell you that we will soon be leaving." He stretched his open palm toward his father, and the last of the dying light splayed across it in luminescent wands.

The old man stood and together they moved to the doorway. A strong man all his life, Reb Shimon had recently been ill. He would not see a doctor. A nodule, the size of a walnut, bulged at his neck. His urine was stained with blood. His children were vanishing. With whispered voice and cushioned step they drifted out of his life. His son Mendel had gone to America and lived in the great city of New York where buildings as falsely proud as the Tower of Babel swept the sky. Mendel sent back snapshots of himself, clean-shaven and wearing the clothing of the goyim. He had married an American girl, a Jewish girl, but in their wedding photograph her unshorn hair streamed loose about her shoulders, her arms were bare, and her hand rested carelessly on Mendel's arm. Mendel sent money too, crisp sheets of currency as green as the leaves of early spring, wrapped in business letterhead that proclaimed Martin Wasser to be a manufacturing furrier. It took Reb Shimon a while to realize that Martin Wasser was his son, Mendel Wasserman. He ran his fingers across the raised lettering of the address and concealed the dollars between the pages of a heavy tractate.

His daughter, Haline, had married a scholar who took her to Argentina, where the talmudic tomes were abandoned for the dull sheen of uncut gems. A visitor brought Reb Shimon a rough, ugly green stone. It was an emerald and could be converted into passage money to South America, to New York, to Berlin.

"I study in Kharkov," Reb Shimon said and he wrapped the jewel in cotton wool and hid it in his wooden citron case.

Reb Shimon's wife and Ezra, his youngest son, for whom Yehuda had named his own lastborn, had died years before in a diphtheria epidemic. No Russian doctor would come to treat the Jewish sick, and their own physician was himself in the throes of the fever. Death beckoned Reb Shimon. He was old and alone and now Yehuda too was leaving him. He would not see his son again, and this final loss overwhelmed him.

Yehuda was his eldest, and when he was only eight he could commit an entire Talmud passage to memory. The boy had delivered a dissertation at his bar mitzvah over which learned rabbis had argued for days. But in class he asked questions that puzzled and disturbed. If God had given the land of Israel to Abraham, why were they, the children of Abraham, living in Kharkov? The rabbis' explanations had not satisfied him. He had sought answers in the dimly lit meeting rooms of the Chovevei Zion and secular knowledge in the lecture hall of the gymnasium. He had married a girl who recited love poetry written in the holy language of the Torah. His eldest sons, the twins, played with gentile youngsters on the forest paths. It was said that they swam naked with the uncircumcised ones in woodland pools. Yehuda's daughter, Sara, spent hours alone with a socialist freethinker who had never completed his bar mitzvah.

All this grieved Reb Shimon but it was a grief he could sustain. His son was here, in Kharkov. When he left the study hall at night and looked down at the lights of the city, he could pick out the brightly lit windows beyond which his grandchildren laughed and played. On Sabbath mornings, his grandson Ezra stopped at his house to carry the faded brown velvet bag that contained Reb Shimon's prayer shawl. He was not alone. But now Yehuda was leaving. He was here to say goodbye. Final solitude had come to Reb Shimon. He would be a deserted old man, the perennial guest at other people's holiday tables.

"Where are you going, Yehuda?" he asked, and Yehuda thought that it was the first time in many years that his father had called him by name.

"To Palestine. To the land of Israel. I will buy land there. A farm. Orchards."

Reb Shimon stood tall in the black caftan woven of finest wool, a gift from his son-in-law, the gem dealer of Buenos Aires. He quivered as anger replaced sorrow and wrath swept grief aside. Pellets of red dotted his cheeks and righteousness glinted diamond-bright in his eyes. He could sustain loss and he could tolerate sadness but profanity must be fiercely fought, brutally rejected.

"What you do is *chilul haShem*. You profane the name of God. Is it not written that we shall be returned to the land only when the Messiah comes? Has the Messiah come?"

"I don't want to argue, Father" Yehuda kept his voice low. Within the study house, the scholars were returning their heavy volumes to the shelves, dropping weary kisses on the frayed bindings. They glanced curiously at the father and son who stood in the narrow doorway. The hour for evening prayers was approaching. The worshipers stretched and yawned. They toyed with their embroidered velvet phylactery cases. Two men edged past Yehuda and Reb Shimon on their way to the outhouse.

"How can there be an argument? There is only one way. The way of truth. The way of righteousness. You choose the path of those who do not believe, who will not believe. You follow the Zionists who work on the Sabbath and eat on the Day of Atonement."

"That's not true," Yehuda said wearily. "Many Zionists observe the Sabbath and live by the Torah."

"I know what I know." The old man's lips were set in a thin line. Just so he had stood when Yehuda told him he was leaving the yeshiva to study at the gymnasium. He would not relent. He would not forgive.

"Father, I want your blessing." Yehuda's voice was very soft.

"I cannot bless you. I will bless Ezra. He follows you but it is you who are responsible for the desecration."

"Reb Shimon. We are waiting."

He was being summoned to evening prayer. He looked up and saw that the sun had formed a crimson crescent in the darkening sky. Pale swallows soared toward it, their wings bloodied by the dying light.

"I'm coming," he said and turned without looking back at Yehuda, whose face glowed in the fiery dusk and whose heart burned with a familiar, unvanquished grief.

Reb Shimon had come to the house to say goodbye to Rivka and the children. He took a walk with Ezra, who returned home red-eyed, clutching a large commentary newly bound in black leather that smelled of the tannery. The boy tied the book around with cord and packed it among his own things. Yehuda had not seen his father again nor did he ask to see the book that his father had given Ezra. His son had been granted the blessing and the inheritance. He himself had had neither a farewell nor a benediction. Rivka's parents had demonstrated their grief; his father had displayed his anger. It was, after all, a consistent pattern. Even at the hour of separation, she remained the beloved daughter and he was ever the rebellious son.

Perhaps, Yehuda thought now as he looked across the waters of Jaffa bay, he would send a postcard to his father. Joppa, his father would call this city which, Yehuda saw now, was not really a city—not if one thought of Odessa and Kharkov—no, Jaffa was more of a seaside hamlet. Reb Shimon was honored each Yom Kippur with the reading of the book of Jonah, and Jonah had set sail from Jaffa to preach God's word to the sinners of Nineveh. Of course Yehuda was disembarking at the ancient port, and in his father's eyes he was the sinner.

"All right then," Yehuda Wasserman said aloud, oblivious to the curious glance of a passing deckhand, "I am no Jonah but I am sailing into Jaffa to do a Jew's work in what will be a land of Jews."

He looked down at the clear green waters. Bright pebbles shimmered in the viridian depths. Frothy patches of foam skittered across the gentle waves. Yehuda suddenly yearned to strip off his heavy European clothing and cool himself in that wondrous water. He wanted to cleanse himself of musty book-lined rooms and muttered words. He wanted to forget a language that was not his own and shed a name, carelessly endowed, that had trailed his family from land to land. Wasserman—a name granted in Germany and carried to Russia. Wasserman. The name spoke of Diaspora, of Jews endlessly

tossed upon foreign waters. He was now a Jew come home
to his own ancient shores, to his own waters. Wasser, his
brother in America called himself. Wasser—*mayim*—water.
The Hebrew word pleased him and he mouthed it again
aloud. Mayim. No—Maimon. Yehuda Maimon. The joined
names pleased him and he smiled.

"I am Yehuda Maimon," he said.

A dhow sailed beside the *Vittoria*.

"Bread. Pita. New baked. Fresh. Very cheap," an Arab
boy shouted up at him.

"Yes."

Yehuda tossed a coin down, leaned over, and plucked the
flat hot pita from the boy's dirt-encrusted hand. The crisp,
delicious crust melted in his mouth, and as he chewed, he
repeated his new name again and again.

Chapter 3

Rivka Wasserman dressed carefully for disembarkment. She swept her fair hair up into an elaborate coil held in place by gleaming tortoise-shell combs. She wore a high-necked embroidered batiste blouse with the blue velvet traveling suit her mother had bought her as a parting gift. Her feet were encased in silk stockings and her high-button shoes were so tightly laced that a welt of silk-enshrouded flesh bulged over the patent leather trim. Before putting on her traveling cape, she tied a purple chiffon scarf around her neck. The purple hue of the scarf exactly matched the embroidered ostriches that adorned her heavy portmanteau.

Sara watched her mother from the narrow bunk in the cabin she had shared with her parents during the voyage. The girl's dark hair was threaded into a single plait down her back, and she wore a loose blue-and-white striped cotton frock.

"You're going to be terribly hot," Sara warned Rivka. Even in her own light dress she could feel the onslaught of the heat and the hot breath of the harbor wind. Ever since Ezra had wakened her with his urgent cry, the heat had clung to her like a tenacious, ghostly shadow—but a shadow that breathed forth a hot and salt-tinged exhalation.

It was the season of spring and she had been dreaming, when her brother's voice pierced the somnolent dawn quiet, of the tiny flowers that dotted the Kharkov meadowlands during these days of silver sunlight and new growing. Chaim walked beside her in her dream, and they gathered the flowers together. He knew the Latin name of each blossom, and offered her the unfamiliar words as though he were sharing a gift of rare value. The flower's names, a meaningless jumble in her ears, had made her laugh, and she had turned her face up to his bespectacled gaze and was waiting for his full lips to press down upon her own when Ezra's shout penetrated the thick, protective wall of heavy sleep that had become her emotional bastion during this voyage.

"Sara, hurry. We've arrived. We're here."

The penumbral Chaim vanished and she was awake, plummeted back into the tiny damp cabin that smelled of her mother's expensive perfumes and sachets, her father's sweat, and the bromidic salt of the sea.

"All right," she had called to her brother. "I'm coming."

But she had, in fact, pulled the thin rough blanket up to her chin and closed her eyes again. To Ezra this day of arrival meant a new beginning, but for her the dropping of the anchor meant an ending, a finish, a completion and a surrender. They had arrived and there was no turning back. Chaim belonged to the cool spring days of her girlhood, to crisp winter nights when they had walked together beneath patterned stars carved of silver ice, and to afternoons when they huddled together about the embers of a dying fire. Together, they read the books that Chaim knew almost by heart and the journals whose flimsy pages promised a bright new world which would know neither war nor hunger.

There were cool forests in the land she had left behind. Ancient trees cast wondrous shadows. She had left all that to follow her father to a land where the heat would press upon her with an almost corporeal weight, where there was no shade to protect her from the fierceness of a ceaselessly blazing sun, and where desert and swamp encroached ruthlessly upon newly cleared farmlands.

"Do you want to go?" Chaim had asked, holding her small hands between his own large ones, warming her fingers although his own throbbed with cold.

"No."

"Then why must you?"

He was bewildered. His own family was loosely knit and each had chosen a separate way. His brother had emigrated to America and sent a perfunctory annual letter. One of his sisters owned a millinery shop in Moscow. His father had died and his mother had waited only a few months before marrying an innkeeper from Oswiecim in Poland and it was there that his other sister lived. Chaim wrote an occasional postcard to each but did not feel that his life was entwined with theirs. He was Chaim, living Chaim's life in a rented room behind the flour mill.

She could not explain to him that her feeling for her own family was very different. He did not understand the way she trembled when her parents railed against the twins for their truancies and their mischief, or how she plunged herself into the middle of arguments to protect her laughing, carefree brothers who needed no protection. Nor could he comprehend the way her heart turned when Ezra's eyes filled with despair and his questions pelted her with desperate insistence: "Why, Sara? How, Sara? When, Sara?"

Who would answer Ezra if she were not there? Who would protect him from their father's harshness, their mother's vagueness, their brothers' careless taunts?

And then, of course, there was Sara's mother, who needed mothering herself. Often Rivka stood before her open wardrobe like a small girl unable to decide on a school frock. It was Sara who plucked the skirt and blouse from the hanger, who buttoned her mother's cuffs.

"Shall we have duck or chicken?" Rivka would ask absently in the late, afternoon, looking up from the romantic novel which carried her into her rightful world, into rooms where waltz music was played as graceful men and women, who wore silks and velvets and spoke many languages, danced.

"I have already begun stewing the flanken."

"What would we do without you, my Sara? How would we manage?" And Rivka turned back to her book, back to her elusive dreams.

But there was a more important answer to Chaim's question. Sara had no choice. She stood poised between girlhood and womanhood, and she would remain her father's daughter until she became another man's wife.

"I could stay," she told him at last, on a night when the

moonlight fell in a silvery sheath across the paths of Kharkov's public gardens, "if I were married."

The words dropped softly from her lips. Her hands trembled and a strange viscosity suffused her heart.

"Married?" He echoed her as though seeking to understand what she had said. "But you know we don't believe in marriage. Don't you remember the article in *The Young Comrade?* And the poem we read together in *A World United?* Marriage belongs to the old world. We will be together but free in our new society. When there is social justice, there will be no need for an artificial family structure."

His voice became oddly shrill and she stared at him as though seeing him for the first time. There was something pathetic about the small edge of golden down above his lips. Her brothers, the twins, had started to shave with a straight-edged razor only a year after bar mitzvah. Chaim, four years their senior, had the soft skin of a youth.

"I don't think a family is an artificial unit," she said. She shivered and they left the park, walking the quiet streets in silence.

Weeks passed before her family left Kharkov, and she and Chaim continued to meet. He helped the Wassermans with their packing, cleverly finding room for Rivka's fragile china tea service within the barrel full of down comforters. He packed Sara's books himself, placing them gently in the large leather trunk her father had given her. The verses of Lermontov nestled among her embroidered camisoles. *Eugene Onegin* slid into place among her petticoats. The leatherbound Tolstoy volumes were evenly distributed among her boots:

"You'll read them?" he asked. He had given them to her as a birthday gift.

She nodded and added, to show that she forgave him, "And I'll think of you."

"Come with us," she said one day.

"No. The future is here, in Russia."

He did not look at her when he answered, and she did not ask him again.

On the eve of their leaving he brought her the shawl of crimson cashmere. She had never touched anything so soft, and she wept at the feel of the fine-as-cloud wool.

"Don't, Sara." Behind his thick glasses his own eyes were moist. "Don't cry."

They clung to each other then like small children, comforting one another against a grief they could neither comprehend nor sustain. Throughout the voyage, with the shawl wrapped about her shoulders, Sara thought of that last paroxysm of grief and fingered the fringes of her lover's gift.

"Are you coming, Sara?"

Rivka, fully dressed, was pleased with herself. She studied her face in Sara's hand mirror and pinched her cheeks to give them color.

"Should I wear my good hat?" she asked.

"But why?"

"Perhaps we will be met. Your father's friends in Chovevei Zion knew we were sailing on the *Vittoria*. Perhaps the Jewish ladies of the city have a welcoming committee. We had one at Kharkov. The women of the synagogue came to meet a train whenever we knew a Jewish family was arriving. Sometimes we brought cake and sometimes flowers. I always preferred flowers. So much more delicate and meaningful than food."

Sara sighed wearily. Her mother, she knew, imagined a delegation of ladies, all addicted to Hebrew poetry and fashionably dressed in the latest European styles, who would carry her off in a landau to a carpeted room where Rivka's arrival would be clebrated with a poetry reading or the recital of a chapter of a Smolenskin novel. Rivka might take her collection of Ben Ami verses out of the portmanteau and show them the poet's signature. They would exchange insights in precise literary Hebrew, and the lemons that they squeezed into their tea would lightly stain their fingers. Only in Jaffa could Jewish women pluck lemons from the trees that shaded their very own kitchen gardens.

"You don't need your hat, Mama," Sara said in the quiet tone mothers use when they talk to recalcitrant children, "your parasol will be much more fashionable." The parasol would at least protect her mother, and perhaps Ezra too, from the heat.

"Yes. Of course." Rivka whipped out the purple silk parasol, pleased with the suggestion.

"You'll join me soon, Sara?"

"Yes, soon," Sara promised.

She listened for the click of the cabin door, the sound of her mother's feet tapping their way down the narrow corridor.

She waited. Often Rivka returned to the cabin to seek a handkerchief, to dab a drop of perfume behind her ear, to change one hat for another. But this time there was no rush of stiletto-heeled boots retracing their steps, and Sara opened her traveling case and removed the copy of Lermontov. She opened it to the center and withdrew a flimsy sheet of paper—the page of a calendar sent to her father each year by a manufacturer of barrels in Odessa. A date was circled, and she touched it with a tentative finger and counted aloud, making small marks on the edge of the sheet.

"It is seven weeks," she said aloud, as though giving voice to the words would somehow vanish their reality. "Seven weeks."

She touched her breasts and felt their odd tenderness beneath the cotton fabric of her dress. She replaced the paper in the leatherbound volume, which she wrapped in the crimson shawl and put beneath the chemises in the case. She did not follow her mother's steps but went instead to the deserted starboard deck where she mounted the rope ladder. She climbed with the ease of a girl who has been raised in the woodlands amid sheltering low-branched trees. Here, as always, the deck was deserted, and the rusted iron rail hung so low that it did not even reach her waist. Throughout the voyage, anxious mothers had cautioned their children against playing on that part of the ship.

"It's so low there—you'll fall over, God forbid," they had shouted stridently.

But Sara had walked there often, searching out the waters below her as though they concealed a secret that would be revealed to her if she stared hard enough at their fathomless depths. Now, too, she did not look at the shoreline of Jaffa, but turned her head downward to the clear green waters of the bay. Silvery tongues of foam crested the small waves, and pebbles as sparkling as tiny jewels lined the ocean floor. How simple it would be to lean too far over the rotten rail, to lose one's balance and tumble effortlessly into the soft warm air and to fall—for the briefest of moments—and land in that clear green pool, face down on the sea-smooth brilliant stones, dark hair streaming out like a net for tiny bright-bellied fish. How cool the water would be against her face, against her closed eyes. It would be quiet there, in that shallow cove with only the whisper of wavelets—they would obscure her father's harsh demands, her mother's timorous questions, her brothers' harsh quarrels, and the remembered timbre of Chaim's voice, thick with anguish and desire. So easy. She had only to lean forward ever so slightly. She loosed her grip of the rail and swayed dangerously. Sunlight rippled across the water in a ribbon of brightness. How beautiful it was, how beckoning. She took it as a sign and slipped out of her shoes. Barefoot then, she closed her eyes and inclined her head to the shimmering waters.

"Now," she whispered, "now," and her body pressed against the rail and pitched forward.

"Sara!"

Small hands gripped her waist, wrenched her backward, struggled to pull her upright. Ezra's slight form became ballast for her own and thrust her back from the rail.

"What happened? Did you get dizzy?"

He gripped her wrists and she saw that his eyes were awash with tears of fear. Poor Ezra. Poor gentle brother. Gently she pried his fingers loose and cradled him in her arms. She no longer needed his fierce and sudden strength. Her own, so briefly and dreamily lost, had been returned to her.

"Yes. I got dizzy," she said softly, and she stepped into her shoes. She looked again at the sea—mirror smooth now.

"Come. Let's find the family. They will be worried about us."

The deck of the *Vittoria* was teeming with crew and passengers, all scurrying in different directions and shouting to each other in a variety of languages. A group of monks in brown soutanes gathered at the stern and listened in silence as the oldest among them offered chanted orisons. His voice rose and fell as melodically as the waves that rocked the anchored vessel. The halo of white hair around his tonsure was rimmed with golden sunlight. The monks stroked their wooden rosary beads and intoned subdued amens. They had been fasting since the previous night and would not eat again until they reached Jerusalem.

"*Hierusalem,*" they moaned and faced eastward.

The German businessmen supervised the arrangement of their cases and nodded and bowed to the wife of the French chargé d'affaires, who pressed a fine linen handkerchief soaked with eau de cologne to her very small nose and fanned herself frantically with a white lace morning fan. An elderly Jew, wearing an ash-colored caftan which had years ago surely been black, clutched the rail and searched the shore with watery eyes.

The tall young Arabs who had boarded in Constantinople strolled the deck leisurely, garbed in flowing robes of bright linen which were belted with gaily woven strips of cloth and satin sashes. They played with the threaded tassels and fingered their bright amber worry beads, occasionally glancing toward shore with the pleasant expectancy of travelers who know they are happily awaited and will receive a hospitable welcome. Of all the passengers on the *Vittoria* only the olive-skinned young men looked comfortable in the glaring heat, and only they moved without urgency or anxiety.

"Mama! Sara!" Saul and David hurtled forward. "Papa and Ezra have been looking everywhere for you. Look! That's Jaffa. It's a village. It's so much smaller than Kharkov. And look at that rock. It looks like a woman. See, Saul, it even has breasts."

Saul giggled at his brother's words but glanced nervously at his mother, whose forehead had already creased into a frown.

Those boys, she thought, and sighed deeply, but her gaze too was held by the dark sprawling rock just off the shore. She too noted the curving belly, the strong thighs, the rounded, swelling breasts carved by wave and wind.

"It's the rock of Andromeda," Sara said, and suddenly Rivka remembered walking with Ephraim, her tutor, down a sun-dappled forest path and listening to him tell her the Greek legend about the beautiful princess who was chained to a wave-lashed rock as a sacrifice to a vengeful sea monster but who was rescued by Perseus astride a winged horse. The rock had been sculpted to her shape.

"Andromeda the princess," Rivka said. "I remember now."

"Chaim told me about her," Sara murmured, and briefly the eyes of mother and daughter met, acknowledging a secret sharing which they could not articulate.

"Boys, look at you. Aren't you ashamed?" Rivka's voice was harsh, but heavy with defeat. She had tried but the twins had struggled and prevailed. Since babyhood they had reinforced each other and played and laughed in tandem. Saul applauded David's mischief, and David conjured up pranks and escapes that required Saul's cooperation. One such child might be controlled, subdued, but Rivka was defenseless against their combined energy. Now they stood before her barefoot, the legs of their dark serge trousers rolled up to the knees and their jackets knotted about their waists. David's white shirt was smudged with grease and Saul's was ripped at the sleeves.

"Where are your shoes and socks?" Rivka asked wearily.

"In our satchels," David said. "We didn't want them to get wet," he added piously.

The twins' faces creased with laughter. The freckles on their noses trembled and when they shoved each other playfully, their bright copper curls straggled out from under the tweed caps that had, against all odds, managed to stay on their heads.

"Come, Rivka."

Yehuda joined her, with Ezra trailing behind him. Her youngest son, she saw with satisfaction, was neatly groomed and had even tied his narrow string tie into a clumsy bow.

"I've arranged all the luggage," Yehuda said and pointed to a corner of the deck where the trunks and barrels were grouped. He was organized as always, supervising his household goods as he had his sacks of grain.

"Saul, David—bring up your mother's traveling bags. Ezra, you take Sara's case. Here, Rivka, give me that." He moved to relieve her of the embroidered portmanteau but she clung to it.

"No. I can manage that, Yehuda." She would not surrender her books and notebooks, the small Dürer etching that had hung in their parlor, the leatherbound diaries of her girlhood, the slender volume of verse with the tutor's hasty letter of goodbye concealed between its pages. "But how will we get all this to shore?"

A shaft of sunlight shivered its way across the polished stone face of the rock of Andromeda, creating mocking lips.

"Those small boats will carry us to shore."

The small dhows with their brightly colored sails were streaking toward the *Vittoria* now, bobbing about on the playful waves. They swarmed across the inlet that refracted the gleaming sunlight like a polished mirror. Dark-robed Arabs sailed the small ships. Their *kaffiyehs* trailed behind them like white banners in the gentle wind. Their hoarse, unintelligible shouts reached the deck of the *Vittoria*, where clusters of passengers beckoned frantically to one or the other of the boatmen.

"What are they saying? What do they want?" Rivka asked, tugging Yehuda's arm and clutching her bag. The dark men frightened her, and she drew Ezra close.

"Money," Yehuda replied briefly. He gestured to the tall Arab who shouted and gesticulated from the largest of the crafts.

"Over here. Over here," he called and held up six fingers to indicate that there were six people in his family.

The Arab sailed his boat closer to them. Three crewmen, wearing baggy breeches and loose long shirts, looked up at them with puzzled gazes as though wondering what these strangely dressed Europeans were doing in their sunswept port. Their leader shouted a word which Yehuda did not understand. Still, he shook his head from side to side. Another word came in reply to his negative motion. Yehuda understood now that they were arguing about price, and he continued to shake his head until the Arab threw his arms up to the heavens in disgust and motioned to his men to row the boat away. Only then did Yehuda beckon him forward. The Arab flashed him a wide grin of agreement and attached his skiff to a hook that jutted out of the *Vittoria*'s hull. The sailors scurried up the rope and jumped lightly onto the deck. Yehuda pointed to his stack of trunks and barrels, and deftly the men passed them from one to the other, tossing them onto the deck of their boat.

"Careful!" Rivka shouted as they heaved up the barrel that contained her Passover dishes. Its weight caused the small skiff to tremble, and the captain scrambled to balance the barrel in the boat's center.

"What are you doing?" she screamed as they hurled forward a wooden crate heavy with the crystal glasses her parents had brought her from Germany.

"Be more gentle," she implored them in a mixture of Yiddish and Russian at which the laboring Arabs jeered.

There was a sudden splash followed by a woman's keening wail. A large crate belonging to the Feigenbaums, a family from Cracow, had missed the waiting skiff and fallen into the water.

"My bed linen, my blankets. My bed linen, my blankets,"

little Mrs. Feigenbaum repeated again and again in Yiddish while her bearded husband patted her frail, quivering shoulders.

"*Sha*, Shaindel. Not to worry. We'll get new sheets, new blankets. Anyway, in the holy land the sun shines with God's own warmth. Will we need blankets?"

Rivka and Yehuda did not look at each other. Three nights earlier, as they strolled the deck together, Reb Moshe Feigenbaum had told them his last capital had gone to pay for his family's passage. He had barely enough to sustain them for one week in Palestine.

"What will you do there?" Rivka had asked. He had told her that in Cracow he had been a *melamed*—a teacher. His meager income had been supplemented by the kaddishes, the prayers for the dead which he intoned on behalf of widows.

"God will provide," Reb Feigenbaum had answered, lifting his eyes to the heavens as though a message had been left for him amid the stars.

Would God also provide bedsheets and towels and blankets, Yehuda wondered, but he knew that it was not on God that the pious Jews actually relied. It was, in fact, on the charity of the world Jewish community. In Palestine, the indigent teacher would live on donations sent there from abroad. He would become a *halukkah* Jew, one who received support from others and considered that he repaid them with his piety and his learning. Yehuda frowned. Palestine would have to produce a more productive community than that. Still, he sidled over to the weeping woman and pressed a ten-ruble note into her hand.

The noise on the deck of the *Vittoria* reached a shrill crescendo as the Arab sailors shouted to each other and the passengers screamed cautionary invectives. More than one splash was heard as misdirected cargo slid into the water. A brown-cassocked priest, his cheeks red with anger, shook his pudgy fist at the grinning Arab who had allowed a leatherbound box to slide into the deep green waters. The priest clutched his wooden cross and gestured wildly with it, as though invoking God's own wrath.

Now, at last, the passengers were leaving the *Vittoria*. The men scrambled down on improvised rope ladders and some of the women managed the descent as well, but the majority of women and children reached the small boats in the same way their luggage had—their trembling bodies were passed hand over hand and lowered onto the wet and cluttered decks of the longboats.

Little Mrs. Feigenbaum closed her eyes and said the *Sh'ma* as she was swept up and unceremoniously lowered. The wife of the French chargé d'affaires sat regally in a chair held by ropes that had been fashioned for her, but the pale pink parasol which she kept elegantly poised above her head caught in the rope and sailed into the water. It bobbed about on the spumescent waves like a child's plaything until one of the Arab boys fished it out and amused his friends by dancing about the deck with the soggy bit of finery extended in his hand.

Ezra and the twins managed to lower themselves down the ropes easily and Sara, hugging her skirts, also made it to the smaller boat without assistance. But Rivka, still clutching her unwieldy portmanteau, stood nervously at the railing.

"I can't," she whispered to her husband. "Really, I can't do it."

"Of course you can."

He knew that the only way to combat Rivka's timidity was through a fierce display of strength. "I can't," she had whispered to the midwife as she labored to bring forth the twins. "You can. You must." Then as now there had been no choice, and he had given her no quarter.

He pried her fingers loose from the bulky embroidered valise and lifted her into his arms. Within the heavy traveling cloak her body trembled like a small bird he had once held briefly during a courtship walk with Rivka through the Kharkov woodlands. Poor Rivka, he thought. Poor little bird. Gently, he dropped her down to the tall Arab captain who stood waiting.

Rivka stiffened in the new set of arms. She could not stop trembling. The rough fabric of the Arab's robe scratched her cheek. The smell of his body's sweat mingled with the salty fragrance of the sea. She closed her eyes and fought against the sudden nausea that welled up within her. Then another pair of arms took her, and new odors assailed her. A cloying sweetness, the stink of spoiled vegetables, the noxious aroma of reused cooking grease and unwashed men. She would faint. She would lose her balance and tumble into the bay to float face down among the polished pebbles. She would drown.

Tears of self-pity burned behind her closed eyes, and terror strangled her. What was she doing in this blazing hellhole of a land with its guttural, incomprehensible language, its malodorous air and clashing colors? Like the black stone maiden that blocked the harbor, she too was a sacrifice to her husband's dream. She breathed stertorously and then, without warning, the arms that held her were loosened, her body was lowered to a tarpaulin on the deck, and Sara was bending anxiously over her.

"Mama, are you all right?" Ezra's voice was concerned, gentle. He stroked her face with his long, graceful fingers, smoothed the pale hair that had escaped its pinnings. "Poor Mama."

Then Yehuda too was beside her, impatience struggling with tenderness in his face. He wanted her strong, yet loved her weak.

"You see. You're all right, Rivka," he said.

"My books. The satchel with my books, my notebooks. You have it?"

He blanched. The launch boat was already moving but he motioned the captain to stop. Rivka's case stood in lonely splendor on the deck. Urgently Yehuda gestured to one of the Italian sailors, who did not see him.

"Feigenbaum!" Yehuda called desperately, but the small scholar, pacing the deck with his phylateries, was absorbed in his first morning prayers in the promised land and did not hear him. In the end, it was a monk who hoisted the bag up and heaved it over the rail. An Arab sailor in their boat stood poised to catch it.

"*Hawaja!*" he shouted, both his hands outstretched. But the monk's aim was bad. The purple bag gravitated downward and sailed, with a playful splash, deep into the shining waters. Swiftly it sank out of sight and Rivka leaned perilously over the side of the longboat as though she might follow it.

"My books!" she cried, and this time her voice did not rise in a scream but took on the low, mournful whimper of bereavement. "My papers. They are lost. They are gone."

"Mama, don't." Ezra's voice trembled too. He could not bear his mother's misery. He remembered now, with relief, that he had packed the precious volume his grandfather had given him with Sara's books. The thought filled him with uneasy guilt. What sort of a boy was he to think of his own possession when his mother swayed from side to side in the rhythm of grief?

Within a split second Saul had shed his jacket and his shirt and plunged into the water. Breathless, they watched the spot where he had disappeared downward. The Arab sailors looked at each other and shrugged. They could not understand these Jews who arrived in the harbor each Tuesday. They prattled feverishly in a mixture of languages and wept when they looked at the rockbound shore, at the low seabound hills. They were a clumsy lot. What was the boy doing? The Jews could not swim. They would have to dive after that foolish youth with hair the color of fire. Already their captain stood ready with a heavy rope. Well if they had to swim beneath the waters, the journey to the shore would cost that tall, bearded Jew plenty.

But Saul surfaced, gasping and triumphant, the purple bag leaden and soggy in his grasp. He flung it onto the deck and scrambled aboard himself.

"Here, Mama. I saved your books. Just don't make me read them anymore. That's all the reward I ask."

His twin laughed and hugged his brother. Sara looked at Saul as though she had never seen him before. Standing there in his honey-colored half-nakedness, his youthful muscles still rippling with the effort of his exertions, he appeared amazingly at one with the sun-streaked sea and the raucous harbor life. Yehuda too watched his son and thought of his father, wrapped in the black shroud of his caftan. Would he recognize this grandson who lifted his laughing face to the sun of the holy land? How swiftly the generations catapulted away from each other. Already Reb Shimon, his father, was a shadowy figure from another life.

Now David too exploded with laughter, and Sara was aware of an almost angry envy. The twins had felt instantly at home in the new land. They sailed the brief distance into the harbor enveloped in their own private laughter.

Ezra watched the shoreline with quiet wonder, and Rivka and Yehuda stood side by side, their hands touching, as the cluster of tiny waterfront houses grew closer. They could pick out forms and faces from among the crowds that congregated in front of the customs house. They recognized a familiar face and pointed excitedly. Only Sara looked back out to the endless blue-green stretch of open sea, as smooth as glass in the distance.

"Where are you going?" Chaim had asked her. "What kind of life will it be? Why are you going?" How soft her breast had felt beneath his heavy hand.

He did not want to marry her. He did not believe in marriage. But he did believe in love. He had held her gently that last night, in the firelit room behind the flour mill. His body was very white as he moved toward her.

"You mustn't go," he had said, and buried his head in her hair. "You mustn't go." His desire, his longing, burst forth within her, and she surrendered to pain, clawed his white shoulders with joy.

"Why are you going?" he cried. "Why?" His breath seared her shoulder, and the tear that dropped from his eye became a moist jewel upon her breast.

"I don't know." Her throat rasped with dryness, and when she spoke she felt that the pain of her answer would cause her chest to split in two.

"Stay," he pleaded, but she left. Soon, she would write to him. She would tell him about her crossing and about the rock of Andromeda that stood guard at the entry of Jaffa harbor.

"Sara, we're here." Ezra tugged at her and she followed him off the boat, climbing awkwardly onto the splintered dock. She did not look back again to the great expanse of sun-splayed sea beyond which lay the land she had left behind.

Chapter 4

Rivka, as she struggled ashore burdened by the waterlogged satchel, was, after all, pleased that she had worn her good traveling suit. A crowd of Jews stood on the dock, and they too were dressed properly as befit important occasions such as arriving and departing. Oh well, Sara was young. She would learn. Even in this land appearances were important.

The women wore dresses in the wide-sleeved, long-waisted style that had been popular years ago. The men wore dark business suits, and the cuffs and collars of their white shirts were frayed. The shabby clothing was neatly pressed and seemed oddly oversized for those who wore the garments. The women's bodices bulged where air filled the space between fabric and breast, and the men's jackets flapped at the wrists. Of course they lived different lives here, and their bodies had altered accordingly. And perhaps it was difficult to obtain new clothing in the European style. Still, Rivka was very pleased to see them. Her hand darted to her hair and she regretted, now, not wearing her best bonnet.

Really, it was so kind of them to come. She would, in time, do her own share in the welcoming of new arrivals. Most probably a representative group of the Yishuv, the Jewish community in Palestine, came to the dock each Tuesday to greet the disembarking passengers and welcome them to the homeland. Her pleasure at seeing them dispelled the uncertainty and fear she had felt only minutes before.

But she did think it strange that they had not brought flowers and that there was no small group dressed in *rubashkas,* the string-tied Russian work shirts of the pioneers, to sing them greetings in Hebrew. Mentally, she prepared a small speech to thank them for their courtesy in coming. She molded the Hebrew phrases in her mind, forcing them into proper syntax.

"Dear and good friends . . . our hearts are full of joy and optimism . . ." But what was the Hebrew word for optimism? She remembered copying it out of a Hebrew newspaper and inscribing it in one of the notebooks buried in the sodden case at her foot. Never mind. She would think of it.

The Arab sailors were energetically unloading their belongings onto the steps that led up from the sea to the customs house. Other Arabs, sitting idly on the seawall, stared at them without interest. The group of waiting Jews watched them with the bored, regretful gaze of an audience departing a theater, already knowledgeable about the flawed ending of a play which newcomers, queuing up for tickets, have yet to see.

Yehuda recognized a man he had met at Chovevei Zion meetings in Odessa, years before.

"Lefkowitz," he called, *"Shalom aleichem."*

"Aleichem shalom," the man replied in the traditional exchange of greetings of peace. A slight flush colored his cheeks as he moved down the seawall steps to shake hands with Yehuda.

Yehuda remembered Nachum Lefkowitz well. He had been an early proponent of the Bilu, a group of agricultural pioneers who had opted for immediate settlement in Palestine six years earlier, in 1882. They were a romantic, idealistic group of students who spoke passionately, often in poetic similes, of social reform and national fulfillment. Even now Yehuda recalled the febrile glint in the eyes of their leader as he rallied his followers around him. Audiences listened in spellbound silence as Chaim Chissin spoke.

"We cannot afford to wait," Chissin had shouted from the rostrum of the tiny meeting room in the rear of an ancient synagogue where the assembled comrades drank strong tea from enamel cups. The copper samovar shone in a corner of that dark room, bathing those who sat near it in a strange orange light. "House of Jacob—arise and let us go up!" Chissin's voice had risen to a crescendo and his listeners shouted after him, in a frenzy of emotion, "Yes. House of Jacob, come let us go up!"

The Hebrew equivalent of that phrase became the initials of their group. They were the Bilu, in readiness for adventure. Yehuda, the pragmatic businessman, watched as the would-be pioneers surged forward to pledge their allegiance to Chissin.

"We are going," they cried. "We are going up to the land."

The young girls in rubashkas and navy blue skirts sang. The young men linked arms and danced fierce horas that caused the tiny synagogue to tremble. The samovar bubbled and belched forth gentle clouds of steam.

"Where are you going? How are you going? With what are you going?" Yehuda thought as he watched them but he said nothing, and a small group of thirteen had indeed set off, their necks ringed with garlands of flowers. In place of implements they had carried manifestos. Yehuda read their statement in *HaShachar,* the Hebrew newspaper to which all Zionists dutifully subscribed.

"And Israel on its own land, the land of the prophets, will combine a new society with social justice, for that is the function of Israel in the land of Israel."

They had danced a wild dockside hora and sailed forth. News of them had drifted back to Russia. There had been illness and near starvation, exhaustion and disillusionment. Some had retreated to the agricultural school at Mikveh Israel, founded by the Rothschilds. In Russia they had scorned the paternalism of the French baron, but in Palestine their refuge had been the modest shelters the banker had built. Some had returned to Russia, and some few had gone to America.

Nachum Lefkowitz, who moved toward Yehuda now through the sodden heat of Jaffa harbor, had not ascended to the land with the Bilu. He was a married man, and Chissin's followers were not yet ready for families. Instead Nachum and his wife, Chaika, a gentle fragile girl with wheat-colored hair that fell about her shoulders had decided they would go as independent pioneers. Chaika, Yehuda remembered, wrote sonnets in

Hebrew and sang in a high, sweet voice as she accompanied herself on the balalaika. Surely, the young couple had reasoned, they would find a place for themselves in a communal settlement on the sloping hillsides of the Carmel or in the quiet valley of Jezereel. One had to seize the day. The important thing was to go up to the land, to launch the Zionist adventure.

"How are you, Yehuda?" Nachum Lefkowitz said. They shook hands, and the other man's fingers were skin-covered bits of bone in Yehuda's fleshy grasp.

"I am fine. And you? And Chaika?" Yehuda asked.

"Chaika is dead."

There was death, too, in Nachum Lefkowitz's voice. The blue eyes that had been glazed with fervor were faded now. His hair was gray as ash and his threadbare dark suit was a tent for his shrunken form. He walked with an old man's stoop although he was not yet forty.

"And I . . ." the man continued, "I am returning to Russia. From there I will go to America. To Texas. I have a brother in Galveston, Texas. He has a house." His voice seemed to gather strength at the mention of a shelter, an established dwelling in which he would have a bed.

"Good luck to you," Yehuda said.

He did not ask about the death of the lovely Chaika whose slender fingers had so delicately plucked the strings of her instrument as she sang softly, "Play balalaika, spin balalaika, we shall be glad, we shall be joyous." Nor did he ask Nachum Lefkowitz why he was leaving the land. Even back in the meeting room, while brave voices soared and the samovar glowed brightly, Yehuda had known that for all their zeal they would not succeed.

He had watched them dance with sadness and envy while formulating his own plans. He would work in his father-in-law's business until he had accumulated enough money to buy a piece of land suitable for citrus cultivation and the equipment necessary for such a crop. Meanwhile he would devote himself to a study of agronomy. There would also have to be enough money to furnish a comfortable house for Rivka and the children, and funds to guarantee Ezra the education he himself had been denied. With God's help there would be a university in Jerusalem, but if not, Ezra would be able to study in Europe or even in the United States. Like the

frenzied dreamers and dancers, he, Yehuda Wasserman, would
go up to the land, but when he went he would stay and his
family would not suffer. Especially Ezra, in whom all hope
rested.

Nachum Lefkowitz clutched Yehuda's shoulder.

"It is good that you have come," he said. "This is a land
for the strong. *Chazak!* Strength."

Slowly, with the reluctant tread of defeat, he walked down
the seawall steps and settled himself on the same longboat
from which the Wasserman family had traveled to shore from
the *Vittoria*. Other departing Jews, already seated there, turned
their faces seaward, away from the land they were abandoning. An aged, blind Arab sat on an upturned barrel and played
a reed pipe. The mournful music rose like a dirge in the
heat-heavy air.

"And I thought they had come to welcome us," Rivka said
softly.

The short Hebrew speech accepting their welcome still
trembled in her mind. She had even remembered the Hebrew
word for optimism. Slowly she removed her traveling cape,
and she used her parasol to swat the flies that blackened the
air around them.

A caravan of donkeys laden with sacks of grain lumbered
past. The bells on the animals' colorful woven halters jingled,
and their drivers urged them forward, indifferent to the bewildered passengers who stood directly in their path. One animal
defecated and the steaming, green-streaked turd was immediately dark with insects. Beggars scurried about them, their
hands outstretched. An old man who maneuvered his shrunken
body on rag-encased stumps thrust out a blue-veined claw. A
blind man, his head wrapped in a cocoon of filthy bandages,
clutched Yehuda's jacket. Small boys trailed after them in
packs, begging for coins, pointing to Ezra's buckled shoes
and laughing. Their own feet were bare, dirty, and covered
with sores.

Arab women in black embroidered gowns wandered by,
balancing straw trays of newly baked *pittot* on their heads.
Vendors laden with straw baskets of vegetables wandered
about the dock. Tomatoes and cucumbers were thrust at
Rivka, who looked away. A young girl shook a newly slaughtered chicken at Sara. She shoved it away in sudden fear. A
slash of sticky crimson blood streaked her arm and Sara, who

could not bear dirt, screamed. The Arab girl laughed and walked on.

Turkish officials, wearing red tarbooshes on their heads, sat in the courtyard on tiny chairs. They puffed languidly on their narghiles and sipped black coffee from tiny cups. When they opened their mouths, small puffs of smoke soared into the cloudless sky. Now and again a plate of leaves was passed around. They chewed the thick green-black matter and spat the masticated detritus out onto the stone blocks of the courtyard which was pocked with pulpy dark globules foaming with saliva.

Rivka's heel caught on one such soft mass and she swayed dizzily. Her stomach danced in a paroxysm of nervousness. She would lose her footing and sprawl into the filth, the dung, and the refuse. She struggled for balance, and Ezra's small hand steadied her.

"It's all right, Mama," he reassured her. He walked between her and Sara, carrying the purple bag, while Yehuda strode on ahead. The twins had remained at the dock with their large trunks and cases. Together they entered the customs house.

Within the cool, cavernous room, Turkish officials moved among the new arrivals. They passed out faded forms printed in French, Arabic, and Turkish and smiled as the immigrants tried to read them.

"You must need help," a bureaucrat wearing a soiled coat and rimless glasses told Yehuda, who was staring at the document in bewilderment.

His hand was outstretched, and without bothering to answer, Yehuda reached into his pocket and passed him a gold coin. The man's hand remained extended and Yehuda placed another coin in it. Only after a third coin had changed hands did he pull forward a blunt pen and an inkwell and begin to work as his red fez slid dangerously over his myopic eyes.

"Name," he barked.

"My name is Maimon. Yehuda Maimon."

Rivka and his children stared at him in astonishment but said nothing. One by one the names of the family were entered on the form. Rivka Maimon. Sara Maimon. Saul and David Maimon. Ezra Maimon. Without discussion, in a matter of seconds, they shed one name and took on another, just as there had been virtually no discussion when Yehuda told them they were shedding their comfortable middle-class life in Kharkov to take up the life of pioneering farmers in Palestine.

"Ezra Maimon."

Ezra whispered his new name to himself. There was strength and beauty in the sound. He repeated the words again as they walked out of the cool customs house into the narrow streets of Jaffa. He was in his new land and he had a new name. Despite the heat and his hunger, he walked quickly with a new and easy spring to his step as though he had suddenly left behind an old and familiar burden.

"Do you look for a hotel? A Jewish hotel?"

The man who approached them reminded Yehuda of his father-in-law, the grain broker. Here, on the sweltering narrow street, surrounded by beggars who plucked at his clothes, he fondled the gold watch that hung about his waist and smoothed the pockets of his jacket. He was impervious to the shouts of the vendors, the shrieks of the small children who surrounded them with pointing fingers and a strange incessant prattle. He shared the grain broker's instinct for a good and reliable customer. Other Jewish immigrants had hurried past him without meriting his attention. He had not stopped the group of young pioneers who had spent the voyage on the deck of the *Vittoria*, nor had he hurried after the Feigenbaums who shuffled down the street now, following a small Arab boy who had loaded their belongings onto a rickety wheelbarrow.

"I am Chaim Baker," the hotelkeeper said and held out his hand to Yehuda.

"Yehuda Maimon. Shalom aleichem." How easily the new name fell from his lips. Yehuda was pleased. "We will in fact need a hotel for a few days. There are six of us. My wife, my daughter, and my three sons."

"Good. We can accommodate you. The hotel is clean and kosher and the price will be reasonable."

Chaim Baker snapped his fingers and two Arab boys, each lugging a wheelbarrow, hurried to him. Yehuda led them to the dock where the twins stood guard over their possessions and the boys quickly loaded them, motioning to friends to come and help. These Europeans had brought much with them. The baksheesh would be good.

The Maimons followed Chaim Baker up the narrow incline and through the maze of alleyways and dirty warrens of the

port city. Rivka kept her eyes averted as they passed through
the market where huge, bloodied carcasses of young cows
and sheep swung from iron hooks. A lamb's head, severed at
the neck, stared at them, its mouth flapping open in a silent
bleat. The fleshiest cuts of meat were black with flies that the
merchants did not bother to brush away. Skeletal dogs haunted
the butchers' stalls. They licked the pools of dark red blood
formed by the dripping meat and yelped with fear as children
in ragged robes tossed rocks and sticks at them.

Fruits and vegetables were piled in colorful array on stall
after stall. Shining purple eggplants, pale green okra, bright
red tomatoes veiled with thin brown layers of earth, and tiny
cucumbers in noduled green skins were arranged in tenuous
pyramids. Rotting vegetables, through which fleshy white
maggots crawled, had been tossed beneath the stands and out
into the streets. Beggars crawled about and snatched the
moldy bits of okra and blackened tomatoes and ran before the
proprietors could pummel them for stealing the reeking refuse.

It was not the filth that startled Sara but the abundance.
The Russian winter had been a long one and the spring was
late in coming. Aboard the *Vittoria* they had eaten little
besides hard-boiled eggs and the hard cheese and dried meat
they had brought with them from Russia. She had not seen
green vegetables for almost a year. She resisted the urge to
stop at a stall and make a purchase, and hurried to keep up
with Chaim Baker who strode determinedly onward, brushing
away tenacious beggars and groups of whining and cajoling
children.

The twins, however, bought long hot pretzels pebbled with
sesame seeds and munched them happily. They offered a
piece to Ezra, who turned away. The boy who sold them had
running sores on his hands and snow-colored grit was encrusted
about his eyes.

"You'll get sick," he warned his brothers, but they laughed
derisively and continued to munch.

They were strong boys who had not even known childhood
illnesses. They had hiked along snow-laden forest paths and
had gone swimming in the Donets River on the coldest fall
days. They had plucked potatoes from the fields and eaten
them raw on a hike from Kharkov to Paltova without getting
the slightest stomach ache. But despite such physical exertions they were never ill while Ezra, who dutifully drank his

mother's nourishing concoctions and wore the flannel under-shirts that Sara stitched for him, spent week after week in bed, his eyes bright with fever and his skin parchment dry as he shivered beneath the eiderdown.

Rivka watched her sons eat and shook her head in resignation. After their bar mitzvah she had all but surrendered her hold upon the twins. They were too strong for her, and they had recognized their strength very early. She would heed the promise that Saul had laughingly extracted from her when he surfaced from his successful dive to rescue her portmanteau. No longer would she hound Saul and David with exhortations to study and read. They were good boys, good sons, and they would make good farmers. But it was Ezra who had inherited Yehuda's intellect and her love for culture. It was Ezra who would study for a baccalaureate.

The long walk and the morning's adventures had exhausted her and she walked slowly, pausing at one of the many narrow shops that sold a variety of improbable items. Scattered on a counter, in careless disarray, were rusty locks, wonderfully tooled chased copperware, and Bedouin mortars carved from wood. In their center a single impeccable white glove had been placed on a plaster of Paris molded hand. Rivka stared at the glove and fought an irresistible urge to laugh wildly. This was, after all, the ultimate absurdity. Here in this stretch of markets thick with flies, amid these narrow streets that stank of human sweat and animal ordure and were haunted by beggars, a snowy, pearl-buttoned glove pointed its way upward.

The Arab shopkeeper noticed her attention and ran out. A long white apron covered his striped robe and he wiped his hands across it.

"You want? You like? I have the other glove, lady. So fine. From France. Here, lady."

He found the matching glove beneath the clutter and stripped the one on display from the molded hand.

"Yes. I want." Laughter floated from her mouth now. She was so tired and it was all so foolish. What was she doing on this filthy street, in a cacophonous bazaar, buying white gloves that she would never wear?

"Twenty piasters," the merchant said.

"Here are ten," Chaim Baker replied.

"Fifteen." The merchant's voice became a silken whine. "From France, these gloves. The finest work."

"Twelve then." Chaim Baker's tone was firm and the man grasped the money and handed them the gloves.

"You will come in, please? I have other wonderful things. Real gold. Amber. Trays from Yemen. I will make you coffee. There is no coffee like Ali Hassan's."

"Another time," Chaim Baker promised, and they walked on.

"What did you want them for?" Yehuda asked his wife.

Rivka tucked the white gloves into the pocket of her traveling cloak.

"I wanted them because they were so clean," she said, and he heard, for the first time, a seepage of bitterness in her voice.

They reached the Clock Square and Ezra stared up at the clumsy tower with its four-faced clock on which no hand moved to signify time's passing. Patrons in the many restaurants that lined the square stared at the family as they passed. Rivka gagged at the smell of lamb being cooked over sizzling coals, smoky with grease, and Sara turned away from the pyramid of raw meat arranged on the wooden counters from which customers selected meat for their own kabobs. Small barefoot boys fanned away the flies that gathered on the exposed meat.

A group of Arab youths sat at a splintered wooden cafe table, sipping at tiny cups of coffee. As the family passed, one of them shot out a sandaled foot and tripped Ezra who fell, sprawling across the courtyard. The young Arabs laughed as Sara hurried to help her brother up and held her handkerchief to his badly scraped knee. Saul and David moved threateningly forward. Twice, in Kharkov, they had turned on young hoodlums who were threatening the scholars at Reb Shimon's study house. But Chaim Baker grasped their arms and pointed to the police station at the opposite side of Clock Square, where a uniformed Turkish officer was watching the scene with expectant interest.

"Come," Chaim Baker said. "The Turk won't care what happened. He will just be pleased to lock everyone up and to get baksheesh in return for your freedom."

The twins looked at the jailhouse that stood next to the police station. Its grimy windows stared blindly into the street. A manacled Arab in a dirty white robe waited indifferently as a Turkish guard fumbled with the keys that opened the heavy padlock.

"All right, Ezra, let's go," David said, and put his arm around his younger brother.

Walking three abreast, the brothers moved on past the old mosque where three old Arabs sat basking in the sun, manipulating their amber worry beads.

"Good. You understand we must always practice *havlaga*—restraint," the hotelkeeper said with relief.

"Not always," Saul said sharply. "Not forever."

They turned up Bustrus Street and passed shop after shop selling Oriental jewelry and elegantly embroidered colorful gowns, and made their way to Jerusalem Avenue, where Chaim Baker directed them up the stairway of a stone house and into the shadowed coolness of his hotel.

Little Mrs. Baker, a plump woman in a starched cotton housedress, bustled forward to greet them and to show them to their impeccable, simply furnished bedrooms. Busily she demonstrated how the shades and shutters of the window could be manipulated for maximum defense against the bright sun. Much of their lives here, Sara thought, would be devoted to seeking shade, to fleeing from the blinding golden light and its pervasive heat. Back in Russia, during these days of early spring, Chaim would be wearing a jacket and a sweater and there would be a pale silver sun, still veiled by drifting clouds.

The Arab boys, who against all odds had reached the house before them, unloaded the wheelbarrows. Serving girls scurried up and down the stairs with buckets of water which they heated on a copper brazier and poured into a large enamel tub in the bathroom. The tub rested on iron clawed legs and Rivka admired the colored floor tiles, artfully fitted together, which formed a picture of full, petaled flowers and blue birds.

"That's Armenian work," Mrs. Baker said, following her guest's glance. "There are many beautiful things in this country," she added as though sensing Rivka's sadness and disappointment. "I know how you feel, Geveret Maimon. I too was shocked when I first arrived in the country. I could not bear the open markets, the beggars, the filth, and the smells. I came from Vienna, after all. Twice a year my father took us to the opera." She closed her eyes as though summoning up again the image of the opera hall with its blazing chandeliers and velvet seats. "But this is not Europe. This is the Middle East. Smolenskin and Mapu do not speak of the flies and the poverty nor do we read about actual conditions on the pages of *HaShachar* and *Havatzelet*. You will grow used to it."

"Will I?" Rivka asked wearily as Mrs. Baker left the room.

She took off her heavy clothing. The undergarments were soaked with sweat and her fine white skin was blotched with a heat rash. She slipped gratefully into the tub and took up the soap, one of a dozen such cakes which her father brought her each year from his visit to Marienbad. Like her laundry, it had the scent of early blooming lilac, and she thought with longing of the silver-leafed bush that grew in their Kharkov courtyard and the pale purple blossoms that weighted down its fragile branches each spring. Just as Mrs. Baker had never again seen the opera house, so perhaps she would never again see those delicate lilacs.

The heat of the tub formed a cloud of steam. She lathered her body with the soap that smelled of another world and fought back the tears that formed burning pools behind her tightly closed eyes. She had left so much behind.

"Mama," she whispered, "Papa." The tears fell and she hugged her breasts and whimpered. She was an only child whose parents lived in a distant land.

Alone in the bedroom, Sara unpacked her mother's wet portmanteau. She spread the soggy books and papers across the beautiful tiled floor. The notebooks were useless; the sea water had blurred the inked-in words. The frame and glass of the Dürer print were broken. Letters, in a hand she did not recognize, had been saved from eradication by the thick text of Mapu's *Blame of Samaria* in which they had been entombed.

"Dearest Rivka, child of my heart . . ." read one salutation. Sara replaced the letters. Her hand trembled. It had never occurred to her that her mother had had a life and a love before marrying her father. Would Sara's own unborn children ever know that a youth named Chaim had walked with their mother down forest paths and held her close in a firelit room in a land they would never see? Sara realized, for the first time, the enormity of life's possibilities. Weariness engulfed her. For the past several weeks a hunger for sleep had suffused her in the mid-afternoon, and she was aware it had begun at the same time as the new fullness of her breasts. A shiver of fear riddled her body

She gathered up the ruined notebooks and the shards of glass and gave them to Ezra to toss into the rubbish.

Poor Mama, she thought and lightly touched the book that concealed the letters which held secrets she did not want to know. She walked to the window and threw open the shutters. Bright sunlight filled the room and Sara unplaited her braid, brushed her hair loose about her shoulders, and watched a boy and girl dressed in the rubashka of the Zionist pioneers walk down Jerusalem Avenue hand in hand. Their shadows formed velvet patterns across the cobbled street. An Arab girl walked behind them. Her long dark dress fell in graceful folds and she balanced a ceramic pitcher on her shoulder.

Chapter 5

Yehuda left Jaffa the next day. The twins accompanied him. They were gone for two days, during which time Rivka recuperated from her journey under the careful pampering of Mrs. Baker, and Sara and Ezra explored Jaffa. Together, they climbed the hill that led to the monastery of Saint Peter and looked down at the domed rooftops of the city and the outstretched fronds that crowned the palm trees and vaulted above the squat stone Arab houses.

"It looks so beautiful from here, doesn't it?" Sara asked.

The sands of the beach below were pure white, and the Mediterranean stretched in blue-green smoothness against the cloudless sky.

"Yes. The view is beautiful. But this, this is more beautiful to me." The boy dug a clump of earth out of the hillside and crumbled it in his fingers. "See, Sara, how rich it is. When this land gets enough water, anything will grow here. Citrus. Grapes. Even grain."

The granules of dark soil seemed to him to be possessed of a special energy of their own that seeped through his body, invigorating him with a strength he had never felt before.

"Are you playing farmer now, Ezra?" Sara laughed. "You're

our little scholar. Leave the farming to Saul and David and to Father.''

They continued their walk, and Ezra dropped the crumbs of earth from his fingers as though to leave a trail he might discover again one day.

They shopped in the open-air market and bought fruits and vegetables, flat pittot still hot from the low brick ovens that squatted within the bakers' courtyards, and slabs of goat cheese which the Arab vendors wrapped in newspapers from Amman and Cairo. A Jewish tailor peered at them through the narrow doorway of his tiny shop.

''Are you a Jew? Cover your head,'' he hissed at Ezra in harsh Yiddish. He would not profane the holy tongue by using it for daily conversation.

''We are not in the Diaspora, old man,'' Ezra retorted good-naturedly, but he fished a skullcap out of his pocket and put it on. The tailor reminded him of his grandfather, Reb Shimon. The musty Kharkov study hall belonged to another life, another world.

Yehuda and the twins were jubilant when they returned. Yehuda had bought land near the new settlement of Rishon LeZion. He glowed with an excitement and optimism that Rivka had not seen since the long ago days when he had dreamed of studying medicine. He spoke rapidly and swept the air with his arms as he described the breadth of their new holdings.

''Twenty-five dunams. Imagine, twenty-five dunams. With a house already built on the property. And the Altmans, from whom we are buying the land and the house, will also sell us their furniture at a very good price.''

''Why?'' Rivka asked suspiciously. ''Is it a solid table? Of what wood are the chairs made?'' She was the grain broker's daughter who had been driven around Kharkov in her own landau. Her girlhood bed had been hand carved of heavy oak. The twin marriage beds on which she and Yehuda had slept had been purchased in Germany. A cherrywood table with matching chairs had stood in their dining room. They had, of course, sold all their furniture before leaving Russia, but she did not want to replace it with the discarded remnants of another woman's household.

''They are selling because they are going to America,'' Yehuda replied impatiently.

He wanted to tell his wife of the gentle slope of their land and describe to her the young citrus saplings that had already been planted. They swayed so delicately in the mildest breeze, and the scent of their new blossoms filled the air with melancholy sweetness. Why did Rivka speak only of sticks of wood, of tables and chairs? Did she understand him at all? Would he ever understand her?

"If their land is so wonderful, then why are they leaving for America?" Rivka asked.

"They did not plan right. They did not know enough about agronomy and they did not have enough money to sustain them until the land became sufficiently developed to support them. I heard about them through Joseph Feinberg, who saw the possibilities. Saul and David saw it at once. The land is good. It can be cultivated. We shall turn it into a garden, Rivka. We'll have orange groves, wheat fields. Perhaps a chicken run."

"The land is good, Mama," Saul said. "And there is water in Rishon. That's really important. The Baron de Rothschild gave thirty thousand francs so that a well might be drilled in Rishon."

"But the Baron did not bring the Baroness to settle there?" Rivka queried dryly.

"Rivka!" Yehuda's voice was harsh with disappointment. He had not made plans to settle in Palestine without his wife's acquiescence. The move had not been imposed upon her. They had married with the knowledge that they were both Zionists. It had added a new dimension to their relationship. It was she who, during their courtship, had read to him from the dreamy Zionist writings of Kalman Schulman and Mapu. He could not understand her strange bitterness, her strident discontent. He had been betrayed. He had anticipated a helpmate and now confronted an adversary.

"Papa, Mama's tired," Sara intervened. "The heat is difficult for her. She had a bad headache today."

He glanced gratefully at his daughter, startled anew by the gentle wisdom of her perception. But Sara had always been wise beyond her years. She mothered her brothers and from earliest girlhood it had been she who pampered her own mother. The sadness in Sara's eyes grieved him but she would forget the student, Chaim. Soon she would meet a young man and be happy in the new land. And she was right about Rivka. His wife was exhausted and worried about her parents. When she saw the land he had bought, she would feel differently. Poor Rivka. She was so delicate.

"Rishon LeZion. That means first to Zion," Ezra said. "It's a nice name."

"It's a name. What's important is it will be a successful colony. A good place for Jews to farm and live together," Yehuda said.

"Twenty-five dunams," Chaim Baker said thoughtfully. "That's a great deal of land to farm, my good Maimon. How will you manage it all with just the twins?"

"And me," Ezra interposed quickly. "I too will farm."

"You will help, of course," Yehuda Maimon said, "but you're our student, Ezra, you must stick to your books. In Rishon there are learned mèn who can help you to prepare for the baccalaureate exams. Rivka, do you know who lives in Rishon—the poet Naphtali Hertz Imber."

"Really?" A hesitant note of optimism crept into Rivka's voice. A poet attracted other lovers of literature. It was possible that she might have a small salon in Rishon LeZion. Men and women who loved words and music would come together to listen and to talk. She would serve wine in her delicate crystal glasses, and tiny nut cakes. On summer evenings when the air was thick with the aroma of orange blossoms, they would sit outside and read aloud from published works or from their own journals. She herself had begun to write some verse. She had shown it to little Mrs. Baker and the landlady had been dutifully impressed.

"How wonderful that you know Hebrew," she cried. Even after several years in the country Mrs. Baker still spoke only Yiddish with a smattering of Hebrew and Arabic that allowed her to maneuver in the marketplace and instruct the servants who kept the small hotel impeccably clean.

And, Rivka reasoned, Rishon was not that far from Jaffa. They could come in to shop and to visit the Bakers. It was true that Jaffa was only a filthy little port village, but she had already found a seamstress here who was making some light cotton dresses for her and for Sara. A Jewish goldsmith had repaired a brooch for her, and in a musty bookstore she had found a copy of *Love of Zion* to replace her own copy which had been soaked beyond redemption. It was not, after all, a total wasteland.

"You'll see, you'll be happy there," Yehuda said, encouraged by the new brightness in her eyes.

"But Maimon, my friend, I ask you again. How will you work so much land? How will you manage the harvest? Ah, perhaps you will get students from the Mikveh Israel agricultural school to help you," Chaim Baker suggested. There was real concern in his voice. His hotel had housed so many Jewish families who had arrived full of plans and hope and left within a few years bowed by defeat and disappointment. Still, somehow he felt that the Maimons were different. Yehuda was possessed of such strength, such a sense of purpose. And he had planned well. A thick envelope of currency and certificates rested in Chaim Baker's safe.

"Yes, the agricultural students may help. And then of course there are always Arabs seeking work," Yehuda said.

"I thought we were coming to be Jewish farmers on Jewish land," Saul said, "not Jewish overseers of Arab laborers."

"Let us worry about that when we are settled," Yehuda replied irritably. "We leave for Rishon in the morning."

The diligence which Yehuda hired for the journey was owned by a bearded Jew from Yemen whose curling sidelocks danced about his fine-boned copper-colored face.

"Blessings on you who come to the land," he murmured as he helped each member of the family up the lacquer steps and into his carriage. The seats were of glistening black leather, and a brightly embroidered cushion was provided for each of the ladies. The two horses were carefully groomed, and long, intricately woven streamers decorated their reins.

The Yemenite Jew was named Gedalia, and as they drove he told Yehuda that he and his family had traveled in caravans from their home in Yemen. They had traversed the great desert lands of Saudi Arabia, bribing officials with their finely crafted jewelry and meager savings until at last they reached the Gulf of Aqaba.

"After that there was no problem," Gedalia said, winking mischievously. "It took us only two years more to reach Jaffa."

The journey of the Yemenites, by foot and camel, by donkey and dhow, across desert and seaway, had taken almost four years.

"Why did you come?" Yehuda asked. The bearded Orthodox Yemenite, who had delayed their departure so that he might complete his morning prayers, was surely no agricultural pioneer. Nor, Yehuda thought, was he a social visionary dedicated to building a new society.

"I came because the Torah tells us that the exiles must be gathered up and returned to the land of Israel," Gedalia replied, looking at them as though the question was a strange one. "It is what a believing Jew must do."

"I see," Yehuda said, and his face creased in a musing smile. He thought of his father, Reb Shimon, the Talmud scholar whose fists had flailed the air as he shouted that Yehuda's migration to Palestine was a profanation of God's name. Two Jews and you have three ideologies, Yehuda thought wryly. It was too bad that Reb Shimon and Gedalia would never meet.

"And the diligence, how did you get that?" Ezra asked. He had the dreamy child's instinct for ferreting out a good story.

"Ah, the diligence," Gedalia said, and a sweet and wily smile showed teeth scraped to an ivory whiteness by acacia leaves. "The diligence I won from my neighbor Achmed Bey, the Turk, in a game of shesh-besh."

"What's shesh-besh?" Sara asked, glad to be diverted. The ride was making her nauseous and beads of sweat stood on her pale forehead.

"It's like backgammon, I think," Yehuda said and whistled in admiration. Only in the Middle East would a man gamble for his livelihood over a board and a pair of dice.

The carriage moved slowly over the road that led southward from Jaffa. A donkey-drawn cart driven by one of Gedalia's many sons trailed after them, laden with their possessions. The purple portmanteau lay at Rivka's feet. The soaking papers had been dried, and she had added to its contents. In the Jaffa bookstore she had bought Ezra a Latin primer and a geography text. Already the boy had looked with absorption at the wonderfully colored maps. He was a born student with a gift for words and learning.

Clouds of smoke-colored dust hung heavy in the air. The windblown sand stung their eyes. The leaves on the low bushes that clung to the side of the road were bleached to a ghostly whiteness, and the nettles and thorns were pale clusters of overgrowth, sucked dry of life. The empty, barren landscape stretched north and south, east and west. A jackal scurried across the road and shrieked wildly at them. The echo of his keening protest against their invasion of his arid wilderness lingered as they drove slowly on. A few meters further they saw the stripped carcass of another jackal and glimpsed a hawk circling slowly above the fly-infested carrion, scraps of bloody meat suspended in its claws.

Here and there along the roadside, eucalyptus trees with massive trunks and tapering graceful leaves cast pools of gentle shadow. Once they were startled by the sight of a single wild almond tree, its crown a mass of delicate pink-and-white blossoms that drifted gently to the sun-parched ground like the last snows of late winter. Soon the flowers would disappear and clusters of oval-shaped golden nuts would begin to form. They were reassured. Growth was possible, after all, amid the sand and dust.

An Arab girl wearing a loose gown of varicolored stripes passed them, leading two black kids on a frayed length of string.

"Salaam aleikem," Gedalia called to her.

She waved her staff, then leaned upon it heavily, and they saw that she was badly crippled.

"The children's disease," Gedalia said and looked back as though to assure himself that his own sons were still healthy.

Yehuda assumed that he meant the same infantile paralysis that sent a shaft of fear through the heart of every mother. Even Rivka had, in desperation, tied bags of garlic around her children's necks to ward off the dread disease.

"There is Mikveh Israel," Gedalia said, pointing his long finger.

They saw the patch of green emerging in the distance where the fields of the agricultural school founded by the Alliance Israelite rolled southward. Wheat fields had been planted as well as barley, and groves of almond and olive trees stood sentry, shading patches of radishes and potatoes. They saw the new greenery of grape arbors, and as they watched, a trio of small gray birds shot skyward, weaving their way through the sheltering leaves of the young vines.

Two farmers from the agricultural settlement passed them, perched on an ox-drawn cart. One wore a straw hat and the other had shielded his head with an Arab kaffiyeh which he twisted rakishly about his neck.

"Shalom!" the family called back, and Saul and David

stared with open admiration. How tanned the men were, how strong and at ease amid the fields of their own planting.

As they passed the Arab village of Beit Dijon, Sara stared at the squat stone houses and the barefoot children in over-sized dark robes who scurried about. A swaddled infant clung to the back of a girl who could not have been older than six. Three women sat together in the pebbled courtyard and pounded grain against a large flat rock, using another rock as a mortar. Beneath the shade of an ancient olive tree, a group of old men sat on the ground hovering over a single water pipe which they passed from hand to hand. They did not look up as the diligence passed, and Gedalia made no effort to greet them.

At the crossroads they turned left and at last they were in Rishon LeZion. The diligence moved with regal slowness through the main street of the tiny settlement.

"Look, Papa," Ezra called and pointed to the newly built wine cellars adorned with the crest of the Rothschild family.

Housewives carrying straw market baskets paused to stare at them, shading their eyes with work-reddened hands. A white-jacketed pharmacist emerged from the dispensary and nodded while a group of children ran after the carriage, shouting playfully in Hebrew. The men and women who sat at the rickety tables in front of the town's single cafe stared at them over tall glasses of tea encased in metal holders. There was a tentative wave, an exchange of shy smiles. Their welcome was clear.

"Shalom," a tall man who carried a medical bag called to them as he mounted a chestnut horse that stood patiently reined to a railing.

"*Shalom u'vracha,*" Yehuda replied. "Peace and blessing."

"Dr. Schoenbaum," Gedalia said. "A wonderful man. A saint. He is the doctor for all the settlements. Alas, he is a widower. Only last year his wife died. He must find another woman. It is not good for a man to be alone."

They turned in at a rut in the road and continued on to the low-built stucco house where the Altman family stood, dressed and in readiness for their journey. The two Altman sons, who were perhaps only a few years older than the twins, muttered brief greetings and busied themselves with their luggage. Only once did they look at the Maimon boys and then, swiftly, they averted their eyes. Ezra felt a strange stirring of guilt as though he were too early moving into a life his predecessors were reluctant to abandon.

Mrs. Altman was a tall, gaunt woman whose faded dark blue traveling dress had been mended too many times. The heels of her high-button shoes were run-down, and her gray hair hung in carelessly combed wisps about her thin face. Yet her voice was cultivated and the furniture she showed Rivka was well-crafted and tasteful. Surely she had paid dearly for it and selected it with care.

"We brought the furniture from Europe," she said in answer to Rivka's unarticulated question. "But I don't want to take it to America. I don't want to take anything from this place to America."

The woman's hand trembled and her voice rose shrilly. New questions trembled on Rivka's tongue but she remained silent.

"The furniture is very beautiful," she said at last, but the thin woman did not respond to her words.

Yehuda and Mr. Altman discussed the financial arrangements. The deed to the property had been transferred during Yehuda's first visit, and the price of the furniture was quickly agreed upon.

The Maimons watched the Altman family drive away with Gedalia. It was Sara who noticed that they did not look back although the older boy had stooped, just before he left, and plucked up a small stone which he put in his pocket. She recognized his gesture. In the pocket of her brown skirt there were stalks of dried clover grass which she had pulled from their garden the morning they left Kharkov.

"He was a poor manager, this Altman," her father was explaining as though there were a need to justify the other family's failure. "He switched from crop to crop. One year wheat and the next barley. Then almonds. Only now, finally, citrus, but too little and too late. Farming is like business. You have to know the land. You have to know the market. He failed. We, Rivka, we won't fail; we can't fail. And they buried a daughter here. She was the wife of this Dr. Schoenbaum. Mrs. Altman is bitter, very bitter." There was a hidden plea in his words. Take warning from this other woman's sorrow, Rivka. Stand with me. As though she understood, Rivka took his hand and moved closer to him.

Sara walked through the house, running her fingers across

the surfaces of furniture another woman had cared for. The dark wood dining room table gleamed in the encroaching shadows. Somber secrets were frozen into its shimmering surface. A family had sat about this table laughing and singing, and then, trapped by disappointment and despair, had, shared silent meals and avoided each other's eyes. Here the tall young doctor had toasted his bride, the daughter of the house, and at this table he had eaten the somber meal that followed her funeral. Here plans had been made and discarded. Here hopes had soared and plummeted.

"Sara, look." Ezra stood beside her, his outstretched hand forming a cup. Discrete black grains of soil peppered his palm and his eyes shone with wonder as he looked at them. "Anything can grow here on this land. Anything."

"It's earth," Sara said shortly. "Just dirt."

Briskly, she moved away to avoid the hurt in her brother's eyes. She was tired of men who burned with mystic idealism. They attributed strange powers to a clump of earth and sought to become social alchemists. They would alter the world with their ideas and their deeds. New social orders would be born, new nations formed. Deserts would become gardens and the sea water would be freed of its salt.

In Russia, Chaim, whose shoulders glowed white in the darkness, dreamed his dream of universal brotherhood, collective ownership and action. Here in Palestine, her father, the businessman Zionist, plotted his crops and thought to mold a new Jewish national destiny. A Jewish state. A Hebrew university. Her brother trembled as he looked at hillside and field. She was weary of them all.

She wanted only an easing of loneliness, and she feared that she would be balanced always between men who dreamed disparate dreams. She stood alone as the great red sun burned a hole in the sky and streaked the heavens with arcs of gold-tinged flames. Crimson slashes faded into soft cushions of drifting pink and purple that hovered over the vast stretch of barren fields.

The twins cavorted with two speckled kids, and in the distance a donkey brayed mournfully.

Ezra's small solitary figure vanished over a gentle hillock. He stopped to scoop up a handful of earth, which he sifted through his fingers.

Rivka and Yehuda, their arms linked, watched the sunset

from the half-finished flagstone terrace. Reluctantly they walked back to the house. There was so much to do, so much to prepare for against their new beginning.

But at the doorway Rivka turned again. Their fields were ablaze now in the glow of the lowering sun. This then was her home; this newly viewed barren vista would be the landscape of her life forevermore. Sadness and fear gripped her, and when she entered the house her face was wet with tears that sprang from a mysterious source and could not be controlled. Weeping, she took up the broom and swept the dust and debris of alien lives from the floor of the house she would make her home.

PART TWO

Sara, Avremel, and Shimon

1896

Chapter 6

"Shimon!"

The woman's voice, strident with irritation, pierced the afternoon quiet.

The two blue-robed Arab workers lifted their scythes and looked at each other. Shrugging, they glanced at the small boy who scurried ahead of them in the field of golden durra wheat. They hesitated only a moment and then bent to their labor again. Surely the child had heard his grandmother call. Besides, it was not their business. If the Jewish woman wanted her grandson she could come and look for him herself. Besides, the boy was not a baby. He had attained his seventh year. Their own sons, at such an age, already cared for the goats and fetched water for their mothers. Abdul, Hassan's nine-year-old boy, worked in the Jews' wine cellar. But all this small boy, Maimon's grandson and the doctor's son, managed to do was frolic in the fields when he returned from the schoolhouse. They watched him now as he heaved a flat stone into the distance and then bent to find another.

Still, the doctor was a good man. They could not forget that if he had not cut the flesh of Saleem's neck to force the breath out, Saleem would have choked on the relentless green mucus that blocked his throat. Strange and complicated were these bodies that Allah had cursed them with. And the doctor had come in the darkness of the night, riding as swiftly on his chestnut steed as Saleem's own son, who had raced on his stallion to fetch him. Yes, the doctor was a good man and perhaps when the boy was grown, he would learn his father's secrets. He looked like his father, the tall doctor. His long silken hair matched the golden grain and they had remarked the swift grace of his tapering fingers when he helped them with the chaffing.

"Shimon!"

There was a new harshness in the woman's call now and the first hint of anxiety. Rivka shifted her weight from one foot to the other and mopped the perspiration from her brow with the wilted linen handkerchief that had been crisp and fresh only moments before. She wished that Sara and Avremel had taken the boy with them to Jerusalem. She could not manage her grandson any better than she had been able to manage her own twin sons. He had inherited Saul and David's gay propensity for adventure, their indifference to restriction and threats. He would not listen to her.

"We'll just be away a few days, Mama," Sara had said, and of course Rivka could not object. After all, Sara virtually ran the Maimon household. She did almost all the cooking and shopping, and supervised the cleaning and the laundry. And the trip to Jerusalem was an important one. An English ophthalmologist, sponsored by Sir Moses Montifiore, was delivering a series of lectures on the treatment of trachoma at the Shaare Tzedek Hospital. Avremel wanted to hear the lectures, and Sara had never seen Jerusalem. Avremel teased her about it. Imagine—eight years in the country and you haven't yet seen David's Tower or the Western Wall of the temple! But of course there had never been time. Sara and Avremel had been married only a few weeks after the arrival of the Maimon family. Their daughter's hasty courtship had bewildered Yehuda and Rivka. They had barely unpacked their belongings and already they were making a wedding.

Rivka had busied herself fashioning a wedding dress, and Yehuda had made discreet inquiries about the bridegroom and then bought a supply of meats and wine for the wedding feast. Both were apprehensive, yet pleased to see Sara slowly emerge from the cocoon of sadness into which she had been sealed since the day she left her Chaim in Kharkov. Rivka admired her son-in-law's fine-featured handsomeness, and Yehuda, who could not keep himself from balancing accounts, mused that Avremel's maturity would balance Sara's youthfulness. She was seventeen, only a year younger than Rivka had been when he stood with her beneath the marriage canopy.

And that first year Sara had been constantly ill with the pregnancy that ended with a sudden hemorrhaging in the night. Heavy clots of blood had stained the sheets on the featherbed on which Rivka herself had labored to birth Sara and her sons. Even now, after all the years of laundering and bleaching, tiny tear-shaped rust-colored stains adhered to the linen, indelible testimony to that night of pain and terror when Sara had almost been lost to them. But they had been lucky. Sara had recovered, and a year later Shimon had been born.

Gentle Avremel had held his son, his hands still glistening with the milky liquid of the afterbirth that he had wrenched from Sara's body. He had wept.

"Isn't he beautiful?" he had asked again and again although he was a doctor and newborn infants were no mystery to him.

They had all assured him of the infant's beauty and Rivka had swaddled her grandson in the tiny garments sewn by Moscow seamstresses for the layettes of her own children. The newborn had been passed around among his young uncles, who held his tiny body in their large and trembling hands. Ezra, when his turn came, lightly brushed the child's tiny fingers with his lips.

They named the child after Yehuda's father, who had died that winter of pneumonia. The news of the old scholar's death had not reached them until months after his interment in the Jewish cemetery in Kharkov. Yehuda had not even observed the seven days of mourning. It seemed oddly meaningless to him, and besides, the barley harvest was in progress. He had, however, assembled six men of Rishon to join him and his sons in a daily prayer quorum so that he might say Kaddish. They prayed in the lifting shadows of the first light of dawn, before going out to the fields. Wrapped in their prayer shawls, they bound the black leather phylacteric straps around their bronzed muscular arms. Silver sunlight streaked the metallic surfaces of the scythes and rifles that leaned in readiness in the doorway.

"Blessed and sanctified be Thy name," Yehuda intoned, and remembered, with a bitterness that had only now begun to fade, that his father had not blessed him and would not be glad to think that the child that bore his name had been born in the holy land which was being redeemed now, not by God but by man.

The years the Maimons had spent on the land had been active and full, one day speeding after another so that they were startled by the changing seasons, the vanishing years. Shimon galloped from infancy to childhood, living with his parents in the Maimon house because Avremel understood (as Chaim, whose face she no longer remembered, had not) that Sara could not leave her family. Who would do the cooking and manage the household? (Rivka tired so easily, and besides, she was involved now with poetry and painting.) Ezra completed the school at Rishon and studied privately with Imber, who taught him literature, and Feinberg, who knew law and geography. Avremel taught him biology, and an Alliance botany instructor at Mikveh Israel tutored him in botany. Rivka taught him French, which meant that he mastered Rimbaud's poetry but would not have been able to ask a Parisian waiter to bring him bread.

"Why does the Rishon school have to teach in Hebrew?" Rivka moaned. Every other schoolroom in the country was reigned over by French-speaking teachers.

The twins, who remembered how their mother had pursued them across the deck of the *Vittoria* armed with a Hebrew grammar, glanced at each other and smiled. They no longer lived with the family—an arrangement which both suited and saddened them.

Yehuda Maimon's farmlands were no longer the barren waste which the Altmans had sold to him. He had established a four-year cycle of crop rotation. Wheat, barley, corn, and hay grew golden in their turn and were tended and harvested by the Arab laborers who had built a small shack village on the edges of the farm. The citrus trees, carefully grafted and pruned, were reaching maturity. Plump fowl strutted through the chicken run, built far enough from the house so that the ammoniated stench of their excrement would not reach Rivka's delicate nostrils. Shimon always had a new kid to ramble with from among the new litters born to the sleek nannies who haughtily prowled the fields, munching the sorrel grass. A milch cow stood patiently in the small corral which the twins had built near the barley field.

Visitors to Rishon, who came to observe the miracle of successful Jewish agronomy, were always taken to the Maimon farm.

"Who would have believed it?" they said, looking at the rolling fields, crushing a grain of barley between two soft-fleshed urban fingers.

In Europe Jews were shopkeepers, city dwellers, brokers, and bookkeepers. They did not grow the grain they sold. (Who knew that better than Yehuda Maimon, the grain broker's son-in-law?) But here, a miracle had happened. The visitors stripped the delicate skin from the grapes that grew in pale clusters in the Baron's vineyards and sucked the sour juice of the fleshy fruit. They toured the damp wine cellars and marveled at the barrels fashioned in the Rishon cooperage. The year of the vintage was carved in Hebrew characters across each barrel. Vintners in the holy land were using the language of the prayer book and the script of the Torah in their record keeping. The Jews from abroad trembled at the wonder of it.

They were urged to drink cups of wine and they were invited to the school, where the children of Rishon chanted their geography lessons in Hebrew. They heard only vaguely of the years of drought when the villagers rationed every drop of water, washing their floors with the water they had used to boil their vegetables. Yehuda Maimon, the prosperous farmer, did not tell them of the year when Rivka fell ill with dysentery. The infection so racked her body that she could not bear to stand up straight. Her bowels were tarred with blood and bilious vomit soured her throat and mouth. She lost twenty pounds that year and when the illness passed, she painted her cheeks with rouge and rimmed her eyes with kohl because the chalky pallor of her own skin frightened her.

That was the same year that Ezra lay near death because of pappataci, the fever brought on by the sandfly. Throughout one long hot night, the twins took turns in pressing their mouths against their brother's so that they could breathe their own breath into his body, while Sara swathed his thin arms with rags soaked in alcohol. Nor did Yehuda ever speak of the year when the wheat crop failed and there was no harvest. He would not use the capital he would need for pruning implements for the citrus trees, and so for a year they ate nothing but beet root and sourdough cakes and eggs.

"We are fine and we love the country," Rivka wrote then to her parents, who had sold their Kharkov home and moved to Kishinev where her father's younger sister lived. They had thought of coming to Palestine, but Rivka's mother dreamed of Arabs carrying bloodstained daggers who might murder them as they slept. The streets of Kishinev were clean and quiet. Their Ukrainian neighbors nodded politely when they passed the elderly couple. Rivka wrote out the unfamiliar street address. Her tears moistened the flap of the envelope when she sealed it.

But the years of struggle were over. The citrus trees had matured. Yehuda was thinking of buying up additional dunams. Alfalfa would be a profitable crop. He read the manuals sent to him by his brother Mendel in America, his lips slowly mouthing the unfamiliar English words. A dictionary was always at his elbow. Slowly he pushed his callused finger down the columns of words, searching out meaning. Cross-fertilization. Pesticide. Hybrid.

"Why not alfalfa?" he asked Rivka, who did not answer him. He wished that he could talk to his twin sons about it. Saul and David were good farmers. Their hands fondled the earth with the natural pleasure and ease of a sculptor testing a compound of clay. They were strong, lithe men who raced beside the plow horses when a field was being cleared, stooping to heave up loose rocks and earthbound boulders. They swung their scythes in vigorous arcs, uprooting thorn bushes and wild brambles purple with thistle flowers. They delighted in the harvest season, when they rose before dawn and prowled the fields where ripened grain glowed golden in the shadows of unborn day. At day's end their hands were bloodied by the coarseness of twine and stalk but their laughter was loud, and they sang as they doused each other with cold water from the shower barrel.

Rivka listened to them through the open windows with her lips set in a thin line. She had meant her sons to be advocates and professors, scientists or poets—not sweat-soaked farmers with callused, earth-colored palms. Her sons, naked and wet in the half darkness, splashed water at each other and sang.

"We are, we are, we are
Pioneers, pioneers!
On burning field
On barren fields of waste
The first to arrive
Like swallows in spring
We believe . . .
We'll cover the stony fields
With golden bloom."

It was a song she had sung in her youth, but now the words seemed coarse to her and the melody raucous and harsh.

"Ezra," she called. "Have you completed your translation?"

Her younger son, who worked in the field only half a day, sat at the table hunched over his books. He glanced from the heavy text to the open notebook covered with the neat cursive lines of his script. He mouthed the words he read and smiled with a scholar's pleasure.

"Soon, Mama, soon," he said.

Yes, Ezra would make it all up to them. He would compensate them for the twins' indifference to books, for the years of struggle on the Rishon farm, for the illnesses and the small defeats. Soon, very soon, they had to think about sending him to university. Yehuda's dream of a Hebrew university would not be realized in time to benefit his son, but he thought that perhaps Ezra could go to the United States and enroll in one of the great universities there. But Rivka insisted on Paris and the Sorbonne, and the French consul in Jaffa had assured her that Ezra could sit for a matriculation examination in Palestine. The consul himself had studied at the Faculté des Humanitiés, which he recommended without reservation, adding that if Ezra were interested in medicine (as so many Jewish students seemed to be) such a program of study could also be arranged.

"There will be no problems, madame," he had said, bowing elegantly and graciously accepting the pen-and-ink sketch of his wife that Rivka had dashed off as they had tea together in the Bakers' Jaffa living room.

"No problems. The man who represents the country which is trying Alfred Dreyfus for the crime of being a Jew assures us that there will be no problems," Yehuda said bitterly when

Rivka repeated the conversation to him. "Did you ask him about Dreyfus, Rivka?"

"No, of course not. I don't like to discuss such things with him. We meet socially, as friends," Rivka replied stiffly.

Her day trips to Jaffa, the tea parties in the Baker living room, the quiet conversations in French, were important to her. Besides, she did not like to think of the Jewish captain on trial for espionage in a Paris courtroom. She resented the fact that Yehuda insisted on reading aloud the accounts of the trial by a young journalist named Theodor Herzl, who wrote for the *Neue Freie Presse*. The French consul was not responsible for the injustice. In fact, it had been his wife who lent Rivka Émile Zola's pamphlet "J'accuse," because she remembered Rivka had so enjoyed Zola's *Nana*.

The twins had still been living at home then and Saul had looked up and smiled mockingly at his mother.

"We must not let our Judaism interfere with our friendships," he had said.

Rivka had been startled. It had been her first hint of the new ideology which the twins were cultivating and had preceded that fierce and final argument. It was perhaps just as well that they no longer lived on the Rishon farm. They visited often enough and the house was peaceful now. There was a better atmosphere for Shimon. *Where was that boy?*

"Shimon!" she called yet again. The sweat dripped in rivulets between her breasts. She could not sustain the midday heat. Daily, when the blinding sun peaked to a fiery brightness, she retreated into her bedroom. The shuttered windows shielded her from the harsh unrelenting light, and Yehuda had installed a large fan that kept the heavy air moving. If she looked long enough at the slowly rotating blades, she sometimes fell asleep. That was what she longed to do this afternoon if Shimon would only come in.

"Must I come out to the fields to get you?" she shouted now in fresh fury.

The sea of durra wheat parted suddenly and the child's head appeared between the swaying stalks of grain.

"I'm helping Saleem and Abdul, Grandma. Can I stay out for another hour?"

"All right," she called back. He was a wily child. He had wearied her into acquiescence. Oh well, later she would talk to him about his failure to reply when she first called—later, when he was munching his halvah and drinking his lemonade and after she had rested. Later, when the sun was lowering beyond the field and its fierce blaze had ceased to sear her eyes.

Shimon watched his grandmother turn and disappear into the house. He felt a nagging shame. He knew it had been wrong of him not to answer when he first heard her call. He had seen Saleem and Abdul exchange a knowing glance at his willful disobedience, and he remembered his Uncle Saul's admonition.

"You must never give an Arab the opportunity to disrespect you. The only way we can live together in this land is if we acknowledge and respect each other. We must work as hard as they do, fight as hard as they do, and show them that we care about each other and about the land."

Saul had delivered this lesson while he carved Shimon a small gazelle out of olive wood, using the heavy knife with the gem-studded handle he had bought in the Jaffa market. He kept the blade of the knife finely honed and brightly polished. Its lightest touch slashed the thick fruit of the cactus plant and exposed the juicy, pink, seeded flesh. He had used that knife once when he and Shimon, while hiking through a wadi, had come across a limping wounded jackal.

"Poor creature," Saul had said. Like many strong men, he was deeply affected by the weak and wounded.

The jackal lay down on a clump of leaves and writhed in pain, baring its sharp thin teeth in a grin of agony. Swiftly, Saul drew his knife across the animal's throat. Dark blood gushed forth, staining the white neck fur. A rattling moan trembled in the air. The creature shivered mightily and lay still. Saul had wiped the blackened knife clean of blood, and Shimon had helped him to cover the animal's body with earth and twigs.

"If the hawks want it, let them work for it," Saul said, and walked on so quickly that Shimon had difficulty catching up with him. The small boy understood instinctively, then, that his uncle hated death but did not fear it.

The Arabs, Shimon knew, would respect the way in which Saul had dealt with the wounded animal's pain, just as they respected his father for his knowledge of medicine and his willingness to help them. Shimon sometimes went with

Avremel, riding in front of him on his saddle, when the doctor visited Beit Dijon. He had seen how even the sheik who wore the white turban that marked him as a pilgrim of wealth and distinction who had been to Mecca, spoke softly and deferentially to his father.

Adoni HaRaphun, he called him, lowering his head respectfully—my master, the one who heals.

The Arab children waited patiently in line near the date palm tree where Avremel worked. They did not cry when he dropped mysterious liquids into their poor encrusted eyes. They stood rigid while the doctor's sharp steel blades and needles pierced their festering boils.

"*Yaala.* Good boy," Avremel said to each of them, and distributed the lemon drops he bought by the gunny sack in the Jaffa market.

He carried home sacks of olives, dried herbs, and bolts of woven linen. Once Shimon held a speckled heron's egg in both his hands as they rode home. Musa, the sheik's small son, gave it to him and although he knew the egg would not hatch, he fashioned a nest for it out of tall swamp grass and kept it on the shelf in his parents' room. The gift was a mark of the Arab boy's respect.

But the Arabs respected his grandfather too, Shimon knew, although his grandfather felt differently about them. Saul and David were very aware of the men who worked beside them in the field, but Yehuda Maimon sometimes appeared not to see those who worked his fields. But it was true that he worked as hard or harder than Saleem and the other workers. Often he was in the fields before they arrived and still at work when they left. And of course they were impressed by his knowledge, by the new tools he taught them to use, and by the mysterious composts and mulches he concocted for the kitchen gardens he allowed them to plant behind their shacks.

It occurred to Shimon that there was merit in both his uncles' words and his grandfather's actions. Was that possible? He would ask his mother when she returned from Jerusalem, or perhaps he would talk to his Uncle Ezra about it that night. He was glad that Ezra had not left the Rishon farm when Saul and David did; the house would really be quiet then. His father was seldom home and his mother was so busy with the marketing and housework and working with the poultry and in the kitchen garden. His grandmother, of course, could not be bothered with his questions. Her health was poor. Odors offended her and the heat oppressed her. She contented herself with her books and her watercolors, the conversations with Imber and Mrs. Feinberg, and the Sabbath afternoon tea parties when she sat with her friends in the shade of the citron tree and they read strange unrhyming poems to each other and murmured compliments in hushed voices.

"Oh, lovely. Full of feeling."

"What a wonderful use of simile."

"That one you must send to *Havatzelet*. And that one to *HaShachar*."

It was Ezra whom Shimon would seek out that night, and he knew that his uncle would take the time to carefully consider his questions. Ezra had more time to spend with Shimon now that Saul and David had left the farm. That too was strange. Shimon had never thought that Ezra and the twins had much to say to each other, but since the night his brothers had stormed out of the house, Ezra had seemed lonely and at odds with himself. He sometimes wandered the fields alone, as Shimon often did when there was nothing to do and no one to play with. Sometimes he just stood, leaning against the eucalyptus tree and gazing northward. Shimon followed his uncle's glance but he saw only the clear sky and an occasional heron winging its way to the sea.

It was sad that Saul and David had quarreled with Grandpa Yehuda the way they had. Shimon remembered how he had trembled at the anger in their voices, at the sudden shouting and fierce muttering. His own parents always spoke gently to each other.

"Please," they said, and, "thank you."

Even in the darkness of the night, when Shimon lay on his narrow bed in the smaller of the two rooms which his grandfather had added to the concrete house when his parents were married, Shimon could hear them being polite to each other.

"Please, Sara," his father would say, oh so gently.

And then after sweet whispering and the rustle of linen, the creak of bedsprings, Shimon, lying rigid and awake, waiting, would hear his father sigh deeply.

"Thank you," Avremel would say then. "Thank you, my Sara."

His grandmother and his Uncle Ezra also spoke in quiet

tones. It occurred to Shimon that people who spent a great
deal of time with books, like his grandmother and his Uncle
Ezra, spoke softly because they were unused to the intrusion
of sound upon their thoughts. Voices startled them and invaded
their privacy. His grandfather, of course, spoke hardly at all.
He was absorbed in his manuals and account books when he
was not busy with the farm itself. The vitality of the house,
the gaiety, and finally the fierce anger, came from his twin
uncles, those strong handsome men whose copper curls blazed
in the sunlight and whose skin, at summer's end, was bronzed
to the color of the earth they tilled.

Saul and David knew how to laugh aloud and to exchange
jokes that coaxed forth the merriment of other men. They
rode their horses into Jaffa, to Petach Tikvah, to Mikveh
Israel, and north to the foothills of the Carmel and the rolling
slopes of the Galilee. Wherever they went, they made friends
whom they brought back to the Rishon farm. They buckled
ammunition belts around their waists and thrust their pistols
through hand-tooled leather holsters.

"*Yaala!*" they shouted as they rode forth on the horses
they had bought from a Bedouin tribe that had grazed its
animals near Rishon one summer. The horses were black
stallions, twin issue of a valiant mare who had died at their
birth. Saul and David had nursed the motherless colts themselves, feeding them from bottles and spooning mash into
their open mouths. Like their masters, the horses were identi-
cal, each born with a white star that glowed between wide-set
amber eyes.

Sometimes the twins invited young pioneers from the Mikveh
Israel Agricultural School or new arrivals who lived in the
hostel at Petach Tikvah. Small Shimon looked at his uncle's
friends with awe. They used words he did not understand,
spoken in a Hebrew accented with the guttural intonations of
Russia and Poland. They spoke of foreign lands and distant
cities. They talked in solemn tones of pogroms and conscrip-
tions. A handsome blond youth had only four fingers on his
right hand. His own father had chopped off the fifth one, the
pinky, so that the boy would not be drafted. A small scar
grew in a jagged line across the uneven stump.

The young men were always armed. A dagger or a revolver
dangled from their belts. Rifles were slung carelessly over
their shoulders. They ate with gusto the meals that Sara

prepared. It was not often that they had enough to eat, they confided unashamedly to Shimon, who was embarrassed because he always had enough to eat. Of course there had been times when the family had done without meat and chicken, eggs and fresh vegetables—his Uncle David retched now at the sight of beet root, remembering the winter when they had eaten dried beet root for breakfast in order to survive. Still, that was before the citrus trees bore their fruit and before his grandfather had instituted his system of crop rotation.

"Why don't you have enough to eat?" he asked the tall, thin man they called Yossi.

"Because we can't get enough work," Yossi replied, cramming another piece of pita soaked in gravy into his mouth.

"Why can't you get enough work?" Shimon asked with a child's dogged persistence.

"We want to work on the Jewish farms but the farmers do not hire us," Yossi explained.

"But there is work on the farm," Shimon replied stubbornly. "Saleem works on our farm and Abdul and all their cousins. And next week even their children will come to help with the pruning. Do you want to work on our farm? Then you must talk to Grandpa Yehuda."

He turned to the head of the table but his grandfather was already standing, a frown furrowing his brow.

"We will talk about it another time, Shimon," his grandfather said and hurried out without saying goodbye to the young men who sat at his table.

One spring morning Shimon rode with Saul into the village. Their nanny goat had died and Shimon who had been overcome with grief at the loss had been promised that he could pick her replacement from among the herd of a tribe of Bedouin encamped in an open meadowland near Rishon.

He walked with his uncle among the heavy black tents. The air was dark with the smoke of the early morning cooking fires over which the veiled, black-gowned women of the tribe crouched, stirring the grain that steamed in blackened copper pots. Small boys rotated slabs of meat suspended above the low fires, and little girls darted nervous glances at them as they pounded barley between smoothed and flattened rocks.

A tall young man wearing an elegant striped robe led them to the goatherd and stood patiently by as Shimon and

Saul examined each frisky animal. Now and again he would murmur something in Arabic to Saul, who considered carefully before replying in the same language. Shimon wondered how it was that his uncles and his father had learned the language of the Arabs while his grandfather could barely manage a rudimentary greeting.

In the end Shimon chose a goat with great mournful eyes and speckled fur. They sealed the bargain with the Bedouin beneath an acacia tree where he poured them tiny cups of bitter black coffee from a copper *feenjan*. Shimon, who was not allowed to drink coffee at home, savored the thick drink and ate more than his share of the sugared dates which crowned the brass tray that served as a table. He was feeling content as they jogged home. Saul's horse rocked him gently, and the young goat was a warm bundle of fur that he clutched to his chest.

The morning sky was pale green, threaded with strands of gold that would increase and multiply as the sun rose. Soon they would be woven together into an overhang of blinding brightness. Three men approached them, walking slowly along the cambered road.

"Look, there's Yossi," Shimon called. "Where is he going?"

"To the hiring hall," Saul replied. He pointed to a long wooden building that straddled an ancient wadi.

"What's a hiring hall?" Shimon asked.

Saul hesitated for a moment and then said, "Come, you shall see for yourself."

They entered the large bare room where a group of young pioneers had assembled. Like Yossi, most of them wore rubashkas, the typical Russian work shirts, and loose work pants that were now worn and ragged. Yossi's thin gray trousers were held up by a twisted piece of rope. Some of the men wore Turkish pantaloons, and their boots were caked with mud and cracked at the seams. All of them were thin and hungry-eyed. A milky veil clung to the pupils of a bearded dark-haired man who squinted painfully when he looked at them. A heat rash peppered the skin of a pale blond youth whose palms, when he shook hands with Shimon, were so soft and tender that the small boy could not imagine how they could grasp a plow or scythe.

Two Rishon farmers, friends of his grandfather's whom

Shimon had often seen at the Maimon home on Sabbath afternoons, entered the room, surveyed the assembled men, and nodded imperiously to two pioneers who followed them out.

"Good. I am glad that they chose Yaskov. He badly needed a day's work," Yossi said.

"Saul, have you read this essay by Gordon?" the bearded man asked and he flourished a pamphlet. "He says here again, in the strongest language imaginable, that we must pledge ourselves to labor on the land. A religion of work, he calls it. Only through our efforts can the land be redeemed. Jews must till the soil to reclaim it. Do you agree with him, Saul?"

The man's eyes burned feverishly and he clutched the printed pages to his breast with the same fervor as the Rishon Jews embraced their Torah.

"Yes. Of course he is right. You know that I think he is right," Saul replied.

"Then you'll talk to your father about us?" the man persisted.

"Yes. Tonight. David and I will talk to him. And Shimon will back us up. Won't you, Shimon?"

Saul tousled his nephew's hair and Shimon, who would do anything for his handsome, brave uncles, smiled happily.

"I will do whatever you want, Uncle," he said.

"What will the men who do not get work do?" Shimon asked as they rode home.

"They will find something. And those who work will share their wages. They've established a communal kitchen and they share everything. But it is very sad not to have work. Especially when you have come to a land and dedicated yourself to the idea of working its soil," Saul said.

"Like Grandpa did," Shimon offered, but his uncle did not reply.

Shimon was silent for the rest of the ride. A sad secret had been revealed to him and he struggled with it unhappily, just as he had struggled to understand why his nanny goat had died when she was still young and had just birthed a litter. It startled him to realize that there were things in this clear sun-drenched world of his which could not be explained.

It was that night that the argument that drove his uncles from their father's house erupted. The quarrel grew like the

slow storms that overtook the countryside in the early days of
fall, just after the harvest. It began with quiet, almost gentle
talk as they sat around the large dining room table. The men
spoke softly, their voices subdued by fatigue. Sara and Rivka
passed the serving dishes, uncovering each so that the room
was swathed in the fragrance of the food. The ritual slaugh-
terer had visited Rishon that week and there was young lamb
cooked with barley, and baby carrots from Sara's kitchen
garden for dinner. They talked as they ate, and their voices
rose and fell like the gentle soughing of the wind that wafted
over the stripped and barren sheaves just before the fierceness
of the first rains. Saul spoke of his friends, the young pioneers who wanted to work the land. The hiring hall, he said,
was a humiliating experience. The Jewish settlers who were
already established had an obligation to these young men.

"Who had an obligation to me when I arrived in the
land?" Yehuda asked.

The dessert was passed but the men ignored it. Momentum
was building. Contained anger was threatening to overflow its
fragile borders.

"They are good workers, Father," Saul said.

"How can they be good workers? They have come here
straight from the study halls. Their hands are soft. Their
backs know only how to bend over books, not how to use a
plow."

"They will learn." It was Ezra who spoke now. He turned
his eyes from his father's startled stare and looked at his
brothers.

"And I must pay them while they learn?" Yehuda said.
"The Arabs already know how to work and they are used to
the heat."

"You pay the Arabs," David said. "You even let them
build shacks on our land."

"What do I pay them? Can a Jew live on the wages I pay
the Arabs? They don't need much. They have their houses,
their gardens, their small flocks. But can I pay a Jew what I
pay Saleem or Abdul? I would be ashamed."

"Can a Jew live on nothing?" Saul asked, and the anger in
his voice pelted them like the first drops of a new and
gathering rain. "Are you not ashamed that young Jewish
pioneers are starving and ill? Are you not ashamed that they
return to Russia or go to the United States—you who talk of a

Jewish state, a Hebrew university? Before we can have a Hebrew university we must have Jewish farmlands."

The contempt in his uncle's voice made Shimon shiver and he saw his mother and his grandmother exchange nervous glances.

"They are troublemakers, these *chalutzim*—these pioneers of yours," Yehuda retorted angrily. "They would bring their ideas of socialism and communism here. They want to do away with the sabbatical year."

"You have managed to circumvent the sabbatical year by rotating your crops and always allowing one field to lie fallow. And I have not noticed you pouring away the milk of the cow or the goats because it was produced on the Sabbath as the truly Orthodox farmers do. Besides, Father, you know that if you were to stick to the letter of Orthodox thought you would have to wait for the Messiah to arrive before the land could be redeemed. Those who walk the alleyways of Meah Shaarim in Jerusalem would say that you are profaning God's name by reclaiming the land without His messenger," David retorted.

Anger distorted Yehuda's face. A vein at his throat throbbed dangerously. Memory transported him back to the doorway of the Kharkov synagogue and he heard again his dead father's voice and saw the palsied tremble in the old scholar's hand. He stood up, and his shadow darkened the white cloth.

"Listen, my sons, my brave sons who ride black horses and speak in the language of the fellahin and the desert dwellers—if you do not approve of your father and your father's way, do not sleep in his house, do not eat at his table. Join your friends at the hostel in Petach Tikvah. Learn what it is like to have a board for a bed. See for yourselves how it feels to eat your ideals and drink your dreams."

Spittle flecked the corners of his mouth and his right hand flew threateningly upward although he had never, even in the days of their boyhood, struck his sons.

"Yehuda!"

Rivka's hand clutched her husband's shoulder and her body trembled with unfamiliar fear. Even after two decades of marriage Yehuda's fury was foreign to her. She felt suddenly that she had shared her life with a stranger who masked his secret angers, hoarded his private sorrows. The source of his rage was unknown to her and thus frightening.

He had never told her of his last meeting with his father, nor had he shared with her the pain he had felt on the day of his arrival at Jaffa, when he had seen his failed former comrades leave the land they had sworn to make their own. It was not difficult to love Zion on the boulevards of Moscow or in the cafes of Kharkov. He had no patience with horas danced around a samovar and the readings of Zionist tracts and Hebrew poetry in candlelit circles. He was done with pledges made beneath the stars. "If I forget thee O Jerusalem . . ." It was difficult to remember Jerusalem when the body burned with fever and was racked with hunger. Words and philosophy were not enough.

He had worked according to his own lights and he had prevailed. His orchards flourished. Full-headed grain swayed in his sunlit fields. There was meat on his table. His sons rode strong horses and wore leather boots. And yet they defied him. They would have him beggar himself to provide work for dreamers who did not know how to saw a board or dig a ditch. He had worked too hard for what now belonged to him. He would not risk his own achievements for other men's dreams.

Saul and David also stood up, and Shimon noticed for the first time that his uncles were taller than their father. The brothers looked at each other and with that brief glance an agreement was reached. Anger held his shoulder's rigid but when Saul spoke, his voice was deadly calm.

"You are right, Father. We don't belong here. We leave tonight to join our friends. Saleem and Abdul will find you men to do our work. But know this, Father—if there is to be a Jewish state, then Jews must farm their land."

They left the room, slamming the door behind them, and as the family sat in the dining room, their silence was punctuated by the slamming of cupboard doors and the metallic thud of a trunk lid. When the twins returned they carried laden rucksacks and wore heavy sweaters against the evening cold.

"Saul, David, don't go," Rivka sobbed, but she knew they would not listen to her. They never had. They were her rebellious, playful boys grown now into strong men who moved with the certainty and assurance of those who know what they must do.

They bent to kiss their sister goodbye, and Sara, always

practical, slipped a parcel of food into David's rucksack, tucked a scarf around Saul's neck.

Avremel shook hands with his tall brothers-in-law. He had said nothing during the argument but his eyes were sympathetic as they traveled from his wife's brothers to her father. In all things he saw all sides. It was true that the young Jewish pioneers needed the work, but his father-in-law could not afford to take many risks. A farmer's prosperity was tenuous, dependent on wind and rain, dangerous shadows in the evening sky. And the Arabs also had their rights to labor and homes. All sides screamed for a hearing and he heard them all and struggled to grant justice to all, thus assigning right to no one. He was glad that his work called for few moral judgments. He was charged only with healing the sick and he stood by the bedsides of the old settlers and the young chalutzim, the Bedouin child and the Arab villager.

Ezra embraced his brothers. His eyes were dangerously bright and color burned high in his cheeks.

"Father." They would not leave without saying goodbye. Yehuda held out his hands to them and felt the strength of their grasp.

"Shalom," he said and sorrow tugged at him. They were so tall. Their bodies were bronzed by the sun and trained to a graceful muscularity by the hard work of the fields. They were shrewd farmers. He did not want them to go but he could not ask them to stay.

"God be with you," he added softly. His sons would not leave his house without a blessing.

Shimon was tossed into the air and hugged and then the door slammed and they were gone.

"It will be a cold night," Rivka said.

"They have their sweaters. They're on horseback," Sara reassured her.

But in the morning they saw that the twins had left behind their coal-black stallions with the white stars that glowed between brooding amber eyes.

Shimon cared for the horses. He curried their manes and wiped kernels of grit from their eyes and from their long lashes. In three years, when he was ten years old, his uncles would teach him how to ride. Saul and David lived now at the agricultural school at Mikveh Israel, but they often visited the Rishon farm.

"Take the horses," Yehuda had implored his sons on their first uneasy visit home. He was not a man who nursed his grievances. He evaluated his assets and cut his losses. True, he was disappointed, hurt. But his sons would live their own lives. Still, and forever, they were his sons.

"One day, when we have our own settlement, a collective colony of our own, we will take them. Then they will belong to all our comrades. But it would not be right for us to have horses now while our comrades do not."

"Crazy men." Yehuda looked at his sons with resigned despair. He had taken what was given him. Their lives in this promised land had been built on the grain broker's largesse. But he had also worked and struggled and planned. He had nothing to be ashamed of. Couldn't the twins follow his example? He sighed and thought with relief of Ezra. His youngest son, at least, created no problems, caused no difficulties. But then he never had. He was a good boy, a brilliant boy. Avremel was teaching him zoology now. They had set up a rough-hewn laboratory table in a corner of the barn and Avremel had taught Ezra how to pith a frog and how to dissect the large rat which Saleem had caught for them in the barley field.

"He has a wonderful grasp of science," Avremel had told Yehuda, who nodded with satisfaction.

Shimon sometimes hovered about the barn when his father and Ezra bent over the microscope. It was lonely on the farm and his grandmother frowned and nagged when he went over to the Arabs' shacks and played with the children of the workers.

"It's filthy there. You'll get lice. Germs. Don't eat there. Not even pita. You'll get stomach aches."

"And you'll have fun. And you'll learn to speak Arabic and you'll begin to understand how Saleem's children think," Saul laughed, and although Rivka flushed she also smiled. It was difficult to resist the twins. And oddly enough, since they had left her home, she got along better with her older sons. Shimon had seen how they could make her laugh like a young girl when they teased her.

"Shimon—where are you?"

It was a man's voice that traveled clearly now across the field of durra wheat. David's clear tenor. Shimon sprang to his feet at once. Sure enough the Mikveh Israel oxcart stood near the house. His uncles had come to visit. The tails of the huge lazy animals swirled majestically through the air, swatting away the flies that buzzed around the clumps of steaming manure that dropped from their bodies. How angry his grandmother would be that they were standing so close to the house. He laughed. Perhaps his uncles would take him for a ride. Last week they had ridden as far as Petach Tikvah.

"Saul, David, shalom, I'm coming," he called.

He dashed across the field, his bare feet lightly scratched by the fallen hulls and dried stalks that covered the ground.

Chapter 7

Sara Schoenbaum stopped at the fruit stall in Emek Rephaim on her way back to the room she and Avremel had rented in the travelers' hostel at Mishkenot ShaAnanim. The wizened little proprietress offered her half-ripened plums and shrunken apricots. She pointed and gesticulated irritably when Sara shook her head. The shopkeeper was a pious woman. She clutched a worn leather copy of Psalms in her hand, and her white cotton kerchief was tied tightly about her shaven head. The day was warm but she wore a heavy dark dress; the long sleeves covered her arms and the skirt flapped around her legs, which were wrapped in thick stockings. She looked disapprovingly at the young woman in the light cotton frock whose long dark hair was loosely twisted into a chignon. The girl's skin was sun-burnished and she moved with a light briskness that suggested immodesty. The older woman sniffed and opened her book.

" 'I will set no wicked thing before mine eyes. I hate the work of them that turn aside'," she intoned, looking at the young woman who wore a marriage ring although she walked the streets of God's holy city with her head uncovered.

"Come, Mother," the younger woman said coaxingly in a

fluent Russian-accented Yiddish. "Surely you have better fruit than this."

"I have. For those who fear the Lord," she said grudgingly. The young woman smiled.

"I fear God," she said gently and thought that she must remember to share this incident with Avremel. Surely Jerusalem was the only city in the world where you could not buy a decent apple without stating your religious principles.

The fruit seller knelt beneath the counter and took out a basket of apples brought to her that morning from the Arab village of Silwan. She also fetched a basket of pale green grapes and cut loose a cluster which she offered to her customer.

"Sweet like sugar," she said. "They grow in the Baron's vineyards in Rishon LeZion."

"That's where I live," Sara told her, and she paid for the fruit which she placed in the straw basket that dangled from her arm. "Be well, shalom."

She dropped the requisite number of coins into the fruit seller's tin cup and added a piaster for the charity cannister that stood next to it, then continued up the road, walking with the slow languid gait of a woman on holiday, briefly freed of the responsibility of rushing home to prepare a meal or tend to a crying child. It was wonderful, after eight years, to be released from obligations to her family and to lift her eyes to a landscape that varied from the low rolling hills of the Rishon plain.

"You'll love Jerusalem," Avremel had promised her, and she thought now that like all his promises that one too had been fulfilled.

It was not the city itself that claimed her but the gentle Judean hills that majestically circled the ancient wall, and the wondrous coralline light that caused the city to glow pink and gold at the twilight hour. Sara loved the tall cypresses whose velvet-leafed dark peaks lightly brushed the sky.

A long terrace girdled the rooms of the hospice at Mishkenot ShaAnanim, and when she sat outside at the evening hour, Sara saw how the rough-hewn stones of the city shimmered golden in the gloaming. The bells of the low, domed church chimed softly, and a light flickered in the tower of the mosque from which the muezzin would soon sound his cry, summoning the faithful to evening worship.

At such a chimeric hour it was easy to forget the filth in the city's streets and the rotting garbage that filled the ancient warrens where huge families shared a single room and drank sour water from splintered barrels. It was easy too, then, to forget the beggars and pious mendicants who trailed after pedestrians on the streets, displaying their twisted limbs, their fingerless hands and faces disfigured by blindness and disease. The peace of encroaching evening, the magic of changing light, briefly banished thoughts of children who pursued her on the street, their eyes almost sealed by the milky excretions of trachoma, their bones weakened by rickets, and their hair matted with lice and mites.

One such child approached her now as she descended the paved steps that led to the hospice.

"*Lachmun,*" he whimpered. "Bread. Please. A bit of bread."

Beneath his loose-fitting dirty white *galabiah,* his stomach was distended into a rounded hard mass. His legs were spindly sticks and a bone, one broken and perhaps improperly set (if set at all), jutted through his right kneecap. But his eyes were a clear blue and he blinked with gratitude as she gave him an apple, a bunch of grapes, and a pita from her laden basket.

"Allah thanks you and blesses you," he muttered and hurried away as though fearful that she might regret her generosity and reclaim her gifts.

She thought about the boy, in the coolness of her room, as she arranged the apples and grapes in the ceramic bowl she had bought in the Armenian shop on the Via Dolorosa. He could not have been much older than Shimon. What happened to such children? She shivered and concentrated instead on the fruit, crowning the largest apple with a small cluster of grapes. Avremel would approve of that, she knew. He would notice how the subtle green that broke through the apple's redness almost matched the pale verdure of the grapes.

Her husband had a craving for beauty, a love of flowers loosely set in smoked-glass vases, an eye for melancholy sunsets and bits of dry wood arranged into a collage of varied forms and shapes. That, after all, was how she and Avremel had come together on that distant day when she was newly arrived in the land and he still mourned his dead bride, daughter of the house which the Maimon family, in their turn, had made their own; that day when she had watched Avremel as he tended the tiny purple-blossomed cacti he had planted in a lovely pattern about his first wife's grave.

Often, when Sara thought back to those early days in the land, she saw herself as a stranger, as a young girl who was oddly unrelated to the woman she had become. That distant Sara was trapped by fear and melancholy. She moved like an automaton through the myriad details of unpacking the cases and barrels they had brought with them from Russia. She helped her mother organize the kitchen and devised sleeping arrangements for her brothers. With machinelike efficiency, she learned how to control the *petiliya,* the small kerosene burner on which their meals would be cooked, and she instituted a system of bringing water into the house for cooking and washing. Smiling, always polite, she accompanied her mother on visits to other Rishon families and went to the schoolhouse with Ezra to arrange for his enrollment. And all the while she vigilantly awaited the occasional dizziness that overtook her at odd moments. In the mornings she awoke to a vague nausea and could not eat her breakfast. In the afternoons a heavy fatigue overtook her and often she collapsed on the narrow day bed, her head facing the wall.

"It's the heat," her father whispered to her mother. "She will grow used to it."

But Sara knew that it was not the heat. Since the morning of their arrival she had known that life grew within her. She was pregnant. Chaim, gentle dreaming Chaim, who did not believe in marriage and who did not believe in Zion, had fathered a child which she would bear out of the bonds of marriage and in Zion. Soon, very soon, she would either have to go away or confront her parents with the truth. Each morning she awakened resolved to tell them, and each evening she fell into an exhausted sleep and assured herself that another day could not make a difference. She would wait until Rivka had accustomed herself to the house and adjusted to the routine of obtaining and preparing the family's food. She would wait until her father had organized the farm. She would wait until Ezra was immersed in his school schedule. She would wait until they could manage without her.

One week passed and then another. One morning she could not close the button on her skirt and she pulled an overblouse on and saw her changing form in the mirror. There was no

more time to wait. She brushed her long dark hair and
formulated plans. She could go back to Russia and live with
her mother's parents in the Ukraine. Their family was not
known in Kishinev. She could masquerade as a widow whose
husband had been killed in Palestine. Or perhaps she could go
to her Uncle Mendel in America. He was prospering. He
would welcome his niece and her child.

She created diverse scenes in her mind but none of them
involved Chaim, whose first letter had awaited her when they
arrived in Palestine. The czarist police had been making
inquiries about him and he had left Russia to join his sister in
the town of Oswiecim in Poland. Ezra had helped Sara find
Oswiecim on the map of Poland in the atlas Rivka had
brought for him in Jaffa.

" 'Oswiecim, or Auschwitz as the Germans call it,' " he
read from the text, " 'is a beautiful town in the Polish timber-
land. It is of no strategic or historic importance.' "

He looked up at her, proud that he had been able to help
her.

How could she leave Ezra? He needed her. Their mother,
who in Russia had dreamed of Zion, now sought to recreate
an island of European culture within Zion. Her French novels
dominated the living room shelf and her Dürer print, newly
framed, hung in the dining room. Their father spent every
hour of daylight in the fields and in the evenings he either met
with other farmers or immersed himself in his agronomy texts
and catalogues. The twins, too, were constantly in the fields.
Who then would be concerned with Ezra if she were to leave?
He was only a boy, not yet bar mitzvah.

She took a long walk that afternoon, wandering eastward
where scrub cactus and thin-leafed acacia trees lined the
rutted path. Well beyond the outskirts of the hamlet, a field
had been cleared and black iron gateposts had been thrust into
the unyielding earth. She thought it strange and drew closer,
attracted by the blanket of shade cast by an aged palm whose
thick, coarse fronds were weighted earthward by amber clusters of unripe dates. She realized then that she had wandered
into a cemetery.

Half a dozen gravestones were ranged on one side of the
tree, and three others stood on the other side. Just as men and
women sat on either side of a divider in the synagogue, so in
death were they buried separately. Here, in this sunswept

land, a tall palm marked their division, and its comforting
shadow was evenly shared. The names on the low stone slabs
were all freshly carved. Rishon, after all, was a young settlement and had only just begun to bury its dead.

She took up a handful of pebbles and walked from grave to
grave, placing a small stone on each but not reading the
inscriptions. The melancholy she had eluded all that day
settled upon her now and, almost gratefully, she abandoned
herself to it. The last gravestone was unlike the others. It was
of soft white marble and had recently been brushed free of
debris from the field. Plantings of dwarf cacti grew about it,
inset with star-shaped purple thistles. Sara yearned for a
moment to lay her head upon that clear, smooth stretch of
cool white stone. She felt a brief, irrational envy for the
woman who lay within the coolness of that carefully tended
grave. Even in death the unknown woman was cared for. Her
final resting place was tenderly nurtured while Sara, in life,
was charged with the care of others and carried a child within
her whose father now lived in a distant land and walked
streets that were unfamiliar to her.

She moved away from the grave and sat down, instead,
beneath the palm tree, lured by her own tiredness and its
gentle shade. Within that transient coolness she fell asleep.
She dreamed briefly of forest paths and snow-heavy clouds
drifting through purple-hued winter sunsets. Somewhere, beyond
the clouds, an unseen baby cried but it was a distance from
her. She struggled through icy mists, through clear green
waters, but her body had become so heavy suddenly that she
moved only with great difficulty and the baby would not stop
crying. She awakened weeping, the desperation of the dream
clinging to her, and heard the soft bray of a horse at rest, the
slap of iron-clad hoofs on rockbound soil. A man in a light
blue work shirt knelt near the grave. He carried a small hand
broom and a trowel. He brushed minuscule flecks of earth
from the marble and turned the soil in which the cacti had
been planted. When he had finished he stood and put a black
skullcap on his head and intoned the Kaddish, the prayer for
the dead. She realized then that he was Dr. Avremel
Schoenbaum, the man they had seen on the day of their
arrival, the doctor on the same chestnut horse that now impatiently pawed the ground.

The physician's youth and handsomeness startled Sara. His

hair was bright yellow, the hue of grain at the time of harvest. A soft golden mustache grew above the graceful curve of his full lips. He was tall and lean and he stood with the uneven posture of a man who is accustomed to swift and spontaneous movement.

"Shalom," he said, turning toward her.

"Shalom." Her own voice was very soft and new shyness suffused her.

"You were sleeping when I got here. I thought you would not mind if I stayed. I come here to tend to my wife's grave and to say Kaddish for her."

"I hope I didn't intrude on your privacy," she said.

"I have more privacy than I know what to do with."

He laughed bitterly and sat down beside her, bracing himself against the palm tree's trunk. She too leaned back. He opened the canteen he carried in his belt and took pita out of his shirt pocket. They shared the water and bread and he took up a long stick and nudged first one cluster of dates and then another. They found a few ripe enough to eat and made a small neat mound of the oval pits.

The graveside picnic, the heat of the day, the encircling shade of the palm tree, created an odd, swift intimacy. They talked with ease, as though they were old friends who had been parted for many years and were only now sharing encounters and experiences.

Avremel told her that he had been born in Russia, in a small village in the Pale of Settlement. His parents had sent him to Berlin to study medicine. He remained in the German capital for the five-year course of study because there was no money for visits home. During the last six months all correspondence from Russia ceased. No letters came in reply to his own. His urgent telegrams went unanswered. Immediately upon receipt of his diploma, he provided himself with a set of surgeon's implements and journeyed home to his village. But he found neither his home nor his village.

"That was in eighteen eighty-one," he told Sara, "just seven years ago. It seems like another lifetime. Czar Alexander had just come into power and enacted the May Laws. That was like an invitation to our peasants. They gathered one night to drink in the tavern and when the tavernkeeper turned them out, they decided they would get more vodka from the Jews. Why should the enemies of the czar drink his liquor?

They rode through the town in a drunken frenzy and the Jews fled, leaving their doors unlocked so that they would not be broken down. But my mother was sick with a fever and could not leave the house and so my father hid the whole family in the cellar. He thought that they would be safe there. He had been through other pogroms and had mastered small tricks of survival. Once, I remember, he put barrels on the cellar stairs, and another time he left bottles of wine on the kitchen table, hoping, and rightly so, that they would grow too drunk to go into the cellar. But this time the peasants were not content with just looting and raping. They threw rags soaked in kerosene at the houses and lit them with torches. They say that it took only two hours for our little village to become a pile of embers. My parents and my small brother were burned alive. The leader of the burial society told me that when they came to gather up the remnants of the dead for burial, their bodies were clustered on the stairwell. My brother's small hand was clawing the doorknob. They could not loosen his fingers and so they buried the doorknob, too, in that small grave.''

Sara shivered and covered Avremel's trembling hand with her own. She thought of Chaim who had seen a new Russia emerging, a Russia where Jew and Gentile would live in brotherhood. Would that new society obviate a child's weeping, or the drunken, nocturnal shouts of hatred? Would it blot out the memory of a desperate child's fingers grasping a searing, resistant doorknob? Where hatred was so deep and so inbred, could it be uprooted by dreams of a new society, a new social philosophy? Poor Chaim, she thought, pitying him for his dangerous innocence.

''I could not stay there,'' Avremel continued. ''I wandered about the country for a while, working now at one hospital and then at another. A well-meaning Christian colleague offered me a solution. 'You don't even look Jewish. You're blond. Come, my priest will convert you. Or if you don't want to be converted, just take a new name and say that you are a free thinker. You don't go to synagogue. You don't share their beliefs. Why should you share their dangers?' I listened to him as though he were speaking another language. The 'they' he was talking about were my people, whether or not I went to synagogue. Finally, I wandered into a meeting of the Chovevei Zion—the Lovers of Zion. I heard Tiomkin call on

Jews to go to Palestine to farm the land. Well, I thought, farmers also get sick and have children. Jewish farmers should have a Jewish doctor. They said then, in Russia, that the czar had a solution for the Jewish problem. One-third of the Jews would convert, one-third would die, and one-third would emigrate. All right, I thought. Since I won't convert and I don't want to die, I'll be among the third to emigrate, but I'll emigrate to a land that has a chance of becoming my own. And so I took up my surgeon's box and came to Palestine, to Rishon LeZion. The Altman family offered me lodging. They had a daughter, Miriam. We married.''

"Did you love her?'' Sara asked. Her own temerity startled her, and yet it seemed natural to ask this man she had met only minutes before the most intimate of questions. But the answer was clear to her. She had seen him tend his dead wife's grave. She had watched him kneel to cultivate the plantings he had set beside it. He was not a religious man, yet he had covered his head to say Kaddish for Miriam.

"She was always so frail,'' he said, and his own voice was a bare whisper. "In summer, the heat sickened her. In winter she grew ill with colds and fevers. There was an outbreak of malaria in Petach Tikvah. She insisted on coming with me and she caught the fever. In three weeks she was dead. All that last night she shivered in my arms and in the morning she was still.''

He was silent now and his eyes raked the empty landscape. Just beyond the plain, an Arab goatherd led a flock to pasture. The boy piped a small, sad melody on his reed flute and the lonely music drifted out to the couple who sat in the palm tree's shadow.

"It is such a solitary land,'' he said softly.

"And perhaps only those who seek solitude come to it,'' she replied.

"I must go,'' he said. "There is a sick child at Beit Dijon whom I must see.''

She watched the clouds of dust formed by his horse's hoofs as he rode off, and she realized that for the first time since their arrival in the country she did not feel alone.

He came to see her that night and the next. They walked together in the gathering twilight and watched for the evening star. They rode south, into the desert, for a picnic. He showed her how to find streams hidden in the wadis and taught her to peel the thick skin of the cactus fruit so that she could suck the sweet pink fruit it shielded. He took her to Gedera, where he ran a clinic for some of the remaining Bilu who were now private landowners like her father. Their dreams of a Jewish collective had been squelched by poverty and illness. Now they too hired cheap Arab labor and spoke with bitterness of both the past and the future. They complained to Avremel of backaches and insomnia, of soured dreams and vagrant aches. Disappointment sapped their energy.

Sara was depressed as they rode home. She sat awkwardly on the gelding Avremel had borrowed for her. She did not know how to ride and he arranged her on the horse and laughed at her clumsiness. His strong arms were firm about her waist. Suddenly, he rode close to her and leaned forward so that his cheek brushed hers. Then his lips met hers, his tongue sweet and thrusting in her mouth and his fingers wild in her hair. His breath was like a sweet wind and she wept at the gentle urgency of his touch.

They had known each other for only two weeks when they were married in the garden of the Maimon house. They stood together beneath a marriage canopy crafted of fragrant eucalyptus branches and the prayer shawl Reb Shimon of Kharkov had given to his son Yehuda on his marriage day. Three weeks later their bed was soaked with her blood. There was, after all, no need to tell her parents, no need to tell anyone about the child conceived in the firelit room behind the Kharkov mill. She wept in sadness and relief. A year later Shimon was born. Ezra, newly bar mitzvahed, held the infant at the circumcision ceremony. He studied the baby with great intensity.

"How lucky he is," he said, "to be born here, in the land of Israel."

Sara looked across the room to where her husband stood.

"He is lucky because Avremel is his father," she said.

Sunlight poured in through the open window and an aureole of brightness settled on Avremel's flaxen hair.

The light of Jerusalem was so much softer than that of Rishon, she thought now, and wondered if Avremel would ever consider moving south to the ancient capital. There were hospitals here, facilities for research. New houses were being built in this new section of the city, outside the great stone walls. Yemin Moshe, they called the new area, in honor of

Sir Moses Montifiore of England, the executor of the will of Judah Touro, who had given the aldermen of Jerusalem funds to begin building homes for Jews beyond the gates of the Old City. Their own hostel, Mishkenot ShaAnanim, was the first such building to be erected in the new quarter. A windmill, a factory, and a small synagogue had also been built. A family could be happy here, she knew, and imagined Shimon scurrying across the cobbled streets, rolling down the sloping hillsides. Perhaps when Ezra left for university she and Avremel too could begin planning their own lives.

"Sara, are you here?"

The cool wind of late afternoon had reddened his cheeks and a triangular bright green leaf from an almond tree was caught in his golden hair.

"I'm here, Avremel."

She traced his lips with her finger, plucked the leaf from his hair.

"Sara, Dr. Goodman has invited us to his home this evening. Some of the other doctors and their wives will be there."

A brief and giddy panic seized her.

"But my hair is terrible. And what will I wear?"

Avremel laughed.

"You sound like your mother. This is Jerusalem, not Paris."

Nor is it Rishon, he thought, his mind recoiling suddenly from the small room in her parent's house which they called their own. They were man and wife, parents themselves, yet they lived in her father's house and ate at his table. His wife did not belong to him alone but rather to her family, to whom she was at once sister and mother, daughter and companion, housekeeper and nursemaid. She lay beside him in the darkness, their mingled breath hot and sweet, heart trumpeting against heart, when her mother's thin voice called through the night like that of a plaintive child—"Sara, I am cold. Can you find another blanket?"

He arrived home eager to talk with her, to tell her about a difficult case, about a flock of herons he had watched flying seaward. But she would be too busy. She was helping Ezra with his algebra, her dark head bent close to the boy's matching hair, her hand guiding his own. She was doing her father's accounts. She was plaiting her mother's hair. There was no time for them to sit alone and speak of soaring birds.

He had known that this was how it would be when he married her and, oddly, he had welcomed it then. His family had been lost to him. He had lived too long in silence and loneliness, without the guidance of parents or the companionship of siblings. His marriage to Sara had reconnected him to a world where family concerns dominated. He belonged again to a world that extended beyond himself. His first wife's family had been silent, insular. The Maimons throbbed with separate passions, shouted with anger, rocketed with laughter, and swept him along on the tide of their intensity.

He had welcomed that at first, welcomed it and understood why it was that Sara had to remain with her family. She was their ballast, maintaining calm, restoring order, guaranteeing that meals would be served and accounts would be balanced. She was both sister and mother to young Ezra and he, who had been deprived of sister and mother, did not want to see the boy bereft. Their courtship and marriage had been so swift that he did not want to compound its suddenness by wrenching her from her family. And so they had stayed, and the weeks had become months and then years.

But Ezra was almost grown now and the twins had left the house. Surely Yehuda and Rivka could manage on their own. The time had come for Sara and him to separate their lives from those of her family. The time had come for them to have their own home so that they might sit together in the evening, her long dark hair fanned out upon his lap (she would sit at his feet then, he thought, and firelight would splay across her rose-gold skin) while he told her of white-winged birds, of gentle gazelles running in herd across the Galilee or of the heavy-fruited silver-branched olive tree that huddled in the shadow of the windmill.

He watched patiently as Sara piled her hair high on her head and draped a crimson shawl he had never seen before about her plain dark dress.

"You look beautiful," he said. "Where did you get that shawl?"

"I've had it for years," she replied and touched the soft wool lightly. It was the first time she had worn the shawl since the morning the *Vittoria* had docked in Jaffa.

They walked across the terraced fields that separated their hostel from the crenelated walls of the Old City. The crowds that teemed before the city gates during the daylight hours were gone now and only a few beggars lingered, extending their hands piteously as Avremel and Sara passed. Children, holding kerosene lanterns on long sticks, padded across the rock-strewn path, creating strange patterns with their flickering lights. On their heads they carried small sacks or balanced straw baskets laden with twisted breads and vegetables. An Arab porter, his back bent beneath the weight of a huge dark wardrobe, stumbled by, casting a grotesque shadow on the ground. Now and again, a burdened donkey lumbered past them, guided by veiled women who walked with the slow steps of those who have, without battle, surrendered to a bitter and unrelenting fatigue.

They entered the Jaffa Gate and looked up at the square-towered citadel of David. In the distance they saw the incline of the Mount of Olives, darkened in isolated places by ancient, untended vineyards. Slender silvery trees, their leaves lost in the evening darkness, stood sentinel on the sloping hillside.

The Goodmans lived in one of the domed, flat-roofed stone houses that rimmed the winding streets, and Sara was pleased to find herself in a room where books lined the walls and soft carpets were spread across the tiled floors. The evening was cool and a kerosene fire had been lit. The vagrant shafts of flame splashed across surfaces polished to a pleasing glow.

The assembled group sat about two large hammered brass trays, neatly balanced on intricately carved wooden stands. Tiny cups of coffee were passed around. A Yemenite serving girl, wearing a bright embroidered gown, offered Sara a slice of golden sponge cake as light as the cake which Rivka served at the New Year.

The doctors spoke of the lectures they had been attending.

"If we could wipe out trachoma," a black-bearded man who practiced in Jerusalem said, "half my caseload would be relieved."

"And you still wouldn't have time to eat breakfast," his wife added wryly.

She was a tiny woman who spoke Hebrew with a German accent. She taught geometry at one of the Hilsverein schools, academies sponsored by the German Jewish community.

"It is the infant mortality rate that bothers me," an elderly doctor said. "We have four hospitals in Jerusalem but not one maternity ward. Our babies die. They die at birth—they die a few days afterward. They die during the first year. How is it in your area, Dr. Schoenbaum?''

"High. Very high," Avremel admitted sadly. "I include, of course, the Arabs."

"Do they call on you for deliveries?" Dr. Goodman asked.

"When there is difficulty. At Beit Dijon, only last month, I delivered an Arab woman of twins. The second baby was a breech and I used forceps, which frightened them."

"But they allowed it?"

"I think that by now they know and trust me," Avremel said, "and so they allowed it."

"But if the infant had died they would have blamed you?"

"Possibly."

He had heard of a doctor in the north who had performed an operation on an Arab child. The child had died of postoperative infection and two weeks later the doctor's disembowled body had been found in a mountain gorge.

"I've been lucky," he added. "I have their friendship and their trust. But it was many years in the building."

"You see." The Hilsverein teacher leaned forward in her seat. "It is that friendship and trust which we must build on. If we are going to share the land, if we are going to live together peacefully, we must trust them and they must trust us."

"I agree," the bearded doctor said.

"And we must have a common language," the teacher persisted. "It's no good having the Alliance schools teaching in French and the Hilsverein schools in German. All the children must learn both Hebrew and Arabic in the elementary grades."

"We teach in Hebrew in Rishon LeZion," Sara offered, and immediately everyone turned to her with questions. Was it difficult to obtain texts? What subjects were taught? Where did the graduates go for more advanced education?

"We must have more schools," Dr. Goodman sighed. "Secondary schools. A gymnasium. A university."

"And more hospitals. And at least one maternity ward in Jerusalem," his wife added.

"And a uniform language," the teacher said.

"Is there anything we don't need?" Avremel asked and the group collapsed with laughter.

It was that laughter that distinguished them, Avremel thought, and ensured their survival. They were pioneers in this barren, deserted land where jackals howled and newborn infants died. They were gathered in a city renowned throughout the world, but they knew its houses to be largely dilapidated hovels and its small shops to be primitive enclosures where gaping holes often served as doorways. Rotting vegetables and excrement filled the warrens they called streets, and beggars and mendicants wandered, barefoot and blind, amid nobly named valleys and historic mounts.

Those who traveled to the city from the north of the land crossed wadis and stony hills. They needed proper transportation and a network of highways and roads that would link Jewish settlements and Jewish cities. In truth, there was nothing they did not need, but they did not despair and they were not frightened. Mysterious energy spurred them on. Laughter sustained them, and incandescent hope, and the certain knowledge that in the end nothing would be denied them. Their infants would not die, and when they matured they would speak to each other in the same ancient language and sing the same songs. They had come to this book-lined room from many lands—from Russia and England, France and Germany. The beautiful Yemenite girl who circled the room now, offering them pomegranates and the late-blooming plums of the Carmel, had traveled to Jerusalem across the deserts of Arabia. Their separate journeys excited Sara. They had arrived and there was much to do and they would not turn back.

She turned to Avremel as they lay together in the darkness that night. Their naked bodies were smooth against each other, and their limbs were lazy and heavy with desire fulfilled and energy exhausted.

"You know, for the first time tonight I felt part of it all," she said. "Part of this Zionism."

He stroked her hair and waited for her to go.

"I came to Palestine because my family came. I never felt anything for the land the way my father and brothers did. Even my mother, in her own dreamy way, had more connection with it than I did. I came because there was no other place to go and because I knew I had to take care of Ezra."

"You were the good Sara," he said softly. "Always doing for others."

"But tonight I felt caught up in the excitement of it—the

excitement of building a nation. New schools, new hospitals, a new language.''

"Yes. I saw that." Always sensitive to Sara's moods, he had noticed the excited tension in her voice, the brightness in her eyes, when she spoke of the Rishon school.

"Avremel, that first child—the one I miscarried . . ." Her voice faltered, and beneath his hand he felt her heart beat too rapidly.

He widened his embrace and encircled her trembling body in his arms.

"Sara," he said, "there is nothing that you can tell me that I don't know. And nothing that will make any difference. I love you. Sometimes I think that I was born loving you."

Gently, then, he rocked her like a small child until at last she slept. Through a crevice in the thin drape that covered the window, he saw a cluster of stars. Their brightness splintered against the gray mountain haze that drifted through the darkness. It was said that the smoke emanating from his family's burning house had spiraled skyward and formed an ashen veil across the star-studded, death-stained Russian night.

"Mama," the grown man, the doctor, whispered, and fell asleep at last, a tendril of his wife's dark hair caught between his fingers.

Chapter 8

Ezra sat for his matriculation examination in Jaffa. He found the questions astonishingly simple, but because the kind-eyed French consul watched him with great sympathy and solicitously brought him tall glasses of cold coffee, he furrowed his forehead, bit at the top of his pen, and grimaced.

"I have no doubt that you will pass with honors," the consul assured him as Ezra submitted the last page. He was fond of the young man whom he had known since the days of his boyhood. He had watched him grow from a serious-eyed, almost sickly lad to the strong, lithe young man who stood before him now, passing lean nervous fingers through his thick dark hair. The boy's large eyes, fringed by straight lashes, were an odd green, the same color as the brilliant sea glass which his children sometimes carried home after a day at the shore.

"I hope so," Ezra said, but he did not give the examination another thought as he went back to the Bakers' hotel, where he was staying overnight.

The hotelkeeper, too, was reassuring.

"I am sure you will be admitted to the Sorbonne," he said.

"But perhaps you will decide on one of the American universities your father spoke of."

"I don't know," Ezra said uneasily. "I'm not sure I want to go to university at all."

"I see."

The hotelkeeper removed his glasses and rubbed his eyes. Poor Maimon. One by one his children went their own way. First the twins and now Ezra. It was not surprising. Chaim Baker's own son had left Palestine and lived now in a red brick house in Golders Green in London. Dutiful, loving letters were exchanged and the pictures of their English grandchildren, tastefully framed, lined Mrs. Baker's ornate credenza. She displayed them proudly to visitors who came to tea but cried softly in the night because she had never seen her grandchildren and perhaps never would.

But Yehuda Maimon was not a man who easily sustained disappointment. Chaim Baker knew. It was true that he had made his peace with the twins, Saul and David, in spite of what he still saw as their defection, but in truth he had given up on his elder sons even before they had made their break with him. It had always been Ezra on whom he and Rivka had affixed their hopes. Ezra would achieve all that had been denied them—the learning, the academic degrees. He remembered how Rivka, newly arrived in Jaffa, had sought out a bookstore where she could buy her son a geography text and a Latin grammar.

"What do you want to do?" he asked Ezra.

"I don't know. But I don't want to leave the country."

"But you would return."

"I don't want to come back to be a lawyer or a doctor. It's the land I want to work on," Ezra said. "I want to farm."

"Then why can't you stay and work with your father in Rishon? It's a prosperous farm. Perhaps one day it will be yours."

"I don't want to inherit a prosperous farm," Ezra replied. "I want to build something of my own. And I agree with my brothers about Arab labor. I will not be overseer to fellahin. Do you know what we have built in Rishon and in Gedera and in Petach Tikvah? We have built an extension of the shtetl. New small bourgeois villages where small people dream small dreams. Instead of owning shops, we own farms and orchards and vineyards, and instead of hiring clerks we hire

Arab laborers. We sit over glasses of tea and speak of a paved main road, of new kitchen cabinets, of indoor plumbing. I did not come to Palestine for the miracle of having running water in my home.''

"But it is, you must admit, a great convenience,'' Chaim Baker said, smiling. "But please, I do know what you mean. Sometimes I look about me and think, did I come to Palestine to be a hotelkeeper? I too had dreams of farming. Like your mother, I had read Mapu and I dreamed of being a bronzed Jewish warrior, strong and fearless. We came first to farm in Petach Tikvah but my wife developed allergies. She itched when she worked in the vegetable garden and she sneezed when she fed the chickens. It is not easy to live with a woman who itches and sneezes. And so we came to Jaffa, to this hotel. I was ashamed, disappointed. But now I think that the important thing is not where I live or what I do but that I came to the land.''

"It is not enough for me,'' Ezra said. He spoke with the dispassionate certainty of youth. "I want to go north, to the mountains. When I look up I do not want to see smoke pouring out of the chimney of my neighbor's farm. I don't want to scrape and bow when the Baron de Rothschild comes to visit from France and tells his Jewish farmers how they must live their lives. I want to experiment with this new strain of winter wheat, and I want to sell my crops at market value and not set my prices according to the whim of the Baron's overseers. Perhaps I'll even start a small herd. We will need cattle farms in this country. Immigration is increasing and the new Jewish settlers will want meat to eat, leather to tan.''

"Your plans are ambitious,'' the hotelkeeper said. "You will need money. A great deal of money.''

"It is not money that worries me,'' Ezra said.

The two men walked together down to the harbor where small Arab boys were tugging their fishing boats ashore. They waded to the dock, their laden nets balanced about their shoulders. Within the strong mesh, rainbow-gilled fish thrashed about. Ezra watched as a large sea bass thrust his way out of the mouth of the net and catapulted back into the ocean, slicing the air with his shimmering body. He would wait, he decided, until the results of his examination arrived from Paris, and then he would tell his parents of his decision.

But when the examination results arrived, advising Ezra

Maimon that he had passed with distinction, Yehuda lay
dangerously ill with malaria. The illness had overtaken him
suddenly, at a happy and exciting time in their lives, and they
felt betrayed.

It was the year of the corn harvest and the crop had been
exceptionally abundant. Yehuda was especially pleased because
Saul and David had returned to the farm to help. Without
argument or discussion, he hired some of their friends who
belonged to the groups of young Jews who were now arriving
in the country in increasing numbers. There was new determination and strength in the faces and voices of these young
men. Two of them had even attended the First Zionist Congress, held that year in Basel, and they told of how the
assembled delegates, gathered from every country in Europe,
from the United States, and South America, had risen to sing
the new Jewish national anthem, "HaTikvah"—"Hope."

"A song written here, in Rishon LeZion," Yehuda said
proudly. He did not add that Imber, the poet who had written
the stirring words and fashioned the tune from an old Moldavian
folk song, was even now speaking of leaving the land.

"There is so much to see in the world," the poet said. His
cheeks were too bright and he averted his eyes. He would
come back but meanwhile he wanted to see the world—the
great city of New York, perhaps even California and the
Pacific Ocean. Palestine, after all, was such a small country.
Travel folders littered the worn leather briefcase that leaned
against his legs as he sat in Rivka Maimon's garden and read
aloud his lyric celebrations of Zion.

Ezra had little patience with the poet. It was not Palestine
but the petty provincial society of Rishon that stifled the
creative spirit. Imber should go north and seek out the wondrous beauty of the Galilean nights or south into the untamed
desert, instead of sitting on a canvas chair beneath a citron
tree while he read his verses to pretentious listeners.

But it was the young pioneers and not the poet who gave
audience now. They had seen Dr. Theodor Herzl at the
congress. He was a tall, bearded man with a resonant voice.
He attended the congress in formal attire and even carried soft
gray gloves and wore a diamond stickpin in his cravat. But
when he spoke, passion burned in his words and his listeners
sat at the edges of their seats. He had written a pamphlet

called "The Jewish State," and he was determined to wrest a national homeland for the Jews from the Turks.

"He has met with the kaiser and they say the kaiser gave him hope, offered his friendship. And he will travel to Constantinople for an audience with the sultan."

"All that is nonsense," Yehuda said gruffly. "Talk will accomplish nothing. The important thing is for Jews to settle on the land. Only when there is successful Jewish settlement will the land become ours."

"Settlement is not enough, Father," Ezra interposed. "We must have some political guarantees."

He glanced at his brothers and by unarticulated assent they did not pursue the argument. They understood that the years of work and struggle had frayed their father's dreams, dimmed his perspective. Once he had read Pinsker and dreamed of a Hebrew university. Now he read *Bustenai*, the orange-growers' journal, and dreamed of drilling a second well in Rishon. They were done with arguing with him. Youth and the future were ranged on their side. History moved with them. They would create a new nation and a new social order. But for the moment it was good to be at home in the Rishon farmhouse, eating Sara's good stew and their mother's delicate cake. They leaned back and watched Shimon, their golden-haired nephew, play chess with the young pioneer who had heard Theodor Herzl speak in Switzerland. The twins felt the weariness that came from the long day in the field. The next day they would strip the last outlying dunams of the golden crop and then they would go to the settlement of Sejera. They belonged now to a nuclear group, a *garin*, that would pioneer a collective farm in the north.

But the next day Yehuda returned from the fields shivering and complaining of a chill. Although the afternoon was unusually warm, he closed all the windows of the house and drew on one shirt after another.

"It's cold," he shouted when Rivka asked him to take his temperature.

He would not acknowledge illness. He had been too long in control of his life to surrender now to the vagaries of disease. But within hours he could no longer ignore it. His eyes blazed with an unnatural brightness, and though he shivered violently when they peeled the layers of clothing from his body, his skin was hot with fever.

"Malaria," Avremel said at once when he returned.

The disease was raging through the countryside. He had that day treated Bedouin graziers who had traveled south from their encampments in Huleh, where the skies above the swamps were dark with the buzzing mosquitoes that carried the infectious parasites. In Petach Tikvah, the burial society was cleansing the bodies of three young pioneers so weakened by malnutrition that the disease had vanquished them before they could struggle against it. The rabbi had cut his finger on an exposed bone of the corpse, and drops of scarlet blood had fallen across the dead man's jaundiced skin.

The family sat beside Yehuda's bed through the days and nights that followed. They bathed him with alcohol when the fever raged high and they swaddled him in blankets when the chills reduced him to trembling and sobbing.

"I'm cold. So cold. Cover me, Mama," he called in his delirium, and reached for the woman who had died in childbirth so many years ago and was buried in the land he had left behind.

"Don't be angry, Papa," he whispered piteously into the night. "I must leave the yeshiva. I want to be a doctor. I'm a good Jew, but I want to be a doctor. Bless me."

His sons comforted him. They murmured reassurances, and when he would not be calm, they spoke, in dazed voices, the words the old scholar had withheld.

The twins, who hated to be indoors, adjusted themselves to the rhythm of the sickroom. They spooned granules of grain cooked in chicken broth into their father's mouth and cleaned up the sour vomit that flecked his bedclothes and his body. They helped Avremel dose him with quinine, and when the drug was gone, David and Ezra administered laudanum and aspirin while Saul rode to the dispensary in Petach Tikvah for a new supply.

Rivka remonstrated each time Ezra entered the sickroom.

"Not Ezra," she cried. "Ezra has no resistance. He'll get sick too."

She did not see the strong young man her son had become but remembered only the small boy who had fallen ill so often in their Kharkov home. Saul and David looked at their brother and shrugged sympathetically. They told him, in covert glances, that they did not blame him because he was their parents' favorite. They were grown men now and if the grievances of childhood endured, they were understood and forgiven.

A week passed and then another, and the fever did not break.

"Soon," Avremel told them and he noticed for the first time that Shimon's eyebrows grew in a straight line, as Yehuda Maimon's did.

Late one night, as Ezra kept vigil beside the sick man's bed, he saw that his father's face glowed with a perilous heat. Yehuda writhed in a sudden delirium that abandoned all coherence. He threw off his blankets and tried to peel his nightdress from his emaciated body. His beard was matted with sweat and the pupils of his eyes rolled dangerously, like bright, directionless marbles. He screamed shrilly and then laughed with the cadence of a child's voice. He sang a Russian drinking song and minutes later mouthed the words of a Zionist hymn. Then a chill overtook him and he shivered with such violence that the bed itself trembled.

"Avremel!" Ezra shouted fearfully, and his brother-in-law hurried in.

"The fever," the doctor muttered. "The damn fever."

He swathed Yehuda's body in alcohol compresses and ground the last of their aspirin into a powder, which he dissolved in juice and forced through the sick man's parched lips.

Faint with exhaustion, Ezra watched his brother-in-law. He himself felt that all hope was gone. His father would die and he, Ezra, would be left, the sole inheritor of all Yehuda Miamon's hopes and dreams. The obligation of the Rishon farm would fall on him. There was no one else. His brothers had left, and he knew that Sara and Avremel dreamed of a life in Jerusalem. He would live out his life on the low, rolling fields of Rishon, tending the citrus orchards, listening to his mother read aloud. All would depend on him. He felt fear and anger and a heavy, unremitting sorrow.

"Will he be all right?" Sara stood at her husband's side, her face as pale as her long white nightgown. The scarlet shawl was tossed about her shoulders.

Shame burned Ezra's heart and seared his mind. His father lay dying and he, the youngest son, thought only of what that death would mean to him. If Yehuda died it would be Ezra's fault for thinking only of himself at such a time, at such a dark and dangerous hour of the night.

Miraculously then, Avremel's voice broke through the hushed silence.

"He's going to be all right. The fever climbed, reached a crisis point, and broke. He's cool now. Almost normal, I think."

Sara and Ezra drew closer and they saw that their father breathed evenly. He had fallen into an exhausted sleep but his limbs were no longer stiff with tension. He had hovered at the edge of the precipice but, miraculously, he had regained his balance. They were not orphaned. Their father, the strong determined man who had brought them out of Russia, lived and would endure. The brother and sister clung to each other. Tears streaked Sara's cheeks and Ezra trembled.

"I thought that he would die," Sara whispered. "And I remembered how I thought that I hated him when we left Russia. I was so angry then. He took our lives and made them his own. I thought God was punishing me for that anger, for that hatred. But I love him, and he didn't die. He lived. He lived."

"It's all right, Sara," Ezra said and stroked his sister's hair, glad that Avremel had left the room. "It's all right. No one is punished for thoughts and feelings."

But he withheld from himself the comfort he offered his sister. She had trembled with regret for what had happened in the past but he had quivered with fear for his future. Avremel had returned with extra blankets. It was important to keep Yehuda warm so that his fever-free body would not be shocked by sudden temperature change. Ezra bent to help his brother-in-law, and briefly the sick man opened his eyes and looked up at him.

"Ezra, my Ezra," he said. "What will happen to you?"

"Sleep, Father," Ezra said and he lowered the wick of the kerosene lamp that glowed on the bedside table. The dying flame sputtered blue, and at last the room was dark and quiet except for the evenly spaced breathing of the sick man.

Chapter 9

"If you go you'll miss everything. Everything." Sara said peevishly as Avremel methodically packed his saddle bags.

She was pregnant, and she acknowledged that her condition made her cranky. Still, it was so unfair that Avremel would miss both Theodor Herzl's visit at Rishon and the kaiser's visit to Mikveh Israel. For years nothing at all happened in the colony and then suddenly, in a single week, so much excitement was anticipated just when Avremel had to be away. And his journey to the north might be futile, after all. Dr. Mazis himself, who had come to tell them of the epidemic raging in the Druse village of Kafra Museiba, high in Galilee, had acknowledged that, in all likelihood, the villagers would discourage the ministrations of the Jewish doctor. But if they accepted anyone, it would have to be Avremel, who had achieved a reputation among the Arabs and the Jews. *El Zahabun*, they called him—the Golden One—because of his bright hair. *Ibn Rachmun*, they also called him—Son of the Merciful—because of the many times he had relieved racking pain and saved a dangerously ill patient from what seemed like certain death. If the sickness was not controlled and contained within the village, Mazis said, it might endanger the entire country. Would Avremel travel north and see what he could do?

They did not name the sickness, which Sara knew to be cholera. Its very name was taken from the Hebrew—*choleh ra*, a grave illness.

"I'll think about it," Avremel had said, but Sara had known at once that he would go.

Grimly she packed his rucksack, and as she tightened the strap, the child within her fluttered and gave a strong kick. She winced with pleasure and smoothed the ample folds of her blue-and-white checked maternity smock.

"I'm giving Abba my gazelle to keep him company," Shimon said, and he tucked the olive wood miniature which Saul had carved for him into a corner of the bag.

Sara smiled. There were those who thought that Shimon, at nine, was too old to be playing with carved animals, but she was pleased that her son lingered so pleasantly in childhood. Her own years of play had been too swiftly abbreviated by household cares.

"Are you taking a gun?" Yehuda asked Avremel as his son-in-law checked his surgical case.

Yehuda had come in to rest after working during the predawn hours in the orchards; the young orange trees were being shrouded in sacks against the early cold that was anticipated that year. Two years had passed since his illness but the malaria had left him weakened. He easily grew fatigued and he had not yet recovered his full weight. His work pants and shirt hung loosely on his body and his eyes were too deeply set in a face grown long and thin. His eyebrows and beard were almost entirely gray. Studying himself in the mirror, Yehuda recalled that his father's beard had remained dark even in old age; the pictures that Mendel sent from America told him that his brother's hair was barely streaked with silver. Yehuda was oddly disturbed by his early grayness. His vanity was piqued and in some mysterious way, he felt that he had been betrayed.

"I have never carried a gun and never needed one," Avremel replied. "A gun is an invitation to violence."

"Like medicine is an invitation to disease?" Yehuda asked, his voice laced with sarcasm. He liked his son-in-law but was easily irritated by him. Why had Sara always been drawn to these idealistic dreamers who refused to see the world as it was, as he, Yehuda, saw it?

"Please, Avremel, take it," Sara said. "You can keep it hidden but you must have some protection. Only three weeks ago a boy from Sejera was found dead at the irrigation ditch, his throat cut."

"All right. I'll take the small revolver then. Put it in the bottom of the saddle bag."

Avremel checked his bag before he left and saw that the black butt of the revolver gleamed against his instrument case. He smiled bitterly at the absurdity of carrying instruments of life and death in careless contiguity. He lifted Sara's hand and kissed her open palm. Shimon stood, sleepy-eyed, next to his mother.

"You shouldn't have gotten up so early," Avremel said.

He sat astride the chestnut gelding, and the crimson tongues of the rising sun set his golden hair ablaze. He had held Sara close before mounting but he leaned forward to caress her once again. Then he swung Shimon up to the saddle and rode with him for several yards before kissing the boy and setting him down.

"Be good," he said. "Be a good boy."

Then he waved and rode off. They watched until they could no longer see him and then they too hurried off to begin their day. There was still a great deal to do before Dr. Herzl's visit and the Maimon family, along with the rest of Rishon, had been excitedly caught up in the preparations.

A schoolmate had told Shimon that the Zionist leader would fly into the colony.

"He is King David in disguise," the boy had said. "He is the Messiah, come to restore our homeland."

Shimon, who had grown up in the Maimon home where French philosophers and the writings of Pinsker and Kalisher were discussed at the dining room table and where his grandfather and uncles argued fiercely over Jewish destiny, gave little credence to his friend's words.

"Men don't fly," he retorted. "And King David is dead."

But he lingered at the edge of the crowd that gathered in the Rishon town square to listen to the Reverend William Hechler, who had arrived from Germany a week in advance of Dr. Herzl's scheduled visit. The Reverend Hechler was not very different from other Christian missionaries who had

visited the Jewish colony through the years. He too spoke
with messianic fervor and flailed his arms wildly. He too had
the habit of gazing upward to the heavens and then leaning
forward as though to share with his audience a secret newly
revealed by a divine source. But he made no effort to convert
his listeners to Christianity and, unlike his predecessors, he
made no effort to distribute New Testaments especially printed
in Hebrew and even in Yiddish. Nor did he seek to entice the
children with sweets and toys. He spoke only of the fact that
the restoration of the Jewish state at this specific point in
history was God's will. He himself had written a treatise
predicting that in the year 1897 the Jews would be restored to
their ancient land. God's instrument in that preordained restoration was Dr. Theodor Herzl, whom the reverend knew and
admired. He urged the colonists to read Herzl's remarkable
pamphlet "The Jewish State."

Ezra walked home with Shimon after listening attentively
to the Reverend Hechler.

"This could only happen in Palestine," Ezra said. "Only
in this crazy country could Jewish farmers gather to hear a
Christian clergyman tell them to struggle for the establishment of a Jewish state."

Still, Ezra had taken careful note of the clergyman's remarks
and agreed with much that he said. The time had indeed come
for the Jewish people to assert themselves and demand a
national homeland. Like Hechler, Ezra agreed that the northern reaches of the land had to be developed. He had traveled
once again into the foothills of the Galilee and he was certain
now that that was where his own future lay. But because of
Yehuda's illness, he had decided to remain on the Rishon
farm temporarily—at least until his father regained his strength.
It would not be fair to go off on his own while Yehuda still
could not manage a full day's work. Helping his father now
was an unarticulated atonement for the thoughts that had
teased him when he was sure that the malaria would claim his
father's life. He supervised the farm although he yearned to
be in the north, embarked on what the white-haired German
minister described as "the ultimate reclamation of the land."

Rishon was normally a sleepy village but now the atmosphere was electric with excitement. The townspeople shook
off the summertime torpor of heat and the exhaustion of the
harvest and consolidated their energies to welcome the visi-

tors. On the morning of Herzl's scheduled arrival, small girls were dressed in their best frocks and wreaths of flowers crowned their shining hair and hung in garlands around their necks. Schoolboys walked awkwardly through the town dressed in clothing that was generally reserved for the synagogue. Shimon grinned self-consciously when he met a classmate. Sara had combed his bright hair, wetting it so that it lay flat against his head. The collar of his white shirt was starched to an irritating stiffness and his polished shoes squeaked when he walked. He took comfort from the fact that his friend had undergone similar indignities.

Some of the small Rishon houses had been newly whitewashed. The windows sparkled and housewives, dressed in their best, hung blue-and-white flags of their own making in doorways and windows. The community house was festooned with flowers and banners, and a large blue-and-white flag almost covered the entryway. When the Maimon family reached it, every seat was taken and they were forced to sit on the makeshift benches that had been erected in the rear, while Shimon hurried to join other members of the school chorus who were assembled on the hastily constructed stage.

The director of the colony paused to speak to Yehuda.

"It's an awkward business, this visit of Herzl's," he said gravely, fingering the copy of his welcome speech.

"How so?" Yehuda asked. Since his illness he had not been active in the affairs of the colony.

"This Herzl is not beloved by the Baron," the director said. "In fact, his overseers have told me that the Baron will be incensed when he hears that Rishon has given him such a welcome."

"Hasn't the time come when we must stop thinking about the Baron de Rothschild and begin to think about Zion and our own destiny?" Ezra asked. "We act as though we are schoolchildren, fearful of our powerful teacher. We are not children. We are men and we must make our own decisions about this land and be done with trembling when a directive arrives from Paris."

Yehuda and the director exchanged a glance of sympathetic understanding. They did not argue. Ezra, after all, spoke with the impatience of youth, the innocence of idealism. He would learn the same lessons they had mastered. It took capital to drill water wells. The English manufacturers of artesian equipment would not accept payment in dreams and ideals. Scientifically designed wine cellars, with adequate systems of temperature control, were necessary for viticulture. The cool subterranean warrens which the Baron had built for the Rishon colony were costly. Herzl might offer them dreams but the Baron offered them ways and means. Dreams were not negotiable.

A cheer rose from the crowd of young people gathered outside the community center.

"Heidad!" they shouted. "Long live Dr. Herzl!"

An accordionist struck up a song of welcome and the melody was caught by a young woman who played a balalaika and two girl flautists. The accordionist, who had a powerful tenor voice, sang as he played.

"Hevenu shalom aleicheim!"

The crowd formed a mighty chorus.

"We bid you welcome. We greet you. Shalom. Shalom."

All eyes were focused on the tall, bearded man who towered over them as he stood in the diligence. His piercing black eyes raked the crowd as though to search out secrets, penetrate mysteries. Shimon watched as the crowd parted and the Zionist leader was escorted into the hall. Herzl resembled the portrait of an Assyrian prince in one of Rivka's history books. His long thick beard had been sculpted into a point at the bottom. The boy was fascinated by its elegant luxuriance. His father's soft blond mustache grew to a ragged edge and his grandfather's beard was a scraggly gray mass. Shimon was glad that his uncles, Ezra, Saul, and David, were clean-shaven. If one could not have a beard like Herzl's, one should have no beard at all. He touched his own soft cheeks impatiently, as though to coax sprouts of manhood from his unready skin.

There was a hush as Herzl reached the platform The children's chorus, so carefully trained during the weeks since they had learned that Herzl would be coming, sang "Ha-Tikvah," the anthem of hope, in all its choruses. Listening to it, Ezra recalled the party he had attended in Jaffa at the French consulate. He had heard the "Marseillaise" sung there. The song was powerful, forceful, assertive, like "God Save the King," the British anthem. Only a Jewish anthem was tinged with ineffable, prescient sorrow.

But the children smiled as they sang and cast covert glances about the room, as though they must glean every detail and impress it upon their memories. They shared the certain knowledge, as they raised their small voices in song, that this day out of their childhood belonged to history. They had heard their parents speak of legendary visits. Someone's grandfather had seen Sir Moses Montifiore riding in his splendid chariot. They had heard descriptions of the bright summer day when the Baron drank his first cup of wine in the Rishon vineyards, and they knew that one day they would say, to their own children and grandchildren, "When I was a small boy, Theodor Herzl came to Rishon LeZion and I sang in the chorus that greeted him."

The town's oldest settler took Herzl's hands in his own and greeted him on behalf of the colonists of Rishon LeZion. He proffered a gift of welcome—bread, wine, and salt. The loaf and the goblet were awkwardly balanced between the men as the settler told the visitor that the bread was made of grain grown in the fields of Rishon and the wine had been pressed from grapes grown in the colony's vineyards.

Ezra saw their visitor's eyes grow bright with tears. The children's voices singing in Hebrew, the token gifts of nourishment grown by Jews on their own land, the joyful enthusiasm of the crowd—all that was vindication for the journalist who had wept when the epaulets were stripped from Dreyfus's uniform. Ezra grew uneasy suddenly, fearful that their guest would be overcome with emotion.

But when Herzl spoke, he had full control of his resonant voice. His audience listened, mesmerized into rapt concentration. His voice washed over them in waves of passion and even the smallest children, who could not understand German, sat in unnatural stillness as he spoke. He told the farmers of Rishon of his admiration for them. They had fulfilled Ezekiel's dream. They had breathed new life into the dying land. He spoke also, with grave acknowledgment, of the wonderful contribution of the Baron de Rothschild, who had made the success of Rishon LeZion possible.

Yehuda cast Ezra a knowing glance. Herzl might be an idealist but he was also a politician. He listened closely as the impassioned orator told them that the colonists of Rishon had the sole obligation of continuing to till the land so that it would be ready for the masses of Jewish people who would answer the call of Zion and come to settle in the homeland.

Wild applause greeted his address. Again the children sang and the musicians played and the Reverend Hechler, seated beside Herzl on the platform, raised his eyes to heaven. Outside the community hall, young men on horseback rode in wild circles around Herzl's carriage and shouted their approbation.

"Heidad! *Hoch* Herzl!" Rifles were fired in salute and the tall, bearded man waved a snow-white handkerchief and smiled although tears glinted in his eyes.

The young women spoke in hushed voices of his handsomeness. They wondered how they could obtain a photograph of him. Small boys sought his autograph and Joseph Feinberg's beautiful little granddaughter offered him a bouquet of flowers which he cradled in his arms, not caring that the tiny white petals fell like snowflakes across his fine dark suit.

He toured the colony, stopping at one home to taste a barley soup and at another to drain a glass of sweet grape juice. The Maimon family was just completing lunch when there was a knock at the door. Shimon opened it and admitted two members of the town council and Theodor Herzl.

Rivka heard the staccato beat of her own heart, and her hands trembled as they had the night on which Yehuda brought the Hebrew poet to their Kharkov home. Always, she had dreamed of great men sitting down at her table. Her fingers fluttered to her hair and she whipped her apron off.

"Won't you have coffee with us," she said and noted how elegantly Herzl drew back the long skirt of his jacket as he joined them at the table.

"How does your honor find our colony?" Yehuda asked.

"Rishon is very beautiful. I am very impressed," Herzl replied carefully, "but I should have liked to have seen more crop diversification."

"The Baron encourages only the vineyards," Ezra said, avoiding his father's eyes.

Herzl looked at the tall young man with interest but again addressed the father.

"And I would like to see the swamps drained. They bring the illness and the fever, I am sure. We need a program of forestation, financed perhaps by a Jewish national fund that will involve all Jews everywhere. Trees would control the waste, the erosion."

Ezra knew then that despite his impassioned words in the community hall, Herzl had a very realistic picture of the problems that existed for the Jewish community.

"Yes, the swamps cause a great deal of illness," Sara acknowledged as she poured the coffee into her mother's Meissen cups. "Just two years ago my father was seriously ill with malaria. He has only recently recovered his strength. And even now, my husband, Dr. Schoenbaum, is in the north where an epidemic has broken out among the Druse villagers."

"The north. I should like to go to the north," Herzl said thoughtfully. Again his dark eyes were trained on Ezra. "Have you traveled much in the north, young man?"

"Yes. There is wonderful land there," Ezra said. "And the Galilee is very beautiful—open for cultivation, even for grazing."

"Yes. And there independent farming will be possible," the Zionist leader said and looked at his own hands. They were white and soft and his fingernails were manicured and buffed to a sheen. Abruptly, he dropped them to his lap and continued to look at Ezra.

The town councilors remained silent. By "independent farming" they knew that Herzl meant Jewish agricultural enterprise that was not controlled by the Baron. They smiled and nodded. Their guest was surely a great man, a great thinker. But today he sat with them in Rishon and within weeks he would again stroll the Ringstrasse in Vienna. He would sit in a cafe and speak learnedly of Jewish destiny while they struggled with the problem of obtaining new equipment to build a second well. The Baron must not be antagonized. But they were polite hosts and did not argue. They drank their tea and accepted yet another slice of Rivka Maimon's excellent sponge cake.

The family assembled at the door as their visitors left. One by one they shook the great man's hand. When Ezra's turn came, he felt his face burn beneath the searching stare of those deep-set dark eyes.

"The future is yours, young man," Herzl said to him in a low tone. "You must take hold of it."

His powerful grasp bruised Ezra's fingers and the young man watched as Herzl strode to his waiting carriage. The

author of "The Jewish State" did not err. The future did
indeed belong to him and it was time, at last, to take possession of it. They would have to hold a family council when
Avremel returned. There were things to be discussed, decisions to be made.

Chapter 10

Avremel reined in his horse when he saw the storks. The huge white birds flew as a family, observing a hierarchy as distinct as the one Yehuda Maimon sought to impose upon his family. The father winged his way forward, as though slicing a path through the resistant air with his pink-tinged plumage; the mother followed after him, her elegant head mostly bent beneath the wing. She croaked a harsh admonition and Avremel thought, with considerable amusement, that her voice was not unlike that of the Rishon apothecary's wife, who had too many children and not enough patience. The fledgling stork, as though heeding her instructions, flew more slowly. Clumps of white down still clung to his feathers and he flew low enough for Avremel to see the black-beaded pupils that glistened in his narrow eyes.

Avremel watched until the birds had disappeared from sight, taking note of the way the male bird slowed his flight to await the others. It was important that he remember everything so that he could tell Shimon all about it without omitting a single detail. Already he envisioned his son's delight and his insistent questions. Did storks really speak their own language? What was the wing span of the male bird? Why had only a single young stork trailed behind them? Had jackals gotten the baby birds or had the nest been raided by Bedouin children?

Once during a holiday in the north Avremel and Shimon had stood, frozen into immobility, and watched a serious-eyed stork stand importantly on one leg and swallow a jewel-green frog. In a few years' time Shimon would be old enough and strong enough to travel regularly with him on short journeys. Of course even if Shimon had been older, Avremel could not have taken him with him to Kafra Museiba. The epidemic had been a particularly virulent one and the boy would have been too easily susceptible to the disease. Avremel shivered. He was that oddity—an experienced doctor who had never become inured to death and suffering.

He sighed and urged the horse on, suddenly anxious to be moving more swiftly toward home. More than a week had passed since he had left Rishon, although he had promised Sara that he would be away only a few days at most. Still, he had sent a message to her with the Turkish district health officer who had come up to Kafra Museiba to assess the situation.

"*C'est horrible,*" the Turk had said again and again as he followed Avremel from one small mud brick house to another.

He held his heavily scented white silk scarf over the protective surgical mask which Avremel had given him. He was very careful to stand away from the flaking walls so that no dust would drift onto his bright red jacket. He was, in his way, a diligent man. He had gagged when a small girl whom Avremel was examining had choked suddenly on her own mucus. Swiftly, Avremel had lifted the child and flipped her onto her stomach, inserting his fingers into her mouth and freeing her throat of long tensile strips of swamp-green phlegm, which Avremel tossed, like dangerous snakes, into a slop bowl. Still, the Turk had not vomited, nor had he left the small house.

Even when a naked old man, wandering the village in the last stage of fever-ridden delirium, had fallen dead at the official's feet, streaking the shiny black cavalry boots with a thin golden rim of urine, the last excretion of the withered body, he had controlled himself. He had not even bent to wipe his boots until the old man's grieving family had carried the body away. And the Turk, after all, was not a doctor, although it was true that he had briefly attended lectures at the faculty of medicine in Constantinople. It was that brief attendance that had landed him the assignment in Palestine when his gambling debts reached sufficient magnitude to warrant his leaving Turkey for a while at least.

He made small efforts to live up to the demands of his post. He had traveled north and brought Avremel quinine and aspirin and the pitifully small amount of morphine he had found in stores in Jaffa. He admired the golden-haired Jewish doctor although he could not quite understand what he was doing in Palestine. What on earth did these educated Jews want with this godforsaken desert of a land? Still, he had promised to get word to Sara so that she would not worry about Avremel's delay.

"You have my great respect, Doctor," the Turk told Avremel before leaving. "After all, they are not even your people."

"We are, however, distant cousins," Avremel said, smiling. "The Druse say they are descended of Jethro, who was the father-in-law of Moses. And so of course we must be related."

"You Semites," the Turk said, smiling tolerantly. "We will never understand you."

"No, I don't expect you will," Avremel replied good-naturedly.

The two men shook hands and Avremel watched the Turk ride away, his face still shielded by the heavily scented silk scarf. Then a small boy in a tattered galabiah pulled at him, and Avremel turned wearily back to his work.

During his student days, Avremel had spent summers earning a stipend by serving as a locum, a doctor's deptuy, in the poorest districts of Berlin. There too he had seen the cholera sweep through the slums when a water supply grew contaminated and spirochetes swam unchecked in reservoir and sewer. Once, returning from a night call, a huge rat had dashed through the street and brushed against Avremel's leg. He had burned the trousers and washed his body with lye soap.

Yet even in those slums he had not seen the disease reach the proportions of the epidemic he found at Kafra Museiba. In almost every house someone lay ill. In some cases an entire family had been stricken. The stench of putrescent feces hung over the village in a stagnant miasma. The low moans of the feverish converged and rose in an atonal chorus that trembled with agony and fear. Those who were not ill—exhausted men and women and even children—hurried from house to house, carrying in fresh water and emerging with buckets of sour vomit and excrement.

Almost the first thing Avremel had done, after diagnosing the illness and assessing its gravity, was to arrange for a large ditch to be dug a small distance from the village. All waste matter was carted there and each night kerosene was poured over the chasm and the detritus was set afire. He had arranged for all drinking water to be boiled and insisted that all fruits and vegetables be washed in the sterilized water. He knew that the disease had spread so quickly because the old and the weak were particularly susceptible to the cholera bacilli in the water, and the Druse, who venerated their elderly, had at least one aged parent or grandparent living in each house. It was ironic, Avremel thought, that such a people should be so punished for their virtue.

He distributed the medications he had brought and used those given to him by the Turk. Slowly, the epidemic abated. Miraculously, the Druse did not resist his efforts and raised no objections to his techniques. There were hours of respite when the fevers declined and those who had hovered near death opened their eyes in surprise and found that they were still alive. There was the sudden shriek in the night when the death rattle sounded and the women of the family pierced the dark air with their keening. And always, Avremel thought, he would remember the racking sobs of a small boy as he held the lifeless body of his twin sister in his own arms.

"Doctor, she will not breathe," the boy cried, and Avremel gently took the small girl from him.

The boy was perhaps a year older than Shimon. His hair was a mass of black curls, as thick as the hair of the small girl whose body was already stiffening against Avremel's chest. It was said that twins felt each other's joys and pains. He had seen his brother-in-law Saul wince when David cut himself. He wondered if they also felt each other's deaths.

"She feels no pain now," he told the weeping boy and remembered that an old rabbi in his village had said the same thing to him when Avremel had wept for his brother, the small boy incinerated in a flaming cellar. "He feels no pain now." Only the living felt the pain of survival.

He knew then how tired he was and he sent for the child's mother, so that she might claim her dead daughter and care for her living son.

Still, a week later, the illness had run its course and been contained. There were no new cases. The villagers moved down their stone-rimmed lanes and paths, their steps slowed by grief, their long black robes dusting the ground. Two dozen new graves had been added to the shaded resting places in the village cemetery. Long narrow stones marked each grave, and a vertical marker was placed to indicate where the feet rested so that the corpse would be in readiness for its walk to heaven. Avremel stayed in the village until the small girl was buried. He gave the last of his medication to the wife of the village chief, a sensible woman who sat on the ruling committee of elders. It occurred to him that there were no women on the town council of Rishon.

"We thank you for coming, *El Raphun*—O healer," the chief said.

He stroked his curling mustache and adjusted the snowy white folds of his kaffiyeh. There were those who thought the Jews meant harm, but the Druse chief knew them to be the messengers of God. He himself had seen the Jewish doctor loosen the green tentacles of death from the throat of the chief's favorite granddaughter. Gifts were brought for Avremel: a hammered brass tray for his home; a bright woven harness for his horse; a jeweled scimitar for himself. The women packed him pittot, boiled eggs and rice and cheese wrapped in grape leaves so that they would stay fresh on the journey. They knew that he could not eat their meat but they baked sweets for him, baklava and fruit rolls. The fragrant aroma of their baking caused them to smile. With the rising of the sweet dough, death was banished and the village was returned to normal life.

Avremel rode away fatigued but relieved. The epidemic could have been much worse. It might have been impossible to contain it. He trembled to think of what might have happened if the cholera had swept through the country. They had been lucky.

He rode very slowly after watching the storks. He knew that it would be prudent to head for the coastal road but he was reluctant to leave the verdant unmarked byways of the inland Galilee. He had not realized how dry and parched the landscape of Rishon was until he reached the green expanse of the hill country. This was the land that Ezra loved for its wildness and for its uncharted terrain. He understood his brother-in-law's yearning. A man who carved a home for himself out of such a countryside would have achieved something wondrous.

The summer had lingered here in the north, and late-blooming flowers carpeted the green hillsides. Wild roses, pale lilies, and orange-hearted jasmine were scattered across glade and hillock in a rainbow of profusion. He bent to pluck a clump of crimson roses of Sharon that exactly matched the crimson shawl Sara so often wore. He sniffed the flowers and laughed at himself. A two-day ride stood between himself and his wife at Rishon. The flowers would be wilted and dead long before they reached her. Still, he slung them over his reins and rode on.

He was sorry now that he had not left the village at daybreak but had lingered until the small girl had been buried. There was little chance now of reaching a Jewish settlement that would give him shelter for the night. Still, it was not so bad. Two warm blankets were stretched beneath the saddle and he had sufficient food and water. In fact, the thought of sleeping out of doors beneath the huge stars while the mountain wind licked his face excited him. He felt almost like a small boy, keyed up for the nocturnal adventure. He and Shimon would have to begin taking overnight camping trips. It would be important to spend time alone with the boy when the new baby came. He leaned forward and touched the soft petals of the roses suspended from his reins.

"El Raphun! El Raphun!"

A tall Bedouin youth riding a sleek black saddleless horse galloped up to him. The young man's face was streaked with sweat and the horse's coat was damp. The animal's long marbled tongue hung thirstily from his mouth and his hoofs nervously pawed the ground. He had ridden long and hard in pursuit of the Jewish doctor.

The Bedouin spoke rapidly in a dialect which Avremel had

difficulty understanding. He gestured wildly, and finally with grimaces and pantomime he made it clear that he wanted Avremel to come with him. Something serious had happened. There was a grave illness in his tribe. He trembled, cradled his head in his arms, and gazed heavenward. Death threatened. A mask of sadness fell over his face and his dark slender fingers toyed with the jeweled handle of the dagger in the tooled leather scabbard that dangled from the sash at his waist.

Avremel understood the message. The services of the Jewish doctor were needed, demanded. His heart sank. He did not fear the Arabs like his neighbors in Beit Dijon, who were settled in villages. He had not been afraid to go north to the Druse village. But the Druse, after all, were a stable social unit and friendly to the Jews. The Bedouin were divided into many tribes, each with its own ancient enmities, its own patterns of existence. They drifted into the Galilee from Syria and Lebanon, ignoring borders, perpetuating separate cultures, separate languages. Some were peaceful graziers; others were fierce warriors. Some, like those who came periodically to graze their herds near Rishon, were accepting of the Jewish settlers. Others were belligerently hostile. There were tales of murder and pillage.

A young girl, a pioneer newly arrived from Russia, had been on a hike in the Galilee with her comrades when they were attacked by marauding Bedouin. The girl had been seized and kidnapped. The Turkish authorities sent officers into the area but the Bedouin had disappeared, vanishing like ghosts into the night. There was no sign of their encampment. The Turkish officers spoke harshly to the young men who had accompanied the girl. He accused them of raping and murdering her. He asked them incomprehensible questions and even held one of them, the poet son of a venerated rabbi, in the Jaffa jailhouse until the Jewish community raised a bribe for his release. But the vanished girl never reappeared.

Avremel had heard all the tales of the Bedouin. He knew that Jewish settlers seldom rode into the north alone or unarmed, but he himself had ridden into the Galilee under the protection of the Druse. He knew he had no choice but to follow the Bedouin messenger, but he took comfort from the fact that he was still protected by the Druse. Just as the Bedouin tribe had

known that there was a Jewish doctor in the vicinity traveling
south of Paliyah, so his friends the Druse would know that he
had been summoned to the Bedouin camp. News traveled
with mysterious speed and accuracy through the lonely rolling
hills of the Galilee. He patted his horse's neck and fell into
pace behind the Bedouin.

The animals picked their way cautiously across rockbound
fields. Once, as they passed a murky pool of green water,
Avremel was startled by a sudden flurry and the sky turned
white as a flock of egrets took wing, soaring skyward. The
flash of pale wings against the deep purple of the sky seemed
to him a talisman of hope and optimism. He sat more erect in
his saddle, banished fear, and ventured a gulp of water from
his canteen.

Now he took a new interest in their direction. They were
proceeding south, he knew, and west but the untamed landscape offered no clue as to destination. The Bedouin youth
did not hesitate. He rode steadfastly on, turning when a wild
plum tree swayed westward or when he spotted a boulder
across which damp moss stretched to form an obscure map.

At last they mounted a steep hill and on the descent,
Avremel's guide broke into a harsh scream and urged his
horse into a gallop. Avremel followed more slowly and saw
that just below them, in a concealed hollow within the hillside, a new world had been created. Five shaggy black tents
had been erected, and throughout the camp, low fires flashed
their orange flames and licked the copper bottoms of the
black pots suspended above them. A lone speckled kid goat
wandered from fire to fire.

In a far corner of the field, a group of women bent over a
cauldron, dying long desert robes. They did not look up as
Avremel and his guide rode into the camp, although Avremel
saw that one of them stole a secret glance at him. Her eyes
were dark coals against the bit of swarthy skin that showed
above the thick veil covering most of her face, almost concealing the blue tattoo lines that decorated her cheekbones.

A bright carpet was spread in front of the largest tent, and
three bearded elders of the tribe squatted on it. They all wore
traditional black robes and dark pantaloons; the richness of
their checkered and rainbow-striped kaffiyehs testified to their
importance in the community. The eldest of them toyed with
a string of amber beads which he pressed, now and again, to

his lips. Copper pots and brass serving dishes were ranged before them and the aroma of strong Turkish coffee rose from the long-handled feenjan that rested on a huge tooled-metal tray, surrounded by tiny white cups.

"Salaam aleikum," Avremel said and bowed his head.

"Aleikem salaam," the leader replied and looked angrily at the man who sat next to him, who immediately rose and moved to another place. The sheik motioned Avremel into the seat. A cup of coffee was poured for the guest. He tasted it, paused thoughtfully, and finally smiled. The others smiled too, in appreciation. It was important to them, Avremel knew, that their hospitality not be merely accepted but considered and judged.

With delicate ceremony they opened the covered pots and offered him fragrant lamb wrapped in delicate cones of dough, a dish of grain which they scooped up with grape leaves and pita, and tiny cakes of hulled sesame seeds. He ate everything and smilingly offered his praise. He licked his fingers and smacked his lips although his heart beat with a staccato rhythm and a clammy sweat covered his skin. He fought his anxiety and impatience. They had brought him to their hidden encampment in great haste. There had been urgency and fear in his guide's eyes. Yet now they sat and enjoyed a leisurely feast. Still, that was the Arab way. He ate yet another piece of lamb, although the meat all but stuck in his throat, and then accepted another cup of coffee to show that he was satiated and that, for him, the meal was over.

Only then did the old man rise, still moving his amber beads about between slender fingers. They clicked against each other in soothing, rhythmic sequence. Avremel followed him as he moved toward the side of the hill where, Avremel saw now, a small cave had been carved. The hills of the Galilee were studded with such secret natural enclosures—small fortresses of concealment which nature had granted to fugitives and wanderers. Turkish militia often combed the countryside for weeks, pursuing a criminal or a band of smugglers, but the wilderness seldom yielded its secrets. What the Bedouin knew, and had known for generations, they would not share with transient ruling powers. Their hiding places remained their own, uncharted and therefore inaccessible.

This small cave was among their secret refuges, their clandestine retreats. Within its cool, dark interior they had devised a couch made up of soft white sheepskin and brightly colored rugs. A boy, perhaps twelve or thirteen years old, lay upon it. They had built a brushfire within the shelter and two women tended it, feeding it withered branches and fragrant leaves. A cloud of smoke rose from it and was fanned to the mouth of the cave by small boys who moved swiftly and waved bamboo brooms.

The sick child's white desert gown was damp with sweat. He flailed his arms wildly in the air and his sleeves rose like wings, reminding Avremel of the young stork he had seen only hours earlier. His huge dark eyes were bright with pain and rimmed with tears of fever and anguish. He bit his lips and shouted and then suddenly raised his voice in a piercingly sweet shepherd's song. Then his arms crashed downward and he clutched his right side briefly and wept.

"Imma," he cried, and Avremel thought of Shimon during his last illness.

"Imma," Shimon had called out of the fever grip, in the same plaintive voice as this Bedouin child who rolled about now amid rugs and skins. Pain had only one language, one culture.

Avremel opened the musette bag that contained his medical equipment and removed his stethoscope. His hand brushed across the revolver. The steel muzzle was cold to his touch. It occurred to him, irrelevantly, that he had never fired a gun.

He examined the boy as the old sheik hovered at his elbow. He listened for the heart and measured the pulse, ascertaining the fever by touch because he knew that the boy's chattering teeth would snap the thermometer. He lifted the white robe and his gently probing fingers traveled across the boy's body. He applied pressure and released it, moving very slowly, very carefully.

The Arab elders watched with absorption. Their worry beads clicked at an intensified pace. The boy moaned and shivered, and the women fed more acacia leaves into the fire. Avremel touched the lower right quadrant of the abdomen. The boy writhed and screamed with pain. One Bedouin leaped forward, his hand on his scabbard, but the sheik restrained him and motioned to Avremel to proceed with the examination. Again Avremel touched the tender area and again the boy emitted a wild shriek of pain. One of the women pulled her shawl over her head and huddled within it, as though to shield herself from the sounds of agony.

At last Avremel was through. He stood, his head bowed against the burden of his knowledge. The boy was suffering from an inflamed appendix. It might rupture. There was a possibility that it had ruptured already. If it were not excised from the body, the child would die. He summoned every scrap of Arabic he knew, plundering every vagrant word of dialect, in an attempt to explain the situation to the old man. He took a stick and made a drawing on the damp earth of the cave floor. He drew a piece of fruit ravaged by rot and showed a knife cutting the rotten pulp away. He drew a sketch of the boy and showed a knife carving into the exposed flesh.

The old man nodded. He understood. He pressed the amber beads to his lips and bent down to look at the boy. They shared the same high forehead, the same narrow lips. Avremel marked the resemblance. The child was the old man's son or grandson, heir designate to the sheikdom of the small wandering tribe.

"*Yaala*," the old sheik said and nodded affirmatively. He had agreed to the operation. A wave of weakness washed over Avremel.

He had only the most rudimentary equipment with him; a scalpel; a needle and a set of sutures; a few other implements; and some of the Turkish district health officer's morphine, which might just suffice to anesthetize the lad during surgery but would not be sufficient to soothe him during recovery. He had no alcohol but there was a small flask of brandy which Yehuda had insisted he take. That could be used to sterilize the instruments and the incision.

The weakness left him once he had catalogued his equipment, assessed his options. He drew out a hypodermic needle and injected the boy with the morphine. There was a gasp as he plunged the steel needle into the exposed buttock but the old man's acquiescence impelled the observers to stillness. The sheik cradled the boy in his arms and the two other men wept and embraced each other.

A makeshift table was devised from poles and a single plank. Avremel supposed it to be the platform on which the women stretched the dyed cloth woven of goat and camel's hair and of vegetable fibers. It would do. He motioned to the white kaffiyeh of one of the men. The women understood and brought him yards of similar fabric. He took it all. It was clean and would serve to bandage the wound and to soak up the blood during the surgery. He spread the remaining cloth across the improvised table.

Carefully, he picked up the boy and placed him on the covered board. Four men of the tribe, each holding a blazing torch, gathered at each corner. Avremel lifted the desert gown and the boy's skin glowed orange in the firelight. He slept. His dark lashes were long and thick. Dampened by tears, they clung to his finely curved cheekbones. His penis dangled like a wilted blue flower between his dark-skinned thighs. Now the light of the torches turned his body to gold and the flames danced against the steel scalpel which Avremel lifted and lowered with certain stroke.

He made the incision. Crimson blood spurted forth. He ripped flesh aside, working rapidly, racing against the efficacy of the anesthesia. The appendix was exposed, inflamed and angry, swollen with the poison that threatened to overflow through the peritoneum. One of the torchbearers swayed dangerously and his light was passed to someone else. He ran from the cave and they heard the sound of his retching.

Avremel cut the vermiform appendix loose and carefully lifted it from the abdominal cavity. He tossed it to the ground where it landed with a muffled splatter. He had been just in time. Within minutes it would have ruptured. Even now he was fearful that pus had escaped it and oozed into the stomach walls. Quickly, he moved the exposed skin back into place, threaded his needle and made a dermal seam. Only when he was finished did his hands begin to shake. He felt a sudden chill and realized that his own white shirt was wet with spattered blood.

The boy was carried back to his couch, still locked into the drug-induced sleep. Avremel wiped the blood from his scalpel and his probe and replaced the instruments in his bag. He saw, with relief, that an ounce of brandy remained in his flask. He would drink it later, when he had left the encampment. It was enough that the Bedouin had allowed him to sterilize his instruments with the alcohol that was abhorrent to them.

The women hovered over the sleeping boy. By word and gesture he indicated to them that the boy was to drink only liquids for the next few days and that the bandaged incision must be kept clean. The women nodded and bowed their heads, shamed because a man was talking to them. He guessed that the smallest of the women, whose almond-shaped green eyes brimmed with tears above the coarse face covering, was the boy's mother.

The old sheik knelt on his prayer rug just outside the cave, facing east toward Mecca. He offered prayers of thanksgiving; his lips moved soundlessly, uttering verses from the Koran. He rolled back on his heels and prostrated himself once and then again. At last he rose and turned to Avremel. With a sweep of his hand, he motioned to the largest of the black tents, indicating that the Jewish doctor was welcome to spend the night. Avremel, in turn, shook his head and pointed to his horse. The sheik nodded. A guest's volition must not be violated. Imperiously he motioned to the young man who had been Avremel's guide.

Words of instruction were issued. The younger man mounted his horse and brought Avremel's chestnut forward. The sheik clutched the doctor's arms with his powerful fingers. Fear and gratitude pulsated from his flesh to that of Avremel's. He held out a small leather bag, but Avremel shook his head and declined to accept it. But the sheik would not be refused and placed the money bag in the partially opened musette bag. The green-eyed woman filled Avremel's canteen with water from an earthenware jug and put a parcel of food wrapped in gauzy kaffiyeh cloth in his saddle bag.

"Salaam aleikem," the sheik said.

"Aleikem salaam," Avremel replied, and he and his guide rode out of the camp.

They journeyed on in silence. The huge stars suspended in the endless ink-black sky seemed very close. Avremel watched them as he rode, grateful for the soothing galactic companions that guided him through the night. Again they traversed wild marsh and ascended gentle hills, until at last the Bedouin reined in his horse. Avremel, startled by the brevity of the journey, looked about him, his eyes accustomed now to the darkness. He recognized the large boulder and the dwarfed wild almond tree. It was the precise spot where the Bedouin had found him only hours before. The guide saluted and turned. He galloped now, anxious to return to the encampment, and Avremel was left alone in the silent, pervasive darkness.

Exhaustion held him immobile prisoner for a moment and then he realized that he could ride no farther that night, that indeed he would have been well-advised to stay at the Bedouin camp. He had not liked to leave his patient. The boy was not yet out of danger. There could be postoperative shock. Gangrene could set in. Any number of complications might arise. But Avremel knew that there was little he could do to prevail against any such eventualities. In retrospect now, he was shocked that he had operated at all, that he had performed major surgery without proper implements or assistance, in a cave carved into the Galilean hillside. He remembered how torchlight had splayed across his gloved hands as he had reached into the glistening, moist stomach wall. A slow pride stirred within him. He had done it, and had probably saved the boy's life.

"*C'est bon, monsieur le medecin,*" he said aloud, imitating the voice of the Parisian surgeon who had instructed him in surgery. He laughed, tossing the joy of his relief against the quiet of the night.

Relaxed now, he slid from his horse and loosened the saddle straps to release the blankets. He spread one on the cold ground and covered himself with the other. He remembered the brandy then and reached into the musette bag. Fumbling, his fingers reaching for the bottle, he groped at the soft leather money bag but he did not remove it. He had not anticipated payment nor did he want it. He would turn the dinars over to the Rishon council. His hand brushed the cold revolver and he thought to remove it. Only recently a camper in these hills had been gored by a leopard that had wandered south from Lebanon. But he left it in the bag, found the flask at last, and drained the liquid.

He felt it course through his body in a flow of comforting warmth. Soothed, he lay awake, thinking that Sara's eyes were the same green as those of the Bedouin woman, remembering the way his wife's dark hair fell in graceful swaths across her naked shoulders. Shimon had blond hair, a golden crown the same color as the durra wheat that grew in the farthest field of Yehuda Maimon's farm. Perhaps the new baby would be a girl with hair like her mother's and lashes as dark and curling as those of the Bedouin prince. Sara. Shimon.

His family. They must leave Rishon and move to Jerusalem, where there was important work to be done. To Jerusalem, that rose-gold city of narrow streets and ancient dreams. Sara's family could visit them there. They would have a house shaded by a feathery cypress tree and he would plant a citron sapling in their garden. In Jerusalem. He slept at last.

Fatigue and the brandy weighted his sleep. It was not pierced by the muffled sound of horses' hoofs approaching the boulder. He did not hear the muted voices talking softly in the darkness. But at the touch of a hand upon his throat he opened his eyes and saw the shining steel blade. He recognized the jewels inset in the handle of the dagger—the blood-red agates mined in the mountains of the north and the sky-blue turquoise pried loose from the desert's heart. He had watched the sun glint across the dagger's handle as he rode behind the Bedouin guide who slung the weapon through the scabbard at his belt.

"No," he said and thrust his hand upward to grapple with the Bedouin's trained grip of steel. "Why?" he cried and did not recognize his own voice, shrill with defeat and desperation.

But he knew why. The boy had died. Just as he had been the savior, now he was the murderer. He knew their code. Blood must be avenged with blood.

"No," he said again as the dagger plunged through his carotid artery and he saw the crimson fount of his own blood spurt upward and rain down, in scarlet drops, on the sea-scented blanket his mother-in-law had carried to her new home from the Russian woodlands. He knew that he was dying, and he closed his eyes and listened to the rattle and gurgle of his voice.

"Sara! Sara!"

The Bedouin, poised above him, also listened. The woman's name was repeated again and again and then the night was once more shrouded in silence. Satisfied, he wiped his dagger clean of the scarlet vengeance blood of the Jewish doctor, then joined his companion, who had not bothered to dismount. Without looking back they galloped toward their encampment where, before daybreak, they would bury a prince of their blood.

Again, Avremel's hand reached into his open musette bag and his fingers closed about the small carved gazelle that Shimon had placed there. The olive wood was satin smooth to his touch and with brief clarity he remembered the feel of his newborn son's skin and the wondrous smoothness of his wife's dark hair as she dried it in the morning light. His fingers tightened in a death grip about the small carving, so smooth and fashioned with such love. He closed his eyes and did not open them again.

A flock of egrets flew low and streaked by above him. A nesting owl hooted softly and then was quiet, surrendering his nocturnal kingdom to encroaching daylight. The pallor of dawn veiled the dead man's face.

The Maimon family gathered for dinner at the Rishon farm. They were late in eating because Rivka had insisted that Saul and David, who were working in the area, would join them, but in the end the twins had not arrived. Sara had prepared the meal because Rivka insisted that she felt a cold coming on and was fearful of exerting herself. Sara asked no questions. In the fall her mother complained of a chill in the air, and in the summer she became ill with the heat. Her mother's inconsistencies no longer troubled Sara, who remembered how in Russia she had dreamed of Palestine and memorized epic descriptions of the Galilee, while in Palestine she wrote poignant odes to Mother Russia and painted small watercolors of the Ukranian woodlands she had despised when she lived in their shadow.

"Eat, Shimon," Ezra said.

The child looked at his plate, speared an eggplant fritter and held it aloft.

"I want my father," he said. "When is Abba coming back?"

"Soon," Sara replied calmly. "The Turkish district health officer was here yesterday and he saw Abba only a few days before that in the north. Abba asked him to tell us that he would be delayed for a few days but probably he would be home before the Sabbath. The Turk also said that we should be very proud. Abba helped the Druse villagers and brought the epidemic under control. Now, Shimon, you must eat so that I can tell Abba what a good boy you've been and so you can show him how strong you have grown."

"All right." Reluctantly the boy put the food into his mouth. "I hate eggplant," he said when he had finished chewing, but dutifully he cut another piece.

"If you hate eggplant you'd better find another country to live in," Erza said and tousled his nephew's hair. He would miss Shimon, he knew, when he went north.

"Did the Turk bring any other news?" Yehuda asked. He had been in the orchard during the officer's visit, checking the new grapefruit saplings. They seemed strong enough but he had not worked with grapefruit before and was wary of the new undertaking. Still, he was pleased that for the first time since his illness he had worked a full day without feeling the pull of the fatigue that characteristically pursued malaria victims. His new energy renewed his confidence. The illness had taken on a dreamlike quality; it seemed a distant worrying misfortune that had briefly and purposelessly interrupted their lives.

"He told me that the kaiser and Herzl met on the road to Jerusalem and exchanged greetings."

"Imagine a Jew, a man who was a guest in our house, talking to the ruler of Germany," Rivka said.

She had followed the newspaper account of the kaiser's visit with great avidity, noting the cut of his frock coat and the quality of his cravat. Would Ezra need a frock coat when he went to university in Europe? Perhaps one would be required for conferences and formal teas. The tailor in Jaffa could fashion it for him.

"The kaiser will do exactly what the sultan wants him to do," Yehuda observed morosely. "It is always the same story. Talk does not cost anything and so everyone holds conferences and discussions. But in the end the Jews must plan and do things for themselves."

He did not add "as I did," but the unspoken words hung heavy in the air. Success had brought an odd complacency to Yehuda. If the path he had chosen for himself and his family had succeeded for them, then surely it would work for everyone. He assessed his achievements, tallied his assets. Sara was happily married. Ezra would go on to university now that he himself could again assume full charge of the farm. Saul and David remained in close contact with the family. The orange groves brought a plentiful crop and his new grapefruit trees would surely bear large and succulent fruit. Their wealth would increase. He was well satisfied. He had cheated history and charted his own destiny and, more recently, he had cheated death.

Sara and Ezra looked at each other but they said nothing. A tacit understanding existed between them. Just as they sympathized with their mother, they avoided confrontations with their father.

"What else did the Turk say?" Yehuda asked as Sara served the compote.

"He said that some Arab landholders in the north were thinking of selling off some plots. Good land, he said, for farming and grazing," Ezra replied.

He stirred the dish of stewed plums and grapes. He did not tell his father that the Turk had described the land in great detail and had given Ezra the names of the owners. Nor did Ezra offer the information that he himself intended to take a trip to the north.

"He didn't say exactly when Avremel would come home?"

"Not exactly," Sara replied.

Her voice held a vague note of worry and she glanced out the window. The sun was fading beyond the fields and she felt the terrible loneliness of the dying hours of daylight. The child within her stirred and she placed her hand across her abdomen and rocked gently in her chair. Perhaps if she looked out the window long enough, Avremel would come riding up, his bright hair tossed by the wind, one arm draped loosely about the reins and the other outstretched to embrace her. She remembered how, during her Kharkov girlhood, she had sometimes waited for young Chaim in a similar manner, screwing her eyes closed and willing him to appear just as she opened them. And often it had happened that way. On impulse she closed her eyes and within minutes she heard the sound of running footsteps. A smile skittered across her face. She opened her eyes but it was not Avremel who had entered the room.

Yossi Weissbloom, the head of the town council, stood in the doorway. His face was pale and he stood with the limp posture of a man drained of energy.

"Ezra. Yehuda. I must talk to you. Alone."

Wordlessly the men rose and followed him out of the room. They stood together in a solemn trio beneath the branches of the citron tree.

Sara watched them from the window. Their lips moved soundlessly. Her father staggered and was sustained by her brother. The violent shade of twilight drifted across Ezra's face. A new brightness had come into her brother's eyes—a dangerous liquid luminescence. He was crying.

Saul, she thought. David. Something had happened to the twins. She crossed both her arms about her abdomen, protecting her unborn child, and continued to watch the three men as though they were actors in a mime show and she, their audience, was committed to the interpretation of their wordless message.

Yehuda and Ezra reentered the room slowly, reluctantly, as mourners approach a house of grief. Their faces were drained of color. Their eyes were frozen with sorrow and horror. When they did not look at her, she knew the truth at once.

"Avremel!" she screamed and slid to the floor in a faint.

His body had lain for two days on the hillside before a Druse shepherd, searching for a missing ewe, found it. Birds had pecked small holes in the dead man's face and a hawk had torn the flesh from his cheeks. The days had been unusually hot for the season and where the skin had been exposed, the sun had scorched it. It was the odor of the decomposing body that led the shepherd boy to the side of the boulder where the doctor lay. He had recognized him at once by his bright hair. El Raphun, the golden-haired healer, was legendary now among the Druse. A rider had galloped to the nearest Turkish station and the body had been covered with fine linen. The doctor's horse was found grazing in a distant field, a wilted clump of scarlet roses laced about its harness.

The men of the Rishon burial society retched as they stripped the rags of clothing from Avremel's body. They turned their faces as their hands washed the dead man's limbs. They jumped when the small carved wooden gazelle slipped from the dead man's fingers and clattered to the synagogue floor. Ezra took it and washed away the ribbon of blood that trailed across its back before giving it to Shimon.

The funeral was brief. Sara clutched Shimon's hand as the rabbi ripped the cloth of her blouse and the cambric of the boy's shirt. She understood, for the first time, the significance of the ritual. With just such swiftness, her husband, Shimon's father, had been ripped from their lives. Her fingers toyed nervously with the frayed threads of the torn garment. Avremel was dead. She was a widow and her children would have no father. She yearned to weep but tears would not come.

There was no eulogy. The Kaddish was recited in unison at the graveside by Ezra, Saul, and David. The bright-haired man had loved their sister had been friend and brother to them. His life and death were a part of their own lives. Ezra wept, openly and unashamedly.

"Blessed be Thou O Lord our God—magnified and exalted be Thy name," they chanted.

The sun shone brightly down on them and glowed golden across the body, in the coarse white linen shroud, which they lowered into the newly dug grave. There was no coffin. Avremel would soon become part of the earth in the land that he had loved. Sara led Shimon forward. She pressed a clump of soft earth into his small hand and he stood above his father's body, his lips clenched tight and his cheeks flushed although his face otherwise was almost translucent in its pallor.

"Shalom, Abba," the boy said softly, and the women of Rishon turned their faces and wept.

Sara knelt and lowered her own handful of earth onto her husband's body. It was cruel, she thought, that it was not the season of anemones, for he would have wanted those small, bright flowers planted across the earth that covered him. But then Avremel would never again have anything he wanted.

She sat, as though in a trance, through the seven days of mourning. She accepted, with dignity, the condolences of the Druse chieftain who had traveled south to bring her the condolences of his people. His men had searched for the murdering Bedouin but had been unable to locate them. They were not a tribe of Palestine but had come into the country from beyond the Syrian border. The Druse chieftain brought straw baskets of dates and figs and jugs of honey. He gave Shimon a small reed pipe. The child forgot that he was in mourning. Perched on the low stool of grief, the boy played a song his father had loved. "*Anu banu artza, livnot ul'hibanot ba*"—"We have come to the land to build and be built by it."

Sara smiled bitterly. Avremel had come to the land to bring health and life and he had been rewarded with death. She would not again submit herself so quickly to the ideals by which her father had lived and which had led her husband to death. Briefly, that night in Jerusalem, she had caught a glimpse of the source of their excitement but she knew now that she had been deceived. They were strangers in this land. There was no safety here, not for her and not for her children. She was done with submitting to the demands and dreams of others.

The villagers of Beit Dijon came and stood side by side with the young Jewish pioneers. Avremel had been friend and healer to them both. Medical colleagues traveled from Jerusalem and Tiberias. Tea was poured and honey cake was eaten. Ezra watched his sister who had, during the week of mourning, lost all vestiges of youth and moved now with the tired, defeated gait of those who will never again be surprised by life.

Finally the week of mourning was past and the thirty days of grief also drifted away. The family gathered again around the table. It was a Sabbath eve and again Sara had prepared the meal. They were quiet as they ate, looking more at the flickering Sabbath flames than at each other. Their shared grief had made them strangely shy with each other. Fear had stolen into their lives and they knew that they would never again be free of it. Yehuda glanced over his shoulder as he worked in the orange groves. Saul and David rode the countryside with their rifles slung across their shoulders. Rivka woke in the night and listened to the creak of the floorboards, the rattling of a window.

Sara's voice pierced the uneasy quiet.

"I want to tell you all now. I am going back to Europe. Perhaps from there to America. I am taking Shimon and leaving the country."

Her words fell with harsh heaviness upon their ears but they did not argue with her. Yehuda recognized in his daughter's voice an iron, arbitrary tone, reminiscent of his own when he had told his father that he was going to settle in Palestine. Rivka's eyes filled with tears. Her new grandchild would not be born in the land. Where would Sara go and how would she live? They did not ask her. They deferred to her loss and her suffering and accepted her decision.

Alternatives presented themselves to her but they forbore from discussing them. Sara could go to her grandparents in Kishinev, to her aunt in Argentina, to her uncle in America. They were a wandering family, sprung from a wandering people. Letters would be written and possibilities explored. But they did not dare to hope that she would change her mind.

A flicker of an idea grew in Yehuda's mind. He would, he decided, pluck a single saving asset from this grave loss his family had sustained.

"Wherever Sara goes," he said, "there Ezra will also go. He will go to the university and make a home with his sister. When he completes his studies, he will return to us. It is not as I would have wished it, but I see that it is the way it must be."

"No." And now the same note of decisiveness steeled Ezra's voice. "I am not going to university, Father. I am not leaving the country. I am going north. I want to start a farm—a farm of my own."

"In the north?" Rivka's voice was shrill with disappointment and disbelief. The north was a wilderness where jackals frolicked in the night and wandering leopards roared; the north was the prowling ground of the Bedouin murderer who had slit their Avremel's throat and left him to be eaten by scavenger birds. She had not raised her Ezra to be a pioneer in unknown territory. He was to be a man of culture and learning.

"Ezra, what of your studies?" Yehuda gasped, and desperation choked off his words. He covered his eyes and looked up to see that small trees of candlelight blossomed against the books that lined the room. Latin texts and geographies. Anatomy manuals and anthologies of philosophic essays. Books that had traveled across the ocean and others that he had salvaged from narrow shops. The books had been the compass of their lives, the guide to Ezra's future. His son was to be a doctor, a professor. A man of learning, and recognized as such. Ezra was his own lien on posterity. He offered his youngest child that which he himself had been denied, but he now saw that the denial was to be consistent. Age would not grant him that which had not been his in youth. "You cannot do this!" he shouted.

Anguish seared Yehuda's voice and the child, Shimon, put his hands over his ears. He had his own griefs and could not bear those of his elders.

"I'll go on studying, Father," Ezra said. "Reading and

learning is a part of me. But it's the land I want. I want to work my own land."

"And how will you buy that land? Land is not given away!"

Yehuda pounded the table and the flames danced wildly. The final weapon was his. He would give his son no money. Angry, bitter satisfaction laced his taunt. Saul and David looked uneasily at each other. Their own break with their father had been simpler, their reconciliation implicitly granted. Not as much had been expected of them. They had not been charged with redeeming their father's dream.

Ezra stood and went to his room. He returned carrying the thick black talmudic text his grandfather, Reb Shimon, had given him upon their departure from Russia. Always, he had kept the book close by him. He opened it now and turned the flaking pages. One by one he removed packets of currency. Green American dollars. The money that Mendel had sent through the years to his father in Russia. He withdrew a tiny ovoid, wrapped in yellow newsprint, from the binding of the book. He peeled the paper off to reveal a dull green stone— the uncut emerald that Reb Shimon's daughter, Yehuda's sister, had sent so many years ago from Argentina.

"This will pay for my land," Ezra said.

Yehuda laughed with harsh anger. The irony seared him. His father, Reb Shimon, had withheld his blessing from Yehuda because settling the land was a profanation of God's name. But now Reb Shimon had reached from behind the grave to enable Ezra to buy a farm in the wilderness of the Galilee. It seemed there was no end to the tricks his father's God would play on Yehuda Maimon.

"Go then. Buy your land," he shouted.

Rivka sobbed softly. Ezra moved as though to comfort her but went instead out to the flagstone patio. His sister, his brothers, and his nephew followed him. There was no longer any place for them in the room where Yehuda and Rivka sat in silence, their faces lit by candlelight.

Rivka moved closer to Yehuda and placed her hand on his arm. He moved his head to rest his cheek against her fingers.

"It will be all right," she said.

They were alone, deserted by their children. Hard reality had consumed their dreams. Yet they were together, and golden fruit grew on the trees they had planted and filled the air with fragrance.

Yehuda nodded but made no move to rise. The twin Sabbath flames diminished, turned blue, and died.

PART THREE

Ezra and Nechama

1900–1914

Chapter 11

Crimson star-shaped anemones glittered in the fields as Yehuda and Rivka rode northward. The small flowers had reached full bloom, and as light vagrant spring winds blew, they shivered tremulously. The wide-winged petals flew free of the blossoms but fell swiftly to ground, bloodying the coastal road with a brilliant scarlet litter. Rivka shifted in the leather seat of the diligence and remembered that poor Avremel had loved the anemones. Small Shimon had often gathered them in great clumps and proudly offered her the clumsy bouquets to decorate the Sabbath table. Shimon was a tall boy now, Sara told them in her letters. He would be bar mitzvahed soon in another land, in a distant city. In Oswiecim, Poland. Rivka, who prided herself on her sensitivity to words, thought the very name of the small Polish city where Sara had found a home to be harsh against the tongue—ugly in thought. Still, it was there that her daughter had found her happiness at last, traveling almost full cycle only to arrive again at her point of departure.

Rivka sighed heavily and turned her gaze from the flower-streaked fields to the strip of seacoast visible across the rockbound marshes when they passed an incline in the road.

The sea was calm, its green waves beaded with the gold of reflected sunlight. They broke softly at the beach and Rivka watched their foam-tipped tongues lick the shoreline.

"Are you all right?" Yehuda asked anxiously.

Rivka was not a good traveler. He remembered their voyage from Russia. Even now she kept laudanum and smelling salts available for a brief journey to Jaffa, and although they had lived in Palestine for a dozen years and she wrote verses extolling its beauty, she had never seen Jerusalem. He had been surprised when she agreed to make the journey to Sadot Shalom, Ezra's farm in the foothills of the Carmel range.

"Do you think I will miss my grandson's circumcision?" she had asked indignantly when Yehuda suggested that he go alone.

"The family will be represented," he assured her. "Saul and David will be there with Chania and Mirra."

"I am going." A familiar petulance tinged her tone. She was the grain broker's pampered daughter, the vague and fragile wife and mother.

He did not argue with her, nor did he remind her that she had not felt it necessary to make the far less demanding journey to Sejera when Saul and David were married. He had traveled alone then to escort his tall sons through the newly planted grove of olive trees to a clearing where they stood with their brides beneath the marriage canopy, devised of Yehuda's own prayer shawl. It was the same simulated symbolic shelter that had shaded Sara and Avremel on their marriage day. He did not know who had raised the marriage canopy for his daughter when she became the wife of her girlhood love, Chaim. Her description of the wedding had been brief and he had asked no questions, thus protecting himself from her replies.

The twins, joyous bridegrooms, their skin stained amber and their thick hair fiery beneath the white marriage skullcaps, were married on the same day, sharing the wedding canopy with three other young couples because the bearded rabbi who had traveled north from Jerusalem would not come again for several months. Later in the day the same rabbi would circumcise a child born eight days before and affix a mezuzzah to the newly built schoolhouse.

David and Saul had not questioned their mother's absence from the ceremony. They had been too happy, too delighted with their brides and with the new future that was unfolding for them. PICA, the Palestine Development Corporation, formed by the Baron de Rothschild when he finally despaired of controlling the Jewish colonies, had promised their group land for a collective. Now they could start work and build their own settlement, create their own society.

Saul whirled his petite Mirra in a joyous nuptial dance,, loosening her coronet of braids so that the thick dark bunches of hair covered her shoulders like a cape. She was so small that even on tiptoe she barely reached her tall new husband's shoulder; but her size was deceptive. She worked in the fields with a swiftness and fortitude that surprised her instructors at the agricultural school. She had graduated from the Jewish gymnasium in her native Riga and she spoke an accurate spitfire Hebrew, refusing to answer Saul unless his grammar was perfect.

"You see, a wife can accomplish what a mother could not," Rivka said ruefully when she met Mirra, remembering the hours she had spent trying to teach the twins syntax, persuading them to memorize poetry. She liked Mirra but the girl's energy exhausted her.

Mirra was full of projects and plans. On one visit to the Rishon farm she fashioned heavy curtains that were more effective than the shutters against the pervasive sunlight which Rivka had fought since her arrival in the land. She rearranged the kitchen garden, bordering tomato plants with mint, scientifically arranging eggplant seedlings so that the male and female alternated. She had taken the agricultural prize in her Riga Zionist group, she told them proudly.

Rivka preferred to spend time with Chania, David's tall, slender wife. There was a quietness about Chania, a soothing stillness. She moved with the certain step of a woman who has arrived at a chosen destination. Chania had become a Zionist on the day her brother was seized for service in the czar's army. She had been ten years old then, and she had watched him ride away with the recruiting officer while her mother wept and her father swore bitterly. She was twenty when she left for Palestine. Her brother had never returned and they thought of him as dead. Her mother wept when she left for the land but her father did not swear. They might never see her again, they knew, but they would not think of her as dead.

Yehuda had waltzed with Chania at the wedding and was briefly startled by the callused, leathery feel of her long-fingered hands and the ramrod straightness of her back.

"I hope my son will make you happy," he said.

"We will make each other happy," she replied quietly.

He understood then that she and David shared the same steely resolve to live by their own standards, to carve a new life together in the land they had chosen to make their own. He watched as David took her hand so that they could dance a debka. He thought them a handsome couple and felt a twinge of envy for his son, who had chosen a wife who would share his dream and work by his side. The twins had chosen well, he wrote Sara, who sent each of her sisters-in-law fine white lace shawls which they fondled with work-roughened hands, fearful that their touch might rip the delicate embroidery.

Certainly Yehuda preferred the twin's wives to Ezra's Nechama, with her large brooding dark eyes and her pale skin that did not take on color even when the sun blazed and harsh winds blew. He saw in Nechama's pallor the heritage of the ghetto, the shadowed and bloodless complexions of generations of frightened shopkeepers who walked, with their heads bent, through narrow, cobbled streets and earned their livelihoods in tiny stalls banked by counters and rimmed with shelves on which dusty merchandise was piled. He had been surprised to hear Saul and David remark on a likeness between Nechama and their sister, Sara. He saw no similarity between his son's wife and his daughter. True, they were both tall, dark-haired women, possessed of a natural competence. But Sara had been swift and forceful. She had responded with fierce determination to sudden thrusts of fortune. She had seized her own life, made her own future. She was a survivor, a stubborn chameleon who adapted to each new landscape. Nechama seemed a quiescent woman, silent and inward turned, shielding herself from sunlight and adventure. Yehuda had not been surprised to learn that Nechama's family owned a small dry goods shop in a narrow Jaffa street not far from Chaim Baker's hotel.

'They are fine people," Chaim Baker had assured him when Yehuda first learned of Ezra's engagement. "They are newly arrived in the country but diligent and hardworking."

"Newly arrived," Yehuda repeated bitterly.

The Langerfelds, Nechama's family, had come to the country when times were easier, when the Jewish colonists had managed a liveable détente with the Turks and the Jewish population had doubled. They had not been in the land during the days of food scarcities, when his own children had often gone hungry. Then they had cowered in Russia and piously recited their psalms. Even now they reaped the benefits of harvests which they neither planted nor cultivated. Jewish farmers produced reliable crops now. The fruits and vegetables sold in the Jaffa market were grown on the farms of Rishon LeZion, Petach Tikvah, and other Jewish agricultural settlements. But although the newcomers ate the fruit of Jewish farmers, they themselves did not settle on the land. The farmlands of Palestine were as alien to them as the agricultural estates of Russia had been. They had found themselves a small shop in Jaffa, not unlike the shop they had left behind in Kattowitz. When Yehuda Maimon visited it, he grew nauseous and stumbled from its darkness into the freedom of the sunlit street.

Bolts of dark cloth lined the shelves and rows of buttons stared at him from sagging tiers. Nechama's mother, her hair concealed beneath a neat dark kerchief, was hunched over a sewing machine. Her lips moved soundlessly as she worked. She prayed as she turned cuffs and fashioned seams, hypnotizing herself with liturgy. Reb Langerfeld, his beard combed to a silky softness, his skullcap askew, moved restlessly as he stood at the counter. His fingers danced from his account book to the large volume of Talmud always open before him. Occasionally he read a worn paperbound treatise by Rabbi Zvi Hirsh Kalisher or Rabbi Har Alkilai. He knew their writings as thoroughly as Yehuda Maimon knew the works of Dr. Leon Pinsker. During his first meeting with Yehuda, he excused himself to hurry to the neighboring synagogue for evening prayers. He did not suggest that Yehuda join him. At a subsequent meeting he suddenly peered anxiously into his talmudic text. An elusive point had suddenly clarified itself for him. It was then that Yehuda realized that Nechama's father reminded him of his own father, Reb Shimon, whose thoughts were rooted always in mysterious and intricate arguments about wandering goats and laws of ritual purity.

But unlike Reb Shimon, Nechama's father was committed to the idea of a Jewish homeland in Palestine. He was an ardent member of the newly formed Mizrachi, a party com-

posed of Orthodox Zionists who saw no conflict between their
love of the Torah and their commitment to settling the land.
To live in Palestine, he told his children, was an expression
of spiritual devotion. He taught them to face east to Jerusalem
when they prayed, and when he blessed them each Sabbath
evening, he assured them that soon they would celebrate the
day of rest in the homeland.

Yehuda Maimon had dreamed of the fields and orchards of
the holy land, but Isaac Langerfeld was not a farmer and he
believed that cities belonged to the dream of Zion restored.
He was a shopkeeper, a town dweller, and he continued to be
a shopkeeper when at last he was able to settle in Palestine.
There was a need in the country for cities as well as farms.
Businesses were as necessary as orange groves. There would
have to be Jewish commerce and Jewish industy if there was
to be a viable Jewish homeland.

They could not remain forever in Arab Jaffa, in the warren
of alleyways and streets where one shop hovered over another
and the smells of fried chickpea paste and simmering chicken
soup mingled in odd confluence. Reb Langerfeld and his
family took long Sabbath afternoon walks across the dunes
that bordered Jaffa. The fine-grained sand penetrated the
children's shoes, and their toes curled about bits of sea glass.
They whimpered and complained but their father shrugged his
shoulders and walked on.

"Remember the feel of the sand," he told them. "One day
all of this will be paved over and your grandchildren will not
believe you when you tell them that this city is built on
sand."

But he did not discuss with Yehuda Maimon his dream of a
city built where lonely sand dunes now stood. He talked
instead of the marriage gift he would make his eldest daughter, Nechama, and of the linens and furniture he would give
to her and of the money he was giving to Ezra so that an
adequate kitchen could be built onto the farmhouse at Sadot
Shalom. When Ezra and his brothers had built the house, they
had constructed only two rooms, and Ezra had prepared his
meals in the small lean-to between house and barn. The
city-bred daughter of Isaac Langerfeld would need a proper
kitchen.

Yehuda listened impassively. A shopkeeper's talk. A city

dweller's prattle. A Talmudist's bickering. The man was as
pale as his daughter.

"Where did you meet her?" he had asked Ezra when his
son first brought Nechama to the Rishon farm.

"In a bank," Ezra replied. "In the Anglo-Palestine Bank
in Jaffa. She was a clerk there."

"I am not surprised."

Yehuda's tone was sour. It seemed to him that his youngest
son, upon whom all his hopes had rested, mocked him anew
with each fresh decision. The mistress of Sadot Shalom, the
only independent Jewish homestead of the lower Galilee, was
the daughter of Orthodox shopkeepers, a serious-eyed woman
who seldom laughed and who always wore a large broad-
brimmed hat to hide her long white face from the sun's
brightness.

But it was possible that motherhood had changed her,
Yehuda thought, and he winced as the carriage struggled over
an uncleared hill.

"What is Sadot Shalom like?" Rivka asked, turning her
head from the sea.

Ezra had shown her on the map where the farm was
located, nestled just between the new Jewish settlement of
Bat Shlomo and the Arab village of Zalafa, yet far enough
away from both of them to be completely isolated. They
would turn off the coast road at Zichron Yaakov and wait for
Ezra's wagon, which would carry them across the untamed
fields north and east. The diligence they rode in, the same
coach which had carried them on their first inland journey
from Jaffa to Rishon (driven now by the son of that same
Gedalia) could not manage the rough byways that led to the
farm.

"It is not like the Rishon farm," Yehuda replied, "but it is
very beautiful."

He had visited it when Ezra first took possession and he
had looked then with despair at the overgrown foliage, at the
rock-strewn fields and meadowland. It stood on a sloping
hillside and he saw, with a farmer's trained eye, that the early
rains would send the newly planted grain sliding downward,
that the vulnerable sapling fruit trees would struggle to take
root in the rocky terrain. Angrily, he had told this to his son
and Ezra had listened calmly and agreed.

"But I want to try terrace planting," he said, and he

showed his father how he would rim the hillsides with shelves of earth and buttress his crops with borders of stone that would also serve to capture the waters of the swiftly falling northern rains.

"It's a form of natural irrigation," he explained. "The Nabataeans used it in the desert thousands of years ago."

"I am glad you are putting your education to some use," Yehuda said wryly. But he understood the logic of Ezra's plan and he agreed with his son that the fields where the hillside rose to a gentle plateau made for splendid grazing land. Ezra had bought some cattle—a breeding bull and a heifer, a stud horse and a beautiful moist-eyed foal. He had bought two calves from the Druse graziers of Kafra Museiba, who knew him as a brother of the doctor's wife and who insisted that he accept as a gift a litter of newborn kids and a flat-nosed Arab watchdog.

"This will be a good flock one day," Ezra said, carefully ignoring his father's reference to his education. He did not regret the years he had spent studying. He read and studied still, and his thoughts, as he worked his farm, were often filled with the ideas of the philosophers he had read and whose works he read even now through the Galilean nights.

It was impossible to stand upon his hillside and gaze across the valley where date palms swayed and the air was scented with the heady sweetness of the white bell-shaped sand lily and not think of Spinoza and his pantheistic philosophy. Ezra saw God lurking in his fledgling trees and in the pale sheaves of winter wheat that trembled in the wind. Often, working in his fields, he plucked up shattered shards, earth-stained bits of pottery and once, the fragment of a stone awl. Wonder rippled through him as he fondled these remnants of vanished lives. He ordered archaeology books from Europe and wrote to Sara, asking her if she could locate a text on ancient Mesopotamian religions, because he had found a small metal figurine of a full-breasted woman with stumps of arms and wondrously sculpted legs. He was not the first to seek abundance on this rock-strewn hillside.

In the brightness of a spring morning he was pierced by a sudden melancholy and was comforted by the moody French verses of Rimbaud. But his father had urged him to study so that he could hang a diploma inscribed in Latin on his wall and sit in conference with learned men, not so that he could quote French poetry into the chasmic loneliness of a sunswept morning. Still, he did not argue with Yehuda. He had learned, very early, the power of stillness, the strength of secrecy. Saul and David had shouted and even gentle Sara had wept, but Ezra had made his plans quietly and when he was ready, Sadot Shalom had been waiting for him.

Yehuda had understood at once why his son called the farm Sadot Shalom—Fields of Peace, and he tried to explain it to Rivka as the team of horses struggled northward.

"The farm is hilly," he said, "but then it levels off to a kind of plateau. Standing there, you look down across the fields of the Galilee and the land seems full of peace and beauty. There is a quietness in those fields, a sense of richness. It is so green, so tranquil, so full of promise."

"But it is so isolated," Rivka said.

When they had settled on their farm, Rishon had been surrounded by arid lengths of deserted earth, but there had been neighbors, an accessible road, a community. Ezra and Nechama lived a half day's ride from the nearest Jewish settlement and there was not even a path to Sadot Shalom, although there was talk now of clearing a roadway. Ezra had told them that it occasionally happened that he and Nechama did not see another human being for days at a time. Rivka wondered how her daughter-in-law managed to live there, but then she knew that Nechama shared with Ezra a penchant for solitude.

The wife Ezra had chosen was a quiet, dreamy woman who was happiest with her books and her prayers. Nechama wore a neat kerchief over her long dark hair although Ezra did not share her orthodoxy, she observed religious ritual with quiet tenacity. And yet she was not unsophisticated, Rivka grudgingly admitted. She had once startled Rivka's Sabbath afternoon cultural group by objecting gently to their analysis of Theodor Herzl's novel *Altneuland*. The reviewer had described it as an example of the new realistic literature, but Nechama had maintained that the exact opposite was true.

"It's a romantic fantasy," she said. "It suggests the Zionist fairy tales of Mapu. Herzl envisages a fairyland with wonderful modern cities—a peaceful society where Jews and Arabs live like brothers. You can tell that it is a novel written in Vienna and not in Rishon or Petach Tikvah."

She and Ezra were in Rishon when Queen Victoria died

and she read the group her own Hebrew translation of Kipling's *Recessional*. Nechama's voice trembled when she repeated the verse which spoke of Nineveh and Tyre.

"Do you see how the ancient tales of our people influence the whole world?" she asked, and Rivka caught a glimpse of why Ezra had chosen for his bride this pale young woman, three years his senior.

How would quiet, introspective Nechama respond to the demands of motherhood, Rivka wondered, and she touched the neatly wrapped package she had held on her lap throughout the journey. It contained the tiny kimono which her own sons and then Shimon had worn at their circumcision ceremonies. Shimon had bled profusely and the hem of the delicately embroidered garment which her parents had ordered from Berlin was still bordered with the rusted stain of his blood.

"What will they call the baby?" she asked Yehuda.

"I think they want to name the child for Avremel. Perhaps Avraham. What do you think of the name Avraham, son of Gedalia?" he asked the Yemenite driver.

The small, dark-skinned man flicked the reins and turned on his seat to face them.

"Avraham was the name of your son-in-law, the doctor— may his soul rest in peace?" he asked.

"Yes."

"He was very young when he died. We defy the evil eye when we name a child for someone who was taken to God so young."

The Yemenite lifted his eyes heavenward and touched the talismanic silver hand that hung from a cord at his neck.

"Superstition," Rivka hissed angrily. "Ignorant superstition."

She had no patience with these dark-skinned Jews who had lived too long in the deserts of Arabia. Like the Arabs who painted their houses blue for luck, the Jews of the Arab lands hung blue donkey beads above the bassinets of newborn babies. It was true that she herself adorned the cribs of the newborn with strands of scarlet ribbon, but that (she assured herself and her daughters-in-law, who teased her about it) was merely custom. She did not believe that it warded off bad luck. She did it because her mother had done it. Gedalia's family, she was convinced, believed the evil eye to be a real and threatening presence which they fought with charms and secret chants, with mysterious prayers inscribed on parchment and hidden beneath an infant's vest. They named their children for devout Jews who had lived long lives and were survived by many sons. The Sephardic Jews bewildered Rivka. She wrote pious Zionist verses calling for the ingathering of the exiles, but deep within her heart she wished that not so many of the ingathered had to come from the lands where a desert sun had darkened their skin. She had felt a secret relief when her sons took brides who had come to Palestine from eastern Europe.

"Still," Yehuda said musingly, "there is something in what Gedalia's son says." He had felt death breathe heavily in the night and had known himself to be helpless.

"Nonsense," Rivka replied briskly, but she did not argue further. They had reached the appointed turnoff and Ezra was waiting at the side of the road, sitting astride the wooden seat of his oxcart.

He was bareheaded and slats of golden sunlight shimmered across his dark hair. His bronzed arms rippled with muscles and startled his mother, who still thought of him as the sickly child who had so often cheated death. The power in his body awed and bewildered her. It was the harrowing season, and he had been wreaking fierce vengeance day after day on the resistant soil. He would plant sesame this year and begin a peach orchard.

"Abba, Imma. Shalom."

He embraced his parents and felt the fragility of their aging forms. There was a softness to Yehuda's flesh that he did not remember and lines rimmed his mother's slender neck.

"Will you stay for the circumcision of my son, son of Gedalia?" he asked the driver.

The Yemenite accepted readily. He had anticipated staying and knew himself to be welcome. He was, after all, a member of the extended family of Jewish settlers in the homeland, and thus he considered himself related to the newborn child. He had carried with him a blue velvet skullcap, embroidered in gold thread, for the infant and a donkey bead to hang above the child's bed. It was a wonderful thing, he thought, to live in a land where he felt every Jew to be his kinsman, although their skin was fair and their Hebrew harsh and gutteral like the languages of Europe. In Yemen, his mother had told him, his family had lived isolated lives, cowering beneath the shadows of fear. They had dressed like their

Moslem neighbors and even disguised their prayers to sound like the supplications of Islam.

"What is the child's name, Adon Ezra?" he asked as he tied his horses to an ancient terebinth. The animals would be safe there and cool in the shade. The neighboring Arab villagers knew the horses of the family of Gedalia and would not disturb them.

"You know that it is bad luck to tell the child's name before the circumcision," Ezra replied, smiling mischievously. "But I will tell you in secret. The child will be named Amos."

Yehuda turned triumphantly to Rivka and saw—although he knew she would deny it—a look of relief flash across her face.

"We have named him in memory of Avremel," Ezra added, "but we could not name him Avraham because Nechama's brother carries that name."

"In memory of Avremel," Yehuda repeated and he stared northward to the earth-hugging hills of the Carmel slope, covered now with anemones the same color as the blood that had gushed from Avremel's severed throat.

"Amos is a good name," he said at last, turning to his youngest son, so newly a father. He thought to embrace him but a sudden shyness gripped him and he stood awkwardly at his son's side as a sudden cloud drifted across the sun. Briefly, they were trapped in a small penumbral circle until the swift gossamer darkness drifted, and the sun once again turned the wild daffodils the color of burnished gold.

Chapter 12

Nechama watched for the wagon from the window. Her sisters-in-law, Mirra and Chania, had charge of the infant, and they cared for him with the enthusiasm of small girls charged with the care of a visiting playmate's wondrous doll. There were no babies on Gan Noar, their collective settlement, and Mirra had told Nechama that it had been agreed that no children would be born until the collective was self-sufficient.

"What do you mean—you agreed? How can someone else make such a decision for you?" Nechama asked incredulously.

"No one made the decision for us." Mirra's cheeks blazed with indignation. "We voted as a group—as a community—as we always do."

"But that is a personal decision—a private decision between a husband and wife."

"On kibbutz there are no personal decisions," Mirra replied tossing her dark hair.

Everything Mirra did was punctuated with energy and certainty. She belonged to that enviable group of people who move through life confident of their direction, unhampered by doubt and indecision. If they choose blue as their favorite color they cannot understand how others do not share their preference. Having embraced the philosophy of kibbutz, Mirra would not understand why Ezra and Nechama preferred to be independent farmers. It was that very certainty, Ezra had remarked, that gave Saul's wife her strength and exuberance. He understood how draining it was to constantly question decisions. Nechama often told him that he so exhausted himself with questions that he was too fatigued to find the answers.

Nechama did not argue with Mirra. She and Ezra had visited Gan Noar, the settlement just north of the Sea of Galilee where David and Chania and Mirra and Saul planned to spend their lives. They had arrived in midsummer, when the heat hung heavy and stagnant in the air and the arid ground cracked beneath their feet as they walked. The settlers slept in heavy tents whose canvas reeked of dankness and admitted no light. Planks of wood served as beds, and although Rivka had given each of her sons a featherbed as a marriage gift, Saul and David declined to use them. It was not fair, David had explained patiently to his mother in the tone of an adult attempting to communicate a complex situation to a child, for some members to sleep in comfort while others slept on the damp earth or on splintered wood.

"No one should have more creature comforts than anyone else because of an accident of birth," Mirra asserted piously.

"Not everyone is born with blue eyes," Rivka replied. She had always seen life as clearly divided between those who rode in landaus and those who walked, those who owned orange groves and those who spread fertilizer about the roots of other men's trees.

Yehuda, who remembered how the twins had left their horses at the Rishon farm, said nothing. He was pleased that the twin steeds were now part of the communal property of Gan Noar. That was all right, David assured him, because all members of the collective then had use of them.

Everything at Gan Noar, it seemed to Nechama, was legislated, and translated into ideological terms. Was it bourgeois to put flowers on the communal dining room table? Was it antisocial for a member to eat his bread and hard-boiled egg beneath a tree rather than in the noisy mosquito-infested dining hall?

It was not the discomfort of the tents or the austerity of the lean-to kitchen that repelled Nechama; it was the total lack of privacy, and although she had witnessed it for herself she still could not comprehend how people lived in such physical and emotional contiguity. Even their dreams were common property. Their loneliness and fears were interchangeable. The homesick boy from Lithuania (he had not known that the promised land would be so hot, that the skies of Zion would often be dark with mosquitoes and locusts) who wept in agonized sleep shared his tears with his comrades. The chubby blond girl from Hungary who walked beneath the starlit skies with the tall, thin youth newly arrived from Czechoslovakia, admitted them all into the bright circle of her new happiness. Through the darkness of the night they listened to sweet sighs and small gasps as love itself was shared.

Nechama and Ezra had attended a general meeting of the kibbutz membership. They sat on one of the rough-hewn benches ranged about the campfire and listened to earnest discussions about the quality of the food, the rotation of the crops, a new application for membership, one comrade's laziness and another's request to allow his family abroad to send him boots for the winter. Nechama could imagine that the question of having children would be raised at such a meeting and the earnest discussion that would follow. The comrades would talk deep into the night as the fire died and the embers glowed. They would cite economic difficulties and social responsibilities and quote Shakespeare and the Bible, Herzl and Rousseau. There would be anger and laughter. They would grow drunk on their own arguments and weary with their own rhetoric. Harsh exchanges and bitter contradictions would be balanced by statements of affection and friendship. In the end, they would vote and abide by the communal decision. Mirra, a trained agronomist, had accepted the decision that she must work for six months in the communal laundry. Saul and David had accepted the community's decision not to plant banana trees, although they had argued mightily. They were farmer's sons and knew the soil but they had abided by the decision of town-bred theorists who knew nothing of fruit farms. Of course they would let the community decide whether and when they might have a child.

This forced conviviality bewildered Nechama, who could not remember a time when she had not pursued privacy and quiet. She was the eldest daughter of a large and busy family.

Six younger brothers and sisters trailed after her, their laugher and prattle filling every waking moment, their nocturnal miseries invading her sleep. Each child was cared for in turn by an older sibling with Nechama charged with supervising all of them. Their mother worked beside their father in the Kattowitz shop and later in Jaffa. Her fingers flew nimbly across bunched bits of fabric, narrow expanses of satin. Her lips moved as she worked. She alternated prayer with a computation of interest and payments, savings and expenditures. They did not work simply to make a living. They were a family fired with an ideal of personal destiny. They were Jews consumed by the idea of Zion.

They would go to Palestine and fulfill the commandment that took precedence over all other commandments—ascent to the land. This sense of purpose brought order into the household. The children and their parents worked together toward that single end. In the evenings the shopkeeper taught Nechama to read and write in Hebrew, to keep ledger sheets and maintain records. She discovered the secret worlds that awaited her when she opened a book. She found the secret quiet, the mysterious privacy, of the born reader.

She continued to mother the children but words sang in her mind and ideas restled in her thoughts. The family was devout and she too read the prayer book and discovered the poetry of Psalms, the melancholy cadence of Lamentations. She followed the weekly Torah readings closely. The wind whistled through the pine forests of Kattowitz but she walked with the children of Israel through the vast expanse of the Sinai. She saw the spacious verdancy of the Galilee and she dreamed of living alone in the midst of valleys and hills surrounded by silence.

One day the great Rabbi Kook visited her father on Mizrachi business. He was newly returned from Palestine. She prepared tea in the kitchen and listened to him describe the Galilee. There the skies kiss the earth, he said, and the fields breathe peace. Sadot Shalom. Fields of peace. She repeated the words and looked out of the window. In Kattowitz gray snow clung to low rooftops but in the Galilee green fields breathed peace and white birds floated with soft clouds.

When at last they migrated to Palestine (an orderly migration—each child neatly clothed, the house and shop in Jaffa secured in advance), she was twenty and her air of gravity made her look much older. The house and shop oppressed her. She hated the narrow streets of the port city and she was impatient with the young men who came to call on her. They were the sons of other shopkeepers, of leaders in the Mizrachi who would, she knew, seek to contain her within their own small houses, their own narrow shops. Alone, she traveled to the Galilee and felt the sweet breath of the mountain winds, saw the wild purple iris bow to the stately tall pink cyclamen. She listened to the wondrous silence and returned sadly to the crowded noisy city and the crowded noisy house.

"Nechama is an old maid," her younger brothers and sisters teased. She shook a warning fist at them and turned back to her book. She had mothered them for so long that she had difficulty remembering that some of them were almost grown. Her sister Shiffra attended a teachers' seminary. Her brother Avraham shaved three times a week.

"Nechama should get married," her mother said worriedly to her father.

"She has time. God will send her someone. Meanwhile she has a good job. There is no need to worry." He relied on God, as he always had and always would.

Nechama worked in the Anglo-Palestine Bank on Saladin Road. She was responsible for converting foreign corrency into Turkish dinars and she stood all day in a small cage, peering at her clients through iron bars. Her long white fingers rested on a dark green marble counter and she pushed packets of currency across its cold, smooth surface, counting the bills swiftly, expertly. The piles of dinars and francs, of dollars and rubles and gulden, rested on a tray behind her. Occasionally she turned her back to consult a record book or tally an account sheet.

She was thus employed when Ezra Maimon entered the Jaffa bank. He had been living on Sadot Shalom for a year and he had come to Jaffa to convert the reserve portion of his grandfather's dollars into dinars for the purchase of a small combine. This would be his first mechanized equipment. The year of grueling labor had strengthened him and his skin had turned the color of molten amber. His thick dark hair was raddled with auburn streaks as though the sun had burned its way relentlessly through its thickness. Muscle rippled in his arms and back.

His brothers and their friends had helped him to clear the fields and to reconstruct the small house that had been on the land. But they had returned to Gan Noar and he had spent almost the entire year alone on the farm, heaving boulders out of the field and carrying them to the terraced inclines where he would plant his crops. He drew water from a primitive cistern and he had cooked over an open fire until his sister-in-law Mirra bought him a petiliya, which she insisted that he accept in exchange for the stock of apricots from his fruit trees which he had brought to the kibbutz.

He took little pride in that gift. The apricot trees, wild and unpruned, had been on the land when he purchased it. He was prouder of the scraggly ears of corn grown in his kitchen garden than of the overflowing baskets of fruit that he carted to Gan Noar. But now, at last, he was ready to plant the white winter wheat, and the thought of that experimental crop excited him. The combine would make it easier to prepare the fields, to sow and harvest. As he entered the bank he thought of the machine's great iron teeth ripping through the rich black earth of Sadot Shalom. His hands were thrust deep into his pockets and his fingers tapped the roll of dollars which he had removed from his grandfather's Talmud that morning. It was the last of the money. He had, after all, had to purchase Sadot Shalom twice, paying one fee to the absentee Arab landlord who lived in a Beirut villa and a second fee to the family of fellahin who had squatted for so long upon the land that they considered it to be their own. It was not an uncommon transaction, Chaim Baker had told him, advising him to meet the demands of the resident Arabs.

"It will be even more expensive if they decide to make life unliveable for you," the hotelkeeper said.

Ezra did not argue. He had heard of new landowners whose wells had been poisoned and whose cattle had been kidnapped. He had paid the Arabs their price, accepted their blessing and the token gift of a small goat which they gave him with great ceremony. He lived now with his Arab neighbors in simulated brotherhood sustained by mutual vigilance. Occasionally they helped each other. During the drought the Arab graziers accepted Ezra's offer of water from his well. They, in turn, helped to fight the small brushfire that threatened his barn. They were secret adversaries and accommodating neighbors, polarized by history but linked by need and time.

"One day we may live together simply as neighbors," Ezra wrote hopefully in one of his frequent letters to Sara, settled now in Poland. Sara had been gone for more than a year but his heart still ached with loneliness when he thought of her. None of the excitement of that year—his brothers' marriages, his own settlement in the Galilee—had softened the harsh aloneness he had felt since her departure. Sara would not see his winter wheat waving in serried silver wands across the expanse of the farm he was wresting from the wilderness.

The young woman in the teller's cage was bent over her account books. He could not see her face but her long dark hair fell in thick, silken sheaves and her slender white fingers moved across the table with swift competence as she reached for a pencil and wrapped a rubber band around a stack of receipts. He remembered suddenly how as a small boy he had stood at the edge of the kitchen table and watched his sister's fingers dance across its surface, reaching for a knife, a vegetable. He watched the teller's fingers now with the same absorption, the same childish wonder. He had, he thought, been alone too long on his hillside farm. Loneliness and memory played cruel tricks on him and he was startled to realize that the long black hair and the slender fingers did not belong to his distant sister.

They completed their business together quickly, and if she was disturbed by the depth and length of his gaze she did not show it. He explained why he needed the money and she did not seem surprised to learn that he lived alone in the northern wilderness.

"Have you lived there long?" she asked.

"Only a year. But my family has been in the country for thirteen years."

"You are *vatikim*—veterans. We are new arrivals. We've been here only two years."

"Do you like it? The country?" Ezra asked. He said "the country" as though no other nation existed, as though France and England and Russia were ghostly islands and there was only one true country—*HaAretz*—the land.

"The land is beautiful, but I don't like Jaffa."

"But there are wonderful places here. May I show them to you this afternoon? When you are finished working?"

"We have half-day closing today. I am through at noon."

The blood rushed to her white cheeks and settled in them like tiny scarlet flowers against a snowbound field. She lowered her eyes and he saw the thick silken sheen of her black lashes. Her pallor fascinated him, moved him to sudden tenderness. His own family glowed with color. Sara's skin had been burnished in this season.

"May I meet you then? I could wait for you just here at the bank?"

"Yes. Of course."

His heart sang because she had not hesitated for a moment.

"Adon Maimon," she called as he reached the door, reading his name from the currency declaration he had filled out.

He turned.

"My name is Nechama Langerfeld."

"Nechama," he repeated. "I will see you at noon, Nechama Langerfeld."

He put the money in Chaim Baker's safe and hurried to the market, where he bought fruits and vegetables and long slivers of goat cheese which the Arab merchant wrapped in the thin green skin of newly shucked corn. He selected a slender bottle of wine decanted in the shadowed cellars that neighbored his father's orchards, and he plucked up rounded cushions of pittot so fresh from the oven that they burned his fingers when he touched them.

Nechama Langerfeld, wearing a long dark skirt and a high-necked white blouse, waited for him at the bank, and together, without exchanging a word, they climbed the hill that led to the Monastery of Saint Peter. He showed her where to stand so that she might look down at the pearl-white beach and the luminescent sea.

"It is beautiful here," she said.

"I came here with my sister when we first arrived in the country," he said as though some explanation were required. She turned as though to ask a question but instead she pressed a finger to her lips and he was grateful for her silence.

They ate in the shade of an ancient olive grove. She broke up the cheese and slipped it into the still-warm envelope of dough. She borrowed his knife to cut up the vegetables. He had never seen peppers and tomatoes so brilliant with color as those she carved into narrow wands. As he ate, a speck of dirt settled in his eye and he winced with pain. Nechama removed a clean white handkerchief from her sleeve and gently manipulated his lid. Then her fingers touched his face and he felt their softness against his skin, and he thought that he could sit there forever as she moved her hand, oh so lightly, across his cheek. Strength stirred in his body. His fists clenched and unclenched; he sat quietly until the offending speck settled on her finger.

"You see—that wasn't so bad," she said, and blew it lightly away. Sara would have clapped it between her palms and cautioned him, with mock severity, to be more careful, to avert his eyes from drifts of dust. She was stern and protective. Nechama was gentle and soothing. He wondered lazily why Nechama brought Sara to mind. And then she loosened her hair and he remembered how Sara's thick black hair had draped her shoulders, on her wedding day. A wistful sadness washed over him and Nechama sat quietly, as though waiting for it to pass. Her clasped hands rested quietly on her lap. She was a patient woman, accustomed to waiting. His sorrow did not frighten her. He smiled then and removed the wine bottle from its newspaper wrapping. Sara was in Poland, and he sat on a Jaffa hillside with a woman named Nechama.

They drank the wine directly from the bottle. The sun had warmed it, and although he knew the grapes to be sweet and white, there was a sourness to the drink. But he savored the liquid, and when he passed his tongue across the rim of glass he imagined he was tasting the sweet wetness of her mouth.

He told her about Sadot Shalom.

"It sounds wonderful," she said, and there was a note of wistfulness in her voice.

She told him of her solitary journeys to the Galilee, of her longing for space and silence.

"But could you live for long in the Galilee? Surely you would grow lonely," he said, thinking of his mother and her restless search for company and of Mirra and Chania, his brothers' wives, who were always surrounded by a large group of comrades and friends. Sara too had been happiest with friends, surrounded by family.

"Lonely? There in the hills?"

She found the question incomprehensible. She was lonely within the crowded Jaffa house, amid her brothers' and sisters' chatter. Loneliness haunted her as she moved competently through her tasks at the bank and as she dutifully served coffee to her parents' Mizrachi friends. She was not lonely when she walked with a book through the green fields of the Galilee.

He stayed in Jaffa ten days longer than he had intended. He bought the combine and other supplies. He took Nechama to see his father's orchards and they had tea with his parents. His father spoke of crop rotation and his mother spoke of poetry.

"She is older than you are," his mother whispered to him in the kitchen, and her words puzzled him. What difference did it make?

He went to dinner with her family, carrying a bottle of wine and a clutch of pale cyclamens.

"You do not observe the commandments?" her father asked sadly, noting that Ezra had to be asked to wear a skullcap during the meal and that afterward he had stumbled through the words of the grace which the Langerfeld family chanted easily. His own parents had long since abandoned the custom.

"No." He experienced a moment of trepidation and thought to tell Nechama's father about his own grandfather, the Orthodox scholar who had given him a volume of the Talmud stuffed with dollars as a leave-taking gift.

"Never mind. The Rav Kook says that settlement in the land is more important than all the commandments." Rav Langerfeld stroked his wispy beard and looked at his eldest daughter through narrowed eyes. She continued to cut up fruit for the younger children and Ezra Maimon watched her, his eyes soft with longing.

The next week Nechama journeyed with her father to Sadot Shalom, accepting Ezra's invitation. They stood together on the hillside and looked down on the peaceful fields.

"I understand now," Nechama said.

He moved closer and took her hand. Together they stood before her father; their linked fingers obviating the need for words.

"When will you be married?" he asked.

"At once." Ezra spoke for both of them and she nodded.

"Won't you be lonely here, Nechama?" Her father's question was gentle, laced with concern.

"No." Her answer was quiet, assured. "Other Jewish

families will settle in the Galilee and we will not always be alone. We will have a family.''

Ezra nodded. They would, of course, have many children, he and his tall, slender bride who had mothered her sisters and brothers and soothed his own body with passion and tenderness. Small dark-haired boys and girls would scramble across the hills of Sadot Shalom and sing and laugh from their perches on the swaying branches of the crooked apricot trees. His children would work beside him during the harvest and sowing seasons, and through the long winter evenings he and Nechama would study with them. He saw with incandescent clarity the life he and Nechama would share. The days of his future unfolded before him as peacefully and fruitfully as the fields of his land.

:''We will not be lonely.'' He echoed her words and felt her hand tremble within his own.

The Maimons met Nechama's family but their brief meetings were strained. The men did not like each other. Each had wanted a different life for a favorite child. Shopkeeper and farmer, observant Jew and lapsed talmudic scholar, they looked warily at each other and spoke of the inefficiency of the Turkish bureaucrats, the uncertainty of the fate of Jews in eastern Europe. They cursed the czar in bitter Russian and watched the desert wind whip through the trembling dusty leaves of citron saplings.

Nechama's mother and Rivka Maimon recognized themselves as alien to each other but they seized on the fragile threads that women stretch across a social abyss. They spoke of fabric and food, of the difficulties of child rearing, and of their worry over aging parents. Rivka's parents were in their eighties and grew increasingly feeble. They lived in Kishinev still and although they were lonely they were afraid to come to Palestine because of the Arabs. Perhaps Sara would manage to visit them. Little Mrs. Langerfeld's parents lived in Kattowitz. They wanted to go to America. One son had settled in Pittsburgh and another lived in Brooklyn.

The women's eyes grew bright with tears as they spoke. They had left their parents and now their children were leaving them. Briefly, they touched each other's hands, united in grief as they could not be in joy.

Nechama and Ezra were married in the courtyard of the Rishon farm and as he slipped the slender unmarked gold

band on her finger, an early evening breeze wafted the aroma
of the citron tree toward them. Her hand trembled, and Ezra
saw that her dark eyes were moist. His heart turned with
tenderness because the melancholy fragrance stirred her and
because her tears glittered in the near darkness.

When he slipped off her white bridal dress that night, he
saw that her skin was whiter than the soft batiste fabric. He
felt the wondrous touch of her hands gliding across his body
and the soaring joy as, at last, his aloneness was banished,
and he thrust himself within her to ensure that oneness, that
unity of sigh and silence that bound them together.

She, in turn, thought that she understood at last what her
life was meant to be. Tears streaked her long white face but
her full lips curved in a smile, and again and again her fingers
traced the gentle slope of his shoulders, the softness of his
dark gold skin, and the small scar at the bottom of his chin,
the result of his once having fallen across a tree trunk in the
Kharkov forest.

They had not been separated during the time from their
marriage night until the last month of her pregnancy, when
she went to Jaffa to await the delivery. He had followed her
as soon as the crop was sown and he had been at her side
when the child was born. It was, as the doctors had feared, a
long and difficult delivery. She was so narrowly built and the
child was so large that it seemed that the struggling infant
could not force his way through the compressed fortress of
her body. Her father prayed, draped in a prayer shawl that
concealed his face so that they could not see that he wept as
he swayed. Her mother and her sisters read the psalms aloud.

Through the haze of pain and effort, she thought she heard
Ezra say, "Don't die, Nechama. Please don't die."

And of course she had not died and the baby had been
born, ripping his way through her body, his golden ringlets
wet with her shining moisture. He was a large child with a
lusty voice. Ezra's hands trembled when he held the baby,
and she read a trace of fear in his eyes. But that would pass.
The boy was beautiful and healthy and they had brought him
back to Sadot Shalom for the circumcision ceremony. He
would join the covenant of his people on the land that his
father was reclaiming for them.

The baby cried again now—that arrogant and demanding
infant scream. Nechama smiled at the sound and watched as

the wagon drew up to the house and Ezra helped his mother down. Yehuda Maimon leaped from his seat and darted through the door.

"*Mazal tov*, Nechama," he said and bent to kiss his daughter-in-law.

She looked almost pretty, he thought, and he reflected that motherhood did that for some women, flooded their faces with a new softness, a subtle light.

"Where is my grandson?" he asked.

The infant cried again and Mirra entered the room carrying him, her face bent close to the baby's.

"Here he is," she said. "Say shalom to Grandpa."

Yehuda stretched his arms out and took the child. In his embrace the infant was quiet. The tiny fist curled and settled into small pink balls against Yehuda's shirt. The newborn's pale blue eyelids fluttered.

"Shalom, Amos," Yehuda said softly.

His grandson's name pleased him. He had always had a fondness for the fierce and lonely prophet who had cautioned against ease in Zion.

Chapter 13

Shortly before Amos Maimon's fourth birthday, he astonished his parents by demonstrating his ability to read. Playing
alone in a slat of shade, he was the first to hear the bells that
dangled from the harness of the postman's dust-colored donkey, and he dashed off on his sturdy fat legs to collect the
post. The postman, a toothless aged Arab who rode through
the Galilee at irregular intervals trailing his leather mail bag
emblazoned with the crest of the Ottoman Empire, always
had a sweetened lump of sesame candy in his pocket. Amos
accepted the family's letters and his candy and offered his
thanks in perfect Arabic.

"I hope that Allah has brought you good news," the
postman said. He repeated this after each visit and Amos
always answered politely although he could not understand
what Allah had to do with the letters his parents received. He
arranged the letters just handed to him in an elaborate fan,
looked at them, and dashed excitedly into the house.

"Abba, Imma," he called from the entryway and hurried into
the kitchen where Nechama and Ezra sat drinking cold lemonade. It was only ten o'clock on a summer morning but they
had been up since four. During the summer months, when the

heat scorched the earth until it was riddled with cracks and the metal handles of scythe and plow seared their skin, they rose at dawn, worked for several hours, and then rested. They resumed work later in the day, when the sun, as though exhausted by its own incandescent energy, lowered and paled, and the occasional blessing of a shadow drifted across their land.

"There is a letter from Aunt Sara," the child said, waving the pale blue envelope proudly. He knew how his father waited for mail from this unknown aunt who lived so far away.

"And how do you know it's from Aunt Sara?" Ezra asked. He touched his son's fair hair which turned almost milk white in high summer. It perplexed him that Amos was blond and green-eyed when he and Nechama were both dark-haired. Oddly enough, his brother's children too were golden-haired, and Mirra, his sister-in-law, ruefully played with her daughter's golden curls and complained because she had wanted a child whose dark ringlets would match her own.

"You are being punished because you became pregnant without the permission of the kibbutz general meeting," Nechama gently teased her sister-in-law.

"Well, then, so did everyone else," Mirra replied, although a blush stole into her cheeks.

In the end Gan Noar had found it impossible to legislate against having children. One by one the young women became pregnant and the settlers abandoned their discussions of family planning and argued instead about the communal method of raising children and built a children's house. They decided that the children would be raised by the community as a whole and would sleep away from their parents, visiting with them after the day's work was done. This would free the mothers from the traditional tasks of child rearing and make them available for work on the settlement.

"It is part of our new social system," Mirra said, but Nechama had noted that both her sisters-in-law nursed their babies long past the stage when she herself had weaned Amos. Committed communards that they were, they were reluctant to abandon the sweet privacy of motherhood.

"He recognizes the stamp," Nechama said wearily, and she bent to remove a thistle that had lodged itself between Amos's toes.

She was very tired these days and she found it difficult to forgive herself her own fatigue although she understood its source. She had miscarried for the second time that spring, and this time the pregnancy had been more advanced and the bleeding had been profuse. Ezra had been frightened and insisted that she visit Dr. Mazis in Rishon. The old doctor had examined her gently, carefully.

"You must stop trying to conceive," he told Nechama. "Amos's birth damaged your uterine wall. You cannot sustain another pregnancy."

"Please don't tell Ezra," she said. "I will tell him myself."

Dr. Mazis did not argue. He had practiced for many years and he knew that there were things a doctor could not say, things that must be whispered into the night.

"Be careful," he cautioned her gently, and she had nodded. He read her secret in her eyes. She would tell Ezra nothing. One did not rip away a strong man's dreams. Besides, they had Amos—strong, healthy Amos who filled their house with laughter and chatter and rambled through the fields with Achmed, his small Arab friend, prattling urgently in Hebrew and Arabic.

"I didn't recognize the stamp," Amos protested now, shaking the envelope in protest. "It says here Sara Kerzen, Mila Twenty-one. Oswiecim. Poland. Poland is an easy word to read. Oswiecim is harder."

He trailed a finger beneath each word of the return address which Sara had written in block capitals. Her years in Palestine had taught her to have little faith in the literacy of the Turkish postal workers.

"Can you read this?" Ezra asked his son, holding up a copy of *Bustenai*, the agricultural journal which had arrived in the same post.

"Bustenai," Amos said promptly.

"Did you teach him?" Ezra asked Nechama.

"No. I thought he was too young. You must have taught him the letters."

"No."

"I taught myself," Amos said proudly. "I used the primer that Grandpa Langerfeld gave me. Now I am teaching Achmed. But Achmed does not want to learn. He only wants to play." He shrugged his shoulders derisively and hurried off to Achmed.

The friends were building a stone fort in a corner of the orchard.

"He is unusually bright," Nechama said, looking after her son. "We shall have to make arrangements to teach him."

"We will teach him ourselves, here on Sadot Shalom," Ezra replied. "I don't want him to endure all that racing after education and culture that strangled me when I was a child."

He still remembered the choking odors of chalk and sawdust in the Rishon schoolroom and how his fingers had tightened about the pen while the sun blazed and his brothers galloped through the fields on their horses. He had yearned for the land and had been banished to the schoolroom. His parents' dreams had weighted his childhood, their aspirations had shadowed his youth.

"He may want a different life," Nechama said gently.

"We shall see. Meanwhile we can teach him at home. Now that he knows how to read we must get primers, texts."

"I will write to my father," Nechama said.

"No."

There was a strange firmness in Ezra's voice. He would select his son's books himself. He did not want to involve either his own family or Nechama's parents in Amos's education. He was fearful that Yehuda and Rivka, when they learned of Amos's precocity, would transfer the ambitions they had once harbored for him to their grandson. He did not want Amos to be held hostage to Yehuda Maimon's failed dreams of university lecture halls and learned congresses. And Nechama's father was the consummate Zionist; he equated intellectual achievement with a contribution to nation building. One of Nechama's brothers had been sent to study law in Constantinople. He would join a battery of Jewish lawyers who would argue for a Jewish state in Ottoman courts. Another brother was studying architecture at the Sorbonne. He would help to design a Jewish city to be built on the rolling sands of a Mediterranean beach. Her sister Chana was the directress of the Jewish kindergarten in Jaffa. Just as devout Catholics sent their children to convent and seminary, the Langerfelds dispatched their children to work for the realization of the dream of religious Zionism. Ezra did not want Amos to fall victim to their fierce ambition. His son belonged to the land, not to musty libraries and to cities as yet unbuilt.

"What does your sister write?" Nechama asked, abandoning the discussion.

Ezra opened the envelope carefully, relishing the feel of the thick bulk of pages written in Sara's straight, neat hand. His sister did not write often now, but when she did she wrote in great detail, describing the life she had built for herself in Poland.

It had been intended, when Sara left Rishon, that she would go to her grandparents' home in Kishinev and await the birth of her child before continuing on to her Uncle Mendel in America. The child, a girl whom Sara named Sophia, had been born, and visas and passage arranged when relatives of Sara's girlhood companion, Chaim, asked her to take documents and monies which could not be entrusted to the post to her old companion, who lived now in Poland. He would meet her in Warsaw. Reluctantly, she had agreed. Her feeling for Chaim had faded but she could not refuse to do a favor for the beloved companion of her youth. She had no reason to hesitate. She was no longer frightened of his dreams, of his imaginary utopias. She wanted only a quiet existence for herself and Shimon and Sophia, a quiet bourgeois existence in an established city. She dreamed of a small house and garden. She would not be enticed again to soar on the inflated balloon of dreams that were not her own.

The Chaim Kerzen who met her at the Warsaw station was not the passionate youth who had embraced her in the firelit room behind the Kharkov windmill. He was now a prosperous businessman in a broadcloth frock coat, with gray spats protecting his pointed-toed patent leather shoes and a large pearl stickpin thrust through his royal-blue cravat. He and his sister operated a large millinery supply house in Oswiecim. The revolutionary dreams of his youth were hazy memories now.

"Did I say that?" he asked incredulously when Sara reminded him that he had disdained marriage, disparaged personal ambition. "I was young then," he added, meaning that he had not yet known fear and hunger and the betrayal of friends whom he had thought of as brothers. He realized now, he told her, that the world would not be changed overnight. The youth that he had been, fired with revolutionary dreams, was a mythical creature whom he barely remembered, hardly recognized.

"You are more beautiful than ever," he told Sara, and his large white hand trembled like a cautious butterfly on her dark hair.

They were married within weeks of her arrival, and the first thing Sara did, as mistress of the large stone house, was to install double locks on the windows of the rooms where Avremel's children slept. Danger lurked everywhere, and Shimon and Sophia, whose paternal grandparents had burned to death in a nocturnal holocaust and whose father's throat had been sliced open as he slept, were peculiarly vulnerable.

"The children are strong and beautiful," she wrote to her family in Palestine, but she did not add that she haunted their bedsides at night and watched from the window as they played in the courtyard of the house. Shimon missed the family but he was adjusting to life in Poland and making friends. Shimon had sent Ezra and Nechama a small watercolor as a wedding gift. Certain talent revealed itself in the picture of the Rishon farmhouse, drawn from memory, but Ezra had read his nephew's loneliness in the weeping pastels.

Usually Sara's letters contained perceptive descriptions of the political scene in Poland and amusing anecdotes about her life. Ezra straightened the pages of the letter, prepared to be amused and to read the better portions aloud to Nechama. But before he reached the second page, his breath came fast and his eyes grew hooded with sorrow and horror.

"Ezra—what is it?" Nechama dropped her book. "Is Sara ill?"

She sensed Ezra's change of mood, his sudden tension, as she sensed all his moods and needs. She moved swiftly to his side, her hand instinctively finding his shoulder.

"Sara is all right. It's my mother's parents. Here. Read for yourself." He held the letter out to her and she saw that his hand trembled and tears filled his eyes. "We must leave for Rishon at once."

She understood then that if he meant to leave Sadot Shalom during a sowing season, something horrendous had happened, but still, she was unprepared for the words of Sara's letter. The ink itself was pale, as though her sister-in-law could not bear to impress upon the paper a description of what she had seen, what she had experienced. Nechama read slowly, absorbing each paragraph with difficulty. When she had completed it, she read it through again with grief-misted eyes, still unable to comprehend the tortured words.

Sara wrote that she and Shimon had traveled to Kishinev some weeks earlier to celebrate her grandfather's ninetieth birthday. The Russian countryside was beautiful during these first days of early April. Tall buttercups and graceful young cornflowers dotted the fields as their train sped eastward. Sara watched the passing landscape with the intense concentration of those who revisit the vistas of their youth. But Shimon was absorbed in calculating all that had happened in the ninety years of his grandfather's life.

"When Grandpa was born, Napoleon was emperor of France," he told Sara. "And there was no telegraph."

"Yes," she agreed, smiling, "a great deal happened between eighteen thirteen and nineteen three."

"And there were hardly any Jews in Palestine," he continued. "Rishon LeZion was a wilderness."

She did not reply. Inevitably, Shimon directed all conversation back to Palestine and the small town of his childhood.

At a railway station she bought a Russian-language newspaper, and her heart stopped as she read the lead story. The mutilated body of a Russian boy had been found on the outskirts of Kishinev. It was rumored, the newspaper stated, that the child had been murdered by Jews who were preparing wine for the Passover holiday. A provincial newspaper, the *Bessarabetz*, had openly accused the Jewish community of ritual murder. It was the opinion of some local priests, the columnist added, that the Jews also required the child's blood for the baking of their unleavened bread.

Sara had grown up in the Ukraine. She knew what such an accusation meant. Briefly, she considered going back to Poland with Shimon, but they had already traveled so far and if she did not make this journey she might never see her grandparents again. They remained on the train but now she sat bolt upright in her seat and studied the countryside as though a secret, a clue, might be revealed to her. At the Kagal station a grimy hand thrust a crudely printed handbill through the window of their carriage. "Death to the Jews who drink the blood of children!" it read. She shivered and tore it into shreds so that Shimon would not see it.

They arrived in Kishinev on Friday, April 4. Her grandparents wept when they embraced her. They lived on the edge of death and expected each meeting to be their last. The grain merchant was almost blind now and he could walk only with the support of two Malacca canes. Arthritis had doubled his wife's joints and occasionally her mind wandered as she spoke. She called Sara by Rivka's name and asked her if she remembered the handsome tutor who had been so forward.

"Your father was afraid he would take you away to Palestine," she said. "But then you married Yehuda Wasserman and he took you away instead. You see how children play tricks on their parents."

Sara did not correct her grandmother. She had met her mother's tutor once. He was a man called Ephraim and he taught now at an Alliance school in Jerusalem. Once he had lectured at the Mikveh Israel school and Yehuda had brought him to their home. He was a fat, pink-cheeked man who wore rimless eyeglasses, perspired profusely, and coughed nervously into his handkerchief. He and Rivka had stared uneasily at each other and then averted their eyes, as though memory had betrayed them.

Sabbath services in Kishinev were cancelled that week. A delegation from the synagogue called on the grain broker and told him that they thought it would be safest for Jews to stay out of sight. Surely all this unpleasantness would pass.

"Of course it will pass," the old man agreed. They were Jews and familiar with passing dangers. "This too will pass," he added in Hebrew, and Sara stared at him curiously.

The old man drew the draperies and dimmed the lights. He had the maids bring the bedclothes down to the basement. They would sleep there that night.

The old woman wept in the darkness. She moaned and called Rivka's name. Her skull was pink beneath her thin white hair.

"We wanted to go to Palestine, to see your mother just once more," the old man told Sara, "but your grandmother was frightened of the Arabs."

Shimon listened but he could not understand. His grandparents cowered in a basement in Kishinev but feared Arabs in a distant land. His father, Avremel, had never sought refuge in the dank bowels of a townhouse. He had met his death asleep beneath a starlit sky.

The next morning they ventured up to the kitchen. The old woman cautiously opened the back door. The yard seemed

empty. She went out to water the plants that stood on the
veranda. As Shimon watched, a rock catapulted toward her
from the neighboring garden. It struck her forehead and blood
spurted forth in a scarlet spout. Its brightness shocked the
boy. He had imagined that the blood of old people paled into
a pink-gray liquid that struggled in their twisted veins. His
grandmother fell. Her arthritic hands clawed the air. Her
breath rasped painfully, stertorously. Her face turned blue and
the pink tip of her tongue jutted out of her mouth and faded
into the color of darkness. Shimon's mouth tasted of sour
vomit and he realized that the noise at his chest was his
pounding heart.

"Manya!" The old man was out the door before Sara could
restrain him.

"*Zhid*! Death to the *zhid*!"

The young hoodlums were still in the neighboring garden.
They vaulted the wall. One of them pulled the old man's
beard and then strangled him; strong young fingers gripped
withered, aged flesh. The old man dropped with the lightness
of a floating leaf. Sara saw the old man fall. She saw the
gleam of a blade and recognized her helplessness. Swiftly,
she locked and bolted the door and almost hurled Shimon
down the basement steps. She seized a kitchen knife and
hurried down after him.

Hours later, when the street was quiet and Shimon slept,,
his eyes swollen with weeping, she stole upstairs and opened
the back door. The old man, who would have celebrated his
ninetieth birthday that week, lay in a pool of blood on his
own doorstep. His trousers had been ripped from his body
and his flimsy limbs lay naked, stained by the gush of blood
that had flooded forth from the gaping hole in his trunk where
once his penis had been. The severed organ, ripped from his
body, had been thrust into his mouth. The testicles dangled
like pale blue deflated balloons from the corners of his bloodless lips. But his outstretched hand touched his wife's lifeless
body and Sara willed herself to believe that somehow the old
woman had felt his touch, that they had died together, that
their pain had been swift and brief. She covered her grandparents' bodies with the cloth that draped the kitchen table.
She was thinking only of Shimon now—this last at least he
must not see, must not know about.

Later, she learned that their family had in fact been comparatively fortunate. Her grandparents' home had not been among the fifteen hundred Jewish-owned stores and houses that had been looted and gutted. Shimon was safe, unlike poor Moshe Goldstein, the boy next door. They had ripped open Moshe's round belly, the same belly Sara herself had playfully poked for its pudgy roundness, and he had screamed hideously for two hours while blood and guts poured from his riven abdomen. His parents had stood helpless all that time in the room into which the rampaging mob had locked them.

Shaindel, the woman who had shopped and cooked for Sara's grandparents, had been raped repeatedly, her legs spread apart by two men while others battered her until she fell senseless to the floor.

The loss of consciousness had been a blessing. She did not see how her three-month-old infant son was tossed from hand to hand and hurled at last against the concrete garden wall. Weeping neighbors peeled the spongy mass of shattered brain from the stone and placed it gently in the small coffin that contained the tiny body.

Sara stayed in Kishinev long enough to bury her grandparents. Funeral processions moved slowly through the narrow cobblestoned streets. Shawled women shivered and looked furtively about as they walked slowly behind the burial carts. The wheels of the coffin-laden vehicles rolled slowly, and the air shivered with the mournful lament of an endless Kaddish. The soft clumps of spring earth fell soundlessly onto the swiftly fashioned pale pine boxes. Rabbis spoke very softly into the graveside silence. The melancholy fragrance of wild lilac wafted above the odors of death and despair. Children screamed with terror and women moaned. The men of the burial society covered the graves quickly. Tears streaked their cheeks as they worked, and their dark frock coats were soaked beneath the arms with sweat marks.

On the journey back to Oswiecim, Sara sat awake and watchful beside the sleeping Shimon, who had wearied himself by asking again and again what had happened and why. He asserted in a whining mournful voice his child's right to know, to understand. ("Did we do something to them to make them do such terrible things to us?" "No." "Then why?" "I don't know.") The irrational could not be made reasonable. The inexplicable could not be explained.

She came to a decision then, as Russia vanished and the

steel wheels of the train whirled across Poland. It was not an easy decision, she wrote to her brother in Palestine in an uncharacteristically trembling hand. She had decided that she would no longer be Jewish. It was too dangerous and she was too frightened, too weary, to sustain her birthright. She had buried Avremel. She had seen her grandparents' blood flow in thin scarlet rivulets across the veranda. To be a Jew meant that one trod the earth lightly and clung to the shadows. She would no longer be hostage to violence and loss and offer her children as sacrifices on the altar of history.

On her arrival home she confronted Chaim with her decision. He was not shocked. Judaism had long since ceased to have any meaning for him. His sister was married to a Gentile and raised a Christmas tree in her living room each winter. It was a matter of indifference to him.

They moved to a section of the city where they were unknown. She was no longer Sara but called herself Zosia and Chaim became Casimir, a name he had long admired. Shimon was called Simeon. They did not baptize the children but on Easter and Christmas they joined their neighbors at the small church in their quarter and exchanged holiday greetings.

"This is part of the role we must play if we are to be safe," Sara wrote to Ezra.

She did not tell him how each Friday afternoon, as the sun lowered and long shadows streaked her sitting room, she stole down to the basement. There she covered her long dark hair with the scarlet shawl and lit the two candles that stood in the silver candlesticks she had carried with her from Palestine. Shimon, who padded softly behind her and watched her from the stairwell, did not know if she murmured a blessing over the small struggling flames, because her tapering white fingers covered her face. But when she returned to the upstairs rooms a febrile brightness glittered in her eyes and often she hugged Sophia so tightly that the child wept peevishly and shoved her away.

Ezra took the letter from Nechama and studied it again, as though a second reading might reveal new insights, new clues. The closely written sheets of paper fluttered in his shaking hands and he clutched them, remembering suddenly how Sara's body had quivered within his grasp on the day they arrived in Jaffa. Her hands had clung to the rusted ship's rail and she had shaken like a wild creature seeking escape from bewildering and terrifying danger. He realized in retrospect, with a clarity that startled him, that she had been in flight even then. He had known, with a child's certain instinct, that his sister had sought to escape danger by seeking death in the cool green waters of the Mediterranean. He had buried that knowledge deep within him. He, the frightened boy, thrust into a new land, had clung to his sister's nurturing strength and could not afford to acknowledge her weakness.

She had sought escape again when Avremel died. She had fled the land where she was flayed with the cutting whips of dreams that had never been her own. And now again, with this false conversion, she sought a new escape. Always she had grappled for refuge. Survival demanded reversals, grim and terrible compromises.

Poor Sara, Ezra thought.

Grief weighted him, held him prisoner in his chair. He pitied his sister for her terror; he pitied himself because she was lost to him. He looked at Nechama, who sat ramrod straight in her chair. There was strength in that quiet posture. Strength and courage. Her gentle acceptance was deceiving. It cloaked unswerving resolve. Nechama would never seek escape. Her faith would sustain her. He listened, aware now that she was whispering the sixteenth psalm.

" 'The Lord is the portion of mine inheritance—yea I have a goodly heritage.' " Her eyes were brilliant with tears for her unknown sister-in-law who, in fear and trembling, had abandoned that sweet legacy.

"I must go to Rishon," Ezra said.

"How can you tell your parents about this?" Nechama asked.

"Sara asked me to," Ezra said.

He could not refuse his sister, who had never refused him anything. He would try to protect her now, to shield her from their father's rage and their mother's bewildered, uncomprehending sorrow.

Yehuda Maimon read the letter, holding the sheets of paper tight between his calloused fingers. He wore a blue cambric work shirt but when he had read the pages through, he changed into the broadcloth jacket he wore to synagogue and then, with steady hand, picked up his knife and rent a jagged tear across the lapel.

"I rip my daughter from my life and from my heart," he said. "She is dead. Dead to me and to her mother. She no longer lives."

He pounded his forehead with clenched fist and hurled a dining room chair across the room. Silently, slowly, Rivka went to the closet and brought out the rough-hewn low stools of mourning. They sat together in the darkened room, the shutters drawn against the intrusion of sunlight, through the prescribed seven days of grief. Saul and David arrived but Yehuda would accept no comfort. Rivka grew thin and pale. She mourned only her parents, she said. Sara was her daughter no matter what. She would always be her daughter. Yehuda's face became a frozen-featured mask.

"There is no Sara," he said, and he pressed his large hands to his ears whenever her name was mentioned.

Amos, as he grew up, asked many questions about his Aunt Sara. His father offered him abrupt, terse replies. His mother was gentle and patient. The boy saved the stamps from the envelopes that contained her letters. These arrived less and less frequently as the years passed. He knew that other children had been born to her. He had small Polish cousins whose names he could not pronounce. But the only cousin who seemed real to him was the boy named Shimon who had been born in the Rishon farmhouse. Sometimes, his grandmother Rivka called him Shimon and then clapped her hand to her mouth. It was said that his Polish cousin looked like him. Shimon's hair, like Amos's own, was the color of durra wheat in full bloom and his eyes too were sea green, just like Amos's and those of Grandpa Yehuda, who wore thick glasses now and walked with the help of a cane carved from a cedar branch.

Chapter 14

"In blood and fire Judea went down! In blood and fire Judea shall rise again!"

The voices of the assembled men rose in sonorous unison and echoed through the starlit night. Sparks of flame darted skyward, ricocheting off the blazing logs of the fire around which the men stood in a solemn circle. Amos studied the unsmiling faces that glowed golden in the firelight. He trembled with admiration and fear. Reflected firelight danced off the steel trim on the Martini rifles they wore slung from their shoulders on glistening leather straps. The men stood at attention but now and again a hand reached up to tentatively caress a rifle's smooth surface, as though reassurance could be drawn from polished wood and metal. But Saul and David Maimon did not stir. Amos watched his uncles with awe, especially admiring the small topaz-colored mustache which Saul had grown to celebrate the birth of his first son, Elisha.

"When Chania presents me with a son, I too will grow a moustache," David promised them laughingly when they assembled at Gan Noar for Elisha's circumcision ceremony. David and Chania were the parents of three laughing girls.

Abu Banot—the father of daughters—the neighboring Arabs called him.

Amos knew some of the other men in the circle because they were his uncle's friends or because he had met them when they visited the farm and shared a meal with his parents at Sadot Shalom. He recognized Israel Shochat, who had organized the Guild of Jewish Watchmen, the Shomer, whose initiation ceremony they had gathered to witness on this star-streaked night. Strands of silver seamed Shochat's beard although he was a young man still. He had fought in the pogroms of Homel, back in his native Poland, and it was said that his hair had turned white overnight because of the horrors he had seen there. Still, it was in Homel that the Zionist youth group had established the first Jewish self-defense organization and beaten back the czarist attackers. The Shomer, created to defend the Jewish settlements, patterned itself on that partisan army.

"You see, there is more than one way to fight that scum," Saul had said when he first heard of the defense unit. "It is not necessary to surrender, as our sister did."

The twins were bitter about Sara's decision. Only Ezra kept in touch with her, writing her monthly letters although she seldom replied.

"Perhaps she does not want to get letters from Palestine," Nechama had suggested gently. "It may create difficulties for her if she does not want her Jewishness known."

"Don't be ridiculous," Ezra said curtly.

Nechama turned away. It was absurd, she knew, that she sometimes felt jealous of the sister-in-law she had never seen. Once she had asked Yehuda Maimon if Sara had been pretty. The old man hesitated for a moment, as though peeling back layered memories.

"She had a quiet beauty," he said at last and added, "Do you know, Nechama, the first time I saw you, with your long dark hair streaming about your shoulders, I imagined for a moment that you were Sara. Something in the way you stand—in the way you hold your head . . ." His voice drifted off. He was an old man who lived much in memory now.

He struggled to capture a glimpse of Sara—not the woman, but the fiery young girl. Nechama was like her, yes, but very different. Ezra's wife, for all her placid peacefulness, was a tenacious woman who would never be moved from what she believed.

"You are like Sara and yet you are unlike her," he said and smiled at her with the sudden wise slyness of an old man proud of his intuition. "I know why Ezra married you," he added and felt for the first time a rush of affection for the tall pale woman his son had chosen.

His reply was strangely disconcerting to Nechama and that night when she and Ezra went to bed, she turned to him with a fierceness of urgent passion that left them both gasping with delight and fatigue.

"What is my name?" she whispered insistently into the darkness.

"You are my love, my white rose of Sharon, my Nechama," he replied.

She licked the saline sweat of his passion but she was not reassured.

Yitzhak Shimshelevitz stood next to Israel Shochat. Amos recognized him as the man who had once visited Sadot Shalom with pretty, laughing Rachel Yannai. Shimshelevitz's eyes were hooded beneath his heavy brows and he seldom smiled.

"How can you sit here alone in the Galilee," he had challenged Ezra on that visit. He was so used to addressing crowds from podiums that his strident voice had filled the small Sadot Shalom sitting room. "There is work to be done. A nation to be built. We must learn how to govern ourselves, defend ourselves."

Rachel Yannai smiled benignly at her lover.

"Don't excite yourself, Yitzhak," she said. "Did we tell you," she asked Nechama, "that we have applied for a legal change of Yitzhak's name? Why should we carry these ridiculous Russian names? We have our own heritage, our own language. Ben Zvi is the name we have chosen. Yitzhak, the son of Zvi."

"You know, Yitzhak Ben Zvi, every nation must know how to sustain itself. The Jewish nation will need Jewish farmers as well as Jewish soldiers," Ezra had replied, and he himself had declined to join the Shomer.

Still, he had come to Sejera, to this firelight ceremony at which his brothers were being inducted into the Shomer, and he had argued on behalf of the Jewish defense group at the Kinnereth farm school and at the smaller Jewish settlements.

"We can feel protected only by those who truly have our interests at heart. Family members protect each other. The men of the Shomer are part of the Zionist family. We must rely on them."

His throat grew dry with the effort of speech. He had lived so long alone with Nechama on Sadot Shalom that he was uneasy in public meetings, but he knew that he had to speak because the situation was drastic.

The Young Turk revolution of 1908 had weakened Ottoman authority in Palestine. The Arabs no longer feared their Turkish masters and bandits terrorized the countryside. Highwaymen hid in hillside enclaves and attacked travelers. Farm animals were kidnapped, and entire harvests were stolen in the darkness. The much-feared Zabiah tribesmen galloped through the countryside, their colorful kaffiyehs sailing behind them in the wind, their jewel-hilted swords dangling from richly embroidered belts. Their wild screams pierced the quiet nights. Children cried, women trembled, and men slept with their rifles by their sides and wakened suddenly to stand beside their windows and study the threatening night.

Ezra had taught Nechama to use a weapon, and Gedalia and his sons kept pistols at the ready as they drove their diligences from settlement to settlement.

The Circassian guards whom the Jewish settlers had traditionally hired offered little protection. They slept at their posts and there were those who felt that the guards themselves participated in the theft of the cattle.

Gradually, the Shomer assumed the protection of the community. Bedouin attacks did not intimidate the young Watchmen. They sat astride their horses, ramrod straight, with their rifles slung about their shoulders and their pistols loaded and gleaming in waist holsters.

Often Amos had watched his uncles practice target shooting on their visits to Sadot Shalom. They lined jars up on the picket fence that ringed Nechama's kitchen garden and shot them down one by one. Once Amos had seen his Aunt Chania shout at his Uncle David as tears of fury streaked her cheeks. Amos, who knew his aunt to be a gentle woman, was puzzled until Nechama explained that David had sought to demonstrate his skill by shooting at an apple that Hadassah, his smallest daughter, obligingly held out in her hand. It had never occurred to either father or daughter that he could miss.

"Your brother is crazy," Nechama said angrily to Ezra when she told him of the incident.

"No. Only confident," Ezra replied.

But Amos shared his mother's terror. His uncles frightened him. He could never meet their expectations and he felt ashamed when they told him stories of his cousin Shimon. Shimon, they said, had loved to ride into the desert with them. They had taught him Arab war calls and often during Shimon's boyhood on the Rishon farm he had stood guard with them at night although he had been much younger then than Amos was now.

"A boy like you, Amos, must learn to shoot and use a knife," David said. "Come to Gan Noar soon and we will teach you."

David and Saul looked knowingly at each other. They could not depend on their brother Ezra, the dreamer, to teach his son the skills so necessary to a boy growing up in Palestine.

But Amos did not often visit Gan Noar. The young kibbutz had grown since his uncles and their brides had settled there. Small houses had replaced the heavy tents, and the wooden watchtower had been reinforced with steel girders. His cousins slept in the long, low building they called the children's house, and when Amos visited, he too was expected to sleep there. Often he protested that he could not sleep away from his parents because he felt ill.

"I have a stomach ache," he would whine, and he was not oblivious to the glances that his aunts and uncles exchanged. They considered him a weakling, he knew, spoiled by an overindulgent mother. His father reddened with anger at such incidents and Amos avoided his accusing eyes. He had embarrassed Ezra, shamed him before his strong brothers and their exuberant, fearless families. His father was disappointed in him. He fought back tears. He would not betray Ezra further by weeping. Eight-year-old boys were too old to cry. Cramps stirred in Amos's stomach, as the made-up stomach ache became real, and he knew that he would have to use the toilet shared by both the girls and the boys in the children's house. He could not forget how once his cousin Hadassah, perched on her potty seat, had laughed at his penis.

"It's shorter than Yoram's," she had said.

Amos knew that his mother shared his distaste for the communal showers and toilets.

"But it's wonderful," Mirra would protest. "The children know each other completely. They live honestly, openly."

Nechama did not argue. She had long ago recognized the futility of engaging in discussions with those who believed their decisions to be infallible. She tried to share this painfully gained knowledge with Amos. Her son was so like herself—introspective, happiest when he was alone with his books.

"You must try to play with your cousins, but it does not matter that you are not like them. You have other qualities that they do not have. God gives different children different gifts. We all have secrets that we keep to ourselves while we are with other people. When I visit Gan Noar, I do not read as I do when I am at home at Sadot Shalom. I work with your aunts and visit with them although perhaps I would rather be alone to read. You understand, my Amos?"

Amos nodded and placed his small hand on her own. He understood. His mother was so wise, so gentle. He ran off to join the other children and she watched him. She could perhaps teach him how to protect himself from his cousins, but she could not instruct him in the erection of defenses between himself and his father.

The kibbutz children rode the donkeys bareback. They played violent games of war. Sticks became their rifles, pebbles their bullets.

"You be a Bedouin. I'll be a Watchman. You're dead. I stabbed you with my dagger."

They built forts from the rocks that littered the fields and then destroyed them happily.

"Another kibbutz knocked down. Let's go and eat a whole goat."

Sometimes the children allowed the Arabs to win and sometimes the Jews. They were casually indifferent to victory. It was the battle that counted and they played with a fierceness that frightened their visiting cousin.

As much as he liked playing with his neighbor, Achmed, still Amos hated his cousins' games. He was the last to be chosen for their mock armies and the first to simulate death or be taken prisoner. Then he would skulk away to the shade of the newly planted plum orchard, remove his book from its hiding place in his shirt, and peacefully read in the leafy shade until he was discovered.

"Why don't you play with the others?" his father asked him.

"I would rather read."

"We bring you here so that you'll play with other children. At home you have plenty of time to read, and there is only Achmed to play with. Here there is excitement. Enjoy it, Amos. When I was your age all I knew was the stink of the Kharkov yeshiva."

Ezra sighed deeply. When the sun sprayed golden rivulets across the green fields of Sadot Shalom, Amos sought the cool of the house and the books that were his greatest treasures. Ezra and Nechama had selected the volumes for him and taught him. They had recognized his gifts early but even they had been startled by the alacrity with which he learned.

He read the Bible avidly, studying it as both history and literature and committing favorite passages to memory. He had jumped from the rudiments of arithmetic to elementary algebra. He traced the maps from the worn geography text that had been his father's, and his friend Achmed knelt beside him, watching admiringly.

"You see, Achmed, this is the Galilee. Up north is the Lebanon where your uncle lives, and just west here is your grandfather's village in Transjordan."

Achmed nodded seriously.

"North," he repeated. "West."

He was the son of Saleem, the Arab who had worked for Yehuda Maimon on the Rishon farm. When Ezra left his father's house, Saleem had asked if he might come with him. His family had originally come from the northern Galilee and he missed the verdant countryside of his childhood. Ezra had considered carefully and had at last agreed.

"So you too will hire Arab laborers," his father said triumphantly.

"No. I am deeding several dunams outright to Saleem. In return he will help me on the land. It is different from having fellahin live in shack villages on your property. We must be fair and treat them as we would have them treat us. This is the only way Jew and Arab will live together on this land."

"That was what your brother-in-law, Avremel, said," Yehuda replied bitterly. "Go. Take Saleem. The words of

Yehuda Maimon mean nothing to the sons of Yehuda Maimon.''

Ezra had never regretted his decision. Saleem was a good farmer and a hard worker. It was comforting to sit on the veranda of the farmhouse and see the smoke of Saleem's cooking fire. In the evening they could hear the melancholy tunes he played on his reed pipe. It meant that Sadot Shalom was less isolated, less vulnerable to the night shrieks of the jackals and the occasional distant roar of the mountain lion.

When Saleem's wife, Hulda, gave birth, Nechama attended her. She cooled the laboring woman's brow and pulled the shuddering, shimmering infant into life. She had used her mending shears to sever the umbilical cord and had briskly knotted the remaining protrusion against the wailing, walnut-colored infant's abdomen. Hulda left baskets of eggs at their door and during the winter when Nechama ran a high fever, Amos slept in Saleem's house, sharing Achmed's sleeping pallet. The families shared each other's lives, observing scrupulous parameters. They were caring neighbors, resigned to the knowledge that they could never be friends.

But a real friendship had grown up between Achmed and Amos. The olive-skinned Arab boy, whose thick dark hair clustered in ringlets about his finely shaped head, raced through the fields with lithe, golden-haired Amos. Amos devised their games but it was Achmed who lent a subtle elegance to their imaginings. They were Jacob and Esau but it was Achmed who decided that Isaac's legacy should be shared and that the brothers should rule together. They were Abraham and Avimelech bargaining on the road to Hebron. Achmed was a benevolent Avimelech.

''We shall share the caves. Both of us will bury our dead there.''

His scepter was a silvery wand carved from an olive branch and his crown intertwined vines from a failed grape arbor. Amos taught Achmed to play chess. Achmed taught him Shesh-Besh, the Arab version of backgammon. Amos showed Achmed his primers and taught him the Hebrew letters.

''Now you must teach me the Arab alphabet,'' he told his friend.

''I don't know it.'' Achmed was unembarrassed, matter-of-fact.

''Then you must ask your father to teach it to you.''

"He doesn't know it either."

It was Amos's grandfather, Reb Langerfeld, who found them an Arabic primer, and the boys taught themselves to read, tracing the beautiful letters on lined paper.

Ezra watched with mixed feelings as the friendship developed. He would not discourage it. Achmed was a fine boy, bright and industrious. Still, it was important that Amos share more with his own people. As he grew older, the boy seemed inclined only to visit Nechama's family in Jaffa or to spend his days with Achmed. That was one of the reasons why he had decided to bring Amos to this fireside initiation ceremony. Perhaps the boy would be inspired and seek to emulate his uncles.

To earn admission into the Shomer, the Guild of Jewish Watchmen, Saul and David had been drilled in night maneuvers. They had prowled the country in darkness and half-light and learned to find their direction by following the sun and the stars. They spoke Arabic fluently and were capable of taking aim and shooting down a soaring heron as they galloped across wide expanses where only cacti and dwarf palms grew in splendid desolation.

The Arabs—even Saleem, who had known the twins since boyhood—called them *Moscoby*. The term, Saleem explained to Ezra, meant Russians, whom the Arabs visualized as brave men and good hunters.

"It is a compliment," Saleem said, and Achmed had told Amos that the exploits of the Shomer had been woven into Arab song and story.

Saul and David took their oaths together. They stood at attention, their hands on their upswung rifles. The steel glittered and the dark wood was polished to a muted glow. The brothers held their weapons in tender embrace and repeated the oath the men had taken as a group.

"In blood and fire Judea went down. In blood and fire Judea shall rise again. We shall defend our people at all times and in face of all danger. We shall never disobey an order. We shall never turn back."

Their voices reverberated in the silence of the night. A log slid from its piling and crashed into the cinders, shooting bright gold sparks into the darkness. Saul and David slipped back into their places in the circle.

Amos reached for his father's hand. He was cold suddenly,

and he trembled with an unquiet fear. He was frightened of
both blood and fire. Briefly, Ezra held his son's hand and
then released the small trembling fingers. The ceremony was
over and he moved to congratulate his brothers, to grasp them
by the shoulders.

"Now that you are official Shomrim, Watchmen, you must
come and guard the cattle of Sadot Shalom during the *revia*,
the night grazing," he said.

"We will be there, brother. You can depend upon it," Saul
replied and he passed Ezra a bottle of Rishon wine.

Yehuda had not come to the ceremony but he had sent
newly decanted wine, the product of the first vines he had
cultivated in his arbor two decades earlier. His sons drank
deeply, their arms about each other, their voices raised in
song.

> Bring us wine
> Sweet red wine
> From the vineyards of our land.

They sang of the harvest and of the wonder of water and
the beauty of mountains. Softly, they sang of love. They laid
their rifles down and they linked their arms and moved their
feet in circle dances of brotherhood, wild horas, and graceful
debkas.

Amos watched them, fascinated and bewildered, until a
strong hand reached out for him and he was pulled into the
circle that danced about the fire which had dwindled now to
blazing embers which glowed bravely in the unending darkness.

Chapter 15

The *yoreh*, the first rains, arrived early that year, falling just after Sukkoth, the feast of Tabernacles. The huge drops pelted Amos and Ezra as they dismantled the *sukkah*, the hut they built each year which symbolized the temporary dwelling constructed by the children of Israel as they traveled through the desert en route to the land of Canaan.

"It will be a heavy rain," Ezra said.

He was not displeased. A heavy rain was important for his terraced technique of farming. He had planted new rows of young fruit trees and created orchards that rose in slight incline along the hillsides of his land. The young roots would drink in the rainfall and absorb it, and the small stones that pebbled each planted column would stave off the runaway waters. They would have a good harvest.

Amos nodded dutifully. He helped his father on the farm but he was uninterested in agronomy. The only things that interested him in the earth of Sadot Shalom were the small shards of pottery and the bits of ancient metal he had gathered. He had a small collection now and it was of a new discovery that he was thinking as his father assessed the strength of the *yoreh*. He and Achmed had been playing at digging a tunnel. Amos had visited Jerusalem for the first time that winter and had seen the tunnel built by the prophet Hezekiah, and now the boys were obsessed by the construction of underground passages. As they burrowed into the earth, digging a field which his father had not yet tilled, Amos's shovel struck metal. He abandoned the implement and dug the rest of the way with his hands, at last unearthing a metal idol covered with verdigris. The tiny figure was smooth to his touch.

"What is it?" Achmed asked.

"I don't know."

Amos examined it carefully. It was a human figure with wondrously shaped small breasts and a sharply carved penis that jutted forth erectly. He had seen a picture of an archaeological artifact that was not unlike it in his father's large book on antiquities of the Middle East. A fertility god, it was called. Perhaps ancient farmers had buried it in the earth so that their crops would be abundant. Surely one of his Langerfeld aunts and uncles would know about it. He would take it with him on his next visit to his mother's family. It did not occur to him to ask his father about it, although Ezra had his own small collection of mysterious pottery and on occasion had corresponded with a professor at the Jewish National Library in Jerusalem about a particularly interesting find.

It was, as Ezra had predicted, an unusually strong *yoreh*. Nechama stood at the window and watched the rain fall on the parched land. The seven summer months had been hot and dry and the oven-breathed desert wind had blown the dust into their mouths and eyes. The scorched earth had cracked in despair, surrendering to thirst. She herself had felt a small desperation, and the acknowledgment of her own failure weighed upon her as she moved wearily from the house to the fields.

Even Amos had once shyly broached the subject of why there were no other children. He had returned from playing with Achmed, bursting with a tale of a game he and his friend had created, organizing the younger children into rival armies.

"It's fun in a house with lots of children," he had said. "Why don't we have more children, Imma?"

"Sometimes it happens that way," she had replied gently. "But we are lucky, Amos, that you and I are such good friends, that we play chess together and backgammon and read aloud to each other. And Abba likes to play chess with you too. Now sometimes, you even win. Isn't that fun, Amos?''

"Yes," he replied, "Only sometimes it's lonely here. And I think Abba would like someone else to play chess with sometimes—someone who really likes to work in the fields with him.''

And then, as though sensing that his words had wounded her, Amos climbed onto her lap and thrust his bright golden head beneath her chin—a small boy still, who might beat his father at chess but who longed for his mother's kisses.

Ezra talked again and again of having another child. Both his brothers' wives were pregnant again. Chania and Mirra worked the fields of Gan Noar as their abdomens swelled. They carried their children as effortlessly as they did their work. Word came from Poland that Sara had had a fourth child, and they had told Yehuda Maimon of the birth of his grandchild, speaking above the roar of his refusal to listen, to acknowledge, to know. But still Nechama did not conceive, although she and Ezra were drawn to each other night after night, their bodies locked together in sweet and breathless consort.

Nachama expressed ignorance, shared his disappointment, and evaded his hesitant suggestion that she visit a doctor. At such times her own dishonesty pressed against her breast as though it had a corporeal weight of its own, and she found it difficult to breathe. Ezra did not know that she had journeyed years before to a clinic in Tiberias where a young Dutch doctor had fitted her with a small rubber device which he called a diaphragm. He explained that she must fill it with a cream that acted as a spermicide.

"In America they call it a Dutch cap," he said. "It is not much in use now but soon its value will be recognized. Something must be done to control the population." Outside his clinic on the narrow, dusty streets, Arab women sat, swollen in pregnancy, one baby in their arms and two or three tugging at their skirts. The children wore rags; puss ran in pale rivulets from their eyes and their bare feet were covered with running sores.

"If they would only listen. The diaphragm would solve so

many problems," he said and gave Nechama several extra tubes of the ointment.

He was justly confident. Nechama did not become pregnant. She watched the rains moodily and thought that her body was like the dry, unfertile earth. Her womb would grow parched with disuse; not even the fiercest explosions of her husband's potent sperm would renew it.

When the rain stopped, the dark, moist soil was soft beneath their feet and malleable in their hands. The air was damp and fresh against their faces. Ezra mounted the combine and plowed the fields of Sadot Shalom, turning the earth, creating the straight furrows where he would sow the seeds of the next season's harvest. Achmed and Amos followed after him, beating at the land with their harrows. The heavy steel tines bit into the earth, pulverizing the clods, stirring the soil, unearthing hidden weeds and seed covers.

Achmed worked swiftly, moving from furrow to furrow, his narrow face bare in the damp earth. He swayed to his task with effortless rhythm, singing softly. He sang the ancient Arab tunes and hummed bits of melody. Amos also sang, his high sweet voice rising in the harvest songs written by Bialik. Occasionally he sang one of Achmed's songs and now and again Achmed sang in Hebrew.

Ezra looked back at the boys as he moved the tractor along. Amos moved so slowly, as though his heavy work boots weighed him down. Ezra marked Achmed's swiftness and his easy grace. He felt oddly jealous of Saleem, who worked beside him, and he spoke harshly to him because the Arab had failed to load the sacks of seed properly.

They planted alfalfa and winter wheat, corn and barley. Ezra thought now in terms of fodder crops. His cattle herd was growing. He had oxen and cows. The black blood-eyed bull he had bought from the Bedouin graziers of Turcoman was a prize stud. Farmers traveled from distant *moshavim* to bring their cows to Sadot Shalom for insemination. He kept horses and mules, and Nechama had her own goat herd. She loved the sleek, clever nannies and the sleepy-eyed kids. Always she chose one kid from a litter and fed it herself, holding a nursing bottle to the animal's thin carmine lips. There were horses and Amos's piebald pony. Ezra had bought Achmed a pony as well, a chubby black animal with soft large eyes, as a reward for his help on the farm.

The crop came up with rare abundance. Even the locusts that had plagued them year after year were scant.

"Why don't you plant citrus?" Yehuda asked Ezra when he traveled north with Rivka to survey his son's farm at full bloom. Oranges and grapefruits, lemons and citrons had made Yehuda Maimon a wealthy man. Great crates of his golden-globed produce were shipped to Europe and the United States, to South America and New Zealand. Jews in Canada and Australia prayed, during the feast of Tabernacles, clutching citrons grown on the Rishon farm. His sister-in-law in New York made lemonade from the wondrously thin-skinned fruit that grew in his shaded groves.

"There is room on the land for many different kinds of farmers," Ezra replied. Not everything has to be done your way, he thought, but did not put his thoughts into words. His wars with his father were waged silently, the lessons of childhood well learned.

Amos listened attentively although he did not look up from his book. There was room in the land for men other than farmers, he thought, but he too did not speak. Like his father, he sought refuge behind an impenetrable wall of silence. He turned back to his book, a collection of poetry. The words of each verse trembled at the edge of his mind.

"It is good that you like poetry," his grandmother Rivka said approvingly. "Did I ever tell you about the night the poet had dinner with us in Kharkov?"

Her voice grew wispy and tinged with reverance. She was a frail old woman now, remembering her youthful days in a distant land.

"No," Nechama lied. "Tell us about it."

Yehuda groaned and followed Ezra out of the room.

"Your farm is beautiful," he said. It was his first acknowledgment that Sadot Shalom was a success. Ezra touched his father's arm, and together the two farmers studied the green mantled fields that stretched before them. The grain hung heavy and golden; the full-headed kernels were luminous in the half-light of evening.

"It will be a good harvest," Yehuda said. "And your cattle will grow fat in the revia. Have you hired the Circassians to stand guard during the night grazing?"

"No. I have made arrangements with the Shomer. Saul and David will be here."

Yehuda nodded. He had never told his sons how he trembled when he thought of them riding through the night, their horses' eyes luminescent, the steel of their rifles angular lines of silver against the darkness. He grew frightened because he recognized his sons' courage and the vulnerability such courage brought. He was proud of them, yet angry that they should give him cause for fear. He had lost one child and did not want to lose another.

The revia began during the second half of the rainy season, in the month of Shevat. The grass in the meadowlands had grown to a height at which it brushed the boys' bare knees. Achmed and Amos played at being explorers now. They moved through the tall grass shouting to each other in their secret language. Nechama picked sorrel grass and cooked it into the cold green *shav* that the family ate in the evening with scallions, cucumbers, and hard-boiled eggs. The countryside was luxuriant with growth and the cattle herds grew fat with the rich grazing.

Ezra Maimon's horses and donkeys, his oxen and mules, pulled the harvest wagons of Sadot Shalom, and the seasonal laborers worked through the day on the threshing floor separating the cereal grain from the husks and the straw. They filled huge sacks with grain and when evening fell, the cattle were led out to pasture for the night grazing.

A single herdsman, or even two for the drove, such as were normally employed, would not suffice for the revia in which the cattle roamed freely across wild fields and untamed valleys. The pasture lands of Sadot Shalom even extended to sheltered woodlands where the sweet ferns and grass grew in profusion. The herd wandered in the fragrant glens without bit or rein.

Saul and David arrived with ten other mounted Watchmen. They were followed by a posse on foot, young men in training for the Shomer who were armed cap à pie. Newly sharpened daggers hung at their belts; Browning pistols with ornately tooled handles were thrust through their holsters, and the weapons pounded their hips as they walked. Gleaming bullets were strung across their cartridge belts. Their rifles were held at the ready. They sang loudly as they made their way across the low hills to Sadot Shalom, advertising their presence. They wanted lingering Bedouin to know that they were on their way. They wanted their weapons to be seen, their strength noted. With robust voice, they sang an Arab battle song taught to them by Shomrim who had lived among the Bedouin, studying their ways and their language. These secrets had been added to the small but growing arsenal of intelligence assembled by the Jewish unit.

David himself had spent several months living in a Bedouin encampment. He had always had an easy rapport with the wandering Arabs. He spoke several dialects and understood their culture.

"Sing more loudly," he urged his men. "You cannot see them but they are watching us."

The younger men looked nervously about. There was little movement in the quiet Galilean hills. Birds soared in tranquil flight. It was their nesting time and they settled in tall eucalyptus trees and in the silvery gnarled branches of crouching olive trees. The hillsides were spangled with color. Anemones and irises, bright pink cyclamens, creamy daffodils and goldenhearted ferns stirred lightly in the barest breeze. Butterflies and bees glided lazily above the flowers. But the peaceful scene did not deceive David Maimon. He knew that Arab scouts lurked in hidden caves, in unseen turns, in hillside hiding places. He knew that even if they could not count the armed men approaching Sadot Shalom, they would estimate their strength from the sound of their voices and the hoofs of their animals. Some of the Watchmen carried poles to which horseshoes had been affixed. They banged these heavily as they marched, an auditory reinforcement to their show of strength. Occasionally David fired a shot into the air and emitted a warlike whoop. A desert sheik had told him that the advantage belonged to those who loudly proclaimed their strength and their martial intent, and he knew that he must use every weapon available, both actual and psychological.

Ezra rode out to meet his brothers. He too was heavily armed, and Saul and David read the worry in his eyes. They rode three abreast, across the fields to Sadot Shalom, speaking quietly in the terse manner of men who know each other so well they need waste neither word nor sentiment.

"I wanted to speak to you out here because I do not want Nechama and Amos to be frightened," Ezra said. "But the situation here is not good. One of Gedalia's sons was waylaid only three nights ago by the fellahin of Lubiah. He was carrying two families from Sejera to Tiberias and they were forced out of the diligence. Their money and their wedding bands were stolen. And there have been other incidents. A girl at the Kinnereth farm who was hiking along the northern road was raped. A group of Christian tourists traveling near Kfar Kana was stopped and their camera was stolen."

"It's that damn Turkish constitution," David said bitterly. "The Turks revolt in Constantinople and the people of Palestine must suffer for it. The Arabs no longer fear the Turks. They know there will be neither judgment nor justice in this land. If the Turks cannot govern their own people, how can they govern the fellahin of Palestine?"

"We cannot solve international problems now. It is my revia that concerns me. The Circassians are angered because we have turned the guarding of the cattle over to the Jewish watchmen. I am afraid that they themselves will attempt to seize the herds. Perhaps it might be better to share the guarding of the cattle with them."

David's face hardened.

"We have come too far to step backward now," he said. "The Jewish community in this country must prove that it can protect itself. You are a Jewish farmer and your cattle will be protected by Jewish watchmen. We have had enough appeasement, enough cowardice."

Silence fell between the brothers. The ghost of their sister drifted between them. Saul stroked the cartridges in the belt that draped his shoulder. A jackal skittered across their path and David raised his Browning. The pistol shot echoed across the hillside and struck the moving animal in the head. The scarlet rivulet of blood that trickled from his eyes was the same color as the anemones that clustered in the grassy hillside where the small furry creature died.

"You waste your bullets," Ezra said harshly. "I know your marksmanship." He was no longer the small and sickly child awed by the strength and daring of his older brothers.

But he did not argue further, and it was settled that the Jewish watchmen alone would guard the revia.

The first two nights passed peacefully. The Watchmen patrolled the hills with their rifles cocked to readiness. They rode past the cattle that lumbered clumsily across the grasslands, exhausting the greenery in one area and moving slowly and ponderously onto the next. The younger men assigned names to the cows they recognized and laughed at the donkeys who had to be spurred forward lest they linger wastefully over a field already eaten bald.

On the third night David rode farther than he had on the previous evenings. A brood cow had strayed and he followed the sound of her bell into a field where the smell of clover grass moistened by the night dew was strong and sweet. In the distance he heard the mighty bellow of Ezra's prize bull. Not far away a stallion snorted imperiously at his mare, and a cow moaned mournfully after a straying calf.

David rode on, thinking of the new baby at Gan Noar, his son born at last after Chania had brought forth their three daughters. They had decided to name the child Shlomo for Chania's father but the name pleased David because of its meaning. Shlomo—shalom; peace. It was toward the achievement of peace that they had to train their energy. The land could not be cultivated while men trained for war. David begrudged the time he spent perfecting his aim, arming himself with knowledge of maneuvers and military strategy. He would have preferred to be working in the fields of Gan Noar or building the new communal dining hall. Surely there was enough room in this land for Jew and Arab to live together in peace. It was possible to ride many kilometers in the Galilee, across untilled acreage, passing only a solitary Jewish herdsman or a wandering Arab shepherd boy. The land was waiting for them, but instead of guarding it they fought over it, and the Turkish overseers relished their internecine warfare. Still, there was hope. If he stood guard now and there was a recognition of Jewish will and Jewish strength, perhaps his son's generation would be free to farm.

The cow's bell jingled merrily and David followed the sound, oppressed by his own weariness. The baby had been born only a few nights earlier and he had been up with Chania through the labor. The infant was healthy but too small to be circumcised on the requisite eighth day after birth. They would hold the ceremony after the revia.

Shlomo was Yehuda Maimon's sixth grandson. There was Amos, Ezra's bookbound, dreamy-eyed lad; Elisha, Saul's son; Shimon, the first to be born on the land; and Sara's two younger sons with their odd Polish names—Stefan and Janusz. David frowned at the thought of Sara and felt a familiar heaviness of heart. His son had first cousins who did not know they were Jewish, who knelt on the cold tile floors of Polish churches. But Shimon, David was certain, had neither disowned nor forgotten his religion or the land of his birth.

David's horse breathed hard. They were approaching a hilly area and David guessed that his steed smelled the animals who sometimes created lairs in the hidden hillside caves. He stroked the chestnut's satin-smooth neck, whispered softly in his ear, and urged him on.

They were in a narrow glen now. Two large rock formations shimmered like silvery stone fortresses in the pervasive blackness. David was reminded of the fairy tales his mother had read to them in the warmth of the Kharkov parlor—tales of bewitched castles and mountain kingdoms. He had all but forgotten those Russian stories of his childhood. His own children were nurtured on tales plucked from the Bible. That, he thought, would have surprised his grandfather, the Talmud scholar of Kharkov who had called David and Saul *apekorsim*, atheists, because they had played hooky from the yeshiva and run barefoot through the Russian woodlands. Probably, Reb Shimon had known the name of the valley through which David was now riding. Perhaps the rock formations that towered over him had ancient names. Ezra would know.

A stone skittered down the side of the rock buttress on his left. He reached for his Mauser, released the safety catch, and trained his eyes on the abutment. There was no movement except for the swaying branch of a dwarf palm that had mysteriously rooted itself in a seam of earth hidden within that bed of stone. He studied the harsh surface carefully. The moon was very bright and its silvery light illuminated the micaceous rise. Nothing was visible. David kept the pistol in his hand but restored the safety catch. It would be an easy matter, he knew, for a man to conceal himself on the other side of the boulder.

The cow's bell jangled. It was returning to him after all. Probably, there had been no need to chase after it. He relaxed his posture in the saddle, annoyed at himself for being startled by the slight movement and the even slighter sound. He was a trained Shomer, not a foolish youth looking for danger around every corner.

A cloud drifted across the moon and plunged the landscape into darkness so complete that David groped for his reins. He struggled to adjust his eyes to the sudden blackness, leaning forward to see if he could discern the shape of the cow. A shot rang out. He heard the bullet hiss malevolently through the air and he thought, paralyzed with unfamiliar terror, that he could actually see it wing its way toward him through the night. It was a small and deadly silver meteor that pierced his right eye with swift and stunning impact. The metal splintered cranial bone; blood spurted from the gap in his face where once his eye had been. Sticky rivulets flowed down his cheeks; scarlet pain pounded at him and the black night turned crimson. A pounding filled his head, and he felt his mouth grow sour with the vomit which he spewed on the ground, relieved that he could smell its stink. He was alive then, and conscious. He clutched the reins desperately and whispered softly to his horse. Pain rimmed his words and they emerged a fuzzy whimper but the horse, trained in the Bedouin encampments of the south, did not bolt and run.

His hand trembling, David released the safety catch on the pistol. With one hand steadying the other, he lifted the weapon. The cloud soared eastward and once again the moon rained its silvery light. He saw the silhouetted figure of an Arab mounted on the promontory, his black *abayah* floating behind him in death-colored wings, his white kaffiyeh askew. The Arab's rifle was poised but David shot first. The bullet sang through the night and found its mark. The Arab fell from his perch. His body hurtled down the rocky slope, and his wild scream riddled the darkness.

It was the Arab's scream that brought the other Shomrim to the rockbound slope. Saul and Ezra, riding in tandem, reached David first. Their brother's face was a blood-streaked mask, and a milky puddle of corneal fluid had settled in the crevice of his cheekbone.

He is dead, Ezra thought, and grief washed over him. He had not known that one grew weak and faint with sorrow.

But Saul, bending toward his twin, saw David's hand move, his fingers loosen their hold on the trigger. Gently, he wiped his brother's face and saw how the tear-filled sea-green eye was open. David's lips moved in tortured, whispered query.

"Was anyone else hurt?" he asked.

"No. And the cattle are safe."

As though to give proof to his reply, the wandering cow

moved forward, her bell jangling. Slowly, clumsily, she made her way down the hillside.

They carried David back to Sadot Shalom, and the next day, at a small clinic in Haifa, a Turkish surgeon carved into the battered face. He excised the bullet and hollowed out the eye to reduce the chance of infection.

"It's a miracle," the doctor marveled. "Another millimeter and it would have reached the brain."

"I must remember to thank God," David replied.

A new and unfamiliar bitterness had congealed within him. In nightmare fantasy he shot wildly at black-winged Arabs and plucked his newborn son from flame-filled rooms. Unresolved anger embittered his sleep, and in the cold light of pain-filled dawn he struggled to reconcile grim accounts. Since his arrival in the country, he had dealt fairly with the Arabs. He had learned their language, traded honestly with them, and shared with them his knowledge of agronomy and husbandry. During the droughts of the recent years, he had insisted that the well of Gan Noar be opened to Arab graziers, and when malaria struck a Bedouin camp he himself had ridden to the Turkish district health officer to obtain quinine.

And yet, in the darkness of a night sweet with the fragrance of new-grown grass, he had been shot down for the crime of guarding his brother's cattle. He had been betrayed and half-blinded by those Arabs to whom he had offered help and friendship. He felt a bitter triumph because he had killed his own attacker. That, after all, was the only language they understood—the language of whistling bullets, of conquest by blood and fear. He had been two decades on the land but now, at last, he understood what his father, perhaps, had always known. He was done with meeting local sheiks in deserted khans to make bargains that would be betrayed the next day. From this revia on, his rifle and his pistol would be his instruments of negotiation and he would name his newborn son Joshua, for the warrior of Israel, instead of Shlomo. He knew, with acid certainty, that no temples of peace would be built in this land during his son's lifetime.

A black patch was fitted over the eyeless cavity. David was told that there was an American doctor in Beirut who could affix a glass eye, and his Uncle Mendel wrote from America about a plastic surgeon in New York who did miraculous restorative work.

"Please, go to New York," Rivka pleaded. She did not want her son to be maimed, the object of careless curiosity.

David touched the eye patch and traced his fingers across the thick black elastic rope which hugged it to his head.

"There will be no operation," he said. "This patch will be my mark. From now on they will recognize me. They will know who I am and whom they must fight—the cowardly Arab scum."

Achmed and Amos, playing on the veranda at Sadot Shalom, heard his words. The Arab boy's soft dark eyes filled with tears, and Amos touched his friend, stroked his arm.

"He doesn't mean you, Achmed," he said.

But his own words echoed hollowly and the boys, who had never lied to each other, turned their faces, each unwilling to read the truth that stood in the other's eyes.

Chapter 16

The walls of the Sadot Shalom farmhouse were thin stretches of plasterboard. Amos, lying awake, heard the familiar rocking of his parents' bed, his mother's deep sighs, his father's heavy breathing and throaty murmurs. On alternate evenings he listened to their whispers of endearment and the harsh swift exchanges of their rare anger. These were the nocturnal sounds of all his childhood, and he was neither frightened nor intrigued by them. He awakened and slept to their predictable rhythm. From earliest infancy, he had been a light sleeper, and he had schooled himself to lie motionless in the darkness. His parents' voices rose and fell, and he listened as they spoke sleepily of their relatives in distant countries, of alternate crops for Sadot Shalom, of the difficulties at the Rishon farm: Yehuda Maimon tired easily and his eyesight grew weaker with each passing year; Rivka was almost crippled with arthritis; they relied increasingly on hired labor.

"It would be ideal if Saul or David would leave the kibbutz and take over the farm," Nechama said.

"They would no more agree to that than I would agree to leave Sadot Shalom," Ezra replied.

Gan Noar, at last, was coming into its own. The swamps

that had polluted its terrain were drained, and its fields blazed golden at harvest time. David and Chania, Saul and Mirra had their own white stucco bungalows, and Nechama teased her sisters-in-law because they planted ornate flower beds in their small gardens which were not at all unlike those that decorated the most bourgeois doorways of Kattowitz.

"We do it for the community," Mirra protested righteously, and turned to shout at a Gan Noar child who had plucked a flower from her communal bed.

Nechama worried about her parents. It was a strain for them to uproot themselves yet again and move from Jaffa to the new city of Tel Aviv.

"It is absurd of them," Ezra said, vaguely angered because they had caused Nechama unrest.

"Oh, they will settle in well, you will see." She reassured herself by reassuring her husband.

Sometimes, waking suddenly in the night, Amos thought that his mother was talking to him rather than to his father. The tone she used when she spoke to Ezra matched her voice when she reasoned softly with Amos himself. No, his Uncle David did not hate all Arabs. Certainly, he did not hate Achmed and Saleem. He was going through a difficult time. Amos must try to understand. Yes, she knew that Amos would rather read than ride with his father on the combine to fertilize the westernmost fields. It was true that his father did not need Amos's help, but perhaps he wanted his company. It was, after all, difficult to work alone all day, and his father did not have a friend nearby. Amos was lucky to have Achmed. Come, Amos, be reasonable. Her voice was sympathetic, gentle.

Just so she spoke to his father as they lay abed. It would be good for Amos to spend a few weeks this summer with her family. Her father was growing older and it was a long time since the boy had visited. He had, in fact, never seen the new Langerfeld house in Tel Aviv. He would spend some time in the new Jewish city and return to Sadot Shalom happy to be back in the country with his parents. Come, Ezra. Be reasonable.

She was the arbiter of the family, soothing them with the quiet control of her arguments, the orderly sequence of her thoughts. She sought peace and order in all things. Her books were ranged in careful rows. When she tutored Amos through long afternoons and evenings, she could locate the text she wanted without lifting her head. Her few dresses were neatly hung, and she moved through the kitchen with quiet efficiency.

Ezra, watching her as she prayed alone each Sabbath morning, thought that she loved the prayers and the ritual of religion for their constancy and their order. Sometimes it seemed to him that the careful control that dominated their lives was the anchor that held them firmly rooted to the soil of Sadot Shalom, where to everything there was a season. Without it, they would be cast adrift in this uncertain land, afloat on the capricious waves of their uncertain history.

He loved Nechama more with each passing year. She held him firm and soothed him through troubled nights as once she had soothed his eye on a Jaffa hillside when a speck of dirt had briefly troubled him. He no longer worried because there were no more children. They had each other and they had Amos. And they were young still. Nechama had a youthful stance and walked with the easy grace of the tall woman who has always taken pride in her height. Amos was twelve but other children might yet come. In Rishon a child had been born to a couple after fifteen barren years. He was hopeful still.

But Amos puzzled him. The boy took no joy in the land, found no excitement in the reclamation of the soil. He cared only for the remnants of civilization hidden beneath the earth of Sadot Shalom, the battered shards of pottery, the bent bits of metal. These dried and battered artifacts of history engaged his imagination. His sea-green eyes blazed when he talked of a new find. The small fertility idol he had found was on display in Jerusalem. But the boy was indifferent to the essence of life on the farm. He was uninterested in Ezra's crops, in the fat herd of cattle that roamed the meadowland, and the fruit that glowed through the thick-branched trees. Ezra considered. Perhaps Nechama was right. Perhaps a few weeks in the sand-swept city of Tel Aviv would awaken Amos to the beauty of Sadot Shalom.

All right," he said to Nechama. "Let him visit your parents. We will take him in a week's time, after we have harvested the peaches."

Lying in the darkness and listening, Amos's heart soared. A few weeks away from farm chores—it seemed to him an endless expanse of time. Achmed would miss him, he knew, but he would buy Achmed a present in one of the new shops. His grandfather Yehuda had given him five dinars for his twelfth birthday and he had them still. He would buy Achmed a real knife and he would bring his mother a leather bookmark and satin ribbons for her hair. He got out of bed and checked to see that his dinars were still concealed beneath his shirts and then crept back beneath the thin white sheet. He fell asleep as a night owl hooted at a vagrant tern.

Nechama and Ezra accompanied Amos on the journey to Tel Aviv. They had visited the site of the new city three years earlier, on the day its foundation stone had been laid in the sands of the desert that stretched northeast from Jaffa. They had stood then with Nechama's family and watched the ceremony. Ezra was reminded of Herzl's visit to Rishon LeZion and realized with resigned sorrow that the dark-bearded, burning-eyed Zionist organizer had been dead for five years now. He gripped Nechama's hand. Life moved too swiftly. Death and uncertainty teased them at every turn.

A makeshift platform had been erected on the shifting sands and decorated with flags and buntings of blue and white. The orchestra of Rishon was assembled, their brass instruments polished to a harsh brightness, their threadbare uniforms newly pressed. They marched across the beach in strict formation although their boots were soon filled with sand, and they blinked against the tiny gnats that blackened the air. An honor guard of children preceded them, each young marcher carrying the blue-and-white flag emblazoned with the Star of David. The tallest of the boys brought up the rear. He carried the scarlet and gold banner of the Ottoman Empire, and the two Turkish officials on the dais snapped to attention and saluted imperiously as it passed. Their bright uniforms, the polished leather of their boots and belts, contrasted oddly with the loose holiday attire of the assembled crowds and the simple white shirt and blue trousers of the student who carried their flag.

"It is ludicrous," Ezra whispered to Nechama. "Our destiny is controlled by a country known as the sick man of Europe."

"We must be patient," Nechama replied quietly.

She read history texts late into the night. She knew that nations, like carrion birds, fed upon each other and drifted from power to impotence. The dawn of one dynasty signaled the evening of another. The sick man of Europe would die. The sourness of that impending death polluted the air of the Middle East. Corruption and decay littered the boulevards of Constantinople, even as Jewish architects in Palestine studied the plans for the contemplated garden suburb which would stretch northeast of Jaffa, as far as the shores of the Yarkon River. The same Turks who stood at attention for the flag with the golden crescent embroidered on scarlet silk had sat in Reb Langerfeld's office only weeks before. They had huddled over the smoky paraffin lamp and accepted small pouches of gold in exchange for their signatures and official seal on transfers of land, on building permits, on transportation licenses. Neither the solemn officials of the Jewish National Fund, who passed the bags across the table, nor the officials in their bright uniforms and pomaded mustaches who accepted them (tossing the leather pouches into the air to feel their weight but never counting the coins) made any pretense of believing that the money would find its way into the coffers of the Turkish treasury. Bribery and baksheesh were the norm of the decaying Ottoman Empire, and they did not question it.

Nechama's father had been among the first of the Jewish colonists to join the small development company, Achuzat Bayit, which had conceived of Tel Aviv. He had attended the organizational meeting and listened to Arthur Ruppin, the director of the Jewish National Fund, recently returned from a Zionist congress, announce that plans were under way for an all-Jewish city. Individual plots would be sold to Jewish settlers in Palestine and Europe. Proudly, he unrolled a map and displayed a topographical outline of the area selected. It would be rooted in sand and bordered by the sea.

Many left the meeting before it was over. They did not like Arthur Ruppin, the pedantic German bureaucrat who spoke the language of dry statistics and looked at them with a cold, calculating gaze. Ruppin's Folly, they called the proposed city to be built where sand dunes created the landscape. A garden suburb indeed. They lit their pipes and laughed. Grass would not grow where the slightest wind shifted the earth and formed clouds of sand that blinded the surveyors who came to plot the streets and avenues of the envisioned city. The Arab children laughed at the men and their instruments. They scurried past the makeshift tables, tossing trident and scope into the sand. They hurled pebbles at the tents the surveyors and builders hoisted on the sand.

But Isaac Langerfeld was not deterred. He kept records for the Jewish Council and he knew that there were six thousand Jews living in Jaffa, but their presence had made no impact on the Arab quality of the city. The streets remained narrow and crowded, twisting their way from port to hillside. Sanitary systems failed routinely, and orange rinds and eggshells floated in stagnant pools. At day's end the melodic voice of the muezzin summoned the faithful to prayer while observant Jews scurried into the small synagogues hidden within the crumbling buildings that bordered narrow alleys. He had brought his family to live in a Jewish land but now they made their home in an Arab enclave. The open-air market encroached upon their shops and businesses, and Jewish children hurried through narrow streets to avoid the Arab youths who taunted them and the beggars who plucked at their sleeves. Jaffa was Arab by virtue of history and tradition. The newly arrived Jews, Langerfeld knew, would have to find new alternatives.

Ruppin's voice held the ring of truth; he spoke of viable options. Nechama's father did not hesitate; at the first meeting he wrote a draft on his account in the Anglo-Palestine Bank and became a member of the Achuzat Bayit cooperative. In return he received a formal deed with many ornately scripted signatures in both Hebrew and Arabic. It confirmed that he owned a plot on the strip of sand optimistically designed as number eighteen Herzl Street in the municipality of Tel Aviv.

Proudly, he had taken Ezra, Nechama, and Amos to see the location of his new home. They stood upon a sand dune. Amos kicked at a piece of driftwood and bent to pluck up a glinting bit of rose-colored sea glass.

"Are we almost there?" he asked his grandfather.

"We are there," the old man said. "This is number eighteen Herzl Street."

The boy looked up and down the stretch of beach. Sand dunes rolled before him in lunar landscape. He listened to the breaking of the waves and the whisper of the wind through the coarse dune grass. A lone sycamore tree cast its triangular shadow across the sands where a group of Arab fishermen hovered over a fire brewing coffee in a copper feenjan. Silvery fish writhed in their nets. A gull swooped down above them, shrieked hideously, and sailed westward in a whir of massive white wings.

"And over there, I suppose, is number ten," Ezra said facetiously, pointing to the fire.

Isaac Langerfeld consulted his map.

"No," he said solemnly, "that is number eight."

"It is ridiculous to build a city on a beachhead when the Galilee must be reclaimed," Ezra said bitterly to Nechama that night.

"Not everyone wants to be a farmer," Nechama remonstrated. "You sound like your father, who thinks that all of Zion should be built on Rishon LeZion."

"I am not like my father," Ezra said sharply.

"I like Grandpa Yehuda," Amos said and hastily added, "but I like Grandpa Isaac too . . ." He had learned early that he must always balance uneasily on the seesaw of family affections, distributing his weight carefully, tipping over neither into one camp nor the other.

On the day the cornerstone of the new city was laid, Amos found an ocher-colored bit of pottery in the sand. He fondled it as he listened to the speeches—to Meir Dizengoff's impassioned pleas for peace in the new city, to Arthur Ruppin's scholarly address in pedantic Hebrew calling for a modern Jewish society which would function in a modern city.

"You are privileged to participate in history in the making, to share in the future," the German Jew told the small audience.

Amos wrapped his pottery in a bit of chamois cloth and put it carefully away. It was a talisman of the past that he had unearthed that day when men gathered on the beach to dream of the future.

Isaac Langerfeld had sent frequent letters to Nechama, describing the swift progress of the new city. A name had been decided upon. It was definitely to be called Tel Aviv after the title which Nachum Sokolov had given to the Hebrew translation of Herzl's novel *Altneuland*, but Isaac Langerfeld, merchant and Bible scholar, added that the name Tel Aviv appeared in the writings of the prophet Ezekiel. "Then I came to tell them of the captivity of Tel Aviv," the prophet had said. An emblem was chosen for the new city—a lighthouse with a gate.

"This is symbolic of the city as a gateway to the land of Israel," Isaac Langerfeld wrote optimistically.

"Does he think that many people will actually come and make their homes on the sand dunes?" Ezra asked harshly. "They expect that coven of houses on a beach to be the gateway to Israel?"

"How large was Rishon when your family arrived?" Nechama countered.

"We came to be pioneers on the land. We did not come here to work in shops. We did not build a ghetto and live behind its walls."

"Tel Aviv will not be a ghetto," Nechama replied firmly, suppressing her anger. She had schooled herself to ignore the veiled contempt her husband's family felt for those who had arrived in the country after them and who dared to think that there was a way of life besides that of the farmer. As the oldest child of a large family, she had learned early that peace was sometimes achieved through silence, that argument seldom led to agreement.

Saul and David, during their visits to Sadot Shalom, spoke bitterly about the way in which the city was being built. Both the Shomer and the kibbutz movement had sent letters of protest to the Jewish National Fund.

"They call it a Jewish city," David said, "but even the foundation stone was set by non-Jewish labor."

"Jewish carpenters wanted the joinery jobs but Ruppin is only interested in completing the city as soon as possible. The *yekke* bastard claims it doesn't make any difference who does the work," Saul added.

He shared the kibbutznik's disdain for the small group of German Jewish bureaucrats who administered the affairs of the Palestinian Jewish colony. The officials of the Zionist organization were, for the most part, fastidious men who polished their rimless spectacles with snow-white linen handkerchiefs and wore their cravats neatly knotted beneath their chins and their jackets scrupulously buttoned even on days when the desert wind, the *sharav*, breathed its fiery breath across the land. Those neat, tight jackets had earned them the nickname *yekke*, a derivative of the German word for jacket. Saul, David, and Ezra, in their farmer's open-necked shirts and loose mud-spattered work pants, viewed the city dwellers' dress with the hostility of soldiers in one army who contemplate the unfamiliar uniforms of an opposing force.

"It will be very sad if Jews argue with each other simply because one wears a tie and the other doesn't," Nechama said mildly. "We will have to learn to live in peace on this land—Russian and German, Yemenite and Englishman, city dweller and farmer—Jew and Arab."

"Please. Spare me your lecture on tolerance, dear sister-in-law," David said. His calloused hand flew to the black patch that covered his eye. He touched the pistol at his waist. Never, since the night of the revia, had he gone anywhere without a gun. It was said that Arab children hid behind cactus plants when he galloped down the road and Bedouin shepherds automatically lifted their arms to show him that they had no weapon.

"I would not presume to be your teacher, David," Nechama said, and her brother-in-law smiled.

He did not understand Ezra's tall pale wife but he liked her. Not many women would have had the courage to live alone on a Galilee farm so many kilometers from the nearest Jewish settlement. It was too bad there had been no more children to break their loneliness. But she had done a wonderful job teaching Amos. The boy's store of knowledge startled his uncles. He knew history and geography, literature and poetry. He reminded David of Ezra as a child.

"There is no shortage of teachers in your father's city, Nechama," Ezra said, seeking to appease her. "They have built a school. Gymnasia Herzliah, they call it. It stands at the end of Herzl Street."

"What kind of a school?" Amos asked. "A school like the one father went to in Rishon? A yeshiva like the one you all went to in Kharkov?" He had known only his parents' tutelage and he was fascinated by the idea of formal education. It would be wonderful to trade ideas with other boys, to share questions with teachers, to discuss new concepts. It was true that he and Achmed talked about many things, but Achmed was mainly interested in science, in the way things were born and grew. Ezra had given the Arab boy agronomy texts, and occasionally he shared journals on animal husbandry with him. But Amos wanted to discuss history and philosophy, language and literature.

"No. The school in Rishon taught all grades, and in the

yeshiva we learned only Torah and Talmud. This is a proper secondary school where they teach literature and mathematics, science and language.''

''And archaeology?'' Amos asked.

''I suppose so. They say that the headmaster, Ben Yehuda, has a great interest in ancient history.''

Amos thought about the school as he rode toward Tel Aviv with his parents.

''Do you think the school is near Grandfather Isaac's house?'' he asked his mother.

''I should imagine it's very near. Surely you will be able to walk there and see it,'' Nechama replied.

''You must be sure to take long walks, Amos,'' Ezra said. ''I don't want you to spend the whole summer indoors with your eyes glued to a book.''

Nechama darted a cautionary look at him but it was too late. His lips trembled and blood spots stood on his pale cheeks. Somehow, by being himself, he had betrayed his father, who wanted a son who would scamper gladly through the fields and work diligently at his side. He did not answer Ezra but stared straight ahead, watching the coast road narrow as they approached the outskirts of the newborn city.

Children perched on the stone fences that lined the streets and watched the passersby who thronged the narrow thoroughfare. Housewives sat on the verandas of their newly built stucco houses and chatted quietly. The first cool of evening had descended, and cobalt shadows settled on the red-tiled mansard roofs, but many of the women who strolled through the street kept their umbrellas open, as though the sun had merely teased them by reclining for a brief period. The men clustered in groups in front of the houses that smelled of newly poured cement and fresh coats of paint. Tel Avivians, these first citizens of a brand new city, took proprietary walks each evening, observing progress, marking innovations. They argued over whether the box-shaped houses with their large square front windows were more suited to the beach landscape than the rectangular dwellings with their arched Moorish porticos. Householders hovered over small rectangles of parched grass and tended tiny saplings.

Several strollers waved to the Maimons as their wagon lumbered down the street.

''Langerfeld's daughter,'' some said.

"Maimon's son," others murmured.

The Jews of Palestine were linked by an almost incestuous intimacy. They spoke in a eclectic shorthand, dozens of stories and relationships concentrated in each name, sparkling associations and anecdotes, personal histories and interfamilial connections. There was a fraternal quality to their quarrels, a communal sharing of their joys. They traveled through the country trading scraps of news.

Homesteaders in the Galilee played host to Jewish youths from Jerusalem whom they had never seen before. More than once Amos has shared his room with children vaguely identified as the cousin of a Rishon friend, the schoolmate of a Jerusalem acquaintance. Hospitality was anticipated and extended. All Jews in the country were united to fight their isolation in the land they vaguely dreamed of making their own. But in the new Jewish city of Tel Aviv, that isolation was vanquished.

"Shalom!" they called to Ezra and Nechama as the Sadot Shalom wagon raised clouds of dust.

"*Baruch HaBa*. Welcome."

Pride rang in their voices, and they gestured to their houses and stood beneath the fragile sapling that, at high noon, cast narrow ribs of shade across the sun-drenched street.

Isaac Langerfeld had built his house on stone stilts by a triad of beach pines that cast mysterious shadows across the tiled roof and littered the ·sand-strewn path with fine dark needles. The salt scent of the sea and the freshness of sweet pine filled the wide-windowed front room. Nechama's mother drew damp cloths across the ocher-colored tile floors several times a day, but whenever the door opened, sand flew through the room and coated the floor and furniture. Coarse coatings of grit flew into their food and settled on the bed linen.

"It will not always be like this," Reb Langerfeld assured them confidently. "The sands will settle, and we will build over them with concrete and wood. The trees will help. We are planting many trees in Tel Aviv."

Ezra recognized the longing in his father-in-law's voice that matched his own family's wistfulness. They had grown up in the forest lands of Europe. Their youth had been spent in the shade of great trees, amid greenery and overgrowth. Their eyes thirsted for the landscape they had left behind. Their vision was parched by the beachhead and deserts of Palestine, and their skin was cracked by the harsh sunlight and the unrelenting winds that blew up from the southland. Ezra knew, although Yehuda had never told him so (and would not give him the satisfaction of knowing), that his parents were drawn to visit Sadot Shalom with increasing frequency because of the verdancy of the Galilean hillsides.

"It is remarkable what has been accomplished in such a short time," Ezra told his father-in-law.

"Yes. We have over a hundred buildings now. And our school, of course," the merchant said.

"Yes. The school. Gymnasia Herzliah. An ambitious name for a small provincial academy."

His sarcasm was lost on his father-in-law.

"But the Gymnasia Herzliah is no ordinary academy. Our teachers, some of them, have the qualifications of university professors, and students come to study there from all over the country—even from Europe. Even now we are building a new dormitory. I often think that it would be a wonderful place for Amos to study."

"Nechama and I teach Amos," Ezra said abruptly. "We manage very well. But I agree that the building is impressive."

They had driven past the school which bordered the end of Herzl Street. Twin minarets towered above its main entrance, and the two side wings were built of sunset-colored stone and brick. The finest Arab masons had been engaged to carve the arch-shaped doors and windows and to add the balconies and crenelated peaks that decorated the structure. Young date palms shaded the walkways, their slender trunks protected by wooden frames. The caretaker's camel knelt in the courtyard and brayed at a group of students who walked past, their heads bent close together in earnest conference. Ezra and Nechama had laughed at the camel but Amos had stared after the boys who carried their books in green canvas bags and cast long shadows across the cobbled path.

"The building is not important," said Reb Langerfeld. "What is important is that the school will produce scholars able to go on to university and become learned men."

"Learned men and scholars will not build farms and drain swamps," Ezra said sharply. "And that is what the country needs."

"The country needs many things, different things," his father-in-law replied.

Ezra did not answer. There was an echolalic note to the

argument that wearied him. What was it about these European
Jews—his father, his father-in-law—that led them to dream of
academies and libraries, of sheepskin documents and leatherbound books? He too loved learning and studying, but how
could such a life compare with the challenge of the land? No
bit of dry parchment could match the glory of a golden crop
in full bloom, of serried rows of pale green grain growing
where once only rock and earth had been. Surely Amos, the
child of the fields, would see that.

He turned to his son, who stood with Nechama at the open
window listening to the sounds of Beethoven's violin con-
certo streaming forth from the window of a neighboring
bungalow.

"That is Hopenko, the violinist," Isaac Langerfeld said.
"He always practices at this hour but usually he saves the
Beethoven for last."

Nechama smiled. There was nothing that the citizens of Tel
Aviv did not know about each other. They shared their secrets
and hurried from one house to the other with steaming pots of
food and bowls of fruit. They shouted their news from open
windows, and children dashed through entryways without
bothering to knock. She had noticed that they built fences in
front of their yards and not between them.

"We will come for you before Rosh HaShana," Ezra told
Amos the next morning. "Listen to your grandparents and try
to help them. Write to your mother. She will be lonely and
she'll worry." He did not speak of his own loneliness and the
worry that haunted him whenever he thought of his son.

"Yes, Abba."

They stood together on the sunswept street, man and boy,
father and son, searching for words. Silence stretched between
them and Amos, ashamed, felt tears fill his eyes.

"Now, why are you crying?" Ezra asked irritably. "If you
don't want to stay, come home with us."

"No. It is not that." The boy's voice quivered.

"Then what is it?" He struggled to contain his impatience.

"I don't like to say goodbye."

"It's only for a few weeks," Ezra said gently.

He moved closer to his son and touched Amos's shoulders.
How tall the lad had grown. In another year he would be bar
mitzvah. They would hold the celebration at Sadot Shalom,
invite all of Gan Noar, the entire countryside.

"Shalom, Amos."

He hugged his son and was startled because his own eyes were wet with tears, and there was an odd tremor in his fingers when he tightened the horse's reins.

But Nechama did not weep when she embraced her son.

"Remember, Amos, you are almost bar mitzvah," she said. "Only you can make decisions about your own life. Only you can know what it is that you want to do. I want only what will make you happy. And so does your father. Yes. So does your father."

She looked hard at her son and reached out a finger to gently lift a teardrop from the boy's cheek. Her arms were strong about Amos's quivering body but she did not look back as they drove away.

Two weeks later the Arab letter carrier brought a letter from Amos to Sadot Shalom. Amos had arranged for a meeting with the headmaster of the gymnasia, and despite his youth he had been accepted into the first form. His grandparents had invited him to live with them. Would Ezra give his permission?

Ezra passed the letter to Nechama, who read it and stretched it between them on the table.

"Did you know of this?" he asked her.

"No. Of course not. But it does not surprise me."

"It does not surprise you," he repeated, and she blanched at the pain and accusation in his eyes. She would not argue with him although hurt and misery congealed in a painful weight against her heart.

"What do you say?" she asked.

"My son is not my prisoner. He must do as he pleases."

A strange harshness distorted his voice, and he strode out the door so swiftly that Achmed, on his way to the house to ask for news of Amos, scurried off the path, frightened by the thin set of Ezra Maimon's lips and the anger in his sea-green eyes.

Chapter 17

On Amos Maimon's first birthday Nechama had planted a fig tree in the southwest corner of the garden. Through the passing years, the tree flourished. Its foliage thickened and, in season, the evening wind wafted the street scent of the slowly maturing fruit across the veranda and into their bedroom windows. When the pink flesh of the fruit shimmered through the delicate green skin, Ezra would reach through the open window and pluck two or three figs. He and Nechama would eat them as they lay naked on their bed, allowing the juice to flow in sticky trickles down breast and thigh. Once a bit of cyclamen-colored pulp settled on Nechama's pale umber nipple. Ezra licked it off and crunched the sweet fruit.

He had loved the tree and pruned it carefully. It had been a favorite private play place for Amos and Achmed when they were young boys. Here, they had spread their primers and picture books, their chess and Shesh-Besh boards. "Amos's tree," they called it, and Amos, in his letters home from Tel Aviv, occasionally referred to it. Had there been many figs this year? he wondered, and had his parents shared the fruit with Achmed's mother, Hulda? She made a sweeet preserve, and Amos had told the boys in his form about it. Some of the students who had come from Germany and Poland had never seen a fig before. Their ignorance astounded Amos and he wanted them to taste Hulda's jam.

"Does he think we have nothing to do but cook preserves for him and make parcels?" Ezra grumbled, but in the end he carried the basket of fruit to the Arab's house, collected the jarred delicacy, and posted it himself to the Langerfeld home in Tel Aviv.

Nechama noticed that Ezra spent a long time visiting with Saleem's family, and she suspected that he had been talking to Achmed. Amos's friend was a tall youth now, and although he worked in the fields with his father each day, he spent his evenings reading. Nechama sometimes watched him from her veranda, her eyes fixed to the bottled candle that glowed to give him light as he studied. Like Ezra, Achmed was fascinated by the secrets of the earth. He drew delicate diagrams of root formations. He experimented with fertilizer, expanding on the concepts outlined in a pamphlet on agricultural chemistry issued by the Alliance. As a result of his work, the alfalfa crop was almost doubled and the corn, always a weak crop on Sadot Shalom, grew thick and firm. Erza offered him a stallion to replace the pony but Achmed, shyly but insistently, asked for a bonus in dinars.

"But what will you do with the money?" Ezra asked.

"I am saving to go to school," Achmed said. "I want to study agronomy." He turned his eyes away as though fearful that Ezra might mock him.

Ezra opened an account in Achmed's name at the Anglo-Palestine Bank and wrote a letter to the agricultural institute, asking if the school would admit a promising Arab youth.

The leaves of the fig tree spread an umbrella of shade in the sunny garden and often, on summer afternoons, Nechama sat outside on a canvas chair, sequestered within their small dim island, until it was cool enough to return once again to the fields. At intervals, Ezra sliced at a wild vine that wandered up the slender trunk, and when a visiting child from Gan Noar rammed the wheelbarrow against "Amos's tree," Ezra tended the gash gently, searing the wood with tar so that the bark would grow together.

On the morning after Amos's bar mitzvah, a ceremony that was held in his grandfather Langerfeld's Tel Aviv synagogue rather than at Sadot Shalom (because, as Amos had written so reasonably, his friends and teachers were in Tel Aviv, that location was more convenient for the Rishon family, and he felt that the Jewish city was the place where he had studied and learned all that he would include in the service), Nechama woke to the sound of steel against wood. She hurried to the window. In the pale light of dawn, Ezra heaved his axe in rhythmic stroke against the tree. Dark green sap bled from the harsh wide wound. The tree was in flower, and the starlike blossoms trembled and dropped with snowy lightness on Ezra's dark hair. Impatiently, he swept them away, and they settled in snowy foliage on the coarse grass. Sweat showed in damp half-moons beneath his arms but he continued to beat at the tree without breaking pace. The severed trunk trembled, swayed dangerously.

"Ezra, what are you doing? Why are you cutting down Amos's tree?" The words tumbled out clumsily; sorrow thickened her tongue.

He did not look up as he answered.

"It didn't give enough shade. I will plant a date palm here, or a cypress. And it is no longer Amos's tree. Is this Amos's home?"

She understood then, at last, the depth of his hurt. She had sensed it, of course, but Ezra had acquiesced so quietly to all of Amos's suggestions. He had raised no objection to the celebration of the bar mitzvah in Tel Aviv although Nechama had read the disappointment in his eyes at the phrasing of Amos's letter. The boy had written with the ingenuous frankness of the very young. "Tel Aviv and the Gymnasia Herzliah are really the center of my life . . . I study here, so it seems only natural and more convenient for everyone . . . Grandpa Langerfeld says that Achmed can stay here with us . . ."

"I'm sure Achmed will be very comfortable," Ezra had said harshly, sliding the letter back to Nechama.

In the end Achmed had not gone because an interview was arranged with the director of the agricultural school. No Arab boy had ever applied for admission, the director wrote to Ezra, but if this Achmed ibn-Saleem was qualified and prepared to study at a Jewish school and if Ezra Maimon was prepared to pay the annual school fee, the director could see no problem. Ezra read the letter to Achmed and Saleem.

"The tuition is no problem. You will earn more than that

as your harvest wages at Sadot Shalom. But it is a Jewish school," he said gravely.

"Why should that trouble me?" Achmed asked.

He had lived all his life among Jews. Amos was his dearest friend, his brother. Ezra Maimon had always behaved like a benevolent uncle to him. Achmed spoke Hebrew fluently and read it with ease. He saw no conflict, no difficulty. Ezra and Saleem exchanged glances above the boy's head and looked quickly away from each other. Achmed's casual optimism shamed them.

Nechama had left the farm several days before the bar mitzvah to help her mother with the cooking, and Ezra moved through the house aimlessly, pausing at windows and doorways, snatching a meal without sitting down in the empty kitchen. How had it happened, he wondered, that he who had seen himself living at the center of a large family, building a farm for generations to come, was alone now in this house? His bedroom echoed with the sighs of gentle lovemaking. The lemon scent of Nechama's soap clung to the bedclothes. He slept in the living room while she was away.

He wandered into Amos's room, plucked a book from the shelf, looked at it incuriously and replaced it. Amos's small bed was neatly made. The narrow wooden shelf which Ezra had carved for the boy's archaeological finds was strangely depleted. On each of Amos's brief visits home, he had snatched up one or another treasure saying, "Oh, this one I must show to Yossi. And this one Dr. Ben Yehuda especially asked to see." Slowly, he removed the small artifacts of his life from Sadot Shalom. Ezra took up the reed pipe which Achmed had carved for his friend. He blew on it but no sound came. Dust had settled into the open note holes, and an intrepid spider had woven a web at the instrument's mouth.

Occasionally, on those long and lonely nights, Ezra could no longer bear the silence of his house. He would saddle his horse and gallop swiftly across the fields. Hulda and Saleem, hearing the hoofbeats reverberate through the nocturnal silence, looked at each other sadly.

"He is alone," the Arab said sadly.

He could not fathom the emptiness of the Jew's life. He was a member of a tribe, a man of a family. Seven children had followed Achmed into their lives, dark-eyed olive-skinned boys and girls. There was life in his house. He did not wander through lonely rooms. He turned to Hulda in the darkness, pressed himself against her milk-full breasts, kissed the pale flower of skin where once a spurt of cooking oil had scalded her.

The bar mitzvah was held in the small synagogue on the newly built Rothschild Boulevard. Amos read his Torah portion with resounding voice and Ezra, who stood at his side, noticed that although his son moved the silver *yad*, the pointer, across the yellowed parchment, he did not follow the reading with his eyes. He knew each verse by heart and knew, too, every interpretation that could be offered to explain the reading. His voice was strong and sweet, and he sang the prophetic portion in perfect melody, never faltering.

There was an appreciative release of breath when he finished, and the men and women of the congregation looked proudly and approvingly at each other, as though each worshiper were somehow responsible for the bright-haired boy's achievement. Most of them had been born in Europe and struggled to acquire a reasonable command of Hebrew. It was a small miracle to them that Hebrew was the first language, the natural birthright, of Amos Maimon.

The white woolen prayer shawl—purchased by a Langerfeld uncle in the neighborhood of the Hundred Gates in Jerusalem, where the Orthodox huddled in ancient warrens—was draped about his slender shoulders. A blue skullcap, richly embroidered by a skilled Yemenite needlewoman, perched on his golden curls, and Ezra remembered how the son of Gedalia had brought the infant Amos just such a head covering as a circumcision gift thirteen years ago. The years had whirled past them; and he was startled at their swift and soundless passage. He felt like a runner poised to sprint in a race that, mysteriously, was almost over. He was unprepared for Amos's ascent into manhood, unprepared and bitter at the choices his son had made. The boy's voice rang clear in the quiet synagogue but the worshipers hunched forward in the rough-hewn pews to hear his address. He was of a new generation, and they listened to him as though he were a youthful prophet who would lead them into a new era.

"I am proud to celebrate my bar mitzvah in Tel Aviv," Amos said. "I am proud to be the first in my family to be born in the land and to be bar mitzvahed in a Jewish city."

And would he not have been proud, Ezra thought, to have

celebrated his bar mitzvah on the farm that his father had wrested from the wilderness? Ezra listened stoically but his son's words became pellets of hurt, aimed at his own failure, his own vulnerability.

"I am proud to have had the privilege of studying at the Gymnasia Herzliah," Amos continued, casting a look at the headmaster, Ben Yehuda, who sat with other members of the faculty.

Nechama avoided Ezra's eyes. The boy was young. Young people were insensitive, self-absorbed. Amos could not know how that gaze of appreciation wounded Ezra, nor did it mean that he was not grateful to his father. She would explain. Ezra would understand.

"I want my teachers to know that I have decided to emulate their example. I will spend my life studying the history of our land, exploring the mysteries of our ancient heritage so that we will better understand the gift of Zion."

The audience murmured approvingly. Such a brilliant boy. Only just bar mitzvahed and already in correspondence with some of the country's leading archaeologists. In some subjects he was two years ahead of his form. And so handsome, so blond, although both of his parents were dark-haired. It was a shame there were no other children. Poor Maimon. It seemed he had built that prosperous farm to no purpose. Such a boy would never farm. It must be lonely for them all alone up there in the Galilee.

Nechama heard the whispered comments. She watched her husband and son stand together before the open ark for the service of replacing the Torah. They shook hands. Other fathers and sons embraced at such a moment.

She and Ezra returned to the farm alone. Amos had promised to visit at semester's end but she knew that his visit would be unsatisfactory.

Ezra swung the axe with sudden fierceness. The fig tree cracked and fell. Sorrow plucked at her and she turned from the window. She said nothing to Ezra, who, a few days later, planted a stately avocado tree beside the battered stump.

Ezra had changed, and the knowledge filled her with a sense of her own failure and with misery at the thought of the careful deception she had practiced for so many years. They had dreamed of many children, and there had been only the one child who had left them too soon and would never return.

Loneliness festered within Ezra Maimon like a recalcitrant virus. The sweet, companionable, quiet hours of their marriage became vacuous stretches of silence. Tension stretched between them, uneasily elasticized and strained by all that they could not and would not say to each other. She chastised herself for never having told him of the doctor's warning, but the time for truth had passed. She tried instead to talk to him about Amos, choosing her words carefully, modulating her tone into an anesthetizing evenness.

"Why do you blame Amos? You also left your father's house and chose your own life."

"I waited. I was a grown man. And I did my duty first."

He remembered bitterly the years of waiting and working on the Rishon farm. He had paid his dues. Amos had never even recognized the debt.

The awkward silence between them was broken by the visits of friends who came to stay at Sadot Shalom for brief periods. In worried tones they discussed the situation in Europe and how it would affect Palestine. Germany was arming, gathering allies about her. Austria naturally stood with her Teutonic neighbor, and their war guns would be aimed at France and England.

"Russia will come into it," Ezra Maimon predicted gloomily.

"Perhaps not."

Their guests from Tel Aviv and Jerusalem looked out at the calm Galilean landscape. How fortunate the Maimons were to live here, amid this splendid beauty. They sucked the juice of the peaches Nechama laid before them and gazed at the orchard where the fruit had grown.

"Wasn't there a fig tree here?"

"We replaced it with an avocado. It did not give enough shade."

She avoided Ezra's eyes and fanned the flame of conversation.

"Where will Turkey stand in such a war?" she asked.

"That is uncertain."

The men tamped their pipes, blew smoke rings. Tobacco was the newest agricultural craze in the country. Every settlement had its plantation of wide, dark-leafed plants. Young men and women packed and cured the leaves with great care but the crop was not a successful one. It was nonsense, Ezra thought, to compete with the Arabs in producing a crop they had grown successfully for so many years. The Jewish farmers were skilled at citriculture, at vegetable crops, at chicken farming and breeding. At Gan Noar they had even developed an artificially stocked carp pond. Why then should they bother with a competitive and uncertain crop? The only tobacco on Sadot Shalom grew on Saleem's plot, for his own use.

"Some think it would be good for us if Turkey went in with Germany," a Rishon friend said. "The Russian settlers still remember the Czar and his pogroms. If Russia is on the side of France and England, the Jewish farmers of Rishon will be for Germany and against Russia."

"How can you talk of war? Peace is the only sensible answer. We must all work for peace and forget these ancient hatreds," Amos protested. He was spending his holiday on Sadot Shalom, reading Gibbon deep into the night.

"Ancient?" Ezra's tone was frigid. Only ten years had passed since the vicious Kishinev pogroms of 1903. A yearly candle for his grandparents still burned in their kitchen, and a memorial ad appeared in the pages of *HaAchdut*, the journal of the Workers of Zion movement. "But of course, I forget. You are part of the new generation. You received the gift of Zion on a silver tray."

Bitterly, he paraphrased Amos's bar mitzvah speech. The boy did not reply but his eyes drifted to the southwest corner of the garden where once his fig tree had stood. He left Sadot Shalom the next morning although he had planned to spend another week on the farm.

Nechama's brother Daniel Langerfeld visited them.

"I have assurances that Turkey will remain neutral," he said.

He sat on the council of the Zionist Federation in Jerusalem, and he was traveling north to Syria. The federation had commissioned him to affirm the loyalty of the Jewish community to the Turkish government.

He planned to meet in Damascus with Djemal Pasha, the military commander of Syria and Palestine, and a Jerusalem tailor had fashioned him a new dark serge suit for the occasion.

"If a country plans to remain neutral, they do not mobilize," Nechama said.

She was thinking of a recent visit to Gan Noar and the new group of arrivals at the kibbutz who told of passing through Constantinople. The streets of the Turkish capital were filled with troops, they said, and their own voyage to Palestine had been delayed by two weeks because freighters were being commandeered by the Turkish navy and loaded with arms and equipment. Food was scarce in the marketplace as Turkish housewives hoarded their staples. Crews of German sailors milled about the harbor, and Turkish and German naval officers mingled at dockside saloons and made joint visits to the whorehouses that lined the piers.

"Perhaps the sick man of Europe is merely trying to get a blood transfusion from its lusty German cousin," Ezra said.

Nechama, who followed the war news as closely as he did, was dismayed by his cynicism. A brittle negativism colored all Ezra's thinking these days. When Turkey finally tipped over to the German side, he ridiculed those who had believed in the possibility of neutrality.

"What does your brother say now?" he asked Nechama derisively.

Daniel Langerfeld had not fulfilled his mission to visit Djemal Pasha. His smartly cut suit had been stolen by a customs official, and the Zionist Council of Damascus had warned him that the military governor embraced a radical Turkish nationalism and had vowed to suppress all minority groups in Palestine. Ezra derived a perverse pleasure from his brother-in-law's failure. Deep within himself, he blamed the Langerfelds for the loss of Amos. Still, he listened soberly when Daniel quoted from Djemal Pasha.

"The Jews are a cancer in the country's side," the Turk had proclaimed in a public address. "They cause all unhappiness in the Middle East."

"I wonder," Ezra said, "who would they blame for the ills of the world, for poverty and war and unemployment, if there were no Jews around?"

He was bitter when David Ben Gurion and Yitzhak Ben Zvi, his brothers' comrades in the Shomer, who had so often sat on the Sadot Shalom veranda, petitioned the Turkish authorities for a Jewish militia to share in the defense of the country. That same petition was signed by students at the Gymnasia Herzliah, Amos Maimon among them.

"Can't they read the future?" Ezra asked. "The Turks are

finished here. They will lose the war and they will lose Palestine. It will pass to the English, and then perhaps there will be hope for us. It is a great pity that the wonderful gymnasia has not given my son a better grasp of international politics, so that his farmer father must explain it to him.''

"Everyone is entitled to an opinion," Nechama said mildly.

"And every Jew in Palestine appears to have one," Ezra retorted. "Including you, my dear wife.''

She looked at him calmly but as she turned the pages of her book, her hand trembled. Her face burned and the tips of her fingers tingled. His anger and sarcasm, nurtured by loneliness, was indiscriminate now. It flashed out at unexpected moments, like the swift querulous storms of late fall. Small things irritated him. He was annoyed because she left an unwashed mug in the sink, because he could not find his work shirt, because she misplaced his copy of an agricultural journal. He tried to bait her into small scenes but seldom succeeded. Her priority was calm and peace, and she paid for it with submission and a subdued sadness.

Now and again, she awoke in the night trembling with fear. All that they had built together was in danger. They might live their lives side by side on this beautiful farm as strangers, locked into disappointments and resentments they would not articulate. Once, she awakened and found that he had left their bed. She went to the window and saw him riding his horse across the fields, his head bent low to the horse's ears. What secrets was he imparting to the chestnut steed, she wondered, and her eyes filled with tears at the thought of the loneliness that had driven him from their bed to ride alone through the moist, fragrant night.

Only on Gan Noar, playing with his brothers' children, did he seem relaxed. She watched him toss a ball to Saul's daughter Dahlia. He showed David's son, Joshua, how to tie a slip knot. The boy was successful at his first effort. Ezra smiled his approval. Saul's son, Elisha, was equally dexterous.

"When your cousin Amos was your age, I tried to teach him," he said, "but Amos could not get the hang of it." He kept a careful account. Never would he forget the many times Amos had disappointed him.

Nechama wandered away and joined her sisters-in-law, who were sorting linen.

"Why so many sheets?" she asked.

"We want to be prepared," Mirra said. "If the cities are in danger, the Jewish children will be sent to the kibbutzim. Of course, you don't have to worry, Nechama. Amos is old enough to take care of himself, but it will be hard for the mothers of small children."

"No, I don't have to worry," she said, and ignored the reproving look Chania shot Mirra.

Nechama and Ezra rode back to Sadot Shalom in silence. Halfway there, a lightening storm broke through the heat-drenched night, and as she watched the silver bolts streak across the sky, ripping at the velvet darkness, she thought that her own heart must resemble the nightscape, riven by bolts of loneliness, of electric uncertainty.

The next week she journeyed to Tiberias. The Dutch doctor was still there, his hair thinner, his eyes sadder. He examined her carefully and conferred with her in a consulting room crowded with books and pamphlets in many languages. Two French brochures fluttered to his desk as he spoke to her. He played with them absently, his long fingers turning the pages, folding them in strips. He was returning to Holland. His mission here had failed, he knew. The Arab women brought their children to him for medicines and salves but they were uninterested in his lectures and advice. He did not want to be caught up in a war. He wanted to die in his own country, where windmills turned and soft rains pattered against peaceful canal waters. There was too much sunlight in this land, he told her petulantly, as though that were a problem she might solve. But he was not as pessimistic as Dr. Mazis had been about the results of a possible pregnancy.

"I would say that you do have a chance of carrying a healthy infant. But you would be much wiser not to attempt it. You do have a child, don't you?"

"Yes," she replied, and thought that she also had a husband and that slowly she was losing him.

"I would not advise it," he said finally, "but I do not see the situation as totally hopeless. You will be attended at the delivery by a doctor or a midwife?"

"Oh yes."

He shrugged and washed his hands. Outside the clinic door an infant wailed, and two women quarreled.

Two nights later, when Ezra put on his jacket and said that

he wanted to take a walk, she placed a restraining hand on his arm.

"Ezra," she said, "please."

He looked at her large dark eyes, moist now with desire. Her long black hair, shot through with silver strands, was plaited into a gleaming coronet, woven through with yellow buttercups that matched the long skirt with the dirndl that hugged her narrow waist. She was, he thought, as slender and beautiful now as the day he first saw her in the Jaffa bank. She blew out the candle on the cleared dinner table, and her long pale face was luminescent in the new darkness. She took his hand and together, not speaking, they walked into the bedroom.

He rode her that night with the inflamed gallop of sudden, inexplicable desire. His thighs were tremulous above her. His long loneliness, his secret anger, translated into passion and flooded her body. She felt the rush of hot semen and lifted her legs high in a wild dance so that it might thrust its way deep within her. When he kissed her he was startled to find that her face was wet with tears.

"Don't cry," he pleaded. "Please don't cry. I love you, Nechama. My love, my sweet."

Two months later she told him that she was certain she was pregnant.

"Nechama."

Wonder filled him, melted his heart. Gently he lifted her into his arms and carried her onto the bed.

"You must be careful," he said. "Very careful."

"Not to worry." Her voice was fuzzy with tiredness. She had forgotten how exhausted she became during pregnancy. "We will be fine. Fine."

She slept then, and he remained by her side although it was the season of sowing and Saleem and Achmed were in the field, singing a plaintive Arab melody as they scattered the seed into the deeply dug furrows of his rich earth.

Chapter 18

Throughout the long summer, visitors to Sadot Shalom carried delicacies to the pregnant Nechama and speculated, as they sat in the garden, about the international situation. Rumors fluttered about like the nervous colorful butterflies that hovered over her flower beds. Javid Bey, the Turkish minister of finance, made impassioned antiwar speeches which were duly noted in Palestine. Turkey would never move in opposition to that powerful politician, Yehuda Maimon said smugly. His opinion was strongly supported by the Yiddish newspaper which his brother Mendel sent to him from America. One month later Javid Bey was out of office, and several Turkish district officers in Palestine who had supported him had mysteriously disappeared.

Germany offered the warships *Breslau* and *Goeben* to the Turkish navy.

"If they accept them, it is as good as announcing an alliance," predicted Amos, who was visiting the farm.

"You are right," Ezra replied. This time Amos's perspicacity pleased him. One could not deny the boy's brilliance, his unusual insights.

He walked with his son in the cool of the evening. Nechama watched them, pleased because there had been a surcease in tension between Amos and Ezra. The child within her stirred lazily, shifted position. She smiled. The discomfort pleased her.

"Amos," Ezra said, "could you spend this fall at Sadot Shalom? I do not like to leave your mother so alone at this time."

"You mean miss a school term?"

"Yes."

Disappointment darkened Amos's face. His father's approval would be dearly bought. A seminar in archaeology had been organized for the fall term. Instruction in the Greek language was being offered for the first time. He had already purchased the texts.

"If you want me to—if you think it is the right thing to do . . ." he said hesitantly.

"Good boy!" Ezra pounded his shoulders.

But Nechama would not hear of it. Lose an entire semester? Ridiculous. She felt fine, managed well. It was enough that Amos would spend the summer. Ezra watched his son through narrowed eyes and saw relief flood the boy's face. It took little enough to dissuade him.

"I don't want to upset Imma," Amos offered apologetically. "She wants me to return to my studies." But he turned from his father's steady gaze.

Daniel Langerfeld arrived again from Jerusalem. Nechama's brother carried with him cartons of hastily packed documents and sealed notebooks.

"What do these cartons contain?" Ezra asked. Daniel Langerfeld's self-important attitude annoyed him. It seemed to him that Nechama's entire family conceived of themselves as actors, waiting in the wings for their proper cues before they dashed out to play a role on the stage of history. Amos had caught their fever. Like the Langerfelds, his son did not converse or argue—he offered declamations.

"Important documents from the Zionist archives. The notebooks contain Eliezer Ben Yehuda's notes for another volume of his Hebrew dictionary. We managed to get Ben Yehuda himself out of the country. He's on his way to America now."

Ezra carried the cartons down to the basement and concealed them beneath blankets. It was, after all, the very least he could do. Others were taking more direct action to protect the Yishuv, the Jewish community in Palestine. It was rumored that at Zichron Yaakov a small group that included Aaron Aaronsohn and Absalom Feinberg were actually spying for the British. They flashed coded signals from the coast at night to waiting British warships. They were building collateral. The British would know that the Jews of Palestine were a resourceful and courageous ally.

Saul and David galloped into Sadot Shalom in the early hours of dawn. They had ridden through the night, and their faces were pale with fatigue and streaked with sweat. They pulled the Gan Noar sulky. The small cart was shrouded with blankets, and beneath the covering they saw the wide dark eyes of Joshua, David's son, peering at them.

"Is the child sick?" Nechama asked.

"No. But we told the Turkish cavalry who stopped us that he had a fever and we were carrying him south to a clinic," David said. "And the stupid bastards let us through without examining him for themselves."

His eyes flashed with scorn for his adversaries. He himself believed no one—relied on no one.

Gently, he lifted the boy from the cart and removed the blankets. Rifles and cartridges, pistols, and even a small cannon were packed into the small space.

"You see before you the entire arsenal of the Jewish watchmen," David said, his lips curved into a harsh smile. "All Jewish arms will be confiscated. The Turks have been searching the kibbutzim. We must hide them."

Ezra led them to the barn, which was stacked with neatly baled pyramids of hay. They ripped open the sweet-smelling pillows of dried grass and concealed the rifles within them. The pistols were buried in the gunny sacks of alfalfa and coarse wheat reserved for fodder. As they left the barn, David stared hard at Achmed, who watched them curiously from the doorway of his house. Ezra followed his brother's gaze and discerned his thought.

"I trust Achmed as I trust my own son," he said. He did not add that he would rely on Achmed as he could not rely on Amos.

"And I trust no one," David said, his fingers fluttering at the patch over his eye.

A thick and brutal heat settled over the lower Galilee during the early days of that wartime fall. Ezra drove Amos back to Tel Aviv for the new semester and returned to Sadot Shalom carrying all the newspapers he could find. Nechama read them carefully, sorrowfully, but without surprise. It had happened at last, as they had known it would. Turkey was at war, fighting England and France at the Egyptian, Iraqi, and Caucasian frontiers and at the Dardanelles. She studied the map carefully. The Middle East was a patchwork quilt of international interests, parochial fears, bizarre compromises. They had come here to farm, to study, to build, and they found themselves sitting on top of a volcano, caught between warring nations, a historic perversity over which they had little or no control. The child within her moved suddenly. The force of the fetal thrust dislodged the papers that rested on Nechama's abdomen. She smiled but Ezra's grim expression did not change.

"I'm worried," he said. "About you and the baby."

"But I feel fine," she protested. And it was the truth. She was enjoying this pregnancy. She felt infinitely better than she had felt when she carried Amos. She moved with energy. There was vigor in her step. She slept deeply for long hours and awakened feeling strong and refreshed.

"It is often like that with a second child," Hulda had said knowingly.

Nechama had nodded her agreement, but deep within herself she considered her strength and health to be a sign, a portent. This was a special child she was carrying, a miracle baby who would renew their marriage, revitalize their lives. Joy filled her when the child moved, and she passed gentle hands across the growing mound of her abdomen. She had been right to risk the pregnancy. There had been no other choice.

"I'm worried also about what will happen in the country," Ezra continued. "I saw a demonstration in Jaffa when I went to visit the Bakers."

"What sort of demonstration?" She controlled the anxiety in her voice. During her childhood, *demonstration* had been another word for *pogrom*, for fear-drenched nights and days spent hiding in a basement, listening to hate-filled shouting.

"Oh, just some yelling and pushing."

He did not want to frighten her by telling her of the Arabs who had suddenly thronged Tarshish Street as he rode by, brandishing swords that glinted in the harsh sunlight. They cut the air with wide swaths and shouted at the top of their voices.

"Our blades thirst for blood! God will protect the sultan."

One Arab youth had seized a bearded Jewish merchant by the arm and held his sword to the old man's throat.

"There is no room for you in Palestine," the Arab hissed. "Take your people and go."

The old man had stumbled forward and fled. His swiftly moving shadow marked his terror.

The Anglo-Palestine Bank closed its doors. Grimly, Ezra counted his assets. He had foreseen just such an eventuality and withdrawn most of his funds, advising his father to do the same. But Yehuda Maimon had insisted that nothing would happen.

"We must demonstrate our faith in the government," he had said.

The Turks, after all, were fighting the hated czar. Yehuda thought of applying for Ottoman citizenship, but on the afternoon he received the requested application, Turkish officers arrived at the Rishon farm.

"All Jewish property is confiscated," the mustachioed, booted officer said. His stomach bulged above the black leather belt at the waist of his scarlet uniform. Idly, with drawn sword, he sliced the head off Rivka's tallest sunflower and kicked at the fallen bloom with a polished boot. His foot soldiers wore ragged uniforms and unlaced combat shoes. Rheum dripped from their eyes. They moved through the orange groves plucking fruit from the branches. They carelessly peeled the juicy golden globes and tossed the half-eaten fruit away. A corporal took a machete and hacked at a network of burgeoning branches. Yehuda's heart turned. He had worked his groves for twenty-six years and now, within the space of minutes, they were snatched from him.

"Come, Yehuda."

Rivka's restraining hand was on his shoulder. She led him into the house and quickly packed a few bags. Once again she used the straw hamper and the purple portmanteau, faded now to a pale lilac. Once again they were refugees, leaving a home. They went to Gan Noar, where at least there were strong young Jews who could protect them.

Ezra was relieved to learn that his parents were no longer on the farm and were far enough away from the city to be out of reach of the Turks. Refugees, fleeing north, carried grim reports to Sadot Shalom. They spoke with hatred of Djemal Pasha, the Turkish commander-in-chief of Palestine. Ugly, inconceivable rumor became established fact. He had summoned Arthur Ruppin and told the director of the Jewish National Fund that so long as the Turks ruled Palestine, Jews would be victimized. Saul Maimon himself had been in Tel Aviv and had watched the Turk, his face red with anger, his neck muscles strained to bulging blue ropes, shout at Meir Dizengoff, the mayor of Tel Aviv, "I will hang you right inside that Tel Aviv of yours."

Another enemy of the Jewish community, Hassan Bek, the bowlegged plutocrat, was named the police chief of Jaffa. He walked the narrow streets slapping his leather bastinado against his hips. Strips of flesh, flayed from the bared feet of his prisoners, clung to the coarse thongs.

The municipal hospital was closed, the seaports were blockaded. The once-teeming port of Jaffa was empty, and it was impossible to purchase rice, kerosene, or sugar. Jews could no longer buy exemptions from military conscription. Ezra concealed a letter from Nechama's sister informing them that Reb Langerfeld had been pressed into service paving a roadway. Chaim Baker was thrown into a Jaffa jail because a random search of his hotel revealed several books of stamps issued by the Jewish National Fund. Nechama concealed their Jewish flag beneath a pile of linens. There was a death penalty for the possession of a Jewish flag.

Ezra worked harder than ever, concentrating on high-yield crops. Saleem worked beside him from earliest dawn until darkness fell. Jews and Arabs were starving throughout the country. Ezra's sisters-in-law at Gan Noar ran the communal kitchen on the single staple of maize grits.

"Things will get better," he assured Nechama. "This will pass."

Her father had used those same words during the pogroms at Kattowitz. Always Jews had hovered fearfully in corridors, waiting for threatening shadows to pass.

"Yes. I know."

She felt a nagging guilt because although they lived now through the most terrible time the country had known, she and Ezra had never been happier together. In the evenings he fashioned a cedarwood cradle for the baby, carving an intricate design. She sewed a layette, cutting the tiny kimonos and stitching them carefully. Amos wrote them reassuring letters from Tel Aviv. Studies continued at the gymnasia although there was little enough to eat. Still, they managed. They kept a fire blazing in the school courtyard and buried old potatoes and unhusked corn in the embers. Secretly, they practiced military drills in the dormitory corridors.

"The boy seems to be enjoying this war," Ezra said.

"That's not fair," Nechama protested mildly. But she would not allow herself to be drawn into an argument over Amos. This was too precious a time for them.

"When did the doctor say the child would be born?" he asked one night. His head rested on the rise of her stomach so that he could feel the gentle movements of their unborn child.

"Not until December."

"We will go to Haifa," he said.

Amos had been born at her parents' home in Jaffa, but he would not risk a journey south now.

"No." Her reply was firm. "I want this child born on Sadot Shalom. It will be all right. Hulda will be here."

"Perhaps my mother could come," he suggested.

"Your mother?"

She laughed incredulously. Rivka trembled at the sight of blood. Her eyes were weak. She moved slowly, her arthritic limbs twisted. She spent her days at Gan Noar telling her grandchildren about the luxuries she had enjoyed in Kharkov.

"If only Sara were here," Ezra said.

She did not reply. She had schooled herself to fight the strange jealousy she felt for the sister-in-law she had never seen.

During the first week of November, Saleem received word from the elders of his tribe that their chieftain had died and would be buried in the foothills of the Golan.

"We must be there," Saleem told Ezra.

"Of course you must," Ezra replied. He knew how deeply the Arabs felt their commitment to the tribe and to the ritual and ceremony that marked the tribal life. "But be careful.

The Turks are impressing anyone they can find into military service.''

"We will be careful," Saleem said. He knew how to travel at such a time. He fashioned a crutch for himself and leaned heavily upon it. There was no room for cripples in an army. He taught his sons to feign muteness and deafness.

Hulda embraced Nechama before leaving. Worry clouded her eyes.

"I will be back in time, geveret," she said.

"Of course you will," Nechama assured her. "The baby will not be born for another six weeks."

That very morning Nechama had stood naked before her long mirror, marveling at the fullness of her body. The blue veins stretched across her white stomach skin in delicate map strokes. The child had not shifted position.

"I will be fine," she assured Hulda.

They watched the Arab family leave from their doorway. She and Ezra were completely alone on Sadot Shalom. The thought did not displease her.

She was tired that night and had little appetite although they were having meat for the first time in weeks. Ezra had arranged for a calf to be slaughtered and had the meat sent to Gan Noar, where the children were clutching their stomachs with hunger. But he had set aside some veal steak. She stared disinterestedly at the pink meat and urged him to eat her share.

"Somehow I'm just not hungry," she said.

"But you feel all right?" he asked anxiously.

"Yes. I'm just tired.

She did not tell him about the sudden cramp that had shot through her leg earlier that day, nor did she mention the strange nagging pain where her womb had shifted suddenly. Still, the child moved lustily. It was fine. It had to be fine. This was just a small discomfort, a passing indisposition.

She fell asleep immediately and dreamed pleasantly of the small house she had lived in, in Kattowitz. A stream had flowed by their door. In her dream she held her small brothers and sisters by the arms and suspended them above the moving waters. How lovely those waters had been. How wonderful to float upon them during the heat of the summer's day. In her dream she floated on it again. Lovely warm water. Warm water that strangely coursed down her limbs and soaked the bedclothes. Their bed became a stream, and she floated across it. How lovely to glide easily on gentle tepid waves.

"Water," she called happily and placed her hand, sleep-heavy, between her legs. Liquid gushed across her fingers. "Water."

"Nechama, what is it?" Ezra leaned over her, his face pale, his eyes glazed with fear. She was awake now. The dream was over. She sat up with difficulty and saw that dream had become reality. The bed was soaked with the milky moisture of the amniotic waters.

"The baby is coming," she whispered as the first pang shot through her body. "It will be all right." She took his hand and stroked it gently, as though seeking to soothe and reassure him.

The new pain began slowly and increased in intensity. She squeezed his hand hard, bit back a scream and then submitted to it. Her voice filled the small house and echoed into the dark and empty night.

"Nechama!"

Panic gripped him, locked him in a paralysis. He struggled free and moved quickly, summoning knowledge from secret corners of his memory. He had been a boy when Sara had been delivered of Shimon. He remembered peering fearfully into the doorway and watching as Avremel placed cushions beneath his sister's legs, soothed her brow with cool cloths.

"You will be all right," he said, willing his voice to calmness.

The birth would be a hard one, he knew, because it was early. But she would be all right. She would not die. How could she die? She was his life, his love.

He arranged the pillows and hurried to the kitchen for basins of water, cloths for compresses. The pains came slowly. Droplets of sweat formed above her lips and rolled from her brow. Her eyes bulged with pain, and her knuckles whitened as they gripped the brass bedposts. Ribbons of blood streaked her lips where she bit through them in pain, her teeth bared like those of an animal fighting for freedom— freedom from pain. Then suddenly the waves of anguish subsided. He wiped her face, held a bit of ice to her lips so that she might quench her thirst, and smoothed her hair.

"Talk to me," she pleaded. "Tell me."

"I love you," he said. "You will be fine. The baby will be fine."

"You love me," she repeated. "I will be fine. The baby will be fine."

The words became a litany, a magical chant. She repeated them as another spasm seized her. Agony obscured her thoughts. She screamed, and tears filled his eyes. He turned to the window and wished that he could pray. He touched the leather surface of his grandfather's Talmud.

"Help me," he whispered, but he did not know to whom he spoke. She was so beautiful, his tall and white-skinned wife, so gentle, so wise.

"Oh, save her," he pleaded.

Her arms flailed wildly in the air; he reached for her hand and her fingers bit into his, staining his palms with half-moons of blood.

Night darkness drifted into cerulean-tinted dawn. She slept briefly, drugged into unconsciousness by pain and fatigue. They needed help, he knew now. A doctor. A midwife. But they were miles from the nearest settlement and he could not leave her alone and ride forth. Damn Amos. If the boy had been here, one of them could have left her. Damn him for believing that she had wanted him to go. How could Amos not have realized that they needed him, that his place was here at his home, at Sadot Shalom?

"Ezra!" Her voice was weak but there was wonder in it. "The baby is coming. I can feel it moving down. I can feel it." Then another scream poured from her throat as anguish replaced the wonder.

He passed his hands across her lower abdomen and felt the writhing outline of the unborn infant struggling to gain entrance into life, the tiny prisoner breaking out of the maternal fortress. He was not frightened. He had seen life emerge before. Suddenly he knew what to do. He was a farmer, a breeder of calves and foals.

"Bear down, Nechama," he said. "Push. Bear down."

Across the years he heard Avremel issue the same tense commands to Sara in the Rishon farmhouse.

"Again. Once more. Please."

His hands touched the expanded lips of her vagina. Smooth

nacreous membrane glinted against the dark furry canyon. His baby's head inched forward, luminescent. Tenderly he touched it, felt an infinitesimal pulsating begin. Oh live, sweet small life. Be born and live. Prayer trembled at his lips. *Sh'ma Yisrael*, hear O Israel. Lord of the universe—save my wife, have mercy on my child.

"Push, Nechama. One more time, just once."

Her face contorted. Her thighs, glistening with perspiration, strained forward. The baby's head shot through the vulva—a shining meteor of life, thrusting savagely through the vaginal wall, bloody and bloodying. He held the writhing, triumphant infant aloft and bit the long muscular umbilical cord, severing it with a fierce and sudden bite from the maternal source, from Nechama who had labored so hard.

He washed the infant with a ready cloth and wrapped it in the white blanket that had once swaddled Amos. Wondrously, he studied each perfect pink limb and saw that he had a daughter. Her infant wail rose in sweet siren song. The sound thrilled him. He placed her gently in the cedarwood cradle he had crafted through the long summer evenings.

"Nechama, we have a daughter. A little girl."

He went to her bedside. Nechama lay still, her eyes closed, her skin the color of new-fallen snow, her dark hair fanned out about the pillow.

"Nechama. A daughter."

There was no movement, no reply.

He knew then, but he would not believe his own knowledge. He lifted her hand, touched her thin wrist. There was no pulse beat. He pressed his ear to her mouth. Her lips were frozen into a smile.

"Nechama!" His shriek of loss matched her own vanquished cries of pain.

He pressed his mouth against hers and breathed wildly into it.

"Nechama!"

His clenched fist pounded her heart, his hands gripped her limp arms. He shook her as though he would jostle her back into life. But there was no whimper. No answering cry. She was dead. Gone from him, gone from their lives. Dead. In the lightly rocking cradle, the newborn infant girl cried piteously. Full sunlight blazed across the verdant fields of Sadot

Shalom. He went to the window and stared out at the gilded stump of the fig tree and turned at last to tend to his tiny newborn daughter.

"Elana," he whispered, the name coming to him as though in a dream.

PART FOUR

The Great War

1914–1918

Chapter 19

Ezra Maimon stood on the white sand flats of Mudros harbor and looked out across the Aegean. The calm sea waters were ribboned with purple streaks that almost exactly matched the wild thyme blossoms that grew in massive clumps along the crouching hillsides and the rock-strewn gullies of Gallipoli. Small lights were being lit against the encroaching darkness of evening, aboard the ships that lay at bay. Ezra watched them punctuate the darkness with their liquid luminescence. The portholes of the *Queen Elizabeth* became fiery eyes staring out of the massive white body of the ship. Similar eyelets of brightness danced out across the waters from the *River Clyde* and the *Majestic*.

He imagined the Englishmen on board going about their tasks. There was a curious domesticity to shipboard ritual, even in the midst of war. He had observed, during the crossing from Egypt, how scrupulously the British sailors adhered to each small ritual. Surely, even now, the late watch crew were busily mopping the decks. Boots were being polished and uniforms pressed. In the officers' mess, tables were being laid with sparkling white cloths. The officers would dress for dinner and exchange pleasantries while they drank

their sherry. They would talk softly of their gardens in Sur-
rey, marvel at the strange accents of the Anzac troops—the
Australians and New Zealanders now in British uniform,
fighting Turks and Germans to demonstrate their loyalty to
the crown and to a motherland they had never seen. They
would comment on the cruel winter that clung to the Mid-
lands as they felt the soft breath of the Mediterranean wind
waft in through the open portholes.

The shaven ice would melt in their glasses, and perhaps
one of the petty officers would lean across the ship's rail and
look out at the kerosene lanterns that lit up the tent cities of
Mudros and wonder how he happened to be aboard this
particular ship, looking across the Hellespont. Certainly that
same thought occurred to Ezra more than once during the
course of his work day. He was a farmer from the Galilee.
Only a year ago his only interest had been the breeding of
heifers and the cultivation of fruit orchards. How had he
come to be a muleteer, in the service of the British army,
charged with driving stubborn pack animals across this patch
of inlet that by geographic chance overlooked the Dardanelles—
that scissoring waterway that severed Europe and Asia from
each other?

Wearily, he turned his eyes landward, where cooking fires
were being lit in the mess tents along the beachhead. The
smell of charred bully beef filled the air, and men shouted to
each other in an odd commingling of accents. Ezra wondered
if the Dominion soldiers, summoned from the veldt and the
outback, shared his perplexity at finding themselves on
Gallipoli. Did they too wonder, as the sky darkened, what
they were doing there and why they had come?

But of course he knew why he was there, and his own
brooding irritated him. He could trace, with reasonable accuracy, the sequence of events that had carried him across a
desert and an ocean to this stern rock-rimmed cove beneath
the jagged peaks of the Sari Bair range. It was a logical
conclusion, in its way, to all that had happened to him in the
brief months that had passed since Nechama's death. *Nechama's
death.* He recoiled from the words, from their harsh finality.
Often, too often, he thought of her as still alive. He would
read an essay and mark a passage, thinking: I wonder what
Nechama would say to that? He watched the sun evolve into a
blazing crimson ball that sank slowly into the Aegean and

thought that he must find words to describe it to Nechama, who had reveled in the mysteries and colors of nature. Immediately, he chastised himself for the thought. Nechama was dead, he reminded himself sternly. He would never share another thought or sunset with her. He told himself this solemnly, routinely, repeating it as though it were a particularly elusive axiom which he had difficulty committing to memory. It was an exercise in the assimilation of grief, a conjugation in loss and bereavement.

Nechama is dead, he repeated to himself and, although sorrow settled heavily upon him, he still could not invest her loss with reality.

That same sense of unreality had clung to him at her funeral and throughout the mourning period which he and Amos had observed at the Langerfeld home in Tel Aviv. It was during that week of mourning that Saul and David had come to tell him that the Turks had taken over Sadot Shalom. They had announced that all land sales were negated. The Maimon brothers, who had received advance warning, had barely managed to remove the concealed weapons from the barn before the Turkish troops swept down and set up their barracks in the farmhouse.

"They can't do that!" Amos's voice reverberated with anger. A Turkish soldier slept in his bed. Militia overran the rolling fields that had been the playground of his childhood. They had no right. His fury pierced the cocoon of sorrow and guilt that had entrapped him since his mother's death.

"They can do anything," David replied. "We have no power in this land. We do not have the force to support our claims."

"Is force the only answer?" Amos asked. Sadness replaced the anger in his voice, and he left the room before his uncle could answer.

Ezra thought then of his fields and of his orchards and of the new grove of peach trees which had yet to yield its first fruit. The leaves were still furled, forming pale green fingers, and the branches were fragile networks of slender boughs.

"Have they allowed Saleem and his family to remain?" he asked.

"Yes. They are not as threatened by the Arabs as they are by the Jews," David replied.

"Saleem will see to the farm," Ezra murmured. "And how is Elana?"

His infant daughter was at Gan Noar, where Mirra and Chania cared for her. A new mother on the kibbutz nursed her. Elana was a powerful suckling, the woman reported proudly. She cried lustily to be fed and was at the breast feeding long after the woman's own infant had fallen asleep. It was that way sometimes with orphaned children, the woman had heard. In Europe her mother had once nursed a baby whose mother had been killed in a pogrom. That child too had delighted her wet nurse with her strength and greed.

"It is as though they know that something has been taken from them and they must be doubly strong to make up for it," the woman told Mirra, who thought her foolish and superstitious, although years later she would remember the nursing mother's words.

"Elana is fine," David assured him. "And it appears that the Turks have no plans to lay claim to Gan Noar. It is too hot and uncomfortable for them there. They are content to let us farm and then to requisition our grain. They needed Sadot Shalom for strategic reasons."

"Why not come to us at Gan Noar, Ezra? At least until the war is over," Saul suggested.

"I'm sorry."

Ezra turned his head. It was too soon to revisit places where he and Nechama had walked together. It was too soon for him to hold the child whose entrance into life had caused Nechama's death. Amos's eyes followed him pleadingly as he paced the room, but Ezra turned away. It was too soon for him to forgive Amos, who had not been there when Nechama soared beyond his reach on waves of pain while he struggled with his own helplessness and loss.

He lived, during those first few weeks, in a nether world of loss and sorrow. He slept fitfully and awakened soaked with the sweat of desperate dreams. Amos returned to his studies. The Langerfelds picked up the strands of their lives and returned to their daily rounds of duties. Ezra took long walks along the seashore. He watched the ocean and plucked up small, wondrously shaped stones which he tossed back into the roaring surf. He waited restlessly for something to happen. He felt himself to be abandoned on the shoals of sorrow

and he awaited rescue, apprehensively, as drought-plagued
islanders wait uneasily for a sudden storm.

"What will you do, Ezra?" his father asked worriedly.

"I am not sure."

Was it necessary, always, to have a plan, a program? He
recognized a strange redemptive quality to this sudden freedom from Sadot Shalom. He acknowledged to himself that he
was relieved that there was no need for him to return to the
farm where he and Nechama had shared a life that had so
suddenly ended.

Nechama is dead, he told himself.

"They need you at Gan Noar," Yehuda argued.

"We will see."

He made no promises, offered no guarantees. He had been
cut loose from his life and welcomed his new rootlessness.
He waited with a strange, perverse calm for some external
event to catapult him off the edge of his sorrow.

The last vestige of warmth left the air. Cold winds whistled
through the narrow streets of Tel Aviv. Housewives went out
to shop wearing several sweaters. Children roamed the beaches
dredging up bits of driftwood and lengths of dried reptilian
seaweed which they burned at small beachfires. They twisted
their fingers into writhing knots and held them suspended
above the flames. Ezra's mother-in-law polished the Chanukah menorah and took out the molds she used for shaping
candles.

"How will I get enough wax?" she worried aloud, and
Ezra stared at her in disbelief.

Nechama, his wife, her daughter, was one month dead.
The earth was raw above her narrow grave and Geveret
Langerfeld, who had loved her firstborn best of all her children, worried about the availability of wax for candles. She
worried about getting enough food and mending Amos's socks.
Reb Langerfeld was grieved because the cypress tree he had
planted in front of their house did not flourish. Their lives
continued apace, Nechama's death notwithstanding, their own
grief not discounted. Reb Langerfeld worried too because
bolts of cloth he had promised to customers did not arrive.
The embargo of the Jaffa port was complete now. Only the
Arab fishing boats left the harbor each morning. They sailed
slowly, in desultory loneliness, and returned with half-filled
nets.

"The British have poisoned the seas," they whispered to each other.

The absorption in their daily lives in no way minimized his in-laws' sorrow, Ezra knew. He too worried about the torn button on his shirt, which he repaired with trembling fingers. He stroked the seam Nechama had sewn—her stitches as neat and careful as her life had been. She was dead but he was alive, and when his boot ripped he took it to the cobbler in Jaffa to be mended. The dead were not quickened if those who grieved for them stumbled about the street in unsoled boots.

It was evening when he returned, carrying the newspaper-wrapped boot as though it were a sleeping infant. He hurried through the dark streets of Tel Aviv, his eyes narrowed against the drifts of cold sand that blew against his face, blinding him with a fierce and painful gust. Two children scurried ahead of him and disappeared into one of the small squat houses on Rothschild Boulevard. There were only two street lights in Tel Aviv but they had not been lit for weeks, and the windows of the small houses were dark because supplies of kerosene were dangerously low. The low branch of a pine tree scratched his face and he cursed softly. For a brief moment he imagined that he was all alone in this dark and silent city, just as he had been alone on his farm that morning, alone with his dead wife and his wailing newborn child. But a clock chimed in a nearby house and he heard a low murmur of voices as men checked their watches by its sound.

"A quarter to nine, Moshe."

"My watch says ten to nine."

"A quarter to nine."

The first voice grew irritated. When war and winter, famine and fear hover over a city, men argue over small things—the set of a watch, the price of an orange. Ezra increased his pace. The Turks had imposed a nine o'clock curfew on the city, and he did not want to give them any excuse to arrest him. In Jaffa that afternoon he had seen a group of Jews being marched off in chains. Some said they were being sent to prisons in Damascus or Brusa. Others insisted they were destined for slave labor in the granite pits of Tarsus. The arbitrary cruelty of the Turks was no longer mere rumor.

Ezra was almost running now, but he stopped when he

saw the small notice posted on the communal bulletin board on Herzl Street. The official white paper glowed in the dark, and the crescent of the Ottoman Empire was rimmed with gold as it was on all official documents. The crudely printed message was brutal in its brevity: THE JEWS OF TEL AVIV MUST LEAVE THE CITY BY DAYBREAK TOMORROW OR BE EXECUTED.

Ezra's heartbeat quickened. When had the notice been posted, he wondered. At nightfall—so that the Turks would be spared the harangues of the community, the crying of mothers, the distress of men whose property and livelihood resided within this beachbound hamlet? Perhaps it had been posted in the late afternoon so that even now, as he hurried to his in-laws' house, still cradling his boot, families were packing, organizing their bundles, loading their wagons, stringing their pots and pans together—mutely assembling equipment for survival. Jews were skilled at such tasks—the lesson of the generations had been well learned. He ran the remaining yards to his in-laws' home and saw Reb Langerfeld standing at the window, searching the darkness for him. The old man held a length of hemp, and Ezra knew that his wife's family was already preparing in the darkness for the expulsion.

The old man pulled him into the house just as Abu Halil, the Turkish police officer, rounded the corner, flashing his torch importantly into the shadows.

"Amos was here to say goodbye," his father-in-law told him. "He was sorry that you were not at home. All the Herzliah students are being taken north."

"I would have wanted to see him," Ezra said. That much was true, yet he was relieved to know that Amos would be safe and that he himself was relieved of all responsibility for his son. Was he an unnatural father, he wondered, to have thus relinquished responsibility for his infant daughter and his youthful son—to feel freedom because others cared for them? He turned from the window, where pine trees trembled in a timorous wind and a woman's thin weeping voice shattered the stillness.

At daybreak he helped the Langerfelds load their wagon. They were going to Petach Tikvah, where one of their daughters lived. Briefly, but without conviction, they asked him to go with them. Politely, but without regret, he declined.

"I will be needed," he said and wondered what he meant by those words. He was certain, however, that he could not spend the war hiding in a hut built of eucalyptus branches on the outskirts of Petach Tikvah.

Reb Langerfeld shook his hand. The old man's skin was paper fine but his grasp was strong and his keen eyes were soft with regret.

"It was God's will," he said.

"God's will," Ezra replied hollowly.

He bent to kiss Nechama's mother, the fragile old woman who had wept when her daughter went to live on Sadot Shalom but who sat bravely now on the wagon seat, holding the newly polished Chanukah menorah in her blue-veined hands.

"God go with you," she said, and Ezra thought it a small miracle that newly bereaved parents, exiled from home and city, spoke with such calm trust in God.

He watched their wagon join a train of other improbable, clumsy vehicles and vanish down the road, raising a small cloud of dust and sand. He stared after then and hoisted his own rucksack onto his back. He was headed for Jaffa, for Chaim Baker's hotel, when a Turkish patrol stopped him and demanded his identity papers.

"Aha! Born in Russia!" The sergeant was triumphant. He had discovered an enemy alien.

"I have been in Palestine since I was twelve," Ezra protested, but to no avail.

That night he and seven hundred other Jews, randomly rounded up, were herded aboard an Italian steamer heading for Alexandria. The Turks were indifferent as to where the expelled Jews would go but simply dispatched them on the first available transport. Egypt was as acceptable a dumping ground as any other. It was, after all, in a British sphere of influence, and the Turks took some satisfaction from the knowledge that they were saddling the British with those damn Russian-born Jews.

Ezra leaned across the rail and watched the colored lights of the Jaffa suq disappear. A man standing next to him wept, and a young boy cursed in vicious Arabic, but Ezra Maimon watched the ship's lights streak across the dark waters and remembered the cerulean verdancy of the bay that distant morning when another Italian steamer had carried his family into Jáffa harbor.

*   *   *

Alexandria teemed with the energy of a city caught at the crossroads of war. British soldiers in mufti thronged the streets of the bazaar and bargained urgently with patient, smiling merchants who pressed endless cups of coffee on them.

"Drink. You are my friend. You are my customer."

Inevitably, the merchants triumphed. English pounds weighed down their leather money bags. They, after all, had all the time in the world to smile cajolingly, polish their copper, and wait until the price was right. The pale, fair-haired young men whose skin turned feverishly red in the relentless sunlight were in a hurry. Any moment they might be shipped out to fight for king and country. They bargained swiftly, recklessly, and wrapped their parcels of linen and copper, of brightly colored prayer rugs and rough-carved scarabs, and addressed them to cottages in Shropshire and council flats in red brick Midland cities.

The cafes of Place Mehmet Ali were filled from earliest morning until late at night. Shrewd proprietors lit long wicks in the brightly shaded lamps that crouched on the tables streaked with grenadine and clotted with chickpea paste. The cafe owners knew that in time of war no one sits alone, and darkness must be fought and vanquished. Each cafe had its own particular national group. The English soldiers ordered their neat gins and traded rumors as they assembled beneath the checkered canopy of the Cafe Sherif Pasha. They were going to march across the desert to Saudi Arabia. They were going to free the Dardanelles. They would liberate Jerusalem. Always, before the evening was over, a group of Welsh fusiliers rose to sing "Britannia Rules the Waves."

The French gathered at a brasserie on the Rue de Rosette where they untied their ascots and sang rude songs. The Armenians had dominion over a narrow coffee stall whose owner could not afford to light kerosene lamps. Colored candles burned on the plank tables, and the sad dark eyes of the patrons made passersby uneasy. Word of the Turkish massacres of Armenians had reached Alexandria, and stories of the forced march of entire communities into the Mesopotamian desert circulated in the city. The haunted survivors created an atmosphere of unease, an odd sense of guilt. The British and French soldiers, the hard-eyed journalists, walked more quickly when they passed the coffee house where the

Armenians sometimes sat for hours without exchanging a word, as though they could not bear to speak the language that belonged to their lost and vanquished homeland.

The Palestinian Jews lay claim to a cafe run by a coreligionist on the Place Ibrahim. There, in the shadow of the Nebi Daniel mosque, they sipped hot tea from glasses, ate sesame seed cakes, and pondered their alternatives. Ezra watched as their circles grew smaller. Two men who had crossed on the Italian steamer with him received visas and tickets from their families in America. Others found positions with Jewish firms in Alexandria. A Jaffa ironmonger opened a stall in the bazaar. Two Rishon farmers organized a currency exchange.

"What do you know about currency?" they were asked.

"Nothing. But when we came to Rishon, what did we know about farming?" They shrugged with the nonchalance of the born survivor.

At the cafe, letters from Palestine were read aloud and information was traded and exchanged. Tel Aviv had become a ghost town. Cobwebs clung to the windows of the small houses, and the sea air had rusted the hinges of doors that were never opened. A plague of locusts had blackened the skies of the Galilee and destroyed the crops. There was famine throughout the land. Bedouin children ate scrub grass and died, their bellies distended, their legs frozen into rigid sticks. The Turks had seized all cattle. Ezra knew that when he returned to Sadot Shalom he would have to begin again. He would be a cattle breeder without cattle, master of an empty house, a father whose children had no mother. A man whose son studied with Amos at the gymnasia told Ezra that Amos was in Jerusalem.

Ezra was glad to have confirmation of his son's safety, but he wished Amos had chosen to join the family at Gan Noar. Always when he thought of Amos, pride and relief mingled with disappointment. But he could not blame Amos for anything when he himself divided his days between the Mafruza refugee camp and the Place Ibrahim cafe. He slept fitfully. His body, trained to the life of the fields, felt soft and unused to him.

"We must do something," he said fiercely one day to one-armed Josef Trumpeldor, who stood ahead of him on the breakfast line.

"We will."

Trumpeldor's voice was calm. He was a tall, startlingly handsome man who towered over the men who stood around him. Young women turned to look at him as he strode down the boulevards of Alexandria. Often his friends forgot that one sleeve of his jacket dangled empty. He had lost his arm in the Russo-Japanese war, and somewhere in his battered refugee suitcase was a tarnished medal which the Russian government had awarded him for outstanding heroism. He was a member of the Shomer, and Ezra had met him occasionally at Gan Noar although Trumpeldor himself belonged to a neighboring kibbutz.

"What then? Perhaps we could form a Jewish legion. We could help the British liberate Palestine."

"They are not in a great hurry for our help." Trumpeldor expertly juggled his breakfast tray with one arm, placed a lump of sugar between his teeth, and drank his tea.

"What shall we do?"

"We shall wait, Maimon. Something will happen."

Trumpeldor knew how to wait. He had spent months as a prisoner of the Japanese in a Port Arthur camp. Here, at least, he was among Jews, and only weeks had gone by, not months.

Ezra was sitting with Trumpeldor one cold morning when a somber-faced Russian Jew approached them. The man's fingers were ink-stained and he carried the inevitable correspondent's notebook in his breast pocket.

A war correspondent looking for a human interest story about the poor Jewish deportees at the Mufruza camp, Ezra thought. But he noticed with surprise that the stranger carried a book by Croce, an Italian writer whom Nechama had admired greatly, and he was astounded when the man addressed them in an accurate, almost literary Hebrew.

"I am Vladimir Jabotinsky," the stranger said. "I was in Italy serving as a correspondent for the *Russkiye Vyedomosti* during the Russo-Japanese War, but I heard of your work at Port Arthur."

"And I, of course, know of your work with Jacobson in Constantinople," Trumpeldor replied. "And of course I read the proceedings of the Helsingfors meeting."

They sat on backless hardwood benches in a refugee camp on the edge of the Egyptian desert and spoke the elegant,

courteous language of academics meeting at a learned conference. Jabotinsky's dark business suit was mapped with sweat,
and he squinted against the brilliant sunlight. He was an
intellectual from shadowed northern climes plunged into the
unnatural brightness of a Middle Eastern morning. Ezra followed the conversation with interest. The Helsingfors meeting, he knew, had been convened to argue for a resolution in
favor of equal rights for Jews and all other minorities in the
Russian empire. And Jacobson had been the representative of
the Zionist executive in Constantinople. Clearly this Vladimir
Jabotinsky was something besides a journalist tossed up by
the fortunes of war on the shores of a refugee tent city.

"I have been thinking that there is a great opportunity for
us here," Jabotinsky said, adopting a conspiratorial tone. He
was, Ezra thought, the sort of man who might order tea in a
whisper and comment on the weather in code. "We could
make ourselves very useful to the British—perhaps by forming a Jewish legion to fight in Palestine in British uniform.
This would tilt the scales in our favor when the British take
control of the country."

He spoke with the certainty of one who has full knowledge
of the future; it was clear to him that the British would win
the war and Palestine would fall under their governance.
Vladimir Jabotinsky would never waste his time with the
endless discussions that dominated the cafe on Place Ibrahim.
There, men speculated for hours on eventualities and proba-
bilities. Turkey was lost. Turkey would revive itself. Turkey
had sold her soul to the Germans. Enver Pasha might yet do a
turn around and betray his German masters by signing a
secret pact with the British. Turkey might yet prevail, and its
position over Palestine would be reinforced. Vladimir Jabotinsky
would listen contemptuously to such arguments. He knew the
truth. It had been revealed to him as a sacred gift. The future
of the Jewish cause lay with England.

"Ezra Maimon of Sadot Shalom shares your feelings,"
Trumpeldor said.

The Russian's cold eyes studied Ezra. He took note of the
farmer's sinewy arms, his muscular back. He saw how Ezra's
fingers played impatiently with the crude silverware. He was
a man of action consigned to gossip in mess tents and cafes.

"I am glad to meet you, Ezra Maimon," he said. "And
what is your opinion, Josef Trumpeldor?"

Trumpeldor reached for the empty sleeve that dangled at his side. He used it to wipe a rim of moisture from his mouth, then dropped it and passed his hand through thick sand-colored hair.

"I think that there will be difficulties," he said. "Still, we shall try. We have no other choice."

The three men went together to see General Maxwell. He listened to them carefully, staring all the while at the photograph on his desk. The first snows were falling in Sussex and the children in the photo, his son and daughter, would be dashing through the cold whiteness in their brightly colored anoraks. But he would celebrate Christmas on this bloody desert, fighting to capture territory that only madmen would want to call their own. He turned to the three men who sat before him. An odd trio—the one-armed Russo-Japanese War hero who was also, of all things, a dentist; the thin-lipped Russian correspondent for an unpronounceable newspaper (it was General Maxwell's opinion that English should be declared an international language); and the Jewish farmer from Palestine whose skin was stained the color of topaz. A different kind of Jew, each of them, he reflected, than those one came across in the East End or in Golders Green. They were strange people, these Jews. Interesting. General Maxwell justifiably prided himself on not being anti-Semitic. He had once left a mess table at Sandhurst because of a blatantly anti-Semitic remark. Still, one had to admit that the Jews were cut of a different cloth.

"You propose a Jewish legion which would wear the uniform of the British army?" he said as though he were having some difficulty conceiving of the idea.

"Naturally. Inasmuch as the Jewish legion would be part of the British army," Vladimir Jabotinsky reminded him, matching his tone.

"Yes. Quite." This Jabotinsky was no fool, the general thought, studying the dossier provided by his intelligence officer. He was the author of a profile on Turgenev. The general himself was partial to Tolstoy but he was not adverse to having a good joke about Turgenev.

"I'm afraid that wouldn't be possible," he said, and there was real regret in his voice. He liked these three men and would not have minded having them on his side in a war which he had difficulty understanding.

"Why not?" Ezra Maimon asked. Farmers had no patience with Machiavellian arguments, academic courtesies.

"Because the British army has regulations against foreign nationals serving in His Majesty's forces. And because, as residents of Palestine, you and Trumpeldor here hold Turkish papers. If you and your compatriots were taken prisoner while wearing British uniforms, you would be summarily shot as traitors. And let me tell you, gentleman, the Turks excel at summary executions."

"We have that knowledge," Ezra said dryly. "We have lived under Turkish rule."

"Also," General Maxwell continued, "although your knowledge of the Palestinian terrain would be invaluable to us, there is as yet no plan to open a Palestinian front."

"But the general has another idea?" Josef Trumpeldor suggested, twirling his empty sleeve.

That damn sleeve is a weapon for him, Ezra realized suddenly. He uses it to remind others that he is a warrior, that he has wandered through pain and loss and would repeat that wandering. He uses it the way a beautiful woman, bent on seduction, uses her body. He teases and taunts. He will seduce Maxwell into allowing us to serve in his bloody army.

"Yes. I have another idea," Maxwell agreed equably. He reached down and held up a campaign map, which he unrolled with elaborate ceremony.

They looked down at a map on which the island of Lemnos was colored green and the island of Imbros was a bright fuchsia. The coast of Asia was peacock-blue and the coast of Europe a pale purple. Between the two coastlines floated the narrow blue waterway called the Dardanelles, peaked by the peninsula of Gallipoli, overhung with mountainous escarpments, colored brown by a fanciful artist. Gallipoli. Was the name Italian, Ezra wondered, or was it Greek? Nechama would have known. She collected such odd nuggets of knowledge. *Nechama is dead*, he reminded himself. He trained his eyes on the map once again and saw that the word *Gallipoli* was encircled in red.

"We intend to take Gallipoli," General Maxwell said, keeping his voice very low as befitted a military conspiracy, even though he was discussing it with three foreign nationals. "We must control the Dardanelles. A long campaign is projected—surf landings and trench fighting to reach the heights where the Turks are bedded in. Our problem will be getting supplies and equipment from the beaches to the trenches. That is where you people can be useful.''

"Us?" Jabotinsky was honestly bewildered. He took a handkerchief from his pocket and wiped his brow. Always Ezra would remember that handkerchief, spotlessly white and neatly ironed.

"We will be using mules. We need a transport division, preferably men who are trained to work with animals.''

He looked at Ezra Maimon, the farmer, the cattle breeder of the Galilee.

"You are speaking about a mule corps,'' Ezra said.

"Precisely.'' General Maxwell smiled benignly. They were quick, these Jews. He had always said that. He even recalled mentioning it to his wife, whose country upbringing limited her a bit, he had to admit. She claimed to dislike Jews although she had yet to meet one.

Trumpeldor turned to Jabotinsky.

"As I see it,'' he said, "any anti-Turkish front would lead to Zion. I say we do it.''

"Do you agree then?'' General Maxwell asked.

The three men looked at each other and nodded affirmatively.

"It is agreed,'' Vladimir Jabotinsky replied. "After all, it is written that the Torah will go forth from Zion. But nowhere is it written that mules will not go forth from Zion. We, General, shall be your Zion Mule Corps.''

The Jews laughed and General Maxwell smiled uncertainly, uneasily. These Jews were damn difficult to understand. He had been afraid they might be insulted. He was, after all, offering them the kind of work the darkies did in the bush wars, and here they were laughing.

Two weeks later Ezra Maimon, Zev Jabotinsky (who had surrendered his Russian name when he volunteered for the corps), and Josef Trumpeldor sailed for Gallipoli wearing plain uniforms devoid of military marking except for the Shield of David on their shoulder lashings. The refugee camp was left half emptied when more than six hundred Jewish men volunteered, and the owner of the cafe on Place Ibrahim removed half his tables.

Ezra Maimon stood between the lights of the cooking fires on the beachhead and looked again at the great ships of war that listed in the bay. He knew exactly how he had happened to come to Gallipoli. He had begun that journey to war, and to the strange sense of personal oblivion which war brings, on the morning he stood over his wife's body and acknowledged the terror of his incomprehensible grief.

"Ezra!" Trumpeldor called to him across the darkness. "You want to eat—no?"

"I'm coming."

He hurried across the beach to the encampment of the Zion Mule Corps, where a small Jewish flag fluttered in the evening breeze.

Chapter 20

The Zion Mule Corps had sailed from Alexandria in January, and within a few days time disembarked not far from Cape Hellas. The mules brayed in protest as they were herded onto the flat landing boats. They shifted their weight angrily and bared their teeth. They shivered with fright. The muleteers were not deterred. Sacks of equipment and provisions were loaded onto the animals and strapped securely into place. The familiar weight of their burdens seemed to calm the mules, who opened their large mournful eyes wide and stared reproachfully at their masters.

Ezra Maimon supervised the operation, pressing a piece of lump sugar into one animal's mouth, adjusting the protective wrap of another.

"You must lead him and not let him go his own way," he advised the pale young man named Eleazar who had never seen a mule before.

Eleazar had stumbled into the war from a yeshiva near Tiberias. One day he had been a Talmud student and the next day he was stopped in the street and deported to Alexandria, where he had been swept into the Zion Mule Corps. At the refugee camp he had still worn the long black frock coat of

the student, and Ezra himself had cut the boy's earlocks at
Eleazar's request.

"I will grow them again when I return to the yeshiva,"
Eleazar said. "Now we serve God by fighting for Zion."

Ezra smiled, recognizing Jabotinsky's words. He was still
mystified by the scholarly Russian journalist's ability to totally
control his audiences by the sheer energy of his delivery and
the intensity of his message. The small crowds who gathered
to listen to Jabotinsky stood transfixed as the man spoke. His
voice rose and fell with melodic resonance. His hands danced
in the air, pleading for understanding. He shouted. He thun-
dered. At last, he asked questions, speaking so softly that
they leaned forward to hear him.

"Do we want to claim Zion?" His voice trembled at the
edge of a whisper.

"We want to claim Zion!"

His question became their answer.

"Who will fight for Zion?"

"We will fight for Zion!"

Within minutes his listeners were his disciples. Young
Eleazar had drifted to the edge of the circle of listeners,
wearing a caftan and holding a prayer book. Three days later
he wore a uniform and held the reins of a mule.

Ezra sailed to shore on the first of the long flatboats. His
hand steadied a nervous young animal who pawed the bottom
of the boat and shifted dangerously under the weight of the
heavy wooden cartridge boxes. But he lifted his eyes and
studied the grim terrain. He saw the jagged peaks of the Sari
Bair mountain range, and he sought out its central crest, the
Chunuk Bair. A man who perched at the top of the crest
could see Mount Ida and the Trojan plain. A westward view
would reveal the islands of Imbros and Samothrace. The
Dardanelles flowed in a slender river, severing the continent
of his birth from the continent of his destiny. He would come
here again in peacetime, he vowed. He would make the climb
at dawn, with the whole of the Gallipoli peninsula stretched
before him as far as Cape Hellas, where surely the cliffs
dropped suddenly seaward and vanished into the blue waters
of the Aegean.

"What is that?" Eleazar asked, pointing north.

"The town of Chanak," Ezra replied.

He had studied the maps with Trumpeldor and listened

intently to the descriptions of the landscape and the battle
plan offered by Lieutenant Colonel John Henry Patterson,
who commanded the Zion Mule Corps with Trumpeldor
acting as adjutant. The key to the entire military operation
was the narrows guarded by two ancient fortresses—a square,
crenelated building in the town of Chanak on the Asian shore,
and a heart-shaped fortress on the opposite bank. At these
strategic points, high above the beaches, the Turks had dug
themselves in at the onset of the war, deploying their main
defenses there.

"Make no mistake about it. The Turks are not stupid,"
Patterson had said, biting down hard on his pipe, newly
packed with the fine Turkish tobacco Jabotinsky had carried
with him from Constantinople. The rich fragrance filled the
air, an aromatic testimony to Jabotinsky's genius. The Russian had known that a gift of tobacco could buy friendship
and confidence.

"They've built themselves eleven forts manning approxi-
mately seventy guns," Patterson continued. "We've had intelligence reports telling us they even had those damn torpedo
tubes that can fire on ships sailing upstream. They've laid
down a mine field, and I would guess they have a wire mesh
net against submarine penetration. And, of course, the Krauts
have probably given them some howitzers."

All this Ezra remembered, but he did not share his knowledge with Eleazar. The yeshiva student, after all, was only a
boy—perhaps two years older than Amos.

"There are newly reinforced installations at Chanak," he
said. "But they're not our concern, Eleazar. Our job is just to
get the equipment from the beaches to the trenches. It's up to
the Tommies and the ANZAC people to keep advancing and
digging in."

He did not add that as the British troops advanced, so too
would the Zion Mule Corps, and that with each advance they
would come closer to the sightings of Turkish deployments.
Eleazar would learn. He had, after all, never before heard a
gun fired, and when Ezra cut his finger the boy blanched at
the sight of the blood.

They herded the laden mules out of the flatboats and onto
the beaches. It was a daily operation—monotonous, exhausting, and demanding all their strength. The smell of the ani-

mals clung to their skin, to their hair. They shoveled mountains of offal into ditches.

Gradually, as the days turned into weeks and the weeks became months, the barren beachhead acquired the look of a functioning community. A Jewish flag hung from the make-shift flagpole in front of their tents. Men strung up bits of rope between the outstretched branches of scrub bushes and hung up the clothing they had washed in the sea water. They played chess by the light of the low cooking fires and com-mented on each other's moves in a mixture of languages—Hebrew, Yiddish, Russian, German. Eleazar and another yeshiva student opened their Bibles and argued vehemently over a Rashi commentary. Muleteers from settlements along Lake Tiberias fashioned nets and showed them how, at low tide, they could catch fish being swept to the shoreline. Eleazar examined the catch carefully, to ascertain that they had gills and scales and were therefore kosher. They fried them over the embers and ate the sweet fish flesh with their fingers, telling each other of fish dinners they had enjoyed in other countries, at other times.

And all the while, the battle raged beyond them and they watched it from the beach as though they were spectators at a theater, watching a play that somehow failed to engage their interest. They looked up from their chess game, saw the flares of the rockets, and knew that only miles away men were dying. Yet there was nothing they could do, and they bent to their game and spoke very softly in the languages of their native lands.

The Turkish forts were being attacked from the sea. French and English warships moved steadily, firing fierce cannon-ades. The entrenched battlements were veiled by clouds of dust and smoke and then harshly illuminated by a sudden flame shooting upward from the debris. The ships plowed through surging fountains of water and keeled beneath plumes of spray. They shuddered mightily against the onslaught of the howitzers firing from the hills, and even the ground along the beach quaked against the impact of the guns. The Pales-tinian Jews saw small fires break out aboard the ships. The foremast of the *Inflexible* became a rod of fire. A heavy shell penetrated the magazine of the *Bouvet,* and explosions ripped in rapid lightning bolts through the air.

"What if all the ships are lost?" Eleazar said.

"They will not all be lost," Ezra assured him. "But the British must change their strategy or Gallipoli will be lost."

"Yes. I see that," the boy said thoughtfully, and Ezra looked at him in surprise.

In only a few weeks Eleazar's deportment had changed. He had lost his student slouch and moved with swift determination. He still prayed three times a day and would not touch the meat supplied by the British, but he had assumed a field soldier's casualness in dress and language. He tended the mules gently but firmly, clouting a recalcitrant animal and then carefully cleaning grit from the beast's infected eyes. He had, during the short period of the campaign, slipped from boyhood into a new maturity. Was Amos undergoing similar changes? Ezra wondered, and he felt a sharp and bitter sorrow because his son's passages had been lost to him. Their child, his and Nechama's, grew to manhood among strangers.

Winter drifted into spring. The sea battles became more sporadic and finally, an uneasy quiet hung over the peninsula. Shells were fired at uneasy intervals from the Turkish fortifications. The answering fire from the Allied ships was desultory, irregular.

"They must be planning a new offensive," Trumpeldor said musingly.

"Perhaps," Ezra replied, but he did not look up from his letter.

A mail ship had docked that morning and there were letters for him from Gan Noar. His parents were well. Elana was growing wonderfully. At six months she already pulled herself up, and Mirra was certain she would walk before she was a year old. Every member of the kibbutz was entranced by her wide smile. She enclosed a snapshot of the little girl. Wide dark eyes, long-lashed like Nechama's, stared out at Ezra. The full lips were curved in laughter and the child's finely molded head was covered with black ringlets.

"The kibbutz has adopted her," Mirra wrote.

No one can adopt her, Ezra thought angrily, although he knew his sister-in-law was not writing literally. She is mine. Mine.

He pressed the small photo to his lips and slipped it inside his shirt so that it adhered to his skin. Mine. He remembered Elana's infant arms flailing in the sunlight and her tiny lips struggling to suck up the milk he had fed her with an eyedropper because Nechama lay dead. Her skin was cold and white as marble, and the liquid that dripped from her breast clung to the nipples in frozen milky teardrops.

His brothers were very much involved in Shomer work, Mirra wrote guardedly. David had undertaken an important project. Saul rode from Jewish settlement to Jewish settlement and was distressed because so many Jews had left the country. Famine and fear had driven them out. Others, like Ezra himself, had been expelled. Amos had visited Gan Noar. He seemed well and healthy and had grown taller. (Then he must be my height, Ezra thought. Amos had almost reached his shoulder when he last saw him during the days of mourning in Tel Aviv. He tried to remember the toddler Amos, with hair the color of durra wheat, who had rushed toward them across the fields of Sadot Shalom. He had no photograph— neither as a child nor as a youth. How had it happened that a father had gone to war without a photograph of his son?)

Ezra ventured up the marshy roofs and wandered inland where cornflowers, poppies, and tulips grew in colorful profusion. He plucked a yellow tulip, felt its soft velvety petals against his cheeks. The cornflowers were of a deeper blue than those that grew in the Galilee. He wondered if Saleem had remembered to prune the peach trees. He looked across the harbor and saw that new ships had sailed in during the night. The *Queen Elizabeth* flew its brightest banner, and he could make out the ensigns ranged on her deck, dressed in their white dress uniforms. A high-level conference was in progress, he knew. A new offensive would be launched. He hurried back to camp.

"It has been decided," Trumpeldor said to him the next day. "They are going to force a landing on the peninsula itself."

"But how?"

Ezra had walked the beachhead. He had studied it on maps. Twice he had been aboard the small gunboats that patrolled the coast. A forced landing would require an attack from at least five different beaches. And how could the Zion Mule Corps supply such widely dispersed divisions?

"The British will attack by both sea and land. We will be deployed to Anzac Cove. New mules have been brought in for us. I am placing you in charge there. Can you manage?"

"I can manage," Ezra said. "But don't you see that they

are just repeating the same technique that has already failed with the seaborne attack? They act, they wait for the Turks to react, and then there is a stalemate. It makes no sense, Josef.''

Trumpeldor's lips narrowed. The empty sleeve of his shirt trailed in the strong sea wind.

"We are invited guests to this war, Ezra," he said. "We do not plan the strategy. We only follow their orders. A good guest accommodates himself to the requirements of the host. When we have our own country, we shall plan our own wars and those who serve under us will complain that our wars also make no sense. Does it make sense for young men to die on a summer's afternoon?" Bitterness burned his words. Gallipoli was not his first battlefield, and it would not be his last.

"I will assemble my men," Ezra said.

Eleazar joined him as an aide, and a dozen muleteers volunteered as soon as he announced their destination. They were eager to leave Mudros harbor. The Palestinian Jews, who had little patience with conventional military discipline, were not popular with the British. They often forgot to salute and they did not police their camps. They seldom buttoned their uniforms, and when the sun burned fiercely they discarded their jackets. There had been repeated incidents of insubordination, and on several occasions British officers had ordered public floggings.

"An Army cannot be maintained without discipline," Colonel Patterson said angrily when Trumpeldor protested. "What kind of soldiers will you Jews be when you have your own army if you will not submit to discipline?"

"Different men fight in different ways for different things," Trumpeldor replied.

His eyes bore into the colonel's own. There were no more floggings but still the Jewish muleteers were impatient to leave.

They sailed for Anzac Cove on a moonless May night. Eleazar stood at Ezra's side polishing his pistol and murmuring the prayer for travelers. He saw no inconsistency between these actions.

Once again the Palestinians drove the mules forward, leading them from the beach to the trenches. Day after day they crouched as they pressed on through ravines and gullies. They heard the strange war cries of the Turkish troops.

"Irsh'Allah! Fight for the Prophet!"

They saw the steel glitter of bayonets poised on either side
of the battle lines as they edged in between, cajoling the
animals, forcing them forward. They unloaded them swiftly,
passed the provisions to the trench fighters, and hurried back.
The animals' hot breath soured the air, and often they were
caught in crossfire. Ezra, hurrying back, one mule in tow,
saw two men fall on either side of him. Instinctively he bent
and lifted a New Zealander whose leg had been shattered by a
shrapnel and an Irish infantryman whose face had been
mashed to a scarlet pulp. He put them on his mule and
hurried forward, shutting his ears to their groans, looking
away from the bright blue marbles in the Irishman's face
which were the man's pleading eyes, brilliant with fear and
pain. He took them to the hospital tent where a French officer,
his uniform soaked scarlet with other men's blood, cursed
him briefly and brandished a red-stained surgical saw from
which pellucid bits of muscle dangled.

"Why do you bring me dead men, Jew?" he asked bitterly.

"They are alive."

He sat them down gently and saw a tear form in the
Irishman's bright blue eyes.

"Thank you," the wounded soldier whispered and reached
up to touch the Jewish star on Ezra's shoulder lashing.

"There will be a truce tomorrow," Eleazar told him when
he returned to the muleteer's camp. "A truce to bury the
dead. They have sent word that they will need the mules to
carry the water and the shovels."

"All right," Ezra said wearily and went to water the
animals, who looked at him with their large mournful eyes.
One mule had waded through a gully filled with corpses.
Clots of blood clung to its leg and Ezra wiped them off and
disentangled a silvery length of human intestine from its hoof.

They assembled at dawn. Each man wore a white armband,
and a white flag fluttered above each animal. It was a wet and
cold day, and those who had greatcoats shivered within them.
They crossed the beach and traced their way to the battlefields
across cornfields blazing red with poppies. The smell of death
mingled with the fragrance of early spring and then overpow-
ered it. The air was thick with a sickening putrescence. Figs
hung heavily on dwarfed trees, and they crushed the fallen
fruit beneath their boots. Ezra fought nausea, fought the

memory of the fig tree that had grown in his garden and the taste of the pink fruit when he licked it from Nechama's breast. *Nechama is dead,* he told himself.

They climbed a plateau and descended into a gully overgrown with purple thyme, and still the stink pursued them. Eleazar removed his helmet and put on a skullcap. He prayed softly as he led his mule, laden with shovels for the digging of graves.

"God full of mercy, hear our prayer. Oh Lord, magnified and sanctified be Thy name."

And yet they were startled by the first dead they stumbled across, because the fallen men were frozen into the posture they had held when the bullets found them. Only the breath of life was missing. The young soldiers grasped their bayonets. Their heads and shoulders were thrust forward. Their legs were curled as though for a sprint. They were spread across the wet earth in small mountains of bodies—whole companies of soldiers, assault unit piled upon assault unit. One sandy-haired corpse grinned at them wildly. Another clutched a snapshot. Ezra felt Elana's picture against his heart. For a wild suspended moment, he imagined himself dead, caught unawares by a bullet while he studied his daughter's face.

He buried that man first, taking his identification papers. Lance Corporal Dennis Miles from Newton Farmship in Queensland. The snapshot showed a freckle-faced young woman smiling shyly into a bouquet of spring flowers.

That first single grave was a luxury. Thereafter they dug communal graves. The Turkish and Allied troops worked together. They heaved the bodies in, offered each other cigarettes, and chatted in English and Arabic—enemies briefly transformed into confederates.. They exchanged badges plucked from the uniforms of the corpses and traded pocket knives and tobacco pouches.

Moslem imams and Christian chaplains moved from one gravesite to another. The clergymen were pale and muttered their prayers through compressed lips as though fearful that they might vomit if their mouths opened wider. The stench of the slaughterhouse grew stronger as the rain stopped and sunlight sprayed the fields golden. Ezra thought that the stench would be in his nostrils forever; it clung to his hands, to his clothing. If he opened his mouth the stink would slide down his throat and settle in a fetid pool in his stomach.

He glanced at Eleazar. The boy was bent over his spade, and he shoveled with a consistent rhythm. His white palms had grown calloused.

They were through at last. The Turkish corpsman who had worked beside Ezra opened a gold cigarette case, newly removed from an infantryman's body, and offered Ezra an English cigarette, which was declined. The Turk then opened his wallet and showed Ezra a photograph of himself standing in front of a white stucco bungalow and a sepia-tinged snapshot of two small boys dressed in neat school uniforms.

"My sons," he said. "Big. Strong. Smart."

The boys wore hesitant smiles, as though fearful that the camera might somehow betray them.

Ezra slid Elana's picture out of his shirt.

"My daughter," he said.

"Pretty." The Turk's approval was immediate. "We have no daughters," he confided sadly.

"Perhaps one day," Ezra said, and he studied the shy smiles of the Turkish boys while the Turk smiled back at the infant Elana. They had each wiped their hands carefully before exchanging pictures. The muddy earth of the freshly dug graves encrusted their skin and was ingrained beneath their fingernails. They did not want war to soil their children's faces.

"Goodbye," Ezra said. "Shalom." He pointed to his shoulder lashings.

"Salaam. Shalom," the Turk replied, and he flashed his gold teeth in a happy grin that denied the ambience of death that surrounded them. "Smiling may you go. Smiling may you come again." He repeated the valediction Ezra had heard from every Turk he had known since childhood.

Ezra watched the man disappear down the edge of the ravine and wondered if the two shyly smiling boys would grow up to wear red uniforms and carry rifles they might one day aim at Amos's heart. Men lived at the edge of madness, he thought, guests at each other's wars, flirting with death and making life a mockery. The mule lagged, and halfway back he met Eleazar leading his own pack animal. The boy had pocketed his skullcap. He wore his helmet now, and he murmured no prayers as they walked back to their surfside tents.

"Do you think any cause is worth this?" Eleazar asked suddenly.

Ezra could give him no answer. Fatigue and sorrow choked his words, blocked his thoughts.

The days on Anzac beach assumed a pattern of their own. The men lived suspended between war and brief respites of quiet. Each day might bring death yet they washed their underwear on the off chance they might survive. They cooked their meals on fires which they kindled in small crevices in the cliffs. Eleazar fashioned a shelf for his books. Jabotinsky hooked up a lantern for reading and turned the pages while rockets burst and in the distance a man shrieked as a sniper's bullet pierced his chest. Trumpeldor created a lair for himself in a hillside cave with a blanket for a door.

Ezra set up a smithy near the telephone exchange. His mules, placid when there was no gunfire, were sheltered in the gully until nightfall when once again they began their rounds. Under cover of darkness they carried ammunition and supplies to the men in the trenches. He worried inordinately over supplies for the animals, begged water for them, and calmed them when an unexploded bullet fell into the flames of the smoking incinerator and set off a small explosion. Eleazar worked at his side.

"I want to visit your farm, Ezra," the boy said one day.

"Of course you will visit Sadot Shalom."

"I will not return to the yeshiva. There is no point."

"If you want, you are welcome to live with me on Sadot Shalom," Ezra said.

Some sons were born and some were chosen. Had not he himself always turned to Chaim Baker for advice, for wisdom and understanding? Amos was his son but Eleazar had followed him into battle, across bloodstained fields.

"Wherever I am, you will have a home," he told the boy.

Eleazar nodded and turned back to his meal. He ate the bully beef now and did not offer a blessing before biting into his bread.

Soft spring became harsh summer. The green earth faded to a brown barrenness, and wherever the men walked, clouds of dust trailed after them. The mules chomped on the fading purple flowers of wild thyme and brittle, dried asphodel. The air was electric with the clicking of cicadas, and they walked carefully to avoid scorpions and lizards, tarantulas and centipedes. The men in the trenches fought in their underwear. The intensity of the heat melted the fat of the tinned meat but they ate it anyway, their taste inured to the greasy rations. There were no wells on the Cape Hellas bridgehead. Their water was transported from the Nile, pumped ashore from the tankers of the ships, and carried to the men at the front by the Zion Mule Corps. After a while they learned how to distill sea water for the animals.

They ate, slept, and worked through a veil of flies, often swallowing the insects with their food because they hovered everywhere, their bodies bloated with the blood of dead animals and men. Dysentery swept through the camp, and men lay trapped in their trenches, soiled by their own feces. Eleazar grew ill and Ezra nursed him. He carried the boy to the latrine and begged a bit of muslin for him from the medical officers so that his face would not be exposed to the flies.

"It's not worth it," the boy cried out from the depths of the fever.

He recovered but he walked slowly, a seventeen-year-old who measured his pace like an old man, rationing his strength, estimating his energy and the length of the day.

The men named the different guns that fired down upon them from the hills. They called the largest Asiatic Annie and the smaller cannons were called Quick Dicks. Their shells ripped the cover off the earth, unshrouded history. A muleteer passed across a recently shelled field and found two huge jars, beautifully carved and each containing the skeleton of a small child. The man had left a sickly child at his home in Zichron Yaakov. He had been in the burial detail and had tossed headless bodies and dismembered arms and legs, blackened with blood at severed joints, into mass graves. But he wept when he saw the small skeletons of children, dead since the days when Trojan armies roamed their battlefield. Ezra found a small cup winged with delicate handles. Eleazar watched him as he polished it in the darkness of their bunker, coaxing it to a muted glow with repeated rubbings.

"For your son?" he asked.

Ezra nodded.

"For my son."

He did not add that often now he forgot that he had a son,

that he had been a husband. Even the fields of Sadot Shalom faded from his memory, and it seemed to him that he had always lived on this barren beachhead, listening to the sounds of war and the bleating of wearied pack animals.

He walked the beach one night, a cigarette clamped between his lips, after bringing his mules in from the trenches. The cigarette's tip glowed in the darkness. He did not smoke for the taste of the tobacco but for the companionship of the tiny light.

"Hey there, mate, you're making yourself a walking target with that butt," a sentry with an Irish brogue said.

"Sorry." He stubbed out the cigarette.

"Well, now, you're Lieutenant Maimon, aren't you?" the sentry asked.

"Yes. I am."

"Don't ye know me, then?"

Ezra looked at the man's face. There was a jagged hole in his cheeks where a bullet had been wedged out of the soft flesh. A deep gash severed his forehead, giving the man the appearance of two separate visages. But his blue eyes burned with a familiar warmth and Ezra knew that he had seen the man before.

"Of course you don't recognize me. My mates tell me my face was a bloody mess when you grabbed me. Even that Frog medic thought I was done for, but he pulled me through all right. I've been wanting to thank you. Halloran's my name. Liam Halloran."

"I remember now. I picked you up near the gully—put you across my mule."

"A mule's a handy animal to have. I've got three myself on my farm in Derry. Use them for plowing—but mostly haul with them."

"I used them, too—on my farm in the Galilee. In Palestine."

"The holy land, is it then? I'd like to see the land where our Lord walked."

"Come to see me there after the war. My farm is called Sadot Shalom—Fields of Peace."

"You're going back there then, when this is over?"

They walked the beach together now, with the easy, comfortable step of men who are newly friends.

"Of course I'm going back."

"They say the holy land is half desert. And they say what

ain't desert is rocks. And the bloody Arabs want you Jews off, and they come killing you in the night. What do you want to go back there for?''

"It's our land. My home. We're building it," Ezra replied. "You know, they say Ireland's full of bogs and the landlords beat down on the tenants and sometimes there's nothing to eat there but potatoes, and sometimes there aren't even potatoes. Are you going back there, Liam Halloran?''

"It's my land," the Irishman said. "Or at least we'll make it ours one day.''

"You see, we Jews have something in common with you Irish," Ezra said.

They shook hands then, the Irish farmer and the Palestinian farmer, who met on a beachhead littered with crates, wearing the uniforms of a king who was not their sovereign and fighting for a victory that would not be their own.

In August the Zion Mule Corps received orders to move toward Suvla Beach where, it was rumored, a strong offensive had been launched. Grimly, Ezra and his men mended the canvas water bags which were worn to a dangerous thinness.

"I do not think you should go," Ezra said to Eleazar, who had been sick again only the week before.

"I am going." He packed his kit with slow deliberation, forming intricate knots.

"I don't want you to go," Ezra said.

"You are not my father.''

"No, I am not your father.''

And he was glad, after all, to have Eleazar at his side as they approached the Suvla front. Again, they smelled the rotten sweet stench of putrescent corpses. Again, the casualties on both sides had been heavy but there was no talk now of a truce so that they might bury the bodies. They had passed that stage.

The earth beneath their feet trembled with the roar of heavy guns and howitzers. Rockets fired from the battleships sailed above their heads in a blaze of molten fury. Nearer the battleground, the air shivered with the war cries of the light-horsemen, who advanced in waves from the trenches and mounted the shoulder of Battleship Hill. Medics hurtled past them carrying stretcher loads of the wounded. A soldier, his head wreathed in bloodied bandages, who used his bayonet as a cane, bent to lick the moisture from the water bag that dangled from Ezra's mule. Ezra lifted it so that he could drink, and the soldier gulped down the water and then fell to the ground. Eleazar bent over him, but Ezra jostled him forward.

"Come, Eleazar. We must move on. The medics will pick him up."

The soldier was dead, Ezra knew. The tongue that jutted out of his mouth was swollen and black. They passed other fallen soldiers now. The mules dug their hoofs into mounds of corpses and plodded steadily on. Ezra envied the dumb animals. Twice, he turned to vomit into a ditch.

The trenches, when they reached them, were choked with the dead and the dying. The men who grabbed their arms stared at them through a haze of fatigue and babbled incomprehensibly about victory and water. They cursed their leaders and gasped for water. They cursed the Turks and begged for a drink.

Ezra and Eleazar advanced up the hillside, crouching to avoid the fusillade of bullets that rained down on them from the Turkish strongholds. They passed a mule that had been caught in the crossfire and lay rigid in death, its sturdy legs pointed skyward. Their own animals sniffed at the carcass and plodded on.

"Water! We need water up here!"

The shout rang out from a trench tiered upward on the hillside, concealed behind an oleander bush flaming with blossoms.

"We will never make it up there," Ezra said. His own canvas bags were empty. "We must start back."

"I have two more bags," Eleazar said.

"They will need the water at the base camp. Eleazar, be reasonable. There is no cover if you climb upward. You are a clear target."

"Water!" The man's voice was pleading now. It bubbled into a sob.

Eleazar moved forward, his lips moving.

"The voice of the Lord is upon the waters—the Lord is upon many waters."

"Please. Water . . ."

"Eleazar!" Ezra screamed in warning but his shout met the

whistle of a volley of bullets and was obscured by the sudden burst of a rocket.

The bullets penetrated the canvas bags. The water that had been transported across an ocean spurted forward and was soaked up by the bare earth. The impact of the rocket tossed the slender boy into the air like a fragile doll. His body landed softly on the newly moist ground. Silvery strands of gut poured from his open abdomen. A ribbon of blood trickled from his mouth but his lips were curved in a smile and his eyes, wondrously, had closed by themselves so that he had passed into death unseeing, as a small child drifts into sleep.

"Eleazar." Ezra rushed forward, forgetting his own urgent injunction. The boy's limp wrist rested in his hand. How pale were his veins, how translucent the skin. Drops of moisture fell on Eleazar's hand, and Ezra realized that his own tears were falling in a steady stream. He wept openly and freely for the innocent youth who had been almost a son to him, for the men he had buried and those he had left. He wept for boys who would not become men and for small boys in neatly pressed school uniforms who would be fatherless. Lost in an accumulation of grief, he did not hear the sound of renewed firing and he did not realize, until pain gripped his leg, that he had been shot. A bullet had shattered his shin bone, he knew, and a scream formed at the back of his throat. Then, mercifully, the pain overcame him, and he too lost consciousness and fell across the body of Eleazar, the yeshiva boy from Tiberias who would never know whether any cause justified the carnage of war.

Chapter 21

"Will you have more tea?" Chania asked the Turkish officer who sat opposite her in the Gan Noar dining hall.

"Alas, madame, I am partial to coffee," the Turk said. "It is the English, you know, who prefer tea. You have much in common with the English."

"I regret that there has been no coffee at Gan Noar since the war began," Chania said. "Perhaps if your excellency will do us the honor of visiting us after the war, we can accommodate you properly then."

The Turk laughed jovially, as though Chania had said something extremely witty. He was, in fact, enjoying himself with this tall well-spoken Jewish woman, although her red, work-roughened hands repelled him. It was obvious that if she would protect her face from the sun her complexion would be as fair as that of his French mistress, who had left for the mountains of Syria when the summer heat swept through Palestine. These kibbutz women were unfathomable, electing to work as hard as their husbands—indeed as hard as their own farm animals. In any other country Chania Maimon would be the hostess of a salon, pouring tea from an elegant china pot, not from a battered aluminum kettle.

"I am sorry to have missed your husband. I always look forward to a little chat with David Maimon," the Turk said.

He feared the one-eyed Jew, and David Maimon despised him. He wondered what this Jewish woman was like in bed. A tigress, he suspected. Often these cool efficient women were wild when it came right down to it.

"My husband is traveling in the north. He is trying to buy some grain so that we may have cereal for the children," Chania said. "Our own crops were decimated by the locusts."

"Yes, indeed. The locusts and grasshoppers caused terrible damage. And that despite the valiant efforts of your Dr. Aaronsohn. Do you know Dr. Aaronsohn, my dear madame?"

"Dr. Aaron Aaronsohn? Of course, everyone in Palestine has heard of him."

"Yes. Of course. But despite his efforts, the locusts did more damage than the poor British were able to inflict against our forces at Gallipoli," the Turk said, and he laughed again. Like many humorless men, he believed himself to be possessed of a great wit, and he laughed disproportionately at his own unfunny jokes. Chania smiled politely. She was proficient at entertaining Turks like Jhaval Pasha.

"I am afraid I am not familiar with events at Gallipoli," she said. "We are very isolated here at Gan Noar."

"How very odd that you should not know about Gallipoli. I had heard that your brother-in-law, Ezra Maimon, was there with the so-called Zion Mule Corps." The Turk's lips set in a thin line. It was true that he was a good-natured man and it was also true that he preferred the Jews to the Arabs, but he did not want this superior Jewish bitch to think that he was stupid.

"We know nothing of that," Chania said. "But you know that the Maimon family has always been loyal to Turkey. If my brother-in-law is indeed in this mule corps, the British must have impressed him into service."

"Ah yes," the Turk said. "And do you think that all six hundred members of the mule corps were impressed into their service? Including the man to whom they recently awarded a Distinguished Conduct Medal? Come, madame, we are not foolish enough to believe that."

"I have no knowledge of my brother-in-law's activities," Chania said. "We have not even had mail from him since he was expelled from the country." That at least was true. All news of Ezra had been transmitted by family members of his comrades in the mule corps. They knew only that he had been on Gallipoli, that he had sustained a leg injury, and that he was in a British field hospital somewhere on the mainland.

"You Jews are a miraculous people. You do not need letters or telegrams to maintain contact with each other. How is it done, madame? Perhaps you use pigeons?" He laughed again.

"Pigeons?" Chania's heart sank. "Yet again you confuse me, Jhaval Pasha. I know nothing of pigeons. If you will excuse me, I must attend to the child."

A baby who had been quietly sleeping in the battered wicker perambulator in a corner of the dining hall had cried suddenly. Chania picked her up, whispered into the soft pink shell that was Elana's ear, and passed her fingers through the dark curls, damp and tousled from sleep.

"Come say hello to the nice uncle," she said to the child, who happily gummed a rusk of bread.

The child stared at the Turk. Her dark eyes were enormous and were rimmed with long lashes. Her skin was as white and as soft as the jasmine blossoms that entwined themselves around every building and bungalow on Gan Noar.

"She is a beautiful child," the Turk said appreciatively. "Is she not the daughter of your brother-in-law who fought at Gallipoli?"

"She is Ezra Maimon's daughter," Chania said patiently, evenly.

"Is it not benevolent of the Turkish government to allow the child of an expelled traitor to live in Palestine? Do you know what would happen to such a child in other countries?" He chucked Elana under the chin, and she trained another of her brilliant smiles on him. Encouraged, he dangled a gold dinar before her, and inexplicably she began to cry.

Chania held her close.

"She is a nervous child," she said. "Her mother, you know, died in childbirth."

"We know. We know everything, my dear Madame Maimon. We even know that there is no grain to be had in the north. If your husband had asked our advice we could have spared him such a foolish journey. But perhaps he had other errands?"

"I am only a woman," Chania said. "I know nothing of

my husband's affairs.'' She stood up, still cradling the child in her arms. ''Will your men be much longer searching our buildings, Jhaval Pasha?''

The Turk laughed.

''They are not searching your buildings. They are merely checking the construction. It is our duty to ascertain that everything is well built, properly constructed. What could they find in a search of your buildings? Pigeons? Do you have pigeons on Gan Noar?''

''No. We have no pigeons,'' Chania replied in a faint voice. ''Surely we have no pigeons.''

''I, however, have a dove cote,'' Jhaval Pasha said. ''Such a pretty dove cote. Sometimes it even attracts strange birds who fly from Lebanon and Syria. Sometimes the birds come to us from the coast and sometimes from the desert. I think perhaps I will take your beautiful niece to see my dove cote.''

He stretched out his arms to the child, but Elana hid her face in her aunt's shoulder.

''Why is the child crying? And why are you so nervous, madame? The innocent have nothing to fear. So it is written in the Koran. The innocent have nothing to fear, and you yourself are innocent. Can you be blamed if your brother rides with the troops of the Czar against the armies of the faithful?''

''I have not seen or heard from my brother since I was a small child and the Czar's army conscripted him,'' Chania said. ''I hate the Czar.'' That, at least, was true. She was relieved at last, on this humid day, to utter one sentence that was not studded with lies.

But she was unpleasantly startled by the Turks' knowledge of her brother's existence. Their intelligence network must be more efficient than she had assumed, or perhaps they had simply paid special attention to the connections and activities of the Maimon family. Although it was true that she herself had heard nothing of her brother since he had been conscripted so many years ago, a cousin, newly arrived in Palestine, had told her that there were rumors that he had become a high-ranking officer in the Russian army. It would be the final irony, she thought, if she were to be penalized because her brother had been forced into the army of a despot she despised.

''I am pleased to hear that,'' Jhaval Pasha said. ''Of course you hate the Czar. Time and again I have told my superiors that the Jews would never spy to gain intelligence for the man who forced them to flee Russia. And now it appears that my soldiers are returning. Your buildings appear to be in order. Gan Noar is well constructed. You are to be congratulated, my lady.''

"You must come and see us again," Chania replied. "Say shalom to the uncle, Elana."

Again the child's face was lit with the magical smile.

"Next time, madame, I may take the daughter of Ezra Maimon with me. She will love my doves—my pretty doves."

He clicked his boots together self-importantly, bowed to Chania, and straightened the well-pressed jacket of his scarlet uniform.

Chania waited until the cavalry unit had disappeared from view before she hurried over to the wicker perambulator. She lifted the straw mattress and removed the stiff little bodies of two gray carrier pigeons. They had been in her hands, having newly returned to Gan Noar, when she had seen the Turks from the window. She had crushed their fragile heads between her fingers and hidden them beneath the child's mattress before the Turks entered the room. She untaped the coded messages from the rigid yellow legs and hastily thrust the birds deep into the compost heap beyond the cooking area.

Clearly, the Turks suspected something. They could no longer take any risks at Gan Noar. There were children here, and old people. David would have to explain to Aaronsohn that any further work for the British would have to be done at Zichron Yaakov or at the Atlit Agricultural Station. She wished now that Absalom Feinberg, David's boyhood friend from Rishon, had never sought them out and enlisted David's cooperation. Absalom was engaged to Rebecca Aaronsohn, the younger sister of the famous agronomist. It was imperative, he told David, that communication be established with the British and information passed on to them. David, as a provisions officer for his movement, had a valid reason for traveling the country. He could easily observe Turkish troop movements and concentration. And he was a farmer who always had a good excuse for visiting the agricultural station.

"The only way we will get a Jewish state is by cooperating with the British," Absalom said. "Your brother Ezra must share my belief. This is our chance. This is what we dreamed of in Rishon. This is the hope that Imber saw when he wrote 'Hatikvah,' " Absalom said. His eyes burned with a lover's fire, a patriot's zeal. "We have a chance to realize the hope of two thousand years."

"Imber is safe in America," David said dryly, "and I have an obligation to the kibbutz. If the Turks should find out . . ."

"They will never find out," Absalom assured him. "Never."

And yet they had found out. Perhaps not everything, but enough. Enough.

"What will happen?" Chania asked David that night as they lay across their bed in nervous wakefulnes. She whispered although they were alone in their bungalow. Sometimes it seemed to her that she would never again speak in full voice or walk without shifting her eyes to see if she were being followed, or fall asleep with a full stomach and an easy mind.

She worried over the affairs of the kibbutz, which had undertaken the care and protection of the families of members who had been driven from their homes by the Turks. Elderly couples and young children crowded the communal buildings and the small bungalows. A member's cousin, a member's elderly parents—all Jews in need of refuge. Chania and Mirra used fodder as food now, cooking huge pots of gruel from coarse grains meant for the animals that had long since been seized by the Turks or slaughtered for food.

She worried about David, who was acting now as a courier for the Aaronsohn network. NILI it was called, an acronym from *Netzach Yisrael Lo Yishaker*—the defender of Israel will not lie.

"I don't know what will happen," David said. "But Aaron Aaronsohn is right. The future, our future, lies with the British. If we help them now, they will help us after the war."

"How can you help them?" Chania said wearily.

They could barely manage to keep their own children from starving. They were impotent against the clouds of locusts that had destroyed their crops. They were powerless against the Turks who expelled them from their cities and roamed at will across their farms. How could they be of help to the forces of Britain fighting in a distant theater across an unknown terrain? And besides, there were many in the kibbutz movement who did not trust the Aaronsohns. They were private landowners who openly and harshly disavowed socialism and even hired Arab labor.

"Our weapon is information. The British must have knowledge of Turkish strength and troop movements."

"And that was the information the pigeons were carrying," she said, and she thought of how the skulls of the small birds had been so easy to crush. Their soft cranial bone had slid beneath her fingernails, and her dress stank where she had wiped her hands across the skirt when she saw Jhaval Pasha.

"Yes. And the British returned them with questions. They want to know the Turkish troop density in the Jerusalem corridor. They want to know if howitzers have been moved into the Jordan pass." He passed a hand across his eye patch. His good eye was red with fatigue.

She knew that nothing she could say would deter him from his work, but he could no longer use Gan Noar as a base. It was too dangerous. The Turk's references to Elana had not been lost on her. There were no children or old people at the Atlit station. Let the Aaronsohns take the risks and be the heroes.

"You cannot work from here," she said. "The risk is too great. Jhaval Pasha knows about the pigeons. He hinted. He threatened."

David nodded. He agreed with her. It was hazardous to work against the Turks. The fate of the Armenians haunted the Jews of Palestine. Mothers in Petach Tikvah clutched their children tightly when they thought of the dark-eyed Armenian women who had been marched into the desert, some of them holding nursing babies to their breasts. There had been stories of children who died with scimitars in their hearts and of the dismembered bodies of young men strewn across the streets of deserted villages. The Jews of Palestine had much in common with the Armenians. They too were an isolated, powerless minority group living on the edge of the desert. They too had little to protect them from the fury of their Turkish masters. They felt themselves to be imprisoned in a mysterious maze, darting backward and forward between former enemies and current oppressors—choosing the protective banners of strangers because they had none of their own.

David Maimon agreed with Aaron Aaronsohn and with his old Rishon friend Absalom Feinberg that the days of the Turkish reign in Palestine were numbered.

"Their edicts against the Jewish community are their death cry," the agronomist had told him.

Aaron Aaronsohn's words rang with certainty. He had the confidence of the Turks, who respected his work in the development of a sturdy strand of indigenous winter wheat. He had been authorized by Jhaval Pasha himself to travel to Berlin to do research. Often the Turks talked too freely in front of the bespectacled, introspective Aaronsohn. He listened very carefully. He knew their secrets; he sensed their destiny.

"I must go to Zichron tomorrow," David told Chania. "I must warn them."

"Why you?" she asked bitterly. She turned her face so that he would not see her weep. Why must David Maimon always ride in the vanguard of danger?

Elana, who slept in a corner of their room, cried in her sleep and Chania went to rock the child's cradle, to pull a coverlet over her. Her own children had always slept in the children's house, but she kept the motherless baby with her. Elana was so alone, so vulnerable. She had been snatched from death and thus her life was doubly precious.

"Chania, be patient. These are dangerous times for us."

"You are only happy in dangerous times," she said harshly.

When would her life and their children's safety be as important to him as clandestine meetings held in dimly lit farmhouses and isolated khans? When would their life together outweigh his bitterness?

"Listen to me. You must be careful not to endanger Gan Noar," she said, and her voice was strangely cold.

"And you must listen to me," he replied gently. "If they do know that I am involved, if they have information on the network, it may be necessary for me to leave the country. The others can disguise themselves but I—I am too easily recognized."

"David."

Her anger melted. She was suffused with love for him, for all that he risked for her and for their people. She turned to him in the darkness and passed her hands across his narrow shoulders, his muscular arms. The strength of his body thrilled her. Her father had been a stooped and fragile man—a shoemaker who spent his days bent over a cobbler's bench. Her husband was a tall farmer, a soldier who wore the black badge of his own courage. She trembled at the thought of losing him. All anger was gone, and only her terrible need remained.

"David."

Now his name became a whisper. She thought it the most beautiful name in the Bible. David. The warrior poet, the brave and sensuous king who had fought fiercely and made love unwisely. She drew him to her, and they sank down together on the bed while the toddler Elana stared at them through the bars of her cradle, her face glowing like a soft white flower in the darkness.

David mounted his horse the next morning before the first light of dawn. A silvery light shimmered across the wild meadowlands that led to Zichron. It would be a cool day in the village. But he did not go to Zichron that day. A NILI messenger intercepted him—a bearded youth who had hidden in the pass, waiting for him. David noticed his trembling hands. The Turks had arrived at Zichron the previous day. (At almost the same time Jhaval Pasha had sipped his tea at Gan Noar, David thought, trembling himself now.) They had arrested Sara Aaronsohn. They had beaten the old man, her father, with whip and bastinado, and even now they were torturing Sara. They had tied her to a door, crushed her fingernails, pressing burning bricks on her breasts. The man wept as he spoke. She would not survive, and no one from the network was safe.

"You must leave the country, Maimon," the messenger said, and he rode off, leaving David alone on the coast road.

His stallion nervously paced the road as David held the reins loosely. An Arab shepherd wandered across the meadow, playing his reed pipe and leading a flock of goats. When he saw David he turned back and led his animals across the wadi. His music was stilled, and the silence hung heavy in the morning air.

Sara Aaronsohn would not speak. Of this David was certain. She would die before she would betray her comrades, but still he was in danger. He had to follow instructions. He had to get out of the country.

Often he had heard others complain of the smallness of Palestine and how claustrophobic it was to live in a country bordered by hostile nations. How cut off they were, such people said. How isolated. They bought picture books of

London and Paris. They hung up prints and paintings of
landscapes they had left behind. His own mother spoke long-
ingly of Moscow, of Baden, where she had vacationed with
her father the grain broker. David had never understood such
feelings. He could not imagine why anyone would want to
leave Palestine at all—even for a day. For him all beauty, all
destiny, was contained in the lunar landscapes of its southland, the verdant wilderness of the Galilee, the snow-capped
mountains of the north, and the gentle waters of the south-
ernmost sea. The land was a daily miracle to him. Its soil was
an extension of his own being. And yet now, he realized, he
himself was a prisoner within the land that he loved.

There was no exit. The Turks blocked every seaport, every
mountain pass. The only possible way out was across the
southern border, into the Sinai and then to Egypt, where the
British were in command. Absalom had given him the name
of a British officer who was organizing an expeditionary
force. "Just in case," Absalom had said. Someone else had
told him of an Englishman named Lawrence who was sup-
posedly organizing an Arab revolt against the Turks. Aaron
Aaronsohn had met this Lawrence and spoke of him with
some bitterness.

"He is your typical Russian anti-Semite but he happens to
speak impeccable English," Aaronsohn had said. "The British mask their hatred."

No. If David got across the border he would seek out the
other British officer and forget that Lawrence, who was mad
with dreams of Arabian splendor. They were fascinated by
Arabs, these Englishmen. They thought they knew them, that
they could trust them. They would learn. As he had learned.
He touched the eye patch. Grit accumulated in the empty
socket. Soon he would have to rinse it. Soon he would have
to figure out a way to get across the border. Damn it. There
was no way it could be done.

"David Maimon. Salaam aleikem, David Maimon."

Ezra's neighbor Saleem, astride Ezra's white stallion, rode
up to him.

"*Yaala*, Saleem. Aleikem salaam," he replied.

He could not imagine what Saleem was doing on this
lonely byroad, miles away from Sadot Shalom.

"Have you news of my brother?" he asked.

"No. There has been no word from your brother. But this morning the Turks came looking for you at Sadot Shalom. They left a party of soldiers at the kibbutz. They told me that I must tell them if you come to Sadot Shalom. They even gave me baksheesh against the time that I would tell them of your arrival."

He tossed David the leather purse that contained three gold coins, the conventional bribe on account.

"And you took it?" David asked.

"It would have been foolish not to take it," Saleem said. "I took it, and I listened when they told me that all Jewish land titles had been cancelled. 'Your master will not come home. Sadot Shalom will be yours,' they said, then I, their faithful servant, kissed their feet. It is necessary that they think I am their friend, or else we are both betrayed."

"And you would not betray me, Saleem?"

"I would not betray Ezra Maimon's brother," the Arab replied. A levantine answer, David thought, but one that he had earned. His face twisted in a painful grin.

"I must leave the country, Saleem," he said.

"Yes. And the only hope lies across the desert to the south."

"Yes. But they will be watching for a Jew who wears a black eye patch."

"True. They would be watching for such a man. But they would not be looking for a blind Arab on his way to the baths of Luxor, perhaps being led by his grandson. Such a man would pass without challenge," Saleem speculated. His voice was dreamy, as though he were telling a story to a small child.

"Such a man would be safe," David agreed.

"You must come with me," Saleem said.

He led David to a cave and cautioned him to stay there. He left him his own water bottle and a supply of dried meats and fruit. Achmed arrived at the cave before evening, carrying a bundle which contained the white abayah and kaffiyeh of a tribal elder, and white muslin used to bandage the eyes of the blind so that they would be protected from the desert sand. A cedar staff was added to the costume. When David was dressed, Achmed laughed.

"I myself would have been deceived," he said.

It took them almost a week to make their way through the desert to the Rafah gap, south of the Gaza strip. The blind man and his grandson aroused no suspicion. David had learned Bedouin dialects during his Shomer training and was able to converse with the few tribesmen they met, who always courteously exchanged greetings, shared their food, and directed the travelers to the next water hole. The landmarks of desert passage were the secret sources of water. The man and boy talked little as they walked but there was an unarticulated mutual respect which they acknowledged with small courtesies. Achmed always offered David the canvas water bag first. When David killed a desert hare and they roasted it on an open fire, he carefully cut out the sweetest meat for Achmed. At night they lay awake together and listened to the odd chorus of hyenas wailing against the fall of darkness.

"This is a fine thing you have done for me," David said to Achmed on their last night together as they looked down on the lights of El Arish from their hillside cove.

"I do this for my friend Amos—for his children, for my children," Achmed replied. "Together we will free the land from the Turk, and Jew and Arab will live in Palestine. It is possible. Feisal the Hashimite has said it is possible. But we cannot build on hatred, Adon Maimon."

David did not answer. The boy's statement was a plea he could not yet accept, an idea that caught him by surprise. He had too long seen the Arab as an adversary. Yet Achmed was an Arab, and Achmed had saved his life. But how many Achmeds were there among the Arabs of Palestine? The question wearied him. It had been easier to cling to his anger, to his memory of the dark night of the revia and the treacherous whistling bullet that had claimed his eye. He derived his strength from his hatred.

"I leave you here," Achmed said. "You do not need the disguise to go into El Arish. I will send word to Gan Noar that you are safely arrived."

He extended his hand and David took it. The boy's fingers were slender but his skin wore a farmer's callouses and there was strength in his grasp. They looked at each other for a long moment, remembering the days and nights of their dangerous journey, thinking that it might be the will of the separate gods they worshiped that they might never see each other again. Then Achmed turned and rode off, a slender figure on a black horse, riding across drifts of sand, between pillars of calcite, to disappear into the desert as David Maimon crossed the border into Egypt.

Chapter 22

The lights of New York City were distant pinpoints of brightness but the blazing torch of the Statue of Liberty cast a shivering cone of light across the ink-dark harbor waters. A small cheer rose from the passengers—the traditional emission of relief and excitement of those who have been long at sea intensified now because they had crossed the ocean in time of war and had felt themselves pitted against both the forces of man and of nature. A group of returning Americans, who had spent most of the voyage playing cards in the ship's lounge, suddenly burst into song.

"Give a cheer for the red, white, and blue," they sang. "Hello my honey, hello my baby, hello my ragtime girl . . ." They sang loudly and held their arms out to the approaching shoreline. They clapped and did rapid little dances. They embraced each other and exchanged addresses and telephone numbers although they would not disembark until the morning. Already they had relegated the voyage to the past, and they were thinking now of those who awaited them on shore, their land arrangements, the weeks ahead.

Ezra Maimon leaned heavily upon his cane and watched them with the amused condescension of an adult observing small children at play. The young women were pretty and gay. They huddled within their furs and their warm coats. The war had interfered with their grand tours, with their studies at conservatories and studios, with the fun of being young and in Europe at last. But they had been duly compensated by the thrill of the unexpected and the atmosphere of danger that had haunted their crossing.

"Do you think there might be U-boats nearby, Lieutenant Maimon?" the pretty auburn-haired girl from Connecticut had asked him every time the S.S. *Orangeton* hit an unusual swell.

"I don't think so," he replied.

"But remember the *Lusitania* and the *Sussex*," she said. Her eyes opened with wide anticipatory fear.

"I was on Gallipoli when the *Lusitania* went down," he said and immediately regretted his words.

"Was that where you were wounded?" she asked.

At last she would get the story. All the young people on the boat were so curious about the tall, amber-skinned British officer who spoke such an oddly accented English and whose uniform was adorned with shoulder lashings on which a Jewish star had been mounted. Some said he was Egyptian. Others thought he might be a spy or an agent provocateur.

"Probably sent over to try to coax us into their bloody war," one young man said.

"We ought to be in it," another replied. "That damn Bryan lives in the sixteenth century."

"Yes, I was wounded on Gallipoli," Ezra told the girl. "On Suvla Beach," he added perversely, knowing that she probably had never heard of Suvla Beach and would have difficulty finding Gallipoli on the map. He was immediately ashamed of himself. She had meant no harm. She was just a child, snatched from her game and given a real war in its place. "If you will forgive me, I must go below," he said. "The night air is not good for my wound."

She smiled understandingly. He had redeemed himself, he knew, by admitting her into the drama of his suffering.

Alone in the cabin that he shared with another Palestinian, he had been annoyed with himself and his own evasiveness. Although, he acknowledged, in all probability his full story would have disappointed her. A muleteer, even a wounded one, was not a glamorous figure, and his mission to New

York was not an errand of dramatic secrecy. He had been sent
to collect funds and to encourage young American Jews to
enlist in the Jewish legion which Jabotinsky was now trying
to organize.

"I am not equipped to be a *schnorrer*," he had told
Jabotinsky when they spoke in the British field hospital to
which he had been evacuated.

"What are your options?" the Russian asked shrewdly. He
was not a man who wasted time or effort. "You cannot return
to Palestine. The Turks will almost certainly arrest you and
try you for treason. You are no good to the British here, even
if they would use your services, until your leg wound heals.
Gallipoli is lost, and the usefulness of the Zion Mule Corps is
ended. But when a Palestinian front is opened there will be a
need for a Jewish legion, and that is where you can be useful.
They will need you and the other Palestinians because of your
knowledge of the terrain and the language. But we will need
many more men. We must get volunteers and money from
Europe, England, and the United States. And that is where
you have a role to play." He spoke with the considered
thoughtfulness of a director assigning roles to be acted on a
stage of his own improvisation. He would determine the lead
and the supporting characters; he would manipulate financing
and publicity.

"What role?"

Ezra's leg throbbed. The discomfort was a good sign, the
doctor told him. The bone was knitting together and the ache
was part of the healing process. Would the doctor think it a
good sign too, Ezra wondered, that he awakened night after
night drenched with sweat, feeling anew the pain of Eleazar's
death, licking his own lips as though he might taste the ribbon
of blood that had streaked the dead boy's mouth?

"The role of the brave Palestinian warrior-farmer. Our
American cousins will be duly impressed by a tall, bronzed
Palestinian who has plowed the fields of the Galilee and been
wounded on Gallipoli. You will lean on your cane and stare
out at the audience. You will tell them how beautiful the
nights are on your farm and how Jews died fighting to
keep their world safe for democracy on Gallipoli. They will
open their wallets. They will give you their checks, their
promises, their gratitude. You will ask the young men if they
have examined the meaning of their lives. Do they not want

to live toward some purpose? Have they thought about the contribution they will make to history, to the Jewish people? Do they not want to proudly wear a uniform as you do?''

"And immediately they will sign away their lives for a country they have never seen and a cause that is new to them?'' Ezra asked dryly.

"Didn't your father sign away his life for a country he had never seen?'' Jabotinsky asked. He smiled. "I myself have never seen Palestine, Maimon. I have never walked through the hills of the Galilee and the deserts of the south. Yet I have signed my life away.''

"All men are different, Jabo,'' Ezra replied, remembering Nechama (*who was dead*) cautioning him in the same words. "All men are different,'' she had said. "You are not your father. And Amos is not you.''

"All men are different,'' Jabotinsky agreed, as Ezra himself had not. He had turned his head and heart away from Nechama's pleading voice. He was a father betrayed, and he wrapped himself righteously in the cloak of his own disappointment. "But all Jews everywhere must be united by one common cause—a Jewish homeland in Palestine. And each Jew must do what he can to bring about that miracle. Some will give their lives and some will give their money.''

The Russian's eyes burned with passion. His voice, which rose to a crescendo when he spoke from the podium, was soft now, but still hypnotic. There had been no refusing him, and so Ezra stood at the rail of the ship steaming into New York harbor and listened to home-coming Americans sing songs he could not comprehend.

From England he had written to his father's brother, his Uncle Mendel, to tell him of his arrival, enclosing the notice in the *London Gazette* which announced that a Jewish legion was in formation and would be attached to the Thirty-eighth Battalion of the Royal Fusiliers. The Zionist organization in England had furnished him with other material which he did not send his uncle. The situation of the Jews of Palestine had grown desperate. Expulsions, emigration, and death had reduced the community from one hundred thousand to fifty thousand, and those who remained were barely sustained by funds made available through the good offices of Henry Morgenthau, the American ambassador to Turkey.

"You must tell the American Jews what is happening in

Palestine—how Jews are hunted down by both the Turks and the Arabs, how Jewish girls are selling themselves to Turkish and German soldiers so that their families will not starve to death,'' a Palestinian envoy in London had told him. The man himself was extraordinarily thin, and his left eye danced nervously as he spoke. He had brought news of the Maimon family. Except for Amos, everyone was at Gan Noar, but David Maimon had disappeared and was presumed dead. Some said that he had been involved with the Aaronsohn spy ring and had died of thirst, trying to escape across the desert into Egypt. There had been no word from him for months.

"My brother is not dead," Ezra had said.

The envoy did not argue with him. He had, in recent weeks, met many men who would not believe that their brothers were dead.

Would his uncle be waiting for him, Ezra wondered as he packed for disembarkation. And if so, how would they know each other? Yehuda himself had no clear recollection of the brother who had left so many years ago for America. His Uncle Mendel was called Martin Wasser—just as Yehuda had Hebraized the family name, so his brother had shortened it; there was no time for long names in a land where speed and brevity counted for everything—and he lived in New York City. He had replied warmly to the letter Ezra sent from London, offering his help, his assistance. But Ezra would not predict how far that help and assistance would extend. His uncle might be a man of modest means, and besides, it had never been Ezra Maimon's way to ask for help from others.

He had some money given to him by the Zionist committee in England and a small notebook filled with addresses from the same source. He had noticed the names of David Ben Gurion and Yitzhak Ben Zvi, who had occasionally visited him at Sadot Shalom. It seemed that they too were involved in the business of raising money and recruiting volunteers for the Jewish legion, Ezra smiled. The last time he had seen the two men they wore the red tarbooshes of the Turks and were afire with plans to earn law degrees in Constantinople and argue before the Turkish courts for the establishment of a Jewish national home in Palestine. But that had been a war ago, before the expulsions from Tel Aviv, before Palestinian Jews had been conscripted to build roads in Armenia.

They docked in the early hours of morning, and Ezra

emerged from the customs shed and stared at his provisional British passport, neatly stamped now and affirming that he had entered the United States as a tourist. He held his cane in one hand and his Gladstone bag in the other and allowed himself to be swept along in the excited crowd of disembarking passengers.

The auburn-haired American girl kissed him goodbye as she rushed past him.

"I just knew you were a hero," she whispered breathlessly, "and the next time I see you, I'm going to get you to tell me all your secrets."

He realized now that she had wanted to sleep with him, and the thought bemused him. Two years had passed since Nechama's death. He had fought in a war and traveled across two continents but he had not yet made love to another woman. He stared after the girl and felt the strange stirring of regret.

"All right," he said softly.

"Excuse me. Are you perhaps Ezra Maimon?"

The man who stood before him wore a fur-collared chesterfield coat buttoned high against the early spring chill. His thick silver hair was crowned with a fedora and his mustache was brushed and waved so that the crumbs of tobacco from his cigar slid off the silver, pomaded hairs. His eyes, like Ezra's own and like Yehuda's, were sea green.

"Uncle Mendel," Ezra said in astonishment. He knew that his uncle was at least five years his father's senior, but the man who stood before him looked ten years younger than Yehuda Maimon. His skin was soft and he moved with the effortless ease of a man who has not abused his body. Ezra's father walked slowly and moved with careful deliberation, as all men do who know that they must live by their physical strength. Ezra had not realized before the toll the pioneering life had taken on Yehuda. He himself had grown up on a farm but Yehuda had come to his life there as a middle-aged man.

"Uncle Marty," the man corrected him and suddenly threw his arms about Ezra, engulfing him in a fierce and powerful embrace. "Yehuda's son. My God, you're Yehuda's son, and I never thought to see any of my family again."

Marty Wasser smelled of tobacco and pine, of fine wool and newly laundered linen. Tears stood in his green eyes, and when he released Ezra his cheeks were bright pink. Passersby stared at them curiously, wondering what the relationship could be between the limping British officer and the prosperous American businessman.

"Forgive me, but you don't know what it is to go away and leave everything and everyone who was ever a part of you," Martin Wasser said.

"But I do know," Ezra replied.

His uncle's tears had stirred his own heart, and he thought of his distant sister and wondered if he would ever see Sara again. He thought of his children and of his brothers and of their children. David is alive, he thought suddenly. *I know that he is alive.* It had not occurred to him before that he had even considered for a moment that David might be dead.

"Let's get your luggage." His uncle recovered himself and was once again the organized man in control of a situation.

"This is my luggage." Ezra pointed to his Gladstone bag.

"I see. We shall have to outfit you then. It will be no problem. I have many friends in ready-to-wear. One, two, three, and you have a whole wardrobe."

"No. I have enough—my uniforms. And I will be staying only long enough to do my work. But I thank you, Uncle." He knew instinctively that Martin Wasser needed the recognition of gratitude.

Martin Wasser in turn took measure of his nephew and decided that he was not unlike the brother he had not seen for many decades. Yehuda too, even as a young boy, had always had a plan and had proceeded with deliberate determination, living sparsely in the present, planning for the future. "I am going to Palestine," he had said when he was still a youth, and Martin had known that he would surely go. Yehuda was fortunate to have a son so like himself. Martin Wasser did not share his fortune. His own son, Alex, a doctor who practiced dermatology in a northern New York city, was nothing like Martin himself. Even his name was different. Dr. Alex Wade he called himself. It was better for the practice, he explained to his father. "Why? Girls don't like to get their pimples cured by a Jew?" Martin had retorted. "You changed your name." "To make it shorter!" But Alex had turned away. Ezra Maimon, though, had kept his father's name, and dreamed his father's dream.

"You are so like your father," he told Ezra now.

"He would be very surprised to hear you say so," Ezra replied.

In his uncle's apartment, high above the broad street called Park Avenue, which strangely did not overlook a park, Ezra explained his purpose in America.

"We must raise money for the Jews in Palestine who are only just barely managing to survive," he said, and the plea in his own voice startled him.

He had never imagined himself capable of asking other people for money. He remembered how bitter his father had always been about the Jews in Palestine who existed on the charity of the Jewish community abroad. But these were different times. There could be no pride, no contempt, when lives were at stake, when his own children and his brother's children lived at the edge of starvation. Little Elana was two years old now—a toddler. He had seen the malnourished children of the Gallipoli villages balancing themselves on legs weakened by rickets. His child must be sturdy and strong. And he was not asking strangers for money. He was asking Jews to support their brothers and sisters in Palestine.

Martin Wasser looked about his comfortable living room and studied his highly polished black shoes, neatly encased in gray spats and planted in the deep blue carpeting. Claire, his wife, sat opposite him in an easy chair upholstered in fuchsia taffeta. She was a handsome woman who had only recently begun to color her white hair blue. Gently, she urged Ezra Maimon to drink more tea, to eat another pastry. She had walked three blocks to a special shop to buy them especially for him. Ezra Maimon spoke of famine. The children were eating coarse grain meant for animals. Nursing mothers had no milk. The whipped cream oozed out of the thin pastry shell and drizzled across the rose-colored flowers on the patterned china plate. He remembered how the fat on the cans of bully beef had melted in the hot Aegean sun and oozed in white trickles across the marbled pink meat. Nausea swept across him in a treacherous wave. He excused himself and limped to the fine tiled bathroom, where he vomited into a toilet bowl the color of the sea.

Martin Wasser took his nephew on a tour of New York. They rode the subways and were hurtled through the great metropolis in minutes. He had never imagined that a city could be so huge, so diverse. He sat on the train and watched black people and Orientals, red-cheeked Irish girls and bearded Chassidim. People had come here from every country and found new lives. If it had happened in the United States it could happen in Palestine. Jews could come from all the countries of the dispersion and together forge a single nation.

He visited the great department stores and rode an elevator to the top of the Empire State Building, where he looked down on Manhattan Island. He was swept into the rush of urban life. Everyone was in a hurry. Martin Wasser rushed to his factory on East Broadway each morning. Claire Wasser rushed to Macy's and Ohrbachs. She rushed to meetings of her synagogue sisterhood and her study group. She rushed to meet her friends for lunch. Ezra's cousins rushed to meet him and then they rushed to keep other appointments, to go to the theater, to attend meetings. Ezra watched them and thought of the long quiet days and nights on Sadot Shalom where the pace of life conformed to the needs of the earth, to the turning of the seasons. He remembered how the sun set in the Galilee, the gentle fading of light and the wondrous sweep of purple shadow across low hillsides.

The sun set in New York in heartrending splendor: color shattered the sky; avalanches of pink and purple clouds cascaded into the waters of the Hudson River. He leaned against a railing each afternoon and watched the dying sun bloody the rocks of the Palisades. Pedestrians looked at him curiously. They were accustomed to people looking up at their great skyscrapers but it was seldom that a man paused to mark the setting of the sun.

He grew attuned to the momentum of the city. He too rushed to meetings in dimly lit railroad flats on the Lower East Side and listened to old friends explain their strategy. Ben Gurion and Ben Zvi had been feverishly busy. They had met with Zionist leaders. They had met with Louis Brandeis, the lawyer who headed the Provisional Committee for Zionist Affairs.

"America is a neutral country," he had said guardedly although they could see that he himself did not feel neutral.

"Neutrality is a luxury we cannot afford," they said.

They talked to staid businessmen and intense young men and women. They demanded money. They pleaded for commitment. They had traveled to the South and collected sub-

stantial checks from old men who lived with the memories of
childhoods spent hiding in the cellars of Eastern Europe,
listening to booted feet march across the carpeted floors of
their homes. They lived in Atlanta and Charleston now, in
Chicago and Detroit. Their businesses were prosperous and
their children were becoming doctors and lawyers but they
had not forgotten the stench of fear and the tyranny of violence. Ben Gurion told Ezra how a prosperous merchant in
Chattanooga had wept to hear of the abuses which the Jews of
Palestine suffered at the hands of the Turks. He had written a
generous check but had looked at Ben Gurion incredulously
when he asked if his teen-age son would join the Jewish
legion.

"They will give us their money but not their sons," the
short Russian, whose hair stood up in disarray, said wonderingly. It was incomprehensible to him that Jews would not be
magnetically drawn to fight for Zion. Like Jabotinsky, he had
the zealot's impatience with those who could not believe as
he did.

Ezra addressed meetings of Zionist groups. He traveled the
city, taking the subway from Brooklyn to the Bronx, sometimes addressing three meetings in a single day. He spoke to
crowds of young people in synagogue social halls and in
Jewish community centers. He spoke on the boardwalk of
Brighton Beach flanked by an American flag and a Jewish
flag. Across the way an Irishman with a rich brogue held a
satin banner emblazoned with a bright green clover and exhorted
his listeners to fight for a free and independent Ireland. A tall
bearded black man mounted a wooden crate and reminded
those about him that a war was brewing on the Russian
steppes and in the boulevards of Saint Petersburg. "A war for
justice, for righteousness, for equality. The great Bolshevik
movement of Russia is ready to throw off the chains of
capitalism and war. Working people of the world unite!" the
black man shouted and distributed mimeographed sheets which
small boys seized and fashioned into paper airplanes.

Ezra spoke of the need for a Jewish homeland and for a
Jewish legion to fight against the Turks and the Germans.

"Must Jews always live in fear?" he asked. "In Palestine
we have shown that we can farm. On the battlefields of
Gallipoli we have shown that we can fight. Join us! Help
us!"

High school students, members of Zionist youth groups wearing coarse white linen bands on which blue Jewish stars had been stitched, circulated in the crowd, shaking their cannisters. Coins and bills were thrust into the blue-and-white containers. Sheets were passed around calling for volunteers for the Jewish legion. One of them was passed back to Ezra with an ugly scrawl. "Give the kikes guns. Let them kill each other." One afternoon the Irish speaker gave Ezra the contents of his collection box.

"Your people have the greater need of it now," he said and solemnly shook Ezra's hand.

Ezra thanked him and thought of Liam Halloran. He wondered if he was back at his farm in Ireland now and if he remembered their conversation on the Gallipoli beach.

It was during such a boardwalk address that he first noticed the small dark-haired young woman who stood at the edge of the crowd and listened to him solemnly. She did not shout or nod as his other listeners did. She stood quite still, wrapped in a bright plaid cape with a red beret perched jauntily on her smooth dark hair. Something in her quietness attracted him. He set his gaze on her, sensing the intensity of her attention. But when he stepped down from the podium she had disappeared. She was in his audience again that night when he addressed a Zionist meeting in the Bronx. This time she removed her cape because the crowded synagogue hall was overheated, and he saw that she wore a schoolgirl's dark skirt and a rose-colored cardigan over her white blouse.

"She is a child," he thought. "A young girl."

But he realized at once that the clothes deceived. She was not a young girl. She was a full-breasted, wide-eyed young woman. He looked for her at the end of the meeting but again she had left. Two days later he saw her again at a midtown meeting held in a union hall. She sat amidst the weary pale-eyed garment workers. There were fewer people than usual in the audience, and he looked directly at her. She stared placidly back at him, and he was certain that he saw her cheeks turn briefly russet. He would speak to her that night, he decided, and he rushed through the last phrases of his address. He kept his eyes fixed on her. She sat, as always, at the rear of the room, and as always she was alone and regal in her own stillness. He hurried off the platform at the end, determined to reach her before she left. Already she was buttoning her plaid cape; arranging her books and a parcel.

"Lieutenant Maimon. I have a question about Jews using force." A pale bespectacled boy wearing the red-and-white button of the Young People's Socialist League stopped him. "Isn't force contrary to Jewish principle? Don't Jews believe that all people should work together for peace and equality?"

"We would, of course, rather not use force," he replied. "But history has denied us the luxury of that choice. We must defend ourselves and fight for what is right."

She was putting her red beret on now, edging toward the door. He ignored the questioner and moved forward.

"Lieutenant Maimon," an old man said, clutching at his sleeve, "if Palestine is freed of the Turks, will the Jews and the Arabs be able to work together?"

"Why not?"

She was almost at the door. If he leaped over a bench he would reach her.

"Lieutenant Maimon, I'm with the *Journal American*. If you can spare a few minutes we'd like to run a story on your efforts here." The man in the belted leather coat flashed a press identification card at him.

Ezra sighed. This was a request he could not refuse. Newspaper coverage was vital to their cause.

"One newspaper story is worth a hundred boardwalk meetings," Ben Gurion had said, and Ezra agreed. He buttoned his tunic and followed the reporter to a small conference room.

"Just a few questions," the reporter assured him, but the interview took an hour. When he emerged she was, of course, gone. The meeting room was empty. A red scarf hung forlornly across the back of the chair she had occupied. He plucked it up. The fragrance of wild flowers clung to it.

A small black leather notebook lay on the corner of the chair. He surmised that it had slipped from her pocket when she pulled the scarf out. He leafed through its closely noted pages, searching out a name or an address, but saw only dates and times. Meetings of committees, appointments at clinics. On the last page of notations—a schedule for the following week—a meeting was scheduled on Fenway Square in Boston, and a railroad schedule was clipped to the page. She had circled the Yankee Clipper, which departed from Back Bay

Station for New York late in the afternoon. He too was
scheduled to be in Boston on that day. It would not be
inconvenient, he thought, to try to return to New York on the
Clipper.

He folded the scarf and put it in his pocket. He placed the
small notebook in his wallet. During the days that followed,
he occasionally removed the book and studied the delicate
strokes of her handwriting. She used a violet ink and was
scrupulous about margins. He touched the softness of the
scarf now and again as he traveled through the city. He
realized that he was looking for her on bus and subway,
searching for her in the audiences that flocked to hear him
and in crowded restaurants and half-empty coffee shops. But
there was no intensity to his quest. He was certain that he
would see her again, that somehow he would find her on that
New England train. It occurred to him that the Yankee Clipper was an incongruously romantic name for a diesel-drawn
train that sped steel-encased cars through the New England
night.

The newspaper story appeared with a picture of Ezra in
uniform. The headline read, "JEWISH FARMER FROM GALILEE
CALLS FOR INTERNATIONAL JEWISH LEGION. HERO OF GALLIPOLI
PLEADS FOR JEWISH VOLUNTEERS!"

His Aunt Claire bought fifty copies of the newspaper and
distributed clippings to visitors to her Park Avenue apartment.
His uncle framed the story and hung it in his office. Copies
were sent to Jabotinsky and Trumpeldor, and Martin Wasser
sent an enthusiastic letter to his brother Yehuda Maimon. "In
this country your son Ezra is a hero," he wrote. Rivka shook
her head wonderingly when they received the letter. He could
not mean her Ezra. He had been such a sickly child. He had
wept in the night and run high fevers. But he did mean her
Ezra. She studied the newspaper picture and showed it to
small Elana.

"See Abba. Strong Abba," she said, but the child was not
interested in the frayed photogravure picture of a man she had
never seen.

Ezra traveled to Boston for a meeting of the Provisional
Committee for Zionist Affairs. Louis Brandeis acted as chair-
man. He listened to him carefully, his gray-blue eyes fixed on
Ezra's face.

"You are of the opinion, then, that the sympathies of the

American Jewish community should lie strongly on the side of Britain, Lieutenant Maimon?'' he asked.

"There is no doubt about it," Ezra replied.

"You are aware, of course, that the Turks hold the Jews of Palestine hostage and that the Germans have a similar situation with their large Jewish community. Quite frankly, we are afraid of reprisals,'' a tall bearded man said.

"Rabbi Wise's point is well taken," Brandeis noted softly.

Ezra was startled to learn that the man was a rabbi. He wore no hat, and when an attractive secretary entered the room Ezra had seen him stare after her with undisguised appreciation. America bred strange rabbis, he decided. He turned back to the question at hand.

"I am certain," Ezra said, "that no matter what the risk, the future of the Jewish community of Palestine lies with the British cause. There are dangers, of course. We are not unaware of them. There have been losses and there will be other loses. But the Jews of Palestine have always faced danger and sustained losses. My own family has.'' His voice trembled slightly.

"I agree with your opinion, my friend," Louis Brandeis said. "The American Jewish community stands behind the Jews of Palestine. What is needed is men, money, and discipline."

Ezra waited alone for the train to New York in Boston's Back Bay Station and felt the chill that permeated the cavernous terminal. Light fell in coruscated beams from inefficient ceiling bulbs, and more than one waiting passenger shivered against the loneliness and the cold.

Ezra searched the vast room, his fingers worrying the soft wool of the red scarf that nestled in his overcoat pocket. A crowd of new arrivals surged through the door and he studied each face, his breath coming in short, swift gasps. He shivered with the anticipatory excitement of a young man at a large party, waiting for one face to project itself forward from the multitude of guests. Suddenly, he glimpsed a petite woman walking swiftly ahead of him, burdened with a heavy briefcase. Her hair slid down her back in sleek, dark folds. His heart soared, and he hurried after her. She turned at the sound of his steps, her elegantly curved eyebrows raised in bewilderment, her almond-shaped eyes touched with fear. He stared into the confused face of an exquisite Japanese woman.

"I'm so sorry," he muttered. "I thought you were someone else."

His excitement was transmuted to dejection. He was amazed
now at his own naïveté. Had he really expected to intercept
her? His own foolishness stunned him. This was not the tiny
train station at Abu Tor in Jerusalem. It was a vast terminal
through which thousands of passengers passed each day.
Indeed, he had no way of knowing she would even be here.
Her plans might have changed. The notebook and timetable
might not have belonged to her at all. He had been a romantic
fool, embarked on a fool's errand which had earned him a
fool's reward.

He sat down on a wooden bench and waited, with resigned
patience, for his train to be called. Lassitude overtook him.
He was in no hurry to reach the empty room and the narrow
bed at his uncle's apartment. But he was grimly accepting
now of the unending aloneness of his life.

Waiting passengers turned the pages of their newspapers
with thickly gloved fingers. The headlines screamed news of
the war in Europe. Each day it breathed more dangerously
near them. They trembled for their safety and their sons'.
Two men standing near him shared a single paper and read
with outrage of an attack on an American freighter by a
German U-boat.

"Those damn Huns. They can't be trusted. Wilson ought
to go in there and teach them a damn good lesson," one man
said angrily.

Ezra wondered if he had been similarly outraged when
Germany overran Belgium or when British passenger ships
had been attacked by submarines and U-boats. American
opinion on the war had been divided until its own interests
were threatened. That was, he supposed, not unnatural. Nations
fought in their own self-interests. It was a lesson which the
Jews of Palestine must master.

He went to the newsstand and asked for a copy of the *New
York World*.

"Just sold my last one," the tradesman said. "That pretty
lady over there bought it."

He pointed to a small figure in a plaid wool cape with a
bright red beret perched on shining dark hair. Ezra's heart
turned. Sometimes it happened that fools triumphed.

The stationmaster's voice echoed over the loudspeaker.

Trains were departing for Chicago, for Atlanta, for St. Louis. Crowds of waiting passengers poured out of the checkrooms and coffee shop and cut him off from the small figure, but this time he moved quickly.

"Excuse me, miss, but did you lose this some time ago?" he dangled the red wool scarf in front of her, and she smiled. Then he produced her notebook.

"Lieutenant Maimon. Thank you. I seem to leave that scarf everywhere."

He was unprepared for the musical quality of her voice, for the delicate beauty of the face he had seen only from a distance.

"You have the advantage of knowing my name. May I know yours?" he asked.

"I am Dr. Sonia Lieberman," she said. "I know your name because I have often heard you speak, Lieutenant."

"And I have often observed you listening, Doctor," he replied, and smiled with delight at the elaborate game they were playing. "Shall we make a bargain? If you will forego the Lieutenant and call me Ezra, I shall forget that you are a doctor and call you Sonia."

"It's a bargain." She extended her gloveless hand to him. Her fingers were very cold but there was a confident firmness to her handshake.

Their departure was called and they found seats together in a dimly lit coat car. The train hurtled them southward, and they talked through the hours with mysterious swiftness. He told her of his meeting with the committee, of his dislike of appearing as a supplicant. She had also come to Boston to plead a cause. She had appeared before the disbursement committee of a wealthy foundation to present a proposal for a tuberculosis clinic on the Lower East Side of New York. She had been nervous during her presentation, she confessed, and she knew that being a woman weighed against her. It seemed to her now that she should have sent a male colleague in her place. He breathed with relief that she had gone herself.

They reached Providence and the dome of the state capitol glowed golden in the darkness. He bought hot coffee and sandwiches. They continued to talk, their words falling effortlessly and their conversation increasing in tempo, as though they were afraid they would not finish their stories before they reached their destination.

Sonia was the only daughter of a Jewish merchant, the owner of a large department store in Phoenix, Arizona. Her grandfather had gone west to California in 1849, trailing behind the prospectors who rushed off to pan for gold in the creeks and streams of California. The Jew from Latvia carried no prospecting equipment, no shovels or strainers. His packs were bulging with fabric and thread and needles. He grew weary before he reached California and ended his journey in Arizona. It made no difference, he said later. A Jew can make a living anywhere, can find a home anywhere. He sold the contents of his pack from a shack by the side of the road, which he converted to a one-room store. The city grew up around his store and he expanded. The one room became two and then three. He prospered. He married a Jewish woman from Chicago who had ideas about ready-to-wear dresses when most women bought fabric and stitched their own. The small store became one of the first department stores in the West. They built a house. Children were born. A rabbi was sent for, to teach Sonia's father Hebrew and to train him for his bar mitzvah, but they did not remain kosher, and slowly the vestiges of Jewishness disappeared from their lives. Still, during the Days of Awe, Jews from the neighboring communities, gathered together to pray. A synagogue was built and generously maintained. Sonia remembered that her grandfather, who rode on the Sabbath and ate unkosher meat, always kissed the mezuzah that hung on his front door. He had brought it with him from Latvia. She thought of the gesture as oddly symptomatic of his generation.

Their son, Sonia's father, did not marry a Jewish woman. Sonia's mother was the daughter of a prospector and a Cherokee Indian woman. Her grandfather did not attend the wedding but her father continued to work in the family business, and Sonia was always welcome in her grandfather's home.

"Remember that you are Jewish," the old man said to her, but he did not tell her what that meant.

She went to church with her mother, and during an Easter sermon she was astounded to hear the minister claim that the Jews had betrayed Jesus to the Romans. She did not believe it. Her grandfather was Jewish and he had never betrayed anyone. She decided then that religion was largely foolishness, and no one contradicted her. She grew up neither Jewish nor gentile but her favorite grandparents were her

Jewish grandfather and her Indian grandmother. They were both cloaked in the fierce, proud loneliness of the dispossessed, the uprooted.

Sonia was a precocious student and it was decided that she go east to school. She studied science at Bryn Mawr and went on to study medicine at the Women's Medical College of Pennsylvania. Her work absorbed her totally, and she went home infrequently. Each fall her grandfather sent her a message written in Hebrew letters. She understood this to mean that he wished her a Happy New Year and that he undertook yet again to remind her that Jewish blood flowed in her veins. She became a doctor, moved to New York, and married a colleague—a tall, handsome man who was the son of a pale-eyed, fair-haired New England family. They were married quietly because it was clear that his family was not pleased by his half-Jewish, one-quarter Indian bride. They shared regret that his family was imprisoned by prejudice, but she saw it as their problem. Her work took her to the clinics of the Lower East Side, which were flooded with the Jews who were fleeing Eastern Europe and arriving in New York in great numbers. The bearded, sad-eyed men reminded her of her grandfather. The energetic women who pushed two-wheeled carts through the streets of New York and hawked merchandise in a language they barely understood brought to mind her grandmother who had turned a small shop into a thriving department store. The small railroad flats she visited pulsated with life and warmth. Families cared for each other and for those who had come from the European villages of their vanished childhoods. She remembered the tales of tribal life her Indian grandmother had shared with her. Somehow she had stumbled into a heritage she had never known was lost. She felt at home as she walked through the narrow warrens and alleys carrying her black medical bag.

Her husband practiced on Gramercy Park. He grew irritated because she was so often with her Jewish patients, and he was not pleased when she went to work at the Henry Street Settlement House with Lillian Wald. Vital work was being done there, she told him. Mothers brought their anemic children. The near-blind were treated for glaucoma. He understood why Lillian Wald was involved. She, after all, was Jewish.

"I am Jewish too," she said, remembering her grandfather

and the way the Arizona sun splayed bright light across his
thick-veined hands.

They began to quarrel. They quarreled over small things—
the situation of the sofa in the Gramercy Park living room,
the quality of a cut of meat, a visit to his parents, the
disposition of their money. They quarreled at night because
he wanted to make love and she was tired or because she
wanted the light on to read and he had an early surgery the
next day. One night he discovered a large error in their
checking account. His fury mounted.

"Why can't you be more careful, you Jewish bitch?" he
hissed.

The next morning she left their apartment, and within the
year they were divorced. She used her maiden name again.
There was no need any longer to remind herself that she was
Jewish. It had been emblazoned upon her soul.

"I first heard you speak by chance," she told Ezra as their
train sped through northern Connecticut. "You were at a
settlement house where I service a clinic, and I stopped to
hear you. I had never before heard anyone speak with such
passion about being Jewish."

"No," he corrected her gently. "I spoke with passion of
Palestine and a Jewish homeland. Not of being Jewish."

"I see." She took a moment to absorb the difference. That
stillness of hers which he had noticed from the podium was a
natural part of her demeanor. She absorbed ideas quietly,
with a rare depth. Long training had taught her always to
commit herself to comprehension, to carefully weigh her
judgments.

He told her about his life, about Sadot Shalom, about
Nechama, and finally about Amos and Elana.

"Poor Amos," she said and touched his wrist. "Poor
Ezra."

The train grew too warm. He removed his coat, and she
draped the plaid cape across the seat. She wore the simple
sweater and skirt that he now knew to be her usual costume.
Her color was high, and he put his hand to her cheek and felt
her warm skin. It was natural that he should touch her. He
bent to kiss the nape of her neck, lifting the shining dark hair
that fell in thick waves about her shoulders. It was natural
that he should kiss her. The conductor smiled at them as he
passed. It was a fine thing to see a man in uniform with a

beautiful woman. The candy butcher left a package of sweets on their seat. Ezra held her close as the train pulled into Grand Central, and it was natural that he should go with her to her small flat on lower Fifth Avenue. They made love as dawn broke across the city in a slow rise of rose-streaked clouds, and they fell asleep as the milkman's cart rolled down the broad urban thoroughfare.

His time, during the weeks that followed, was divided between Sonia and his work. He hurried from her flat each morning to attend a rally or a meeting and returned at night, often just meeting her at the door. They ate at small Greenwich Village restaurants or in the bustling dairy cafeterias of the Lower East Side. Occasionally he accompanied her when she made a house call. He had assumed the general prosperity of the American Jewish community but now he saw the raging poverty of the immigrant community. He grew familiar with the small flats shared by many families and the communal toilets that stank of urine and feces. He walked with Sonia down narrow streets strewn with garbage, and he thought of the alleyways of Jaffa. Large-eyed, thin-bodied children trailed after her on the street. She stopped on Pitt Street one afternoon, slipped out her stethoscope, and listened to the heartbeat of a small boy who had tugged at her plaid cape and coughed strenuously. Her brow creased into a frown. She hailed a taxi, and Ezra rode with her and the boy to the Beekman Downtown Hospital.

"Tuberculosis," she said. "I must see the mother, the other children in the family. God, there is so much to do here. We need another clinic, another hospital, more doctors, nurses, midwives."

They slept together on her wide, white-sheeted bed. She was comfortable with her own body, admiring of his.

"You're such a wonderful color," she whispered, licking his skin as though the color might come off on her tongue. The long years in the sun-drenched fields had leathered his skin and burned it to the shade of amber.

"You are an apple." Her breasts were the color of the russets that grew wild on Sadot Shalom. He nibbled at one and then the other. "I love apples."

He taught her phrases of Hebrew. She taught him bits of American slang.

They drifted into Chinatown and ate spaghetti in Little Italy. They listened to street-corner orators. New York hummed with causes—socialism, communism, trade unionism, Zionism. Three weeks had passed since their meeting in Back Bay Station but they felt that they had known each other always, that they had never been apart, that they would always be together.

Ezra introduced Sonia to his aunt and uncle and to his cousin Alex Wade, who was visiting from Rochester.

"You want to be careful with these women doctors, Ezra," Alex said jovially. "They're too damn independent."

"That's good," Ezra replied.

Sonia was neither amused nor offended by Alex's remarks. She asked his advice about an eczema condition that was troubling patients at her clinic. Ezra was surprised when Alex offered to visit the clinic and explore the situation. His cousin had evidently recognized Sonia's uniqueness, and he was grateful to Alex for his intuition.

Independence, quietness of mind, strength of intellect were qualities Ezra admired in a woman. Independence had made it possible for Nechama to live alone all those years on Sadot Shalom. Sonia's independence pleased him. It strengthened his love and did not diminish his passion. He loved her as he had loved Nechama, and he would marry her as he had married Nechama.

Ezra went with David Ben Gurion to meet a man named Eliezer Margolin, an American Jew who would be a commander of the Jewish legion. Margolin was full of plans, enthusiasm, optimism. He had been made a lieutenant colonel, and he wore a wonderfully tailored uniform. The Shield of David flashed from his shining new buttons, and the menorah glinted on his epaulets.

"We have almost two thousand men ready to march with us," he told Ezra. He was impatient to be off to war.

Margolin planned for the Jewish legion volunteers to tour the Northeast. It would be good for morale, he said. They rode in a special train with blue-and-white bunting decorating their cars. An honor guard carried a Jewish flag and a Union Jack. At each stop they stood to attention and sang their anthems. Crowds gathered to see them. Children ran forth with candies, and young girls tossed flowers to them. Synagogue sisterhoods presented them with cartons of bandages and antiseptic. The uniformed young men accepted them with thanks but they did not truly believe that they would ever need them. They were young and strong. Their uniforms were new. Their weapons sparkled. Their eyes blazed with their dream. They would not be wounded. Only the weak and uncertain fell in battle. Besides, they had right on their side. Ezra thought of the day they had buried the dead on the Gallipoli battlefield, but he said nothing.

They were proud because they were almost two thousand strong, and groups of like numbers drawn from the Jewish communities of Great Britain and Palestine awaited them across the ocean. They were the first army in two thousand years to wear the Shield of David, and they trembled with pride when they sang "Hatikvah." They felt themselves to be invincible. In Bangor, Maine, a rabbi stood waiting for their train with a Torah. Lieutenant Colonel Margolin was photographed in his new uniform, embracing the scrolls of the law. The photograph was clipped from newspapers all over the country, framed, and hung in hallways and living rooms.

Ezra phoned Sonia from Bangor. She was tired. She missed him.

"But I think I have enough funding for the clinic," she said. "Alex has been a help." He could hear the excitement in her voice and felt an unfair jealousy.

"God, I miss you," he said in atonement.

"I miss you too." Her voice was a whisper.

"Soon," he said.

"Soon." The word was a caress.

They returned to New York, weary but exuberant. Ezra was pleased that he walked now with only a slight limp. He seldom used his cane.

Ben Gurion and Ben Zvi had already left for Egypt but at a rally Ezra met the American nurse whom Ben Gurion had married.

"How are you, Paula?" he asked.

"It is difficult now but soon I will join David in Palestine," she replied.

He wondered then if he and Sonia should follow Ben Gurion's example and be married now in New York or whether they should wait until the war was over and she could join him in Palestine.

Plans were under way for their leave-taking. A troopship

was being readied for them. They would rendezvous somewhere in Egypt with their Palestine and British counterparts
of the Thirty-eighth Battalion of Royal Fusiliers. It was rumored
that the opening of a Palestinian front was imminent.

The Federation of American Zionists undertook the organization of a medical unit, and Sonia accepted Lillian Wald's
invitation to a reception for a middle-aged woman from Bal-
timore who headed an organization called Hadassah, which
was involved in sending medical personnel and supplies to
Palestine. Ezra accompanied Sonia, and they were both
impressed by Henrietta Szold.

They rode home from the reception atop a Fifth Avenue
bus, huddled together for warmth, and shared a bag of chest-
nuts they had bought from a street vendor.

"How long will it be before you leave?" she asked.

"Only days. What do you think? Shall we be married
now?"

He felt a sudden rigidity in her body. The stillness closed
in around her, cutting him off.

"Married?" The bus paused for a light as her voice lifted
in question.

"Yes. Of course. We love each other. We will be married." He felt no ambivalence, envisioned no problem.

"Yes. We love each other."

"We could be married now, and perhaps you could join the
medical unit being sent to Palestine."

"But, Ezra, my work is here. The clinic. The settlement
house."

"I don't understand." The paper bag filled with empty
shells slipped from his fingers to the floor of the bus. Silence
grew between them. They descended at her stop, and for the
first time they walked together without touching.

She made tea in the small kitchen and bent over the kettle,
still wearing her plaid cape and warming her fingers over the
sudden breath of steam that surged from the spout. He slipped
the cape from her shoulders. She was shivering. She was
cold. She felt as though she would always be cold and now,
for once, his strong hands, his amber-hued body could not
warm her.

"You must understand," she said. "I am an American.
This is my country. Yes, I am Jewish, but the Jews here in
New York are my people. I know that you must go back now

and fight with your unit, but after the war, when you come back, we can be married. Or if you want we can be married now. That is not the problem."

"I didn't think there was a problem," he said.

"We never talked about it. But I thought you saw."

"Saw what?"

"How much my work means to me."

"You could be a doctor in Palestine."

"No," she said. "I've thought about it. I belong here. I've come too far to leave everything now. Palestine is not my country. I don't speak the language. I don't want to begin again. I've had so many beginnings."

She had left a home and a family. She had left a husband. Her grandfather had exhorted her to remember that she was Jewish, and she had not forgotten. She worked among Jews—Jews who had come to claim the land of her Indian grandmother. She lived in a confusion of heritages but at last she had found her way. She had thought that he understood the various loyalties that tugged at her.

"You said that first night—when you heard me speak—that you understood how important your Jewishness was to you," he reminded her.

"My Jewishness is important," she agreed. "But being Jewish doesn't mean that one must settle in Palestine."

"For me it does. Yes."

They drank their tea in silence, each of them feeling the acrid bitterness of betrayal. He had thought she loved him above all else—above her work, above her history. She had thought that his love for her could exceed his commitment to Zion. He could farm anywhere. He could work for the Jewish cause anywhere. Wasn't she working for a Jewish cause in the streets of New York? She could not practice medicine on Sadot Shalom, that distant farm that he himself feared might have been plundered beyond redemption by the Turks.

"You can work for the Zionist movement and organize Jewish youth here," she said. Ideology was mobile, portable. Her clinic on Montgomery Street would be stationary.

"To be a Zionist means to live in Palestine."

"If you love me you must understand that my work is part of me," she said. Could he have forgotten her joy when the clinic hovered on the edge of reality? Could he have forgotten how she trembled beneath his touch, how her body arched toward him with tenderness and desire? She leaned across the table. Their tea sat in cold golden puddles in their cups. Her fingers wove their way through his, rosy against his honeyed skin.

He lifted her hand and kissed her fingers one by one. The fragrance of the wild flower cologne she favored mingled with the odors of her profession, the antiseptic and the carbolic soap.

"I love you," he said. His eyes were the color of a wintry sea.

She looked at him, and he saw that her dark eyes were awash with tears.

"I love you."

Their love was not in doubt. It was their destiny that hovered in the balance across that kitchen table.

"I will never leave Palestine."

"Not even for me?"

"Not even for you. Come with me."

She heard the plea beneath the firmness of his tone. Her fingers crushed his.

He acknowledged to himself that he needed her. She had penetrated the armor of numbness that had shielded him since Nechama's death. She had released the floodgate of feeling stanched since Eleazar had died in his arms. He could not lose her.

"Stay with me." Her voice was husky with desperation.

"I can't. You know that I can't."

There was nothing else to say. They made love that night but their coming together was a loosing of sorrow, an acknowledgment of loss. His body wept within her own, and tears moistened their shared pillow.

Two days later he was aboard a troopship streaking its way to Egypt. He stood on deck in the cool of the evening, watched the serried waves, and reached into his pocket to touch the soft red wool scarf that somehow he had always picked up after her and, finally, had forgotten to return.

Back in Egypt, the months in the United States took on the amorphous quality of a dream. Gritty sand filled his combat boots, and he had difficulty remembering that only months ago he had dashed across Fifth Avenue, Sonia's hand tight within his own. Her face remained vivid in his mind's eye. He wrote her long letters, destroyed them, and sent brief notes instead. She sent him a long urgent plea for compromise.

"There can be no compromise," he wrote back. "Palestine is my home."

But he was not in Palestine. Once again he was cast adrift on the sands of Egypt, stranded with other members of the Jewish legion in the Tel-Al-Kabir camp. He felt the stress of a traveler anxious to reach his destination, impatiently awaiting a train that somehow does not arrive.

"When will we be leaving here?" he asked Lieutenant Colonel Margolin day after day.

"We must wait for our orders."

He chided his men for impatience but could not control his own frantic fear that after all their efforts they would be stranded in this camp, poised on the edge of a war that eluded them although much depended on their fighting it.

He bought the Egyptian newspapers and pitted his meager Arabic against the stories in the *Mukkatam* and the *Ahram*. The Palestine campaign had been launched. The British were committed to the idea of defending the Suez Canal by marching across Sinai to the strategic flanking position near El Arish. They had accomplished this before the Jewish legion reached the Egyptian camp. The Turks were fleeing across the desert but their strongholds had been established in the Gaza-Beersheva area.

"We know Palestine. We know the desert. Why the hell don't they use us?" Ezra asked Margolin angrily.

"They are waiting for another unit of volunteers from Palestine," the American said wearily. He studied the field maps spread before him on a camp table and valiantly tried to pronounce the names of the cities that had become battlefields.

The Palestinian volunteers arrived and joined the British and American troops. Ezra haunted their tents, seeking news of his family.

"Does anyone know anything of Saul and David Maimon of Gan Noar?"

His brothers' names were recognized at once. A youth from Petach Tikvah had seen Saul only a few weeks earlier. He looked well and even had managed to keep his horse, although the Turks had confiscated virtually all the livestock.

But Saul Maimon had the job of overseeing the provisions of Jewish settlements throughout the country.

No one, however, could offer news of David. It was still rumored he had died attempting to cross the desert alone. When the subject was raised, men cast uneasy glances at each other. They busied themselves with polishing their buckles and checking their rifles, and tried to divert the attention of the man whose brother had crossed the wilderness. Ezra wanted to tell them that they were wrong, that he would know somehow if it were true that his brother had died. But they would not believe him.

The days passed. He listened to the Jewish legionnaires mutter angrily against British discipline. He agreed with them, but he was an officer and so he conducted his inspections, supervised drills, and waited.

In March a new group of Palestinian volunteers joined them—a much younger contingent than the previous arrivals. They were sixteen- and seventeen-year-old boys who played soccer and blushed at the obscenities that increasingly peppered camp language as the waiting was prolonged.

"Where are you from?" Ezra asked a tall blond boy whose face was speckled with blotches of acne.

"We were all students at the Gymnasia Herzliah. We heard Jabotinsky speak at a rally in Rehovoth and we joined up."

Like Eleazar, they had followed the pied piper of Jewish militarism. He could imagine Jabo standing on a soap box in Rehovoth. That was fertile territory for him. There, students turned into soldiers before his eyes, intrigued by the historic privilege that was theirs.

"Do you know Amos Maimon?"

"Yes. Of course I know Amos. Everyone knows him. He's at the head of his form."

"Was he at the rally?"

"No. He's been in Jerusalem for a long time."

It seemed to Ezra that the boy blushed, averted his eyes, the way men did when they spoke of David. Did they imagine that they were somehow protecting him by refusing to meet his gaze, by withholding what they believed to be the truth? What could Amos be doing in Jerusalem?

The Turks remained entrenched in Gaza but now the British were determined to unseat them. Word went out from division headquarters, and the Jewish legion readied itself.

This was the offensive they had been waiting for. Men wrote long letters to their families. Ezra wrote to Sonia.

"I cannot imagine life without you but neither can I imagine living outside of Palestine. If anything happens to me remember that I have loved you—that I died loving you."

He felt his words to be maudlin, foolish. As he reread them, a letter was handed to him. He recognized Sonia's handwriting and his hands trembled. The letter was brief. She had been married, she told him, to his cousin Alex Wade. She was sure that they would be happy. Alex had agreed to move to New York, to help her with the clinic on the Lower East Side. She knew that Ezra would be happy for them. He crumbled his own letter and hers. The sheets of paper formed a clumsy wad which he tossed into a cooking fire. The paper burned swiftly.

Finally, as March drew to a close, they proceeded toward Gaza. They were confident, exuberant. Might was on their side. Five reinforced British divisions would oppose three Turkish units. They were on their way to liberate Palestine. But within days they had withdrawn in defeat, leaving the battlefield littered with their dead. The sands were red with blood. Helmets dangled from cactus bushes. They were numb with disbelief.

In April another attack was launched but the Turks had German reinforcements now, and again they were driven back. The Jewish legion carried their dead with them. A college student from Boston. A Russian-born tailor from Manchester. The acned youth from Gymnasia Herzliah. They had not liberated Palestine but they had died on her soil.

They retreated to El Arish. Rumors circulated. They were no longer impatient for battle. Now they were grateful for the respite. They washed their uniforms, beating them free of the sweat and sand that caked the coarse fabric. They wrapped themselves in their blankets and shivered against the cold of the desert night. They learned to sleep through the nightmare screams of men who saw themselves covered with blood, weakened by thirst. The seriousness of their losses staggered them. Over ten thousand men in British uniform had died in the frontal assault.

"Ten thousand. Imagine it. There ain't ten thousand people in my town," a boy from Shropshire told Ezra as they stood in line in the mess tent.

Sir Archibald Murray, their commanding officer, was recalled. It was rumored that the entire expeditionary force would be dismantled. The Jewish volunteers were incredulous. How could Palestine be abandoned?

"You act like it's the center of the world," an Australian soldier said contemptuously. "Why, we could fit your whole frigging country into a corner of the outback. And it ain't even your country besides."

"But it will be our country." The firmness in Ezra's tone closed the argument. The Australian went off to find a game of darts.

A new commanding officer arrived. The Jewish legion was relieved, reassured. General Sir Edmund Allenby, who had commanded the Third Army at Aaras, would not easily surrender Palestine. The British soldiers called him the Bull. He was a harsh and stubborn man with a lightning military intelligence.

"The prime minister, Lloyd George, wants us in Jerusalem by Christmas," he told the assembled troops, "and by God we'll be there!"

A cheer arose, and a Bedouin tribe encamped nearby moved southward the next morning. The Jewish soldiers embraced each other. They transposed Allenby's message. They would be in Jerusalem for Chanukah. They polished the menorahs that glowed on their epaulets.

Under Allenby's command they moved quickly. Ezra was grateful for the action. There was no time to think of Sonia. By October thirty-first, Beersheva was captured, and a week later Gaza fell. The buttons of his uniform were caked with desert grit. The fabric of his field jacket was stained with the blood of a Brooklyn boy who had fallen into his arms as they pursued the fleeing Turks across the desert. The boy's body had blocked a bullet that, seconds later, would have pierced Ezra's heart.

"He will be all right," the harried medical officer said when Ezra carried the boy into the tent, but within hours the American was dead. There was a scarcity of water. Wounds could not be properly irrigated. Men who had survived mortar and bullets died of infection and thirst.

The British launched a full attack on Turkish communications junctions. They jumped the barricades, shouting in a mixture of languages.

"Kadima!" Ezra shouted. "Forward!"

He did not recognize his own voice. It reverberated with force and hatred. He had seen too many young men die. He stretched himself across a stone wall, his rifle poised, and he fired volley after volley. Scarlet-uniformed Turkish soldiers, like toys in a child's game, rushed toward him. His bullets found them and he watched them fall, his finger desperately pressing the trigger. He realized, vaguely, distantly, that he was killing men—fathers and sons, brothers and husbands. He remembered suddenly the Turk who had shown him the snapshot of his young sons as they stood on the Gallipoli burial field. The man's face flashed before his eyes but he pressed his trigger and watched a young Turk clutch his side and topple to the sands. The fallen enemy soldier was very young—the same age, perhaps, as the Jewish boy from Brooklyn. Tears misted Ezra's eyes. He wept, senselessly, for the soldier he had killed so that he himself might live.

And then the battle was over and they were marching toward Jerusalem, weaving their way through the rolling Judean hills. They were no longer participating in a defensive holding operation. They were fighting a major offensive, and victory was within their grasp. Their tanks and motor transport rolled across the only two roads that could accommodate them. Camels, horses, mules, and donkeys, laden with supplies and munitions, paraded through the undulating hills. Like Gallipoli, Ezra thought, but this time they were winning. Their dead had been martyred for victory.

"Jerusalem!" they shouted with a single voice, the British soldiers and the Jewish legion.

The Jewish legionnaires held their banner high.

"If I forget thee, O Jerusalem . . ." The white satin words were embroidered on a shimmering triangle of blue, and the standard bearer waved it proudly. They had assembled from all the countries of their exile to liberate their city.

They attacked from the west and the south. They intercepted General von Falkenhayn's intelligence messages. The Turkish troops were in disarray. The Germans were planning to evacuate, to flee northward.

They advanced steadily now, through the wondrous hills where civilization had been nurtured, where Christ had preached and David had sung his sweet songs. Jerusalem. Men saw the gold-rimmed city and stretched their arms toward it as they fell dead in pools of their own blood.

Ezra and his unit were detailed for a march forward, where a small pocket of Turkish resistance had been spotted. They fired a small cannon, loosing the deadly discharge into ranks of British infantrymen. Ezra crept forward slowly, the men following behind him. They snaked across the pebbled hillside on their bellies. The small stones and briars cut into their uniforms, pierced their flesh. The cannon would find them before they could demolish it with grenades. Ezra's heart sank. Once they were detected, a single discharge would wipe them out. He took aim, found the gunner in his sights, but he knew that to shoot him would mean a betrayal of their position. A replacement would come up and loose a volley within seconds.

"What do we do, Lieutenant?" a Palestinian soldier asked him.

Before he could answer, a grenade was tossed from the rear. It exploded, knocking the cannon out. The gunner and his reinforcements were tossed upward like small rag dolls and fell to earth, still and lifeless.

Men poured over the hillside—men in blue work shirts with bandoliers of cartridges strung across their chest, men who waved their rifles in exultation. Shomrim—Jewish watchmen who had indeed watched and protected their city.

"Shalom!" their leader called to him across the smoke and blaze. Ezra blinked and trained his binoculars on the advancing figure. The small form came into focus, and he saw the copper-colored hair, the smiling mouth, the black eye patch. He saw his brother David, who had not died crossing the desert into Egypt.

"David!"

He dashed across the field, tears streaming from his eyes.

The brothers embraced and did not look up to see the white-robed figure of the chief of the Jerusalem municipality who walked across the battlefield from the city, a set of huge keys dangling in his hands. A standard bearer carrying a white flag trailed behind him. Jerusalem was free. The Turks were gone.

General Allenby accepted the keys of the city. He removed his hat and dismounted. Like Alexander the Great before him, he entered Jerusalem on foot. A Jewish legionnaire followed behind him, carrying the blue-and-white banner that trembled in the wind and suddenly unfurled in a strong breeze.

"If I forget thee O Jerusalem . . ."

The men saluted, a hand upon the heart. They had not forgotten. They would never forget.

Ezra and David Maimon stood with their arms about each other—brothers once lost, now reunited.

PART FIVE

Amos, Ezra, and Mazal

The Balfour Years: 1920–1922

Chapter 23

Elana Maimon lifted the dappled kid goat to her shoulder and stroked the small animal's limpid ears, her fingers lingering where flesh glowed beneath the sparse fur. The young goat crooned softly, contentedly, and burrowed more deeply into the friendly space between the child's shoulder and her inclined head.

"Abba, look, he likes me," Elana said, turning to the chair where Ezra sat reading the newspaper, his forehead creased by a frown. The bloody British Parliament was still arguing the ratification of the Balfour Declaration, four years after it had been drafted. When would they implement the damn thing? His brother David had been right after all. The British had gotten rid of the Jewish legion with a lick and a promise.

"Did you hear me, Abba?"

"Of course I heard you." He folded the newspaper carefully. He would pass it on to Achmed. Elana would take it when she went over to the Arabs' house to play. "And why shouldn't he like you?" he asked his daughter. "Don't you feed and bathe him? Didn't you make him a nest in the back of the barn? Don't you pet him? So he likes you."

"That isn't why he likes me." There was certainty in Elana's voice. "He likes me because I'm me—because I'm Elana Maimon."

"All right. It's nice that you think so," Ezra replied agreeably.

He watched as Elana sought out a patch of shade on the veranda and settled herself within it, seeking out the dark cool center just as a bee targets the sweet core of a flower's heart. And she was much like a bee in other ways, he reflected, this whirling little girl who buzzed through the Sadot Shalom farmhouse from early morning until her bedtime. She was feeding the goat now, forcing the pale yellow nipple of a nursing bottle into the small blind animal's frantic lips, sliding it expertly across the tender pink gums. Ribbons of milk streaked her sturdy golden arm, and when she shook her head, thick black ringlets of hair tumbled into her eyes. Her hair had to be cut, Ezra thought. He would ask his sister-in-law Chania to do it before she returned to Gan Noar.

"Tilt the bottle upward," he called to Elana.

"Oh, Abba, I know what I'm doing. I fed lots of newborn kids on the kibbutz," she replied impatiently, but she flashed a smile at him to show that she was not really annoyed. Such signals of reassurance were necessary for them. They had come together as father and daughter too late to rely on simple acceptance.

He smiled back, bemused as always by his daughter's confidence and determination. He had been home for two years now, and for two years she had lived with him at Sadot Shalom, yet she remained an enchanting enigma to him. She had, after all, been an infant when he left Palestine, and throughout the years in Egypt, Europe, and America, he had retained that image of his daughter. His brothers and sisters-in-law had written to him through the years, recounting her development, enclosing sepia-tinted photographs. Elana was walking, they wrote. She was talking in sentences. She was enrolled in the kibbutz nursery. She had learned to read. He read their letters carefully and studied the cheerful serious-eyed child in the photographs. But in his mind's eye Elana remained the newborn child he had last held in his arms in the silvery light of the wintry morning that had limned her birth and Nechama's death. Even now, he was occasionally bewildered when she danced up to him as he worked in the fields or when she rocketed suddenly onto his lap as he sat reading.

"Abba," she would say then, comfortingly, as though she sensed and forgave his brief disorientation. She would smile then, and a familiar radiant warmth would light her face. She had her mother's smile. He would look at her with an odd commingling of joy and sadness, and stroke her dark curls with trembling fingers.

"Shalom, Elana," he would whisper. "Shalom, my daughter, my black and golden buzzing bee."

The door behind him slammed, and his sister-in-law Chania came out to the veranda and pulled a wicker chair closer to him. She settled down and balanced the brass mortar and pestle on her ample lap. Methodically, with practiced thrust, she ground the sesame seeds into a thick *tehinna* paste.

"Why must you tease Elana?" she asked.

"I don't notice that she suffers visibly," he replied mildly.

They smiled together then as the small goat yawned piteously, belching forth a rivulet of milk that drenched Elana's bright blue pinafore.

"Bad goat," the child said sternly, and indignantly she carried the offending kid to the barn. Seconds later they watched her dash across the field to the meadow where Achmed was gathering wheat samples. He had recently discovered wild wheat growing amidst the tall grasses, and he wanted to analyze the grain.

"Poor Achmed," Chania said.

"Well, he shouldn't have given her the bloody animal if he didn't want to be kept abreast of its development," Ezra replied.

"Still, she does take care of it very responsibly," Chania noted.

"Yes. She's very responsible. Very independent. It's difficult to remember sometimes that she is only seven."

"Is she perhaps too responsible, too independent?" Chania asked.

She concentrated on her work now, casting on oblique glance at Ezra. The tehinna had a liquid consistency at last, and she tasted it and grimaced.

"It needs garlic," she said and tossed two silvery peeled cloves into the vessel. He waited until she had resumed her work before speaking again, as though their conversation required the punctuation of her metallic pounding.

"What do you mean too independent, too responsible?" he asked.

"She is too alone up here. Children need other children. Friends. Companions."

"Amos grew up here. He too was all alone," he reminded her.

"No. Achmed was his playmate. And things were different then. The house was not empty when Amos was a child. Nechama was alive."

Chania blushed but she did not avert her eyes. There were, after all, things that had to be said, and the Maimon men had the strength to bear the truth. She continued, her voice slow but steady.

"And besides, Amos spent his earliest childhood here. This was the only life he knew. Elana lived on the kibbutz for five years. There were always other children around, and women. Mirra and I took care of her. Your mother was there during the war."

"You and Mirra visit here. My mother comes when she can." But his voice trailed off as he recognized the weakness of his own arguments. It was true that Mirra and Chania visited Sadot Shalom when they could, but the kibbutz found it increasingly difficult to spare them.

The war had been devastating for the Jewish farmers. The Turks had left the land ravished and ruined. Carefully nurtured fields had lain fallow during the years of fighting and were again covered with overgrowth. Orange groves were ruined, and wizened grapes sprouted on uncultivated vines. The members of Gan Noar worked fiercely to reclaim the land that had been lost, and to build for the future that was thrust upon them before they could recover from the grimness of the past. The tentative, uneasy peace had brought new waves of immigrants into the country. They clutched their threadbare rucksacks and their battered valises and blinked nervously against the harsh sunlight of Palestine. They spoke in hesitant, fearful voices of the terror they had fled in Russia. The revolution that was to have brought them equality and social justice, messianic unity and implicit equity had, in the end, visited new and dizzying storms of hatred upon the Jews of Russia. But language had been altered if history remained the same. The revolutionaries disliked the word *pogrom*. They spoke of "purges" and "national cleansing." They frowned upon the use of the word *zhid*. Their epithets for Jews included "reactionary capitalists," "usurers," and "Shylocks."

A weary young woman sat in the communal dining room of Gan Noar and told of how she ahd her comrades had remained hidden in a basement in Zhittomar while mobs rushed through the streets, tossing flaming torches into Jewish shops and homes.

"Down with the Jewish bourgeoisie," they shouted.

The Jewish students, who had organized these same mobs into viable political units and set up distribution centers for food and clothing during the early days of the revolution, shivered in the familiar darkness. Their grandfathers had hidden from the Cossacks, and now they hid from those whom they had called their comrades. But the stink of the dank basements was the same, and the women still moaned softly as rats scurried across the dirt floors.

The girl from Zhittomar had emerged from her hiding place to find that her dark hair had turned mysteriously white and that three hundred Jews of the town had been murdered. Her parents and her brother and sister were among the dead. She tore a clump of newly white hair from her head and stared at it in bewilderment. Somehow she had found a group of young Jews who were bound for Palestine, and she had joined them.

"Where else would I go?" she asked the kibbutzniks of Gan Noar, who looked sadly at her and then at each other. They all had families in Eastern Europe. The mailbag was heavy that night. "You must come now," they wrote, "before it is too late. Come at once. Come soon. Come when you can . . ."

And some did come. Each week hundreds of new immigrants arrived on the ships that cast anchor in the aquamarine waters of Jaffa Bay, and the wooden plank docks trembled beneath the weight of the hopeful and the hopeless who had, at last, made their way to Zion.

"The kibbutz movement must absorb these people. New settlements must be built," Saul Maimon had pleaded at an emotional meeting of the central committee of kibbutzim in Tel Aviv. There had been vociferous argument and outbreaks of applause.

"The Balfour Declaration is meaningless without a strong Jewish immigration. We cannot have a Jewish national homeland if there are no Jewish homesteaders," David Maimon argued.

Yehuda listened to his twin sons and smiled. Despite themselves they had inherited their grandfather's talent for talmudic discourse, for measured argument and irrefutable logic. The lessons of the Kharkov yeshiva echoed through the meeting hall in Tel Aviv. In the end, plans were drawn up for a network of new settlements. A nucleus of veteran kibbutz members was to be sent to help the new pioneers. Advisers and material were offered. Saul and Mirra and Chania and David traveled from settlement to settlement. Even Chania's current visit to Sadot Shalom was possible because she had been sent to help a new settlement, located not far from Sadot Shalom, organize its grain storage units.

"I don't know when I will be able to come again," Chania said. "Mirra and Saul are leaving for a new training farm in the south, and you know that you cannot pretend that your mother is much help."

"I know," Ezra agreed, and he filled his pipe.

Rivka was an old woman now. She had aged too swiftly and too soon. Her fine white skin was wrinkled with webs of worry lines; her thinning gray hair and weak eyes startled and confused her. A stranger stared out of her mirror. She wandered through the Rishon farmhouse as though surprised to find herself in the familiar rooms.

"Where is my china closet?" she asked suddenly, petulantly, referring to a cabinet left behind in Russia decades before.

Occasionally she spoke with the breathy expectancy of a young woman who anticipates the arrival of a mysterious letter or a caller who will change her life. Her palsied fingers trembled but still, each day, she sat at her desk and wrote long vague poems about glittering cities and verdant woodlands. Yehuda cast sorrowful glances at her but he continued slowly, stubbornly, to reclaim his land. He hired a land agent to supervise the Arab fellahin who once again squatted in the shacks of the Rishon farm. He had spent three decades nurturing his orange groves, and he was determined to see them flourish once again. He dreamed of oranges dangling like small suns on slender branches. In all other things he had been disappointed. His sons had deserted him. Sara, his daughter, was dead to him. His wife lived in a world of her own dreaming, and his grandchildren were small, bronzed strangers who chattered too rapidly in Hebrew and sang songs with unfamiliar melodies. Only the land would not betray him. He trailed behind the Arab farm hands and pointed with his cane to a shriveled root, a withered branch.

"Dig that one up," he said. "Prune that one. And that one."

The shriveled wood formed clumsy piles throughout the orchard until the Arab women gathered them up and fed them to their cooking fires. Ribbons of smoke trailed skyward in the evening and drifted above the Rishon farmhouse like wisps of half-remembered misty dreams. And Rivka Maimon dozed in her chair and fondled the white gloves she had bought in a Jaffa stall the day she arrived in the land.

"Then what will you do about Elana?" Chania persisted. "She must go to school and be with other children."

Chania was a tenacious woman, and Elana was precious to her. She had, after all, raised the little girl from infancy and she had begged Ezra, when he returned, to allow Elana to remain on Gan Noar. He had been adamant about taking her to Sadot Shalom.

"We must rebuild our lives," he had said, and something in his tone and in his eyes silenced her ready arguments.

Ezra had been gone from Palestine for five years. They knew little of what had happened to him. A farmer had left and a soldier returned. He had seen men die, and he himself had killed men whose names he did not know and whose blurred faces haunted him in dream and thought. Unknown strangers had become important to him. Twice, during that first week after his return when he slept in their bungalow at Gan Noar, she and David had awakened to his frenzied nocturnal shouts.

"Eleazar!" he had called in desperate sorrow.

"Sonia!" he had shouted in desperate command.

Chania and David clung to each other in the darkness, astounded anew that they themselves had come through the war unharmed, and wondered who Sonia and Eleazar might be. But they mentioned neither name to Ezra. Months later it had occurred to Chania that their American cousin's new wife was called Sonia. An odd coincidence, she thought and immediately forgot about it. But Elana worried her, and she felt impelled to discuss the child with Ezra.

"What can I do about Elana?" he asked her. "She does not complain. These have been busy years for us. Soon, when things are under control, we can make other arrangements."

"All right." Chania shrugged as though to acknowledge a defeat for which she had been prepared. Ezra would not give up Elana. They must struggle toward a compromise solution. Perhaps one of the settlements would open a school nearby. And Ezra was a young man. Surely he would remarry.

"I will see to the dinner," she said at last. "David will be here soon."

She returned to the house, and Ezra stood and looked across the peaceful expanse of his land. The durra wheat had risen to a good height for the first time in seven years. Like the Rishon farm and Gan Noar, Sadot Shalom was slowly being reclaimed. Slowly, his life was once again falling into place.

His war, after all, had not ended when Allenby took Jerusalem. He had spent months drenched by the winter rains, fighting in northern Palestine where the Turks remained entrenched. He and David battled side by side and avoided each other's eyes when tales of Turkish cruelty were told. They were not surprised by accounts of the looting of settlements and the burning of homes and property. Reports of summary executions and interrogations under torture did not shock them. The brothers listened impassively to stories of burning torches held to men's testicles and of women being flogged with the bastinado. But they blanched when a soldier from Zichron told them how a Jewish child had been raped and another sodomized while the parents looked on helplessly, tied to chairs by Demal Pasha's men. Gan Noar was not far from the settlement where the incident had taken place.

"If they have touched Chania or my daughters, or Mirra or Elana," David said fiercely, "my war with them will never end. I will follow them if I have to go all the way to Constantinople."

His good eye was spangled with blood, and his hands trembled as he cleansed his rifle. David and Ezra had not slept more than a few hours a night for weeks. Daily they patrolled the Jordan Valley, routing out snipers and Turkish saboteurs until, at last, in the autumn they rejoined Allenby for a final northern offensive. They were in Megiddo when the Turks surrendered, and five days later they stood side by side at the gate to Damascus in Syria and watched Emir Feisal and T.E. Lawrence enter the city astride their matching white steeds. The Englishman, of whom Aaron Aaronsohn had told them, intrigued Ezra. Lawrence was a short man who sat his saddle well. His full lips curled with contempt as he looked down at the mobs of Arab enthusiasts who surged toward him as he rode. Yet he wore a colorful kaffiyeh, and a jeweled dagger dangled from his belt in the fashion of the desert chieftains.

"He is playing games. The sort of games Achmed and Amos played when they were boys. The desert is just a cribbage board to him," Ezra said. "Do you think the British will ever be able to understand the Middle East?"

"We had better pray that they do," David replied. "We helped them win this bloody war, and I suppose we got something out of it. We have that famous memo Lord Balfour sent to Rothschild saying we might get a Jewish homeland in Palestine out of it. Not bad. One paragraph on a sheet of official paper in return for God knows how many lives."

"And you can be sure that if they find oil in the Negev they'll misplace the memo," Ezra said, and the brothers laughed harshly.

It was a long time, Ezra realized, since they had discussed the ideals of Herzl and Pinsker, of Moses Hess and Achad HaAm. The war had made cynics of them. They were realists and saw, with painful clarity, that Zionism was not simply a dream or an ideal. It had been tossed into the international political arena and had little to do with the orange groves their father had so painstakingly cultivated on the sandy savannahs of Rishon LeZion. It was not influenced by the romantic Hebrew poems their mother had read to them through the long winter nights of their childhood. The dream of Zion was inextricably linked to the black oil concealed beneath the desert sands of Arabia and the slender blue ribbon of water that was the Suez Canal.

And then the war was finally over and the Jewish legion disbanded. Volunteers returned to England and America. Some decided to stay in Palestine. Addresses were exchanged and

promises made. Soldiers from the north promised to visit
comrades who lived in the south. Ezra invited Avraham, a tall
young man who had fought beside him in the Megiddo battle,
to visit him at Sadot Shalom. Avraham, who was a student at
the Technion, gave him his Haifa address.

"Do you know, I have known you all these months and I
have never learned your last name," Ezra said and read the
slip of paper.

The young man blushed.

"My name is Beliss," he said. "My father was Mendel
Beliss."

He touched the Jewish star on his epaulet. No one would
ever accuse him falsely of a blood libel. He was a Jewish
soldier who had served in a Jewish legion and he would
remain in this country that the British had promised would
become a national home for his people. He was done with life
as a wandering stranger in harsh and inhospitable host countries.

Ezra and David traveled home. They said little as they
passed burned-out villages and vandalized farms. Once they
stopped because a calf came bleating up to them on the road.
The animal's neck had been slit but the main artery had not
been severed. Huge tears filled the pleading brown eyes.
David shot the suffering beast through the head, and they dug
a hole and heaved the animal into the crude grave. They
walked on in silence, not daring to share their thoughts. If
such cruelty had been perpetrated on an animal by the fleeing
Turks, what had they done to people they considered their
enemies? David and Ezra dared not share their nightmare
fantasies of what might await them at Gan Noar.

"Elana," Ezra whispered and thought of the tiny girl baby
he had wrenched from Nechama's body. She was all that
remained to him now. Elana. Her name became a secret
prayer, a mysterious incantation.

And in the end they discovered that the Maimon family had
been remarkably lucky. Gan Noar had escaped any major
harm. Twice, bands of marauding Turks had approached and
withdrawn at the last moment. It was widely believed that the
kibbutz had survived because the Turks feared the wrath of
David Maimon.

"They are brave only when they confront women and
children, when they wear shiny boots and hold the bastinado.
They would not want to live with the fear of revenge," Saul

surmised as he sat with his brothers on that first evening of their reunion. Rivka had fainted when she saw her sons, and Yehuda's eyes had filled with tears.

"My sons," he said again and again, speaking the words in Hebrew and in Yiddish and in Russian. "My brave sons." They had been restored to him across all the frontiers of his shattered life.

Saul had manned the slender garrison at Gan Noar and had organized the meager food supplies that had sustained the settlement through the war.

"Farming was as important as fighting," Ezra said.

He held Elana on his lap as he spoke with his brothers. Elana was no longer an infant but a laughing five-year-old whose dark hair grew in thick masses of ringlets about her golden heart-shaped face. Elana. His lips brushed her wondrously soft skin. His fingers probed the flesh of her arms, her sturdy legs and thighs. Elana. The infant become a child. The daughter who lived, whose hair was as thick and dark as that of Nechama; the mother who had died.

He was home for two days before he asked for news of Amos. He had been told by David that his son was well and in Jerusalem, where he had spent the war years. Amos had maintained contact with the family but the war had made travel to the Galilee hazardous, and he had visited the kibbutz only twice.

"Who is Amos?" Elana asked. The burst of talk wearied her but it was nice to have a father now, like all the other children on the kibbutz. No. Not all the other children. Leah and Menachem, whose abbas had gone off to fight with the British army, had no fathers.

"Their fathers are heroes," the kibbutz counselor told the children, and Elana knew that meant they were dead. She was glad that her father was not a hero.

"Abba," she said.

"What?"

"Nothing. I just wanted to say Abba."

"And Amos is your brother," he said.

"Oh, yes. I remember. Blond Amos. My brother. He came to see me once. Maybe twice. Blond Amos."

She smiled and closed her eyes. It was wonderful to lie there in her father's arms. He was nice, and he smelled of tobacco and peppermint, this new Abba who had returned to her just as her aunts had always promised he would.

"Will my mother come back too?" she had asked then.

"No."

Chania and Mirra looked away from each other, the way adults often did when they knew something they did not want to share with a child. Elana had noticed this. She was a child who noticed everything, and she carefully stored away her observations. She was an emotional scavenger, as children who live on the outskirts of other people's lives sometimes are.

"That is because my mother is dead," she told them and watched her aunts warily, sniffing out their disapproval, their displeasure, their sad uneasiness.

"If she knows that Nechama is dead, why does she ask the same question again and again?" Elana once heard Mirra ask Chania.

"That is Elana's way," Chania replied placidly.

Chania loved her, really loved her, Elana knew. Mirra took care of her because she was her aunt. It was an obligation which she accepted without complaint. But Chania understood her. Chania understood that she required constant proof, constant reassurance. Children who have been born into uncertainty require repeated proofs. Only confident swimmers dare venture into water that rises above their heads without clutching at bobbing buoys.

"Blond Amos came to see me once," Elana told her father again. "No. He came twice. Once he brought me a doll and once he brought me some sesame candies. I ate the candies but lost the doll."

Elana did not like dolls. She liked small live animals that breathed softly against her neck and licked her with their smooth, wet tongues. Dolls lay too still, and even the most skillfully contrived button eyes were dead and tearless.

"That was nice of him," Ezra said but Elana was already asleep. She slept as Nechama had, with her mouth curled into a smile and her arm tucked beneath her chin. Sonia, he remembered irrelevantly, involuntarily, had slept with her lips pursed and her arms wrapped about her breasts, as though protecting herself from a mysterious nocturnal onslaught. Did she sleep that way in the bed she shared with his cousin Alex Wade, he wondered, and a frown creased his face. He was only now absorbing the shock of her marriage, but the marriage itself remained incomprehensible to him. His cousin shared none of her social zeal, her professional dedication. Why Alex, and how had she been able to marry so soon after his departure? Had she loved him at all, or had he simply represented a brief romantic adventure, safely programmed to end when his unit was called up? He would never know. He smoothed his daughter's hair and sighed softly.

Saul's voice, sonorous and thoughtful, jerked him back into the present.

"Amos did what he thought was right," Saul said. His tone was reminiscent of their childhood—the elder brother striving to reason with the younger.

"And what did he think was right?" Ezra parried fretfully. "Did he think it was right to cower in Jerusalem while other men fought and died?"

"He did not cower," Saul replied. "He belonged to the civil guard which the students organized. He helped to protect schools. He escorted old people through the city. He transported medicine to the clinics. The Shomrim who worked with him in Jerusalem told me that he worked very hard and that he could always be relied on to help them—to do anything they wanted."

"To do anything except bear arms to defend his country." Ezra's voice was soft but edged with bitterness. Amos had not changed. He had never been where he was needed most. He thought back to the lonely hours of the long night of Nechama's death. Where had Amos been then?

"There are many ways to protect a country," Saul continued. "Didn't you yourself say that farming was as important as fighting in this war? Do you have one set of rules for Amos and another for all other men? Why must your son be judged by different standards?"

"He is my son," Ezra replied. "We shall settle things between us when I see him."

But he had not seen Amos until after he and Elana had returned to Sadot Shalom. He would never forget his first sight of the farm after the years of war and wandering. He had stood on a hillside, Elana's hand warm within his grasp, and looked out across his fields. Fiery tears burned behind his eyes, but he could not weep in front of his small daughter. The earth which he had so patiently coaxed into dark fertility was dried and dusty, blanketed with vagrant overgrowth. The neatly cultivated expanse of Nechama's kitchen garden had drifted back into wilderness. Honeysuckle vines and purple-leafed creepers strangled the vineyard trellises. Saleem had concentrated his energies on the fruit trees and on the terraced plantings. He had chosen well, Ezra thought. It was the season of the second harvest, and the newly ripe purple plums glowed in the sunlight. Elana dashed from his side to pluck one. She ate it with relish, allowing the juice to dribble down her chin and licking at it with a quick dart of her tongue.

"Tov," she said. "Good."

He remembered that he had planted that grove during the first months of Nechama's pregnancy. The growing trees had kept pace with the growing child and now, at last, they offered their sweet fruit. Only a farmer, he thought, understood the peculiar symmetry between life and nature and he was filled with joy because he was home at last.

He lifted Elana high on his shoulder and strode across the field to meet Saleem and his family, who were hurrying toward them. Tears streaked Saleem's face and Hulda, his wife, smiled radiantly. She carried an infant on each arm: twin boys with eyes as black as anthracite.

"You see," she said to the blinking, drowsy babies, "The adon has come home."

"I knew you would return. I knew," Saleem cried and embraced Ezra. He stared admiringly at Elana.

"Allah has blessed you," he whispered.

"Allah has blessed me with a friend like you, Saleem," Ezra said and held the Arab's work-hardened hand within his own. "I thank you for the care you have taken of Sadot Shalom. Now, together, we begin again."

Days later, he and Saleem were working in the wheat field when at last Amos arrived. Ezra looked up and saw Elana walking hand in hand with a tall, golden-haired man. She waved to him imperiously.

"Abba! Come here. My brother, blond Amos, has come."

He walked slowly across the field, shaking loose a clump of dark earth that clung to his wrist. He had not seen his son for five years, but the constraint between them had not melted. His heart turned but it was his hand that he extended to Amos. They did not embrace. They gripped each other's fingers with a wrenching strength—bone biting into bone, the cushions of their palms pressing hard on each other as though to search out a secret weakness.

"Amos."

"Abba."

Their matching sea-green eyes met. Relief flashed between them. They signaled sorrow and separation. They acknowledged the toll of passing years, of vanished hours, but they did not smile.

Saleem, perched high on the combine, watched them. When Achmed returned home, even after the briefest of absences, he kissed his son on the cheeks and Achmed's lips caressed his hands. They embraced and laughed and sometimes even wept. He could not understand how it was that Amos and Ezra Maimon walked toward their house now without touching, without even looking at each other. It was sad when shadows fell between a father and son, he thought, and he concentrated again on his plowing, pleased to see the new darkness of the twice-turned earth.

Amos and Ezra talked that night, after Elana had gone to sleep. She had Amos's old room now. There were new glass panes in the windows and a new mattress on the narrow bed. The Turks had randomly smashed glass and sliced through upholstery during their search for the Maimon brothers. Ezra had replaced everything and carefully packed away Nachama's things. Only her books remained on their shelves, the thick volumes and dictionaries of the solitary student, the wife and mother who had read through the endless quiet Galilean nights. Amos studied the worn bindings and remembered how the lamplight had crowned his mother's thick dark hair.

"How was it that you did not join the family at Gan Noar?" Ezra asked him at last.

"Gan Noar was well populated. There were young and capable adults there. They had enough people to manage the work, and I knew that Elana was safe and well taken care of. But the situation in Jerusalem was critical. There was a great deal to be done there. I worked on concealing the collection of the Jewish National Library. I worked with the children. Even during a war children must be taught."

"Yes. I know how you value education. Education comes before your home and your family. It takes priority over your mother's life and your sister's childhood." Ezra spat the words out, each a pellet of bitterness, of sour anger.

"Abba, please understand that I know exactly what you mean," Amos said, and he kept his tone low and level. "I have thought a great deal about what happened. For a long time I blamed myself just as you blame me now. But then I met Dr. Mazis, and because of what he told me, I understand that there is no one to blame and that my mother would not have lived even if I had been at Sadot Shalom that night."

"Dr. Mazis? What did he know? Nechama hadn't seen him for years," Ezra said, but a memory nagged him. Nechama had occasionally gone off alone. To Tiberias. To Rishon. Had she visited doctors on those trips, and if so, what had they told her? Uncertainty gripped him. His palms grew wet and there was an arrhythmic beat to his heart.

"He told me that she was ill and he had warned her that it would be dangerous to become pregnant. She knew that she might not survive."

"But that can't be! She never told me," Ezra said. The words escaped his constricted throat. She would not have withheld such knowledge from him. And yet he knew that Amos was telling the truth. Even as a small child his son had never lied. His mind traveled back over the months just before Nechama had become pregnant with Elana. He remembered the emptiness of the house, his own silent sorrow, the mute despair that hovered between them. Was that why she had gambled with her life—gambled and lost?

"It was an accident then, that pregnancy," he told his son, reaching frantically for an explanation that would absolve them both. "I never pressed her. I never made any demands."

"I know," Amos said at last, still staring at his mother's books. "It does not matter now."

Nechama was dead and Elana slept in the narrow bed he had built for the child Amos. And it was Amos grown to manhood who turned now to look at him. Amos lit a cigarette. The coarse tobacco was loosely wrapped, and the ashes drizzled in graying flakes onto the bare tabletop. They were men who had shared a meal but had not bothered to spread a cloth on the table when they ate.

"I still cannot understand how you could have left your sister alone on Gan Noar," Ezra persisted.

"I told you that my work was in Jerusalem." There was a weary flatness to Amos's tone. His father would not relinquish his anger.

"And besides, it was safe in Jerusalem," Ezra said. "It is safer to teach school than to go to war. Did you know that your classmates from the Gymnasia Herzliah were in the Jewish legion? I met some of them in Egypt. I asked them for news of you."

"There are many ways to fight, Abba," Amos said. "Some men fight with weapons. Some fight with actions. Other men arm themselves with words."

"And those who are cowards do not fight at all," Ezra retorted harshly.

"I am not at war with you, Abba," Amos replied. "I did not come here to quarrel or make accusations. I came to see you and welcome you home and to see my sister. Tomorrow I return to Jerusalem. Can we say shalom as friends?"

"We are father and son," Ezra answered. "Friends are chosen, not bonded by blood."

The cruelty of his own words startled him but he did not disclaim them. The light of the diminishing paraffin lamp spurted, and the unsteady wick hissed and burned into nothingness. Darkness filled the room, and only the glowing ember of Amos's cigarette could be discerned. They stumbled through the blackness to their beds. Ezra heard Amos roam the house in the night. He listened as a drawer was opened and shut, and he saw the flicker of a match as Amos lit a cigarette. He felt his son's misery and his own grief, and he flexed his legs and his arms as he lay abed.

I must go to him, he thought, but he did not stir.

Amos left before dawn the next day, and he did not return to Sadot Shalom, although he sent Elana playful letters and remembered her each holiday with picture books and packets of sweets. Ezra saw him when they gathered as a family at Gan Noar or at the Rishon farm. Alternately, Ezra blamed Amos and then himself for his son's abandonment of his home. He had driven Amos away by his harshness, his unremitting condemnation. But then Amos had chosen to leave Sadot Shalom because the lecture hall and libraries of Jerusalem took precedence over his father and his sister. But in the end it made no difference. The house was silent and empty. Chania was right. Sadot Shalom was a grim and empty home for a small girl.

"Ezra! Shalom."

Startled, he dropped his pipe. He had been lost in thought
and had not heard the hoofbeats of his brother's horse.

David Maimon swung himself down from the saddle and
clapped a hand across his brother's shoulder.

"David. Shalom. I'm glad you're here. I think Chania was
beginning to worry."

"What's to worry? Haven't you heard? These are days of
peace. The messianic time has come. The lion will soon lie
down with the lamb and Jew and Arab will dance horas
together while the benevolent English smile their approval
and fan themselves with copies of the Balfour Declaration.
And that's all that piece of paper is good for," David said,
and his ready laughter was laced with cynicism.

"Please, no politics," Ezra rejoined. "That's the most
wonderful thing about being a hermit farmer. I never have to
argue about politics because there is never anyone around to
argue with."

"I'm afraid that's a luxury you may have to relinquish for
a while," David said. "I have a message for you from your
brother-in-law Daniel Langerfeld."

He reached into his shoulder bag and took out an envelope
emblazoned with the seal of the Jewish Agency in Palestine.

"You don't even have to open it. I'll tell you what it says.
Winston Churchill, the British colonial secretary, is planning
a visit to the Middle East, and the search is on for an
English-speaking agronomist who has the confidence of the
Jewish Agency and of His Majesty's government. Can you
guess whose name your Langerfeld brother-in-law has put
forth?"

"I can guess."

Ezra removed the crisp white sheet of official stationery
and read Daniel's letter quickly.

"I believe that it would require only a few weeks of your
time to accompany the colonial secretary," Daniel had written, "and it would be extremely beneficial to the Jewish
community in Palestine. I hope we can prevail upon you, and
I know that my late sister would have been proud that you
were chosen for this important role."

Damn Daniel for using Nechama as bait, Ezra thought, but
his brother-in-law was right, of course. Nechama would have
been proud. She too had lived by the Langerfeld credo of

service. (And his son, the guardian of libraries and school-children—he too had inherited it, Ezra acknowledged grudg-ingly. The thought had not occurred to him before.)

He studied the letter again. Winston Churchill. One of the architects of Gallipoli. Bloody incompetent bastard. Churchill would need all the help he could get in understanding Pales-tine. And Ezra would be gone only a few weeks. Saleem could manage the rest of the plowing. Elana would be glad enough of a holiday at Gan Noar, and Chania would be pleased.

"All right," he told David. "I'll do it."

"Of course, you'll do it. Oh yes, there's another letter for you—from America."

Ezra's hand trembled but the letter was from his uncle. She would not write. There was nothing left to say. Casually, he ripped open the envelope and a snapshot fluttered out. He picked it up and stared at his cousin Alex, his arm around Sonia who wore, as always, the schoolgirl skirt and blouse. She held a child in her arms. Her fingers were threaded through her son's golden hair and there was a somnolent sadness in her eyes that Ezra did not recognize. He stared at the photo for a long time. He had known, of course, that she had become a mother, but no one had ever told him exactly when her child had been born. Letters from the States were infrequent. He read this letter carefully, as though he were solving a riddle. All was well, his uncle wrote. Ezra's Aunt Claire had a slight touch of arthritis. Sonia and Alex were very happy although his uncle felt that Sonia should spend more time with her family and fewer hours at her clinic. Sammy was growing by leaps and bounds. Sammy. So that was the child's name. But how old was the boy? When had he been born? The question nagged at him, and he studied the photo again.

"Is something wrong, Ezra?" David asked.

"No. Nothing. This is just a snapshot of our cousin Alex's family. I knew his wife in America."

David looked at the photo.

"A handsome boy," he said. "He looks a bit like Amos when Amos was small. How old is he—three years old, four?"

"I don't know," Ezra replied.

He tore the letter into long strips and allowed them to flutter onto the stone floor of the veranda. But he carefully placed the snapshot in his wallet.

"When does the great Churchill arrive?" he asked David, suddenly eager for the new assignment to commence. He wanted to be totally absorbed, and thus too busy to think back to the months in America and the russet-breasted young woman who had wept in his arms that distant wintry night.

Chapter 24

Winston Churchill, the British colonial secretary, was a man who loved his creature comforts. He had been known to hurl epithets at his valet if the temperature of his bath water was off by even a few degrees. He spat out eggs that had not been boiled to the precise minute. He wore a cashmere muffler during the fall and a double-weave tweed overcoat in the winter lest the slightest chill assail his flesh. His spring suits were woven of a special lightweight cloth. But the most intolerable offense to his physical well-being was the imposition of heat. Even during the mild warmth of the English summer, he contrived to spend as much time as possible in the highlands of Scotland. He had, since his appointment as colonial secretary, thought about the Middle East with considerable discomfort. Something would have to be done about it, he knew. The war had left that part of the world in a state of disarray that was particularly offensive to his orderly English mind.

The Turks had finally been dislodged (Gallipoli notwithstanding, he noted with bitter satisfaction), and the British and French had rather messily sliced up the area. But the arrangements, from a British point of view, were not very satisfactory, and he would have to take a hand. But it was so very hot in the Middle East. The climate alone caused him to deeply resent the intrusion of that area of the world on his professional life. And besides the heat there were multitudes of flies and mosquitoes in the Middle East. He shuddered at the thought of the winged insects. He had visited Cairo as a boy, accompanying his cheerful American mother, and he distinctly remembered a fly that had fallen into his tea cup. It had floated in the tepid amber liquid with its legs up.

"It was disgusting," the colonial secretary told his wife, Clementine, who had nodded agreeably.

Still, the affairs of the world could not be put aside because of the memory of a drowned fly, and in the spring of 1921 Winston Churchill was in Cairo where, he optimistically wrote home, he would make every effort "to sort things out." His white linen suit was stained with sweat, and his thinning hair clung damply to his scalp. He stared up at the long sticky sheet of golden flypaper that trembled beneath the slow revolutions of the propeller fan. Dead flies and mosquitoes clung to it in odd configurations, but no more odd than the map which dominated the broad tabletop. He studied the map impatiently and aimlessly moved the tiny flags about with his pudgy little fingers. (The colonial secretary envied men with graceful hands.)

It was all well and good that the Union Jack waved over Syria, Western Turkey, Palestine, Mesopotamia, and lower Iran. And he grudgingly conceded that they had had no choice but to cede the Syrian coast to the French. Millerand had fought hard for that at the San Remo peace conference and the French, after all, had been allies. The thought that Great Britain required allies at all annoyed Winston Churchill quite as much as the flies that floated in tea cups or were glued to strips of poisoned paper. Still, he had to be realistic, and the Fleur-de-Lys had been hauled up at strategic points along the Syrian coast, where it waved almost unnoticed by the Arab farmers and fishermen who glanced at it absently as they worked their fields or sailed their longboats.

It had been hard on the Arabs, Churchill agreed, to pluck away their support and go along with the French, but Lawrence had overstepped himself and promised them too much. The man had no authorization to promise Hussein an independent Arab nation, whatever in God's name that might be.

At least Balfour had been more cautious in his dealings with the Jews. That memo to Rothschild, which the Jews insisted on calling the Balfour Declaration, could be interpreted any number of ways. Clever man Balfour, Churchill admitted, and folded another paper flag.

It had, after all, been hard enough to work out the military boundaries without listening to the grievances of the Arabs and the Jews. It had been unwise, perhaps, to take the Litania River and the Yarmuk away from Palestine; Churchill was a man who loved the countryside and respected natural geographic frontiers. Compromises had to be made somewhere, however, if they were ever to extricate themselves from the endless squabbling. The continual quarrels were unsettling.

It was all very well for Arthur Balfour to issue statements and memoranda and even arrange for a Zionist leader like Chaim Weizmann to be received by King George. Balfour was in London where the cool mists of early spring greeted him each morning while he, Churchill, was in Cairo where the air hung in a heavy thick curtain of heat and his rather too large backside clung to the seat of his red leather chair. He sighed deeply and replaced the flags in their original positions.

The door of the large conference room was closed but through its thickness he heard the muted cacophony of many voices. Impatiently he lifted the large brass bell that sat on the desk. Its harsh jangle brought a few brief seconds of silence as his door opened and his secretary hurried into the room, closing the door firmly behind him. Almost immediately the din began again, and Winston Churchill pressed his small fat hands to his ears and grimaced.

"Who's out there?" he asked impatiently.

"The usual." Dunning, the secretary, was undisturbed by his superior's outward truculence. He was a veteran employee of the foreign service and had served ambassadors and cabinet ministers in more countries than he could count on his fingers.

"It's the polite ones you have to be careful of," Dunning had confided to his son, who was on his very first assignment as a junior clerk in the Sudan. "They think being polite makes you a diplomat. Half the time they can't find the countries they're assigned to on the map."

Winston Churchill was not polite but Dunning could personally testify to the colonial secretary's familiarity with every border area, his knowledge of minor hamlets in Iraq, and his familiarity with the names of warring desert chieftains of whom Dunning himself had scarce knowledge.

"Could you be a bit more specific?" Churchill asked petulantly. He pointed accusingly to the large silver teapot. "And the tea is cold. Very cold."

"One of Millerand's colonial undersecretaries. Two Bedouin chieftains. An Iraqi businessman. A surrogate from Emir Feisal. The elder son of Emir Abdullah. And a Palestinian representing the Jewish Agency—Ezra Maimon."

"Ezra Maimon," Churchill repeated. He liked the name. He was fascinated with resonance, with the musical quality of words. Ezra Maimon had a good sound—an almost biblical lilt, although of course that probably wasn't the man's real name. He had heard the Jews in Palestine took on new names—they Hebraized those that they claimed were part of the heritage of their so-called exile. A damn fool thing to do, he thought. A name was a name. Still, he'd rather see a Palestinian Jew than a Bedouin chief or an Iraqi businessman.

"Has he been vetted?" he asked, and Dunning glanced down at the dossier in his hand. Churchill's lips twitched with grudging admiration. Dunning was a civil service phenomenon. How could he have known that Churchill would want to see Maimon?

"He's a semi-official representative of the Jewish Agency in Palestine. Born in Russia but came to Palestine as a young boy. Runs a successful farm in the Galilee. One of the few independent farmers up there. He spent some time in America, and he fought in the Jewish legion. Earned a minor decoration. He was with the Zion Mule Corps on Gallipoli."

"Gallipoli." Churchill frowned. Gallipoli had been his creation and his failure. He carried it everywhere with him, an albatross that weighted his memory and hobbled his arrogance. As he drove through London on a winter evening, he averted his eyes from the one-legged beggars and the empty-eyed blind men who thrust their tin cups at passersby and waved their flimsy placards: "I WAS AT GALLIPOLI." "BLINDED AT SUVLA BEACH."

He had almost forgotten the Zion Mule Corps. It was, he reflected, the sort of group that belongs to the fringe of history, a peripheral unit whose service had been contributed to a campaign that had been lost but lingered on in bitter memory.

"Show him in, Dunning. It will be my first encounter with a muleteer."

"Yes sir," Dunning replied, and he removed the tall silver carafe. He would personally see that it was refilled with hot tea. The Egyptian concierge had assumed, given the heat of the day, that the colonial secretary would want cold lemonade. It was bad enough that Churchill had thought it tea. Dunning did not want to risk offending the kitchen staff. Colonial secretaries made brief visits and returned to London, but a concierge ruled a Government House kitchen forever.

"You may go in, Lieutenant Maimon," he said. "Please follow me."

"Mr. Maimon," Ezra corrected him firmly. He was done with uniforms and rank.

"Very well. Mr. Ezra Maimon," Dunning announced, and Ezra strode past him into the conference room. The door closed silently behind him and he looked at the squat, over-weight man who bore an odd resemblance to a wily bulldog.

"I have just killed a large and disgusting insect," the colonial secretary reported with satisfaction. He pointed to the map that dominated the oak table. "It was crawling across Lebanon."

Ezra looked down at the minuscule mess of wing and blood.

"You have just killed a mosquito hawk," he said. "That was a mistake. They are our allies. They kill mosquitoes. But you could not have known that."

"No, I could not have known that," Churchill agreed. He was pleased that Maimon had had the courage to tell him that. There were enough tail waggers in his retinue. "There is a great deal that I do not know about the Middle East. But perhaps you would take the time to teach me, Mr. Maimon. You must be familiar with all its creatures. You know which are allies and which are adversaries. Please sit down and let us talk."

He motioned Ezra toward a red leather chair that matched his own but Ezra shook his head and selected a wicker chair from the other side of the room.

"I know enough about the Middle East to know that one does not sit on leather in the heat of a sharav day," he said. "Perhaps you too will take a straw seat."

He drew one forth to the head of the table and Churchill sank into it gratefully.

"I hope you will be as frank in all things," he said.

"I will try," Ezra Maimon replied calmly.

Churchill lit a fat cigar and gently puffed on it until its light was steady. He liked the look of the tall bronzed Palestinian. There was little those sharp green eyes would miss. Ezra Maimon had the look of a man who had seen and registered a great deal. He was not your usual Jew, Churchill decided. Certainly he was nothing like Weizmann.

Winston Churchill did not like Chaim Weizmann, nor did he believe much that the dapper little scientist told him. Weizmann might know everything there was to know about synthesizing acetone; no one denied that the man was a damn good chemist. And he might have helped Nobel speed up dynamite production. But he didn't know a damn thing about the realities of life in the Middle East. Churchill would not soon forget the letter Weizmann had written him, enclosing documents that showed what Weizmann called "the readiness with which the Arabs are learning Hebrew in Palestine." According to Weizmann, the Arabs couldn't wait for the establishment of a Jewish state. That was an idea, Churchill thought—perhaps they would all convert to Judaism and that would solve the problem. He blew a smoke ring and spat out a grain of tobacco that clung to his lip.

"What do you think, Maimon?" he asked.

"About what?" Ezra had lit his pipe without bothering to ask permission. That too pleased Churchill. Weizmann would not have smoked at all, or he would have been most obsequious about establishing his right to do so.

"I beg your pardon," he said. "Sometimes I think so hard, I imagine that other people can actually hear my thoughts and therefore I ask them questions as though they were *au courant* of my mental processes. It is an unending source of irritation to my wife, as you can well imagine. Are you a married man, Maimon?"

"A widower," Ezra replied.

"I'm sorry."

"It was a long time ago. Before the war."

They sat for a few minutes in silence, acknowledging that anything that had happened before the war had indeed happened a lifetime ago. The years of battle had obscured other losses, other sorrows.

"The question I had formulated in my mind was whether you thought the Arabs in Palestine would welcome Jews to the country," Churchill continued.

"Welcome them? No. But if you rephrased your question and were to ask me if the Arabs in Palestine could learn to live with Jews, I would say yes. Arabs and Jews are not like mosquitoes and mosquito hawks. They are not natural adversaries."

He thought of the tears that had shimmered on Saleem's face when he returned to Sadot Shalom. He remembered Amos and Achmed, the small boys, playing their mysterious games, bound in friendship and love. A Druse chieftain had wept at Avremel's funeral. Hulda had screamed her sorrow at Nechama's death.

"Even Emir Feisal has said as much," he added. Churchill would be more interested in Feisal than in Achmed and Amos.

"I too have read Feisal's letter to Felix Frankfurter," Churchill replied dryly. "Emir Feisal is a clever man."

"Cleverness does not necessarily preclude wisdom," Ezra said.

He remembered how optimistic he had felt when Feisal's letter to the American jurist had been reprinted in the Hebrew papers. The Arab leader had written with sympathy of the Zionist movement and the ideal of a Jewish national home in Palestine. A copy of his letter had been framed and hung next to a reproduction of the Balfour Declaration in Daniel Langerfeld's Jerusalem office.

"I hope the Arabs may soon be in a position to make the Jews some return for their kindness," Feisal had written. "We are working together for a reformed and revived Middle East. We will wish the Jews a most hearty welcome home."

The paper on which that letter had been written was frayed now, and Feisal no longer sat on the Syrian throne. Very few Arabs had wished the Jews who came to Palestine after the war that "most hearty welcome home." Only a year ago Arab-led anti-Jewish riots had broken out in Jerusalem, and the streets of the city of peace had been littered with bodies. Streams of blood had run scarlet in cistern and sewer. Two hundred and fifty corpses had been buried, among them the slender body of Daniel Langerfeld's youngest daughter, who had been raped and killed on her way home from school.

Ezra had come to Jerusalem for the funeral and had met Zev Jabotinsky there. The hero of the Jewish legion was pale with fatigue. His voice was hoarse. Daily he patrolled the city and urged the Jews of Jerusalem to arm themselves and fight back in self-defense. The British took a dim view of his activities, and the provisional government sentenced him to fifteen years of penal servitude. Ezra remained for the trial and went to see his old friend afterward.

"The decision will be reversed," Jabotinsky told him. "But what happened in Jerusalem will not be reversed. Jews will not sit quietly by and watch their children die. The course of Jewish history has been changed. Inevitably. Irrevocably."

He spoke with the same fervor that had impressed Ezra in Cairo and again in London, and Ezra envied him his singleness of purpose, his tenacity of dream and vision.

Jabotinsky had been right. Protests in the House of Commons had reduced his sentence to a single year, and now there was scarcely a Jewish home in the country where a weapon was not concealed. Daniel Langerfeld had not removed Feisal's letter from his wall but a musket stood in the closet that had once contained the clothing of the young girl, buried now in a narrow grave on the Mount of Olives.

But a loaded musket had not helped Joseph Trumpeldor. The handsome soldier who had lost his arm at Port Arthur had survived Gallipoli and arrived in Palestine at last to join a group of pioneers at a settlement in the northern Galilee. They were shepherds who pastured their flocks in the verdant meadowlands and lived in the single building that stood on the property they had bought from the Arab owner. Tel Chai, they called their settlement—Hill of Life. It had become instead a hill of death. The French military government had been unable to protect the settlers from hordes of attacking Arabs, and Trumpeldor had been killed with seven other young men and women as they defended their small encampment.

But Winston Churchill had never heard of Joseph Trumpeldor, and Ezra knew that it would be pointless to discuss him now. His friend's death had shaken Ezra but it had not completely destroyed his hope that Feisal might be right.

There were Arabs in the land who would welcome Jews. He suddenly remembered a recent evening when Elana had fallen asleep in the fields and Achmed had carried her home. Her dark head had been pressed against the Arab youth's shoulder, and when he bent his head, his hair all but matched her own.

"I think, Mr. Secretary," Ezra said slowly, "that we must be very patient. The situation is not hopeful but it is not impossible. We must work slowly. I am a farmer. This much I have learned from my work. Where the ground has not been carefully prepared, even the most carefully selected seed will not produce an abundant crop."

"Have you a few weeks' time, Maimon, to work with me—perhaps to help me prepare the ground?" Churchill asked. He liked Ezra Maimon, who was deceived neither by his friends nor by his adversaries.

"I have time," Ezra said as Dunning entered the room carrying a carafe of steaming tea.

"I know that it is difficult for a farmer to leave his fields. But consider that you are engaged in preparing the ground for a most important harvest." Churchill smiled. The metaphor pleased him. "What is your farm called, Maimon?"

"Sadot Shalom. Fields of Peace."

"A most appropriate name. You are working then in new and different fields of peace." He turned to his side. "Dunning, Mr. Maimon will be joining our mission as an unofficial adviser. Very unofficial."

"I understand, Mr. Secretary," Dunning said and poured out two cups of tea.

"Of course you do." Churchill lit another cigar. He was feeling a great deal better. He had hot tea, and his backside no longer adhered to the seat of his chair. Clearly, progress was being made.

Ezra Maimon sent his brother-in-law Daniel Langerfeld only one letter during the weeks he spent with Winston Churchill. There was little enough time to write, and he was certain, despite the swift and almost improbable friendship that had sprung up between himself and the British cabinet official, that his mail was censored. Churchill himself had told him, half in truth and half in jest, that he trusted his enemies not at all and his friends even less.

"Lesson number one in the art of politics," he had said.

During the hours he and Ezra spent together, hours in which Churchill asked endless questions about Zionist philosophy and the Jewish community in Palestine, the Englishman often quoted the Bible in stentorian tones. He knew entire passages by heart and plucked them from memory as the occasion suited him.

"Amazing work of literature, the Old Testament," he said. "A work of genius. You come from an amazing people, Maimon. Do you know what I once wrote about the Jews?"

"I am familiar with some of your writings, Mr. Secretary," Ezra answered cautiously.

Daniel Langerfeld had briefed him well before his journey and had provided him with an article by Winston Churchill that had appeared in the *Illustrated Sunday Herald* of February 8, 1920. "The Jews," Churchill had written, "have evolved a system of ethics which is incomparably the most precious possession of mankind, worth, in fact, the fruit of all other wisdom and learning . . . But they have also produced Bolshevism, a system of morals and philosophy as malevolent as Christianity is benevolent."

It had occurred to Ezra, as he read, that this cool, intellectualized anti-Semitism was perhaps more dangerous than the pogroms, the mindless eruptions of hatred and violence that had killed his grandparents and frightened his sister, Sara, into a false abandonment of her faith. Churchill's writings were, in fact, not too different from the gibberish that a former Austrian corporal named Adolf Hitler was spewing forth in Munich beer halls. Hitler had recently published an article called "Twenty-Five Points of Why We Are Against the Jews." Churchill's work was more articulate, of course, but basically not too different. Both he and Hitler had, in all probability, read "The Protocols of the Elders of Zion," a forgery that portrayed the Jews as locked into an international conspiracy contriving to control the world. But Churchill, Ezra considered, was more dangerous than Hitler. The Austrian would soon be killed in a barroom brawl or marry a fat *hausfrau* and sink into obscurity. Winston Churchill was the colonial secretary and might even be prime minister one day.

"I wrote," Churchill said dreamily, "that it would almost seem as if the gospel of Christ and the gospel of anti-Christ were destined to originate among the same people and that

this mystic and mysterious race had been chosen for the
supreme manifestation of both the divine and the diabolical.''
He quoted from memory, hypnotized as always by the sweeping
rhythm of his own words.

''An interesting concept,'' Ezra said mildly. ''But I am a
Jew, and I have never thought of myself as either divine or
diabolical. My only obsession has been with the soil of my
farm. My father has only been concerned for his orange
groves. We are simply Jewish farmers, and we have never
been involved with theories of cosmic destiny. I don't think it
is either diabolical or divine to want to see wheat flourishing
or citrus trees bearing fruit in their season.''

''And do you expect me to believe, my dear Maimon, that
that is all the Jews want—fruit-bearing trees and grain-filled
fields? Come, let us be straight with each other.''

Ezra did not argue. He had watched Winston Churchill at
work and he knew that the Englishman appeared to move
slowly but thought quickly. He complained about trivialities
(there was a stain on his linen napkin, a defect in the wrapping of his cigar) but he had no difficulty viewing a situation
in all its historic breadth. Ezra had often remained in the
conference room as various delegations visited the colonial
secretary, and he had watched in amazement as Churchill
formulated a new approach to the unsettled Iraqi mandate.

The military and foreign service officials had gathered
solemnly about the polished oak table at Churchill's invitation. They shifted uncomfortably on their red leather seats
while he sat in statuesque dignity on his wicker chair. They
drank strong tea and puffed on excellent cigars as he spoke on
the strategic importance of the area.

''My good friends,'' Churchill said, and the rich cadence
of his voice mesmerized his listeners, ''the future of the
world is linked to this region. Oil is the key to the future. The
most important international waterways will not be the great
oceans. No. We must fix our attention on the Straits of
Hormuz and the Suez Canal.''

His piercing gaze traveled the table, and the assembled
men shivered against the penetration of his glance. They did
not doubt that he read their souls and that he discerned their
most secret schemes. He had called them all his friends, and
each yearned to believe that he was speaking covertly to one
alone.

"We must have stability," Churchill said, and he spoke so quietly now that they leaned forward to hear him. "Iraq must remain stable. His Majesty wishes it, and the people of Iraq share his wish."

A burst of applause greeted this last remark. It had become the accepted procedure, Ezra noted, to applaud when the will of the people was mentioned, notwithstanding the fact that no consensus had been taken and not one of the assembled personages had the vaguest idea of what the people of Iraq wanted.

Still, Churchill had triumphed. The conference had produced an admirable set of proposals. A general amnesty was declared, and it had been determined that a serious effort would be made to determine the wishes of the Kurdish minority about their inclusion in an Iraqi state. The British foreign officers nodded happily over their progress and finished their excellent tea. This was the way the affairs of the empire should be managed. Churchill held a dinner of celebration at which the food was bad and the conversation excellent.

Dunning scavenged a dinner jacket for Ezra, and he sat at the far end of the table, discreetly distant from Churchill, and observed his country's new rulers. The men were all pink and white, flushed with wine and pleasure. They ate too much but contained their belches with dignity. The soft-voiced Englishwomen laughed politely at unfunny pleasantries. Tiaras sparkled in their upswept hair and their jewels were harshly brilliant against their smooth white throats. They might have been at a dinner party at Chartwell (where the food prepared by Clementine Churchill's cooks was quite as bad as that of the Cairene cooks, they whispered to each other), but in Egypt the heat caused their powder to cake and their maids found it difficult to remove gowns and undergarments that were soaked with sweat. A woman in a peacock-blue gown asked Ezra about the climate in Palestine.

"It is not unlike that of Egypt," he said and struggled to mask his irritation. The Turks had at least understood the climate of the country.

"It must be so hard on your ladies' skin," she said and smiled prettily, touching her own bare peach-colored shoulders. The Palestinian Jew was terribly handsome, she thought, and her fingers brushed his richly tanned hand as she reached for the sugar. Her husband was an admiralty official and too often away from home. It was rumored that he would be assigned to Haifa, and Haifa was not far from the Galilee where, she had been told, the Palestinian maintained an estate.

"One must be careful," Ezra conceded. "My wife's skin was unusually fair but she always wore a hat and did not suffer. My small daughter, however, has a complexion not unlike your own."

"If you will forgive me, I must speak to my friend," the Englishwoman said and moved hastily down the table. She did not like men who spoke of their wives and daughters.

Ezra nodded pleasantly and finished his coffee. He had no appetite for brief liaisons. They were dangerous, irresponsible. Sonia's face flashed before him in memory and he teased himself with the familiar sting of pain, the sad sense of betrayal. It occurred to him that he spoke easily of Nechama now. She had retreated into a concealed panel of memory. He could press the magic button at will and she would appear to him, as pale and lovely as she had ever been. The time of sorrow and anger had finally passed. Nechama was dead, but she had left him their son and daughter—Amos and Elana.

I must make it up with Amos, he thought. I must.

He went out early the next morning and wandered the alleyways of the bazaar until he found what he was looking for in a small antiquities stall. The black Luristan dagger rested on a bed of red velvet, and a single garnet glinted in its hilt. The antiquities dealer watched him with the practiced eye of a master fisherman, awaiting the exact moment at which to haul in his catch. When Ezra hefted it for the third time, the turbaned Copt stood at his elbow and puffed gently on his white ceramic pipe.

"Does that find favor in your eyes, adoni? It is no wonder. You have the eye. It is the most precious of all my treasures. Men killed with that dagger before the days of their Christ and our Mohammed," he said. "And it has not lost its magic. Look carefully."

The dealer ran his finger lightly across the blade of the dagger. A thread of blood gleamed scarlet where the metal had barely grazed the flesh. He sucked his finger and smiled, displaying unevenly matched gold teeth.

"There. I do not lie to my master."

"No, you do not lie," Ezra said.

He bargained dutifully with the Copt, who at last agreed on

a price and wrapped the dagger in sheets of yellowing newspaper. Amos, who loved ancient objects, would surely appreciate the dagger. The relic of abandoned wars would be Ezra's gift of peace to his son. He would also give him the winged cup he had found on the Gallipoli battlefield.

He returned to Government House, suffused with an eagerness to return to his farm, to meet with his son, to hold his small daughter in close embrace.

"The colonial secretary would like to see you," Dunning said.

Winston Churchill stood at the golden oak table and studied the map spread across it. Once again he maneuvered tiny paper flags, the Union Jack, the Fleur-de-Lys.

"So, Maimon, you see what we have accomplished," he said proudly.

"I see that you have accomplished many discussions and that many documents have been signed," Ezra replied.

"Discussions and documents solve more than battles do," Churchill said. A shadow of displeasure crossed his face. The Palestinian Jew was getting a little too familiar. That was the way with Jews. One had to be careful. "Will you be returning to Palestine soon, Maimon?" he asked brusquely.

"As soon as Your Excellency has no further need of my unofficial services," Ezra replied smoothly. "Although I had hoped that we might be able to further discuss the Balfour Declaration and the situation of the Jewish community in Palestine. I wanted to tell you about our agricultural advances. You are, of course, familiar with our citrus exports."

He glanced at the bowl of golden Palestinian oranges that rested on the conference table. Churchill selected a fruit and peeled it with exquisite slowness.

"Ah yes, the situation of the Jewish community in Palestine," he replied. "It seems that His Majesty cannot do enough for the Jews of Palestine. No sooner does Lord Balfour promise Sir Edmond Rothschild a Jewish homeland than further demands are made. A Jew is named high commissioner of Palestine and still that is not enough. What will satisfy your people, Maimon?"

He spat out a scrap of orange and reached for a cigar. His supply of Havanas was dangerously diminished. Thank God his business in this miserable region was nearly completed.

"Sir Herbert Samuel was appointed because he was a

British peer, not because he was a Jew,'' Ezra replied quietly. "His appointment was not especially popular. There are those of us who believe that a non-Jew might have been more sympathetic to our cause. You are a student of history, Mr. Secretary. Surely you know that court Jews have a long history of striving mightily to please the court while often forgetting that they are Jews.''

He thought bitterly of Jabotinsky, whom the British had imprisoned after the Nebi Mussah riots, while Haj Amin, who had incited the Arabs to violence, had been pardoned and named mufti of Jerusalem.

"I think we are of divergent opinions on the Jewish question,'' Churchill said coldly and lit a match. Why did the opinion of this Jewish farmer matter to him, he wondered.

"How could we not be?'' Ezra Maimon replied quietly.

Harsh history, not facetiousness, molded his reply. Winston Churchill's grandparents had not been murdered in a Ukrainian pogrom. His wife had not died on a Galilean farm. His brother had not lost an eye shepherding his flocks along the Carmel hillside. Winston Churchill had been the architect of Gallipoli but he had sat behind a desk overlooking the embankment as young Eleazar died on an incline covered with wild thyme, the words of a psalm frozen on his lips.

"You suffer from historical narcissism,'' Churchill said brusquely. "Is the understanding of Jewish history restricted to Jews?''

"With all due respect . . .'' Ezra began and his voice was dangerously low. There were things he must say to this arrogant Englishman who controlled his people's destiny. Harsh things. Unpleasant things. But he would say them. An urgent knock at the door interrupted him. Dunning burst into the room even before obtaining Churchill's permission.

"Your Excellency—we have had an urgent intelligence communique,'' he said and glanced pointed at Ezra.

"You may speak in front of Mr. Maimon,'' Churchill said, his petulance suddenly gone. "At least I hope you can.''

He smiled broadly and Ezra felt his own anger dissolve. The man was a magician, a scoundrel, a statesman, and a bloody genius.

"Emir Abdullah is in Transjordan with his troops. He is pushing on to Amman, heading for Syria—apparently to aid his brother Feisal. If he succeeds there will be a crisis with France which we can ill afford."

"Damn!" The colonial secretary mouthed the curse softly and stared down at the dead gray ash of his cigar. "May I ask you to delay your return to Palestine so that we may travel together, Maimon? It would be fortunate, I think, for England and for this benighted region if the emir and I had a conference in Jerusalem."

And so Ezra Maimon had journeyed with Winston Churchill from Cairo to Jerusalem. Together the two men had watched the desert flash by. They stared, as though in a trance, at rolling hills of mauve and rose and long dun-colored plains.

"God, it's hot," Churchill said and mopped the sweat that streamed down his fleshy forehead. "But beautiful. One can understand how and why."

Ezra nodded. They were passing through the Sinai desert as the fiery sun melted into darkness. Long shadows danced across the golden sand, and flame-fringed clouds ignited the purple sky. It was clear, at that magic moment, why and how men had fought over the barren stretch of desert, and it was clear how and why prophets had come to this mysterious wilderness to search after an elusive truth, to pierce the mystery of eternity.

They arrived in Jerusalem as dawn lit up the walls of the ancient city. Ezra watched Churchill's face soften as sunlight kissed the sculptured stone. Dawn and sunset were the city's chimeric hours, and men who saw Jerusalem in that enchanted light were often changed forever.

Their carriage rumbled across cobbled streets, and Churchill stretched his neck to see the sun-gilded spire of David's Tower and the golden Dome of the Rock. Church bells tolled from the Greek Mission, summoning barefoot monks in brown soutanes to morning mass.

The plaintive, melodic voice of the muezzin, who stood at an archway of the Al Aksa Mosque, called the faithful to morning prayers. Bearded Jews in long black caftans hurried past the coach. Towels were wrapped around their necks and their earlocks were damp. It was Friday, and they had visited the bathhouse early to prepare for the Sabbath.

They drove through the Lion's Gate and past the Church of

Saint Anne. There had been a drought that spring, and the waters of the pool of Bethesda were low, but still the pilgrims congregated there. The lame leaned heavily on canes and crutches. The blind groped their way along stone walls worn smooth by desperate graspings.

Churchill averted his eyes. He was a man who could design elaborate battles but could not bear to witness a child's pain. He screwed his eyes shut when a leprous beggar thrust a fingerless hand through the carriage window. It was Ezra who placed a coin on the bleached, disfigured palm.

Emir Abdullah waited for them at Government House. He was a cherry-faced, diminutive Arab whose handshake was surprisingly strong.

"Salaam aleikem," he greeted them, bowing deeply. His abayah was milk-white, sewn of the softest linen, and the hilt of his dagger blazed with brilliant jewels.

"Shalom aleichem," he said in correct Hebrew to Ezra Maimon, who had been introduced yet again as an unofficial adviser. Ezra wondered why Churchill had wanted him there as he joined the entourage in yet another dimly lit conference room. Dunning had sent explicit cables. The tea was hot and there were wicker chairs.

Pleasantries were exchanged. Gifts were presented. His Majesty, the ruler of the British Empire, had sent the emir a Swiss watch, each numeral marked by a diamond. A royal gift bestowed by one monarch on another.

"Because we know that your passion for beauty is matched only by your passion for peace," Churchill said, extending the red velvet case. The emir removed the watch and held it to the light. The diamonds twinkled like stars. His hand trembled. It was true that he loved beautiful things.

"Alas, our gift to His Majesty is but a poor and humble offering, as we are but a poor and humble people," the Arab chieftain said. He snapped his fingers, and a satrap hurried forward with a soft leather case which he opened. He removed a diadem of beaten gold which he dangled in front of Churchill.

"We pray that this modest treasure will find favor in the eyes of your great and beautiful queen," Abdullah said.

Churchill bowed deeply.

"I thank you on behalf of my sovereign. He also wished me to convey his thanks to you for your valiant striving after peace in this sadly troubled region," Churchill said.

"Would that peace would come." Abdullah's pudgy middle finger stroked the blood-colored ruby that glowed in the hilt of his dagger. A shaft of sunlight ignited the blade of his scimitar, streaking it with gold, and he smiled yet again. His smile was the crafty grimace of the man who truly believes that war can beget peace and that the instruments of war can protect it.

They took their seats at last around the conference table. Abdullah listened, without removing his hand from his dagger, as Churchill outlined a plan to him.

"We ask you to remain in Transjordan and reign there under the protection of His Majesty, the King of England."

"But then His Majesty would, in fact, be the sovereign, would he not?"

Abdullah's smile was wide and ingenuous. The Englishman was foolish to think that he did not understand the difference between reign and rule. Lawrence had been his teacher. He had explained everything to him. How wise el-Lawrence was. How beautiful. How pale his skin and blue his eyes. Not like this Churchill, whose skin was the color of swine flesh.

"Your Majesty understands exactly," Churchill said. He had, after all, discussed this plan with Lawrence and was prepared for Abdullah's reactions.

The colonial secretary continued the discussion, carefully studying the emir's face as each point was made and emphasized. His diplomatic bargain had been carefully crafted. Abdullah would withhold any further military action against the French. He would undertake the establishment of a viable government in Amman. Transjordan would become part of the British Mandate in Palestine, and it would be the emir's responsibility to administer that area within the terms of the mandate.

"His Majesty," Churchill added, his fingers toying with the gold diadem which had surely beggared more than one Arab village, "was certain that he could rely on the emir's talent and judgment to act for him."

"He will not be disappointed—should I accept the proposal," the emir replied. He stroked the velvet watch case.

"His Majesty would, of course, send you a subsidy each month, one that befits your station and responsibility. And of course the government of England will send trained advisers.'' Churchill reached for a grape, briefly worried that it had not been washed properly, but ate it at last.

"His Majesty is very generous. But my people also have dreams and hopes.''

The emir peeled a fig with his dagger. The pink fruit flesh clung to the blade, and the pale green skin dangled in a reptilian ribbon. Fruit juice dribbled down the emir's chin and moistened his pointed dark beard. His brown eyes were liquid with guile.

"My people want so little,'' he said, and there was a hint of a whine in his voice. He stole a glance at Ezra Maimon.

"They will have their independence. You have my promise. I cannot tell you when, but they will have their independence,'' Churchill replied.

"Then surely we must carefully consider and study these proposals,'' Abdullah agreed.

He took up the maps and papers, summoned his advisers, and they adjourned to small conference rooms while Churchill and his entourage waited. The emir's advisers appeared at rapid intervals. Questions were asked, maps consulted.

Churchill calmly puffed at his cigar. He was removed from the diplomatic fray now and waited for the results of his endeavors with the calm of an architect who has drawn up plans for a building now undergoing construction.

"How will your Jews feel about this arrangement if the emir accepts my proposal?'' he asked Ezra.

"Just as you would feel if you found that Cornwall had been cut out of the heart of Britain and ceded to the French,'' Ezra replied dryly.

He too had studied the maps and agreements and felt his heart sink. Churchill had offered Abdullah all the lands east of the Jordan. It was true that there were no Jewish settlements there as yet, but the area was unpopulated and had always been part of the Zionist blueprint. It had been assumed that Jewish collectives would be founded there when enough settlers had arrived and when the land had been legally acquired. The Jewish National Fund had set aside considerable sums against such an eventuality. The Arabs had never been interested in cultivating the territory and had allowed it to become a wilderness. Now, suddenly, in a whirlwind reversal, the barren dunams, covered with scrub and inhabited by braying jackals, had become an important territory.

Ezra was reminded of a pull toy which he and Saleem had
fashioned for Achmed and Amos when they were small boys.
For weeks both boys had been indifferent to the plaything,
and then suddenly one or the other might have a notion to play
with it and there would be quarrels and tears.

"Share," their fathers had exhorted them, but it was clear
that the toy was desirable only when it was in someone else's
possession. So it was with the pocket of land that had so long
been neglected and ignored. But no one was exhorting the
Jews and Arabs to share that wilderness. It had become a
gift-in-hand, a reward for Arab acquiescence to British domi-
nance. Jewish acquiescence was assured without the tendering
of gifts.

Ezra understood now why Churchill had included him in
the meeting. He was to carry the news of the Arab-English
agreement to the Jewish community. Like a Greek messenger, he was to go to Daniel Langerfeld and Arthur Ruppin
and tell them of the new maps that had been charted and the
new agreements that had been signed.

But he offered Churchill no arguments; he recognized the
uselessness of any debate. It was clear that Abdullah would
accept Churchill's terms. The infrastructure of the Arab world
had been irrevocably altered during these last hours. A new
map had been drawn in this dimly lit room. A new kingdom
had been created in a matter of minutes. Ezra's father, Yehuda
Maimon, had worked the land for three decades, and for
years before that Zionists had written and worked for a Jewish
homeland that remained as elusive as ever. The Balfour Declaration was a teasing note from a marriage broker who has
no real hope for a successful match but hedges his bets. It had
taken years and years to achieve and might never be ratified.
But Winston Churchill and the emir had smiled at each other
and mouthed soft phrases that suited each other's purposes
and cross-fertilized each other's ambitions and dreams. Churchill would make the emir a king and the emir, in turn, might
make Churchill a foreign secretary or even a prime minister.
A diamond-studded watch and a beaten gold diadem had been
exchanged, and suddenly the Kingdom of Transjordan had
rocketed into history. This then was how kingdoms were
created. Ezra understood at last and cursed himself for not
having discerned the truth earlier. His son, Amos, who had

studied history and understood the evolution of dynasties, would have understood at once.

He was not surprised, then, that the emir's aide de camp appeared some hours later to report that the proposal had been adequately studied and found satisfactory.

"It is not quite all we would have wanted," the Arab said, "but because we so revere your great monarch and because we strive for peace, we will accept your terms."

He looked at Ezra Maimon, open triumph in his gaze. The Jew, of course, comprehended what Churchill had never grasped. The emir had succeeded beyond his wildest dreams. He had, with a minimal amount of maneuvering, managed to wrest a kingdom for himself and his heirs. That Jewish national homeland, so rashly promised by Lord Balfour, would not include the territory which would henceforth be known as Transjordan. A wilderness had become a nation, and a Bedouin princeling was now a monarch. The British colonial secretary had thought himself clever but they who had the wisdom of the desert and the mysterious blessings of Allah had outwitted him.

"I am grateful to you," Churchill said.

He looked at the signed treaty with satisfaction. His achievement would make that bastard Balfour squirm. Now, at last, he could return to England and settle down to the business of running the colonial office. Iraq was properly squared away and the damn Palestine problem was almost solved. Maimon did not look particularly happy but then not everyone could emerge from such negotiations the victor. The Jews of Palestine would have to take what they could get and they were damn lucky to get anything at all. One had to admire their courage and persistence, though. Ezra Maimon was a sound man. He combined qualities that Churchill himself prized—a cultivated intellect, passion, and physical courage and energy. If he ever came to England there would be a place for him there.

England. The very name of his homeland filled Churchill with expectant warmth. It was the end of May now. If they set sail at once they would dock at Southhampton just as the white roses broke into full blossom at Chartwell. He glanced out the arched windows at the dust-streaked stone road and the undulating, barren Judean hills that encircled the city. He could see the smoke-colored crest of the Hill of Evil Counsel. The meadowlands of England were carpeted with green now; it was the season of bright berries and the shy wildflowers of early spring. Did berries grow in Palestine, he wondered. Ezra Maimon would know, but something in the firm set of the Jewish farmer's lips made Churchill refrain from asking him. It was a pity. He would have liked to keep Maimon for a friend, but clearly that would not be possible.

"I will be meeting with Sir Herbert Samuel," he said to him. "I shall tell him how helpful you have been in explaining the Jewish position to me."

"Apparently to little avail," Ezra replied coldly.

Dunning looked at him reprovingly but Ezra did not care. He was not Dunning's pawn, nor was he Winston Churchill's satrap. He was an independent Jewish farmer responsible only to himself and his own conscience. He had bought and paid for his land. It had not been legislated into his possession.

"I am sorry that you feel that way," Churchill said pleasantly. "Would you care to accompany me to my meeting with the high commissioner?"

"I regret that I have other obligations in Jerusalem," Ezra replied.

He shook hands with the colonial secretary and accepted, with some surprise, a wrapped parcel which Churchill thrust upon him. He did not open it but shoved it into his haversack. He was in a hurry now to leave this building which stank of intrigue and deceit, of sweat and stale cigar smoke, of cloying perfume and oppressive incense. He would make his report to Daniel Langerfeld and Arthur Ruppin and then go in search of Amos.

He was not a politician yet he had busied himself too long with the affairs of a nonexistent Jewish state. He had sat in too many smoke-filled rooms, listened to too many lies, and understood only when it was too late that all his efforts had been for naught. Great men who knew whole sections of the Bible by heart and could easily quote Shakespearean soliloquies were capable of errors of judgment that would haunt their heirs for generations.

Winston Churchill was a cultivated man. He was incapable of blind violence. It was unthinkable even to imagine him party to a pogrom or involved in overt anti-Semitism of any kind. It was not unthinkable to imagine him, after downing two whiskeys and sodas and puffing his luxuriant cigar, quoting: "How odd of God to choose the Jews." He would not think of that as anti-Semitism. No more did he find Lord Curzon's dark fear of the emergence of a powerful Zionist executive in Palestine symptomatic of anti-Semitism. Ezra recalled a memo he had glimpsed bearing Curzon's signature. "With Zionists already in the ascendancy in Palestine . . . they would become one of the most formidable factors in the East. This would be the 'New Jerusalem' with a vengeance." Like Curzon, Churchill feared such a "New Jerusalem." He did not want an independent Zionist territory. He wanted a puppet kingdom of Arabs, like Transjordan, dependent on the guidance and munificence of Great Britain.

But it did not matter. Ezra Maimon was done with play-acting at the council tables of the great.

It was time for him to put his own life in order, to make his peace with his son and build a proper home for his children on that land he had claimed so many years ago. The jasmine was in full flower at Sadot Shalom now, and his peaceful fields would be redolent with its fragrance. Amos's school term was almost over. Perhaps his son would return to Sadot Shalom with him and they could spend the summer as a family. He looked at the Luristan dagger and was pleased with himself for selecting the gift—pleased because he knew that Amos would appreciate it. On impulse he opened the parcel Churchill had given him and stared down at a row of neatly wrapped Havana cigars. The supreme gift from the great man whose supply was running low. Ezra smiled in spite of himself. He closed his rucksack carefully, heaved it onto his shoulder, and left Government House, pausing briefly to shake hands with Dunning, who had already changed into his dinner jacket.

"Goodbye, Maimon," Dunning said. "You were a great help."

"Was I?" Ezra asked. Softly, he closed the door behind him and made his way down the cobbled road bordered with bramble bushes and star-shaped violet thorns.

Chapter 25

The next day Ezra made his way slowly up the Street of the Jews. His shadow fell before him on the narrow lane. Small boys wearing velvet knickers that shone with age kicked a tattered leather ball. Their earlocks flew and they shouted urgent epithets to each other in a Yiddish he barely understood although it had been the language of his childhood. A bearded rabbi strode down the lane, his fist raised threateningly, and the boys darted into the entryway of a building. Just so his brothers Saul and David had scurried away as their grandfather approached the study hall of their childhood. Ezra paused to read the sign above the doorway—the Yeshiva Etz Chaim—the Talmudic Academy of the Tree of Life. He listened to the boys' voices as they chanted a talmudic tract.

"If two men find a garment at the same moment, to whom does the garment belong?" they asked, singing the question in unison.

The rabbi turned to Ezra and smiled proudly. His lips were very red against his dark beard.

"They are my students," he said proudly. "They learn well, do they not?"

"They learn well," Ezra agreed. The rabbi no doubt would be surprised to learn that this clean-shaven farmer knew the answer to the question they pondered and the exact cadence in which it was sung.

He kicked the ball into a crevice where the boys would find it easily and noticed one student poke his head out the window. The boy flashed a grin of complicity and continued the chant. The child's face was pale and his shoulders were hunched but mischief glinted in his eyes. He himself must have looked like that as a child, Ezra thought, and the face of his grandfather, Reb Shimon, flashed before his eyes. He would visit his grandfather's grave one day—perhaps when he visited his sister Sara, who now called herself Zosia. She and Casimir had recently moved to a country estate not far from Oswiecim and Casimir had been named a town councilor, she wrote. Ezra had smiled bitterly as he read her letter. Casimir indeed. Chaim the bespectacled revolutionary became Casimir the Polish landowner. What odd tricks life played. Did Shimon, who had been born on the Rishon farm, cross himself each Sunday morning and pray for the conversion of the Jews?

"Are you on your way to the Wall?" the rabbi asked him.

"Yes I am," Ezra replied warily.

"Then say a prayer for me, my son. Pray that the Messiah may come speedily in our own time and restore our land to us. Amen."

"Amen," Ezra repeated gently and walked on. He wondered what the rabbi would say if Ezra told him that only days ago he had sat in a room not far from this street and witnessed the signing of documents that all but guaranteed that the land would not be speedily restored in their own time, amen. Messianic assistance had neither been invoked nor anticipated. The rabbi would not be perturbed, he supposed. Most probably he would stroke his beard and speak vaguely of the will of God. Briefly, bitterly, Ezra envied the caftaned Talmudist.

He continued down the narrow lane, cloaked in the melancholy that had trailed him since his arrival in Jerusalem. He had been too long absent from Sadot Shalom, he told himself. It was time for him to return home. He wanted to see sunlight pierce the fragile leaves of his young peach trees; he wanted to touch the rich dark earth of his land and rub the kerneled heart of his new grown grain against his cheek. He longed to stand alone on the crest of a hill as evening shadows swept across his land and then to hurry home and lift Elana into his arms. She would laugh then and whisper a sweet-breathed secret in his ear. He was homesick, he knew, but he could not go home—not until he had seen Amos and made his peace with him.

But Amos was not in Jerusalem.

"He is on a field trip," Daniel Langerfeld had told him. Amos had joined an archaeology seminar on an excursion north to visit a newly excavated site. Ezra was welcome to stay with the Langerfelds until Amos returned.

"If it will not inconvenience you, I will stay in Amos's room," Ezra accepted gratefully.

Daniel Langerfeld had been uncomfortable. He shuffled the papers on his desk and threw a nervous glance at his wife, who left the room, closing the door softly behind her.

"Amos no longer lives with us," Daniel Langerfeld said at last. "He has rented a room of his own not far away. He is no longer a boy. He is a young man now. He needs his privacy. You know how it is when you are young."

"Yes, I know," Ezra said but he avoided Daniel Langerfeld's eyes, embarrassed suddenly because he was a father who did not know where his son slept, where he took his meals, who his friends were. Did Amos have a woman, he wondered. His son had become a man, and Ezra had not witnessed the days of his boyhood.

"I know that it is inconvenient for you that Amos is away just now but I am glad of it. This time of year is so difficult for him always."

He sighed deeply and led Ezra into a small back bedroom.

"How so?" Ezra asked.

He looked around the small room with its arched window and whitewashed walls. No pictures were hung, and the shelves of the small bookcase were bare. The subtle aroma of lilac clung to the room. It was a familiar fragrance, one that pervaded his own bedroom at Sadot Shalom. Nechama's lilac-scented sachets were concealed in drawers and sewn into corners of the mattresses. She had sent them as gifts to her sisters and nieces. He understood, then, that the room in which they stood had been the bedroom of Daniel Langerfeld's smaller daughter who had been killed during the Nebi Mussah riots. Aunt and niece were dead but the scent of lilac lingered on.

"Because tomorrow is Nechama's birthday," Daniel said. "Had you forgotten?"

"By tomorrow," Ezra said, "I would have remembered."

He had always observed Nechama's birthday and the anniversary of her death. Even on Gallipoli he had lit a small candle for her and murmured the Kaddish as British and Turkish rockets streaked across the trembling sky. In New York the candle had flickered softly in the window of his uncle's Park Avenue apartment. He had been fighting in Palestine on one birthday and had whispered the prayer as he moved stealthily across the low-slung northern hills.

He was not a religious man. During these last years of war and loss, he had often doubted the very existence of God. But still, he lit the candle and said the prayer each anniversary of her death and each birthday. He was a Jew, and he followed the custom of the Jews. Besides, Nechama had been a religious woman, unswerving in her belief, in her adherence to the patterned order of religion, the careful separation of time, the consecration of special days.

And so on this day that marked her birth, because he was in Jerusalem and because it would have been meaningful to her, his tall pale bride, his gentle wife, he would go to the Western Wall. He would touch its ancient stones and say a prayer to signify that she had not lived and had not died without purpose. Her life was recognized and remembered. Her death was mourned. Her beliefs were honored.

He continued on his way, stepping aside to allow a procession of black-frocked monks to pass before him on the narrow lane. Their peaked hats cast triangular shadows, and a bone-thin Jerusalem cat leaped fearfully between them and darted into an overflowing rubbish bin. An aged beggar jangled a battered tin cup in front of him as he passed the Courtyard of the Karaites. White mucus sealed the mendicant's eyes shut and his feet were swathed in flesh-colored rags. His white robe was covered with dust and grime and belted with a length of rope. But his black leather prayer book was newly bound, and his skullcap was of clean white linen. Ezra dropped a few coins into the almost empty cup, and in return the beggar offered him his Bible to kiss.

"Today the adon finds joy," the beggar said. "God walks with the man who has given righteously to the Lord and to His poor."

"Go in peace with the Lord," Ezra replied dutifully.

Three women stood at the courtyard gate. They wore the long-sleeved dark dresses of the orthodox matron and carefully affixed a hand-lettered sign to the wall. The huge block letters blared their message menacingly: IT IS FORBIDDEN FOR A DAUGHTER OF ISRAEL TO APPROACH THE WALL IMPROPERLY DRESSED! Their small daughters squatted patiently in the dust and played jacks with gleaming pebbles as they waited for their mothers. Although the day was hot the little girls also wore long-sleeved heavy dresses, and thick stockings that bunched clumsily about their knees. One dainty blond girl glanced up at Ezra, flashed him a smile and then blushed, as though embarrassed by his bare arms and smooth-shaven bronzed skin.

Damn fools, Ezra thought angrily. That child should be running barefoot through the field as Elana did—allowing the wind to ruffle her hair and the sun to color her golden. The small girl coughed and Ezra watched as she took out a handkerchief and spit into the white linen. The small drops of blood sparkled like scarlet teardrops. She looked down at them but there was no fear in her pale blue eyes—only sad resignation. She was ill and would die. It was the will of God, blessed be His name.

Ezra turned away. He remembered the child taken sick on a New York street and Sonia's valiant efforts. But here too she could have waged her war against tuberculosis. Here too, on these grim narrow streets with their beautiful ancient names, there were battles to be fought, victories over poverty and prejudice to be won. But Sonia had chosen otherwise, and just as the child was resigned to her illness, so was he resigned to his lost love's choice. He dropped a wrapped sweet in front of the small girl but realized at once that she would not eat it. She could not be sure that it was kosher.

He walked on more quickly now and paused, as he approached the Wall, to look out at the Temple Mount. The cupola of the Mosque of Omar gleamed golden in the morning brightness; the smaller dome of the Al Aksa Mosque flashed liquid lengths of silver light across the entryway through which Moslem worshipers threaded a path: their brightly colored prayer rugs were tucked beneath their arms, and they kept their eyes downcast as though fearful that the metallic glory of their sanctuaries might blind them.

Ezra crossed the large square until at last he faced the Western Wall. The tiers of ancient stones were veiled by a rose-gold light. The huge rampart dwarfed the worshipers who assembled before it and cloaked them in gossamer capes of shade. Bright green leaves and clumps of stubborn overgrowth thrust their way between the crevices, and a pure white flower dropped in the narrow space between tiers of stone. A dusty bird perched on a single vagrant branch and trilled a song of mournful sweetness. Over and over again it sang the same haunting tune, but the Jews who clustered about the Wall and pressed their faces and bodies against the cool stone did not look up at it. It flew away at last, soaring above the narrow escarpment to wing its solitary way through the cerulean Jerusalem sky. Ezra watched it sadly until it could no longer be seen.

Bearded Jews in black satin caftans touched the Wall gently with one hand and held their prayer books with the other, their lips moving rapidly in febrile supplication. A Chassid dressed in dark knickers and white stockings, draped in a huge fringed shawl, rushed past Ezra, knocking him off balance.

"*Slicha*," Ezra said sarcastically in Hebrew. "Excuse me."

The man glared at him. His narrow eyes were frozen slits of blue in his pale face.

"Do not profane God's holy name in His holiest of places," he said harshly in Yiddish.

Anger gripped Ezra. His father's rage and his father's sorrow burned in his veins, but he said nothing.

An English police officer passed, twirling his billy club. The officer's thin lips were twisted into a contemptuous smile. He paused in front of a group of Oriental Jews who squatted in the center of the large plaza. They wore long abayahs and loose desert cloaks; their heads were covered with bright red fezes and brilliantly colored satin turbans. They formed a circle, and their leader sat in the middle wearing a long white robe and a bright blue prayer shawl. He explained a biblical passage, and his followers intoned his words in a melodic chant. A dark-haired young woman stood at a discreet distance from this group but her eyes were fixed on them, and she held a sketchbook with a drawing pencil poised above it. Deftly she drew a face and then another, working swiftly.

Ezra stared at her and, as though conscious of his gaze, she looked at him in turn. Briefly their eyes met. Flecks of gold danced in her almond-shaped dark eyes. Her features were delicately chiseled and her full lips were wine-colored. She was very tiny, and her bright red dress was gathered at the waist and clung loosely to the rise of her small breasts. She turned away from Ezra and concentrated again on the group of Eastern Jews, working even more quickly now, as though she feared a rare moment might be lost. Her pencil flew, and he glimpsed an outline of her sketch as he walked past her. It was very good, he saw at once, and wished that he could tell her so.

The British officer also looked at the drawing and then at Ezra.

"Wouldn't mind having a picture of that group of worthy Oriental gentlemen myself. My pals in Manchester wouldn't believe they were Jews," he said.

"Wouldn't they?" Ezra responded coldly. He too found the Oriental Jews exotic but he resented the Englishman's patronizing attitude. Someone should have taught that arrogant son of a bitch that a governing power was not necessarily superior to the people it governed—it was simply more powerful.

The British officer blushed, and Ezra was briefly ashamed. The officer was, after all, far from Manchester and riddled with homesickness and a need to hear the sound of his own language. And Ezra knew that his anger was not aimed at the officer but at the fact that the Jewish community in Palestine continued to live under the rule of outsiders. The British Tommie had replaced the Turkish field officer—the billy club had replaced the bastinado. Eleazar's blood had stained his fingers scarlet and at Tel Chai the grass grew in verdant thickness where Trumpeldor's body fed the earth, but there was still no Jewish homeland.

Annoyed with himself, he took a small knitted skullcap

from his pocket, clamped it on his head, and strode across the large square-stoned plaza. But he slowed his steps as he approached the Wall. He was not a religious man but always this place moved him deeply. He stood motionless in its caressing shadow and felt the mists of his people's history surround him. Here, Solomon had built his temple, cementing each stone into place with hand-mixed mortar and wooden trowel because no metal could be used to build a sanctuary of peace. Twice the temple had been razed, and now only this section of the defense rampart remained, its lower tiers worn smooth by touch and washed by tears.

He watched now as two shawled women leaned against the stones, pressing their body weight against the ancient rampart. Their laden straw baskets, each overflowing with round loaves of new baked bread, bright red pomegranates, and the huge amber-colored duck's eggs which the Arab women sold in the market, rested on the ground. The older of the two removed a slip of paper from her pocket, kissed it, and pressed it into a slit between the stone. Other similar bits of paper, folded into minuscule squares, had been thrust into such crevices. Some had fluttered to the ground and lay there in tiny mounds of paper that would be carried skyward by a vagrant breeze. Ezra knew the messages he would find if he opened them. "Dear God, make my son walk again. He is a good boy who has never broken the Sabbath." "Dear God, bring fruit to my womb. I long for a child." "Dear God, find a bride for my son, a groom for my daughter, a livelihood for my husband, for we are poor and in need of comfort."

Desperately they waited for their scrawled messages to be read by heavenly angels. Nechama's father, Reb Langerfeld, came to the Wall each pilgrimage festival and left his own carefully penned supplication, folded into a splinter-thin bullet of paper.

"I plead for a Jewish homeland," he told Ezra one day, and his eyes shone with hope.

"All right," Ezra had replied quietly.

He envied those who believed. He wondered what he himself would write if he could manage a leap of faith and add his message to the multitude of others concealed between the holy stones. He knew. He would ask for an end to loneliness, for peace between himself and Amos. He would ask for days of laughter at Sadot Shalom and an end to the long nights when he awoke from sleep and confronted the ghosts that whirled through the darkness of his room. Soft-eyed Nechama, earnest Sonia, frightened Sara. All lost to him. Distant and lost.

He pressed his head against the cool stone and sniffed its dank, vegetal odor. A pale green vine had twined itself through columns of stone and dangled loosely above him. He broke it off and sniffed it, as though to assure himself that life persisted in this place where Jews came to pray for their dead and make supplication for their living. But the coarse bit of overgrowth was odorless.

He intoned the Kaddish then, his eyes tightly closed. He summoned Nechama's face, her great dark eyes staring up at him from the pale oval.

"God full of mercy," he murmured and wondered anew, with a grief mixed with bitterness, and resigned to that bitter-ness, where that merciful God had been on the wintry morn-ing of Nechama's death (and Elana's birth, he reminded himself with trained reflex). The good must be balanced with the bad. Emotional bookkeeping must be kept strictly in order. One day he would straighten all accounts and deter-mine the exact age of Sonia's son, Sammy Wade. All debts could not be collected, he knew, but it was necessary to maintain an accurate ledger.

He completed the prayer and turned to leave when he suddenly heard voices raised behind him. He turned, startled and suddenly wary.

"Give me that!" The shawled woman shouted in a rasping voice at the young artist he had noticed before. Her hand formed a grasping claw, and she struggled to seize the pad from the younger woman's grip.

"But it's mine," the artist protested, and the musical quality of her voice astonished Ezra.

"To create false images is an abomination before the Lord," the older woman screeched. Her basket trembled, and a pome-granate rolled out and skittered like a scarlet ball across the great stones of the plaza. A small boy plucked it up and scurried away, happily spitting the seeds as he ran.

"Thief!" the woman shouted after him, but she did not release her grip on the artist. "For shame!" she hissed.

She had succeeded at last in ripping the page loose, and she waved it aloft now, her fingers still digging cruelly into the younger woman's arm. Ezra saw the fluid lines of a drawing that had captured the concentration of an old man at prayer, the curved forms of the women. He recognized his own straight back and the circlet of his knitted skullcap.

"For shame!" the woman repeated, and a group of men who sat with their backs braced against the Wall nodded and echoed her.

"For shame!"

The British officer strode up, his cheeks red, his billy club flailing the air.

"What's going on?" he asked and was answered in a barrage of Hebrew, Ladino, and Yiddish. Each spectator bore witness. Vociferously, they corroborated and contradicted each other. The artist was correct and the old woman was wrong. She had every right to draw. She had no right to draw.

The younger woman twisted herself loose and spoke to the British officer in careful English. Her eyes were all golden fire now, and her cheeks were deeply flushed.

"I made a drawing and she took it away and hurt my arm because she believes that it is against religious law to create a likeness. That drawing is my property. It must be returned."

"Well now," the officer said judiciously, "regulations have it that the religious sanctity of this holy place must be preserved and the rights of the religious protected." He repeated this proudly. He had received a fine grade in the orientation course designed by the high commissioner, Lord Samuel. He stared hard at the young artist. He had never seen a full-grown woman so small or a white woman so dark. The women of the Middle East were different from the factory girls he had known in Manchester. But not that different, he was bound to believe.

"I'm afraid I'll have to issue you a summons, miss," he said. (If she didn't want that summons she knew jolly well what she could do about it. He imagined the feel of those small breasts—tiny cushions of softness they'd be beneath his fingers. What color the nipples, he wondered. Berry red, like her cheeks. Berry red.)

"I think your grounds for issuing such a summons are extremely flimsy," Ezra interposed, moving between the officer and the two women.

"Are you a solicitor then?" the officer asked superciliously. He didn't care much for the old bearded Jews with their Hebe mumbo jumbo, but he really disliked these smart-alecky young pioneers who thought they had the country by the short hairs. So what if some of them had fought in the Jewish legion? He'd been in the infantry too, and it wasn't his fault that his regiment never saw action. Pioneers they called themselves, that lot. Pioneers indeed. He knew what they were. Goddamn Bolsheviks like that crowd in Russia. All Jewish they were too. Trotsky. Kerensky. That woman—Rosa Luxemburg. Troublemakers, all of them. He read his newspaper every Sunday, and if Mosley wasn't smart, he'd like to know who was.

"No, I'm not a solicitor. I'm a farmer. But you don't have to have legal training to know that the term *rights of the religious* is subject to interpretation. I don't think a magistrate would agree that executing a sketch constitutes a violation of those rights. And magistrates do hate to have their time wasted," Ezra said.

"And maybe that same magistrate wouldn't be at all happy to learn that a British officer was delayed in the lawful carrying out of his duties by a passing farmer," the officer sneered. "See here—who do you think you are to be pushing yourself in here where you got no place?"

"You might find this of some interest to you," Ezra replied.

He took out his wallet and removed the safe-conduct pass signed by Winston Churchill.

"I assume that you have no difficulty reading the signature of your colonial secretary," he added.

"No. No. None at all."

The officer's face turned a mottled pink. His hand faltered as though he could not decide whether or not a special envoy of the colonial secretary merited a salute. Damn this country, he thought. One could never tell who was who. It was much simpler back home in England, where you knew at once who a man was by the sound of his accent and the cut of his suit. He turned his anger on the small crowd that had gathered around them.

"All right then—what are you lot moping about for? The show's over. Get on with your business. All of you. You too,'' he snarled at the shawled woman who had made the complaint.

In reply the woman shoved the girl forward suddenly and with a quick move tore the sheet of drawing paper into several pieces.

''No!'' Anguish and fury mingled in the girl's protesting cry. She swayed and made a movement as though to retrieve the long white strips of paper that fluttered in the sudden breeze. She stumbled and fell against Ezra, who gently steadied her. His head was bent so close to hers that he smelled the sweet lemon scent of her thick dark hair, and his fingers sustained the fragile column of bone at her back. She trembled almost imperceptibly, and the smallness of her body stirred him deeply.

How old was she, he wondered as he held her steady. But she moved swiftly out of his arms, with elegant grace. Her hands flew across her dress, straightening her skirt and the long black stole that covered her shoulders and arms.

''I must thank you,'' she said.

''I am sorry your picture was destroyed.''

''I have myself to blame. I well know the feelings of the Orthodox, and I saw her watching me. I should have moved away. But I can make other drawings, and when I come here again to draw, the officer will not bother me.''

She glanced toward the uniformed official who stood beneath Wilson's Arch busily writing up a summons against an Arab vendor who waited patiently by with his cart of copper knick-nacks. The Arab, who most probably could not read and would destroy the summons as soon as the officer was out of sight, accepted the flimsy document with a deep bow and offered the Englishman a copper dish.

''I want to show that there is peace between us,'' the Arab said and bent his head respectfully.

''Well now, in that case, I accept,'' the officer blustered. He was pleased. They were supposed to try to get on with the native population, weren't they? In his opinion, some of these Arabs were smarter than the Jews. They, at least, knew who was in charge and how to keep the peace. If the Jews were so damn independent now, who knew how they would react if that bloody Balfour Declaration was ever ratified. He hoped he'd be back in Manchester by then. He had his eye on a greengrocer's shop in a corner of King's Lane, and this copper dish would make a nice note in the window. "Got it as a gift during my Middle East service," he would say. Yes, he liked the sound of that. He walked away whistling softly.

"Perhaps I should have offered him a drawing," the young artist said sarcastically.

"I don't think that was what he had in mind," Ezra said, and the young woman's cheeks again reddened.

"I must go now," she said. "I have a class at the Bezalel Academy."

"Please. What is your name? Where do you live?" His own question and the urgency of his tone surprised him, and his heart pounded too rapidly.

She smiled and her lips moved in answer but he could not discern her words because as she spoke a wood-wheeled handcart rolled noisily by, and the voice of the muezzin rang out from the Mosque of Omar.

"Wait!" he called but she was already out of sight, and he could not reach her through the crowds of Arabs hurrying toward the mosque.

He plucked up the severed strip of paper that had been her drawing and smoothed it out. Her pencil had raced swiftly across the page and captured the profile of the turbaned Jew. She had scrawled her name at the corner of the picture but most of it had been ripped away. He stared at the fragmented Hebrew letters but could only be certain that the first letter was a *mem*. Was her name Miriam then, or perhaps Malcha? The only thing he knew for certain was that she was a student at the Bezalel Academy. What was he to do then—haunt the corridors of the school or lurk outside its gates because a young woman's tiny body and golden eyes had briefly caused his heart to turn? He had no time for such frivolity. He would stay in Jerusalem only until Amos returned. His place was at Sadot Shalom with his daughter and, if things went well, with his son. That was what he wanted now—all that he wanted.

He ascribed it to pure chance that late that evening, and again on the following afternoon, his wanderings through Jerusalem took him to the gentle hill where a small sign on a black wrought-iron gate marked the entry to the Bezalel School of Arts and Crafts. On both occasions, students streamed through the gate carrying sketch pads and watercolor boxes, worn leather kits of sculpting tools and furled lengths of canvas. But although he watched each hurrying novice intently, he did not see the small dark-haired artist with the gold-flecked eyes who had so briefly trembled in his arms on the Temple Mount.

Chapter 26

Amos Maimon, had long dreamed a recurring dream. It haunted him during waking hours, and he puzzled it out now as he hurried through the darkened streets, pleased at being back in Jerusalem after the rigorous field trip in the north.

In the dream he stood always at the edge of a narrow stream and wondered how he might best cross the water. The sun burned down on him and he was dizzy with heat and thirst. Shade trees and tall grass beckoned from the opposite bank, and leafy shadows laced the water. A man and a woman moved with easy grace through the tall grass. The woman carried a broad-brimmed sun hat, and although she spoke softly, the sound of her voice wafted across the stream, but he could not discern the words. The man wore khaki shorts and his muscles rippled mightily through his blue work shirt. He carried a scythe and effortlessly slashed away the vines and overgrowth in their path.

"Save me!" the dreaming Amos called to them, but although he mouthed the words he could not give them voice, and the meandering couple did not hear him. They wandered on, talking and laughing, cool and together.

"Save me!" he called again and this time his words were lost but his voice emerged—a raging scream.

The woman vanished into the leafy copse but the man walked into the water and waded to the other side. He lifted the boy in his arms and carried him to the shaded shore. The boy, Amos, was happy because the man had come to him, had heeded his cry of need and bridged the narrow aqueous chasm between them. Yet, he was also shamed because the water had not been deep after all and he could have easily crossed it alone. The woman had disappeared but he sat with the man in the shade and they shared water from a crystal pitcher that rested magically on a velvet bed of moss. Her disappearance was mutely accepted. They did not search for her but their fingers touched as they drank. They acknowledged that they had been mutually bereft and were comforted that they had been separated yet were together.

Amos thought that he understood much of his dream. His archaeological studies, after all, centered around symbols. He had attended lectures during which scholars, speaking in German-accented Hebrew, explained the meaning of the small fertility idols fashioned with breasts and penises, and explicated on the meaning of overflowing cornucopias and shackled captives.

"Our academic colleague and coreligionist at home in Vienna, Dr. Sigmund Freud, has discovered a new truth— that man reveals himself through his dreams. We archaeologists have always known this," a newly arrived scholar told the assembled students, who understood that the fingers of dreamers had fashioned the idols and artifacts they studied so carefully.

Amos dreamed, he knew, of the inexplicable divide between himself and his father, of the silence that separated them and of the unshed tears that hovered between them—an invisible waterway of grief.

"Be friends with Abba," small Elana had implored him during their brief meeting for a family occasion.

"I try," he said helplessly.

He had waited for years for his father to hear his wordless pleas, his nocturnal scream of terror, and cross the narrow stream to rescue him. Instead, when they met they spoke in the restrained, vigilant tone of men who hoard secret knowledge and cannot share their thoughts.

"How is the farm?" Amos would ask his father. He yearned

for the rolling peaceful fields of Sadot Shalom, for the terraced orchards and the distant hillsides that glowed golden at sunrise. But they lay across the stream of silence, and his father would not help him cross over to pleasant shade.

"Sadot Shalom prospers." His father's answer was always the same. "How are your studies?"

"They go well. I published an article in an international journal of archaeology. I asked them to send you a copy."

"Yes. I received it. It was very good. Exceptional."

Was pride mingled in his father's approval, Amos wondered. He did not know. He could not tell. His Maimon family advised forbearance. His Langerfeld uncles counseled patience. Ezra Maimon had suffered greatly. He had lost his wife. He had done much for the country. (But what has he done for me, Amos asked silently. I am his son, and I too have suffered. I lost my mother. *And it was not my fault that she died.*) He had, during the years of his father's absence, made a mental bargain with himself. He would not blame Ezra if Ezra would only cease to blame him. He would allow all debts to be cancelled. Their shared loss would be acknowledged, and the stream of their grief would be bridged. But Ezra had returned from the war seething with anger, suffused with sadness, wounded by a new loss, and the gulf between them had widened. The separating waters were deeper now than they had been.

Still, Amos was no longer bitter. His long loneliness had at last come to an end. He belonged to someone else now. He was no longer a peripheral guest, an itinerant boarder in his uncle's house—an orphaned nephew for whom an extra place had to be set. He had his own room now in the Yemin Moshe quarter—a sweet private refuge in an old stone villa owned by Professor Amitai, his academic mentor.

It was a wonderful room. The morning sunlight bounced off its whitewashed walls and streamed through its wide arched windows. He stepped out on his narrow balcony and looked across at the Valley of Kidron and the slender stone minaret of David's Tower. His bed was covered with the bright red and orange spread she had brought, and rainbow-colored runners of ancient looming were spread across the tiled floor. She had found brass vases in the suq of the Old City, and she kept them filled always with flowers in season or with branches of fragrant myrtle, dark mandrake leaves, and the slender palm fronds that reminded him of the road to his grandparents' Rishon farm.

His papers and book were neatly ranged on the old oak desk which Professor Amitai had given him, and his small collection of artifacts marched across the narrow shelf. Even in night darkness, he could see the glint of the ancient bits of metal he and Achmed had unearthed during their boyhood days on Sadot Shalom. The small fertility idol they had found in the wheat field glowed gently.

Often, she cooked their shared dinner on the small kerosene burning petiliya concealed behind the curtain of beads he called his kitchen. The professor's wife gave them space in her small icebox for the few perishables they kept. They ate on the balcony in fair weather and watched the sun's slow death; the last blood of the fading golden orb flooded the sky with spans and gashes of mauve and rose that drifted across the wondrous hills and stones of the ancient city—their city unlike any other.

In that room, for the first time since he had left Sadot Shalom as a boy not yet bar mitzvahed, he felt that he had a home, a place that belonged to him, where someone waited for him—someone who cared enough to garnish his life with beauty and fill his room with the pungent odors of food prepared with joy and love. He was intrigued by the spices she used—the strong garlic and harsh cardamom, the essence of lemon and grindings of ginger. She, in turn, laughed when he brought home jars of cold borscht and covered platters of gefilte fish from his Langerfeld relatives.

"I think the Jews were persecuted in Europe because no one could stand the smell of their food," she said, laughing.

He loved the sound of her laughter. It was musical, like her voice. He laughed too and watched her ladle out a stew of lamb, tomatoes, and eggplant. They ate it with relish, scooping up the gravy with snow-colored pittot her mother baked each day.

He studied during the long evenings, and she too bent over her work. Occasionally he looked up and watched her as she squatted on the soft leather footstool, her feet tucked beneath her skirt, her hair flowing about her shoulders, as dark as the night outside their arched window. He marveled then at his luck—at the wondrous miracle that he had found her at all and that she had become his.

It had seemed improbable from the first day of their meeting. She was older than he, and the disparity in their ages had worried her—perhaps because her Yemenite parents were obsessed with worry about her age.

By their lights, she told Amos, she was an old maid, doomed to be a spinster. In the synagogue her father prayed for God's intercession on her behalf, and he brought home young men who looked at her shyly but did not speak to her. They spoke instead to her father, who stroked his beard and twirled his curling earlocks as they talked.

Yes. She was a good girl. An obedient daughter. She could cook and bake. The very cloth on which their meal was spread was of her design and her embroidery. The young men admired the intricate gold and silver needlework, the crimson thread roped about knots of copper satin. Had she made the boys' skullcaps too, they wondered as they looked at her younger brothers' brilliantly colored head coverings. Indeed. Indeed. She had conceived the design and fashioned them herself.

She served the salads, fresh vegetables, and bowls of tehinna ground to a liquid thinness. They spoke of her obliquely but they took note of her thick dark hair, her almond-shaped eyes, her slender waist and fine-boned hands. The young men smiled tentatively but her face remained impassive. When they left, she cleared the dishes angrily from her beautiful cloth, and she would not answer her father except to say that one young man had been a fool and another had been ignorant and yet another behaved as though he still lived in the tents of the Arabian desert. Neither their youth nor their prosperity impressed her. She would not be betrothed to them, she said angrily. Finally, she wept.

Her anger did not move her father but her tears made his heart tremble. He was a gentle man, a metalsmith who spent his days mending broken utensils, severed chains, damaged vases. He could not bear breakage and disrepair. He would not have his daughter broken-hearted.

The young men were not invited back. Her younger brothers and sisters were married but she, the oldest daughter, continued to live at home, to study at the mysterious art school in the city, to fashion beautiful things for each dowry. She passed her twenty-fifth birthday, and now widowers came to call on her. She no longer sat with them at the low table, but her mother told them how she loved children and of her grace with the needle. She was gentle and giving and very beautiful. The widowers nodded. They knew of her beauty. They had seen her in the synagogue during the Days of Awe when she sat beside her mother in the woman's balcony. But she was indifferent to the widowers who sent her flowers and sweets.

"What do I want with a man who has already loved once?" she asked. She laughed and found that laughter worked as well as tears. Her father did not press her. A proposal that evoked laughter could not be treated seriously.

She was often away from home, but her parents seldom asked where she had been or where she was going. They feared her secrets, the mysterious life of her school, and they would not risk the loss of her love by intruding on her carefully guarded privacy. Where is she, her father wondered as evening hours crawled by, but he confessed to himself that he did not want to know. Her silence, their caution, protected their fragile family life.

Amos had met her in the small gallery on the Street of the Jews, where he had been sent by Professor Amitai to assess an ancient urn. She had come to sketch it. She wanted to experiment with the manufacture of modern carvings copied from ancient forms. He found the urn to be uninteresting and of dubious pedigree. She did not like its shape well enough to squander precious drawing paper on it. She embroidered three napkins to pay for each slender pad. But they left the gallery together and walked for hours, that first afternoon, across the hills that rimmed their city. She marveled at his hair, which became a golden aureole in the bright sunlight. He was so knowledgeable, so learned, yet he was so young—perhaps the same age as her brother Yussuf whom she loved the best of all her brothers. He held his breath when she spoke. Her voice trilled musically and he asked her questions, not because he wanted the answers, but because he wanted to hear the lilt of her words. His mother too had had a melodious voice and the gift of listening with rapt attention when he spoke.

Slowly, through the hours of that afternoon, they pieced together each other's lives, peeling away luminous membranes so that they might see each other more clearly. She pictured him on the Galilee farm of his childhood, a lonely, scholarly boy, golden-haired amid fields of golden grain, clambering up fruit trees, hiding in distant hills. She grieved for the silence of his boyhood.

Her own house had been crowded with noise and laughter, with children and adults who lived for their children. Poor Amos. Poor boy. She touched his hand lightly to comfort him, and he seized it and held it in a man's tender grasp. The boy had grown and could not be comforted. A man walked beside her through the rolling hills.

She envied him the vast landscape of the Galilee—the verdant fields, the sheltering hills and mountains. Her family lived on Shimon HaTarsi Street, where the houses converged upon each other, clustered together on the sloping road. The Yemenites of Jerusalem lived within a tight community, a hermetic infrastructure. The women chattered at each other as they cooked outside in their courtyards and strung their laundry on the long lines that spanned the street. The men smoked their water pipes together in the evening, each reclining on a special pallet. They told stories and laughed softly as the children played and darted in and out of each other's houses, knowing that they were welcome everywhere. There was no silence but neither was there solitude. She loved her community but she sought aloneness in quiet galleries and in the deserted silver-treed olive orchards that nestled on the outskirts of her city. She sought it once in the bed of a sculptor, a tall quiet man from Prague who wept in her arms and whispered to her in a language she did not understand. She had been relieved when he returned to his homeland although she kept concealed a small alabaster bust he carved of her. Was that truly how he saw her, she wondered—so small, so fragile? Was that how other men saw her? She felt herself a stranger to his world and to her own.

She had been born in Yemen but she had been a small girl when her parents journeyed across desert and mountain to find a new life in Jerusalem. Not that the new life was very different from the old one. Her father had been a metalsmith in Saana, and he followed the same craft in his tiny Jerusalem workroom. His dark beard flowed long and full, and a high skullcap threaded with rainbow-colored satin covered his thick hair. Her mother still wore colorful embroidered leggings beneath her long full skirts and concealed small amulets within the folds of her embroidered blouses. The blue beads and delicate silver hands dangled from exquisitely wrought chains and frightened away the evil eye. She cooked in the courtyard, and her huge copper cauldron always steamed above the low-burning coals. They prepared their food just as they had prepared it in Yemen. But Jerusalem was the joy of their life. The metalsmith prayed at the Wall as the sun rose, and he pressed his forehead to its cool stone at evening prayers.

"They have a love affair with the city," she told Amos. "Can you understand that?"

He told her of his father, who had a love affair with his farm.

"For me to leave his land was a personal betrayal," he said and she nodded.

He told her how Ezra blamed him for Nechama's death.

"It is I who should blame him. It was dangerous for her to become pregnant," he said bitterly, and she looked at him reprovingly.

"He is your father," she said seriously. "You must try to understand and respect him." Among her people the young stood aside and allowed their elders to pass. They respectfully pressed their lips to the outstretched fingers of their elders, and they bowed deeply to the *Mori*—the rabbi-teacher who governed their spiritual lives.

"How can you speak so about your father?" she asked.

She was honestly astounded that Amos blamed his father for the pregnancy that had cost his mother her life. How strange these Ashkenazic Jews were. Surely it was the joy of a woman's life to love her husband and bear his children. Even she, who had so steadfastly resisted the matches proposed by her family, yearned for motherhood—to have a child who would be flesh of her flesh, bone of her bone. But she would have such a child only with a man who could fathom her heart and whose touch was natural to her body, who would keep her captive yet allow her to roam free. Was there such a man, she wondered as she stroked Amos Maimon's palm and felt the scholar-smoothness of his skin.

Two weeks after they first met, he approached Professor Amitai and told him he had decided to rent the room which the professor had so often offered him.

"You will not disturb us," Professor Amitai assured him. "You see, your room has its own separate entrance." He pointed to the stone stairway that rose gracefully from the side of the house, shaded by a mandrake tree whose fragrance filled the arched-windowed room.

Amos did not tell the professor that the separate entrance was the principal reason for his selecting that particular room.

She brought him a brass lamp which she found in a corner of her father's workroom.

"It is for a friend," she told the metalsmith, and he nodded gravely and polished it to a burnished sheen. A gift must be beautiful to be worthy of giving. His people understood that.

"You must bring your friend to visit us," he said, and she saw the shadow of worried fear dull the glinting amber eyes which matched her own.

"Not to worry." She kissed his hand and hurried away.

That night Amos lit the lamp and they admired the way the room looked, bathed in its golden light.

"We will buy a straw chair in the Arab market," she said.

"And a leather ottoman."

"Let us play house," she teased. "You are the abba and I am the imma."

"No. You are the imma but I am the child." He pulled her down to the tile floor and lifted the loose turquoise blouse she wore. "And the child is thirsty."

He pressed his lips to her small firm breasts and kissed the small dusky buds of her nipples. They undressed in the light of the lamp, their bodies reflected in the burnished metal—his slender and pale, hers small but full-figured and golden. She was so tiny that when he cradled her in his arms he had to bend his head low to find her wine-red lips. Her tongue moved sweetly against his own, and her hands traced the bones of his body.

"You are so beautiful," he whispered. "I am frightened, you are so beautiful."

"Don't be frightened."

She guided him into the secret places of her body. He soared within her, quivered mightily, and came to rest. He kissed her shoulders, stroked her hair, listened with a strange exultant triumph to her long deep moan.

"So this is what it is like," he said and remembered the long nights of his boyhood and the whispers and love sounds that had penetrated the thin farmhouse walls.

"Yes. This is what it is like," she said, smiling. They slept briefly then but she did not stay the night. That would have been disrespectful to her father's house. She was an emotional acrobat, poised between two worlds, careful always to preserve her balance so that she would not fall and shatter long-ordained patterns.

He walked with her through the narrow streets of the silent city until they came to the top of Shimon HaTarsi. She descended the hill alone and disappeared into the house where she was the artistic sister, the beloved spinster daughter. But to him she was all things—lover and friend, sister and teacher.

Months had passed, and still they were together in the whitewashed room. Amos quickened his step and hurried now. She knew he would return from the field trip today. Surely she would be there, sitting in the circlet of light cast by the brass lamp. He ran as he rounded the corner. Their window was dark and his heart sank but he looked up at the small balcony and saw her standing there, her golden-flecked eyes shining in the darkness.

"Mazal," he called, charmed even by her name. Good fortune, they had named her, so that the evil eye would be deceived. Mazal. Luck, happiness. All this she had brought to Amos Maimon.

"Mazal," he called again, and she waved in gentle welcome.

"Amos arrived home last night," Daniel Langerfeld told Ezra the next morning. "Professor Amitai stopped by to tell us. He knows that we worry."

Daniel Langerfeld was embarrassed by his concern for his nephew. Nechama's son was twenty-two—a grown man. Yet Amos called forth a protective instinct. The boy had always been so alone, so vulnerable, with his mother dead, his father absent. For all his intellectual brilliance, there was a vein of almost childish naïveté that caused Daniel Langerfeld undefined worry. He was not comforted by the fact that Professor Amitai had told him that Amos's grasp of archaeology was astounding, his flashes of insight brilliant.

"He must go abroad and earn a doctorate," the professor insisted, and although Daniel Langerfeld agreed, he was uneasy about sending Amos to London or New York. He was so sensitive, so much the dreamer.

"I will go to see him at once," Ezra said.

"No. He has classes all day. But the professor is certain he will be home in the late afternoon."

"All right then. I will go this afternoon," Ezra said and turned back to his newspaper.

But he was disappointed. The city, for all its grace and beauty, had begun to close in on him. He longed for the great open vista of the Galilee, the sweet smell of jasmine and mignonette which permeated the fields of Sadot Shalom during the magic weeks of spring. He wanted to work his fields with Saleem and smell the roasting *friky*, the newly grown wheatheads which the Arabs cooked over small field fires until they were parched and could be peeled and eaten. It was time to go home, to resume his life. Even Churchill was at last on his way back to England. The newspaper he held showed a blurred photograph of the colonial secretary shaking hands in farewell with Sir Herbert Samuel. Churchill had offered the newspaper's correspondent a parting quote.

"The Balfour Declaration must be redefined," he had said, and Ezra grimaced. So much for Ezra Maimon's attempts to influence British foreign policy. But then he had told Ruppin and Langerfeld that he was a farmer and not a diplomat. And after all, he had that box of cigars as a memento.

He spent the afternoon walking through the city and once again found himself at the wrought-iron gates of the Bezalel school. The courtyard teemed with activity. Watercolors and oil paintings, framed and unframed, leaned against wall and gate. Long tables had been set out and covered with sculptures in snowy alabaster, rose Jerusalem quartz, and glittering metals. The art students examined each other's work with covert glance and admiring smile. They laughed and called to each other, and one tall young man perched on the top of a gatepost and sketched the spectators who, in turn, stared at his work as they passed him.

"Come in, come in," a smiling girl told Ezra as she passed. "Today we celebrate. It is the anniversary of the school's reopening after the Turks shut it down during the war."

"Thank God the bloody Turks are gone," a boy said.

The students were swallowed by the crowd but Ezra turned and saw two British officers station themselves at the gate, their hands clutching their clubs. Yes, the Turks were gone but the British had come in their stead. Again he felt the slow anger, the impotence of the occupied in the face of the occupier.

He wandered through the courtyard and admired the profusion of work. The artist Boris Schatz had wrought wonders in this school. All the students were talented but some were extraordinarily gifted. If only these young people could be left alone to draw and paint, to etch and sculpt. If only war would not again intrude on their lives, turn creation to destruction.

He walked on but nowhere did he see a display of pencil drawings signed by an artist whose name began with a *mem*. She was gone. He would not see her again. He was annoyed, impatient with himself and with his own disappointment. Their encounter had been brief. He had seen her only for a few moments but still he remembered the smallness, the fragility of her body as she trembled in his arms and the sweet lemon scent of her dark hair.

Later that afternoon, as the sinking sun brushed the bleached stones of the city with wide-stroked shadows of pink and gold, he walked across the Valley of Hinnom where once the Canaanites had sacrificed their children to the malevolent ox-headed god, Moloch. He threaded his way through the gloomy, rock-encrusted slopes and watched a group of Arab children play tag, darting ingeniously in and out of the ancient stone pilings; the altars of one generation had become the playthings of another. Their voices echoed gleefully in the shadowed enclave. Suddenly, a small black goat leaped across the rocks, chased excitedly by two little girls who wore the long stockings and dark dresses of the Orthodox.

An Arab boy seized the animal and held it close until the girls reached him. He passed it over to them, his eyes averted from their faces as theirs were from his own. The small kindness accomplished, the children dispersed and ran off in opposite directions. The Arab boy passed close by Ezra and reminded him of Achmed as a youth. Achmed was a handsome young man now, a graduate of an agricultural institute. He lived with his family on Sadot Shalom but worked at one of the northern experimental agricultural stations doing research on innovative crops. He had talked to Ezra of his work, and Ezra had felt an uneasy envy of Saleem. Achmed had all the qualities he would have valued in Amos.

Still, he reminded himself, he was done with making such comparisons. He had determined to accept Amos on his son's own terms. They had wasted enough time in fruitless emotional sparring. For Elana's sake, at least, if not for their own, they would have to come together and live as a family.

He left the valley and wound his way through the narrow streets and convoluted alleyways, carefully reading the names on the building-stones that marked each pathway. Professor Amitai, in whose home Amos had a room, lived on the Street of the Prophet Ezekiel. That could not be far from the Road of the Prophet Hosea, which he had just passed. He smiled. Only in Jerusalem were there thoroughfares named for the fierce men of Israel who had bitterly condemned their people. Here, rage was immortalized, castigators were sanctified. He belonged to a strange and complicated people.

He turned the corner and saw the house, recognizing it by the narrow stone stairway which Daniel Langerfeld had described. He suddenly felt uncertain and shifted the Luristan dagger which he had bought for Amos from one hand to the other. Would Amos be pleased with his gift? Would he understand why Ezra had chosen it? Soon he would know.

Slowly he mounted the steps. A stone basin rested on the landing, and a cactus plant had been planted within it. A single pink flower grew from a thorn-covered arm. It pleased Ezra that Amos had thought to keep such a plant outside his doorway. He did not know that Amos's friends used it as a mail drop, concealing messages beneath the cactus branches, but the knowledge would not have surprised him. Nechama had grown miniature cacti—sturdy stubborn plants that flowered at odd times. Did Amos remember that, he wondered.

He lifted the heavy brass knocker and let it drop against the stained oak door. There was no reply from within. His knock had been tentative. He used more force the second time and heard a rustling movement, the clatter of a pot. He sniffed. The aroma of a lamb steaming with vegetables seeped through the door. He knocked yet again.

"What? Did you forget your key again?" It was a woman's voice, musical and oddly familiar, mingling annoyance and amusement.

The door swung open and she stood, framed in the archway, wearing a long striped caftan, her eyes ovals of liquid amber, her long black hair falling to her shoulders.

His breath caught painfully. She stared at him with the perplexed gaze of someone trying to recall a half-forgotten encounter, a vaguely familiar face.

"I know," she said, smiling finally. "You are the man who helped me that day at the Wall."

"Yes, I remember now," he lied, stumbling over his words. He looked down and saw that her feet were bare. He must have come to the wrong house.

"I must have made a mistake," he said. "I know that I am on the right street but I am looking for the house of Professor Amitai."

"This is Professor Amitai's house."

"Then perhaps I have come to the wrong entrance. I am looking for my son's room. I am Ezra Maimon."

"You are at the right entrance." Her voice was very soft, and the blood flooded to her cheeks. "Amos Maimon lives here. I am his friend, Mazal Bat Chaim."

"Shalom, Mazal Bat Chaim," he said gravely and extended his hand.

"You are Amos's father?"

She could not conceal her astonishment. Amos had described his father as a forbidding, morose man, consumed by anger and grief. She had imagined him as much older—perhaps the age of her own father—flint-eyed and stern, a man who had deserted and alienated his only son and belittled the artistic and intellectual life. But the man who stood before her radiated strength and vigor. His outstretched hand covered her own, and she remembered the tensile grasp of his fingers when he had prevented her from falling that afternoon and the flash of pain in his eyes when he had seen the destruction of her drawing.

"I am." Her unconcealed amazement puzzled him. "May I come in?"

"Yes. Of course."

She stepped aside, allowing him passage, and saw his approving glance as he studied the room. She blushed as he looked at the pot of food simmering on the petiliya and the fresh mountain iris she had placed in a ceramic vase.

"Please excuse me," she said, and the coolness of her own voice startled her.

She hurried into the small bathroom and changed into her street clothes, the dark skirt and the loose turquoise blouse which she had embroidered with small golden moons and silver suns.

On impulse she swept her hair back into a loose knot. She

frowned at herself in the mirror and knew that she could not deceive Ezra Maimon. He had known at once. Her bare feet, the steaming food, the clusters of purple-and-white iris had all betrayed her. She was his son's mistress, and there was no concealing that fact, which had been evident to him from the moment she opened the door. Abruptly she shook her hair loose and brushed it to a velvet smoothness. Her sandals were of the Greek fashion, and she laced them about her slender calves. The mechanical motion soothed her. She was what she was, and she was not ashamed. She had loved and befriended a golden-haired boy whose sea-green eyes swam with loneliness. There had been no false promises, no insincere affirmations—only friendship and caring and a tender togetherness. It was all right. She went back into the room, armed with a smile.

Ezra Maimon sat at the table, reading the book which she had left when he knocked. It was a social history of art written in French.

"An interesting concept this," he said and read aloud the very paragraph she had been thinking about that morning—a paragraph which described the way in which a changing society affected the creative artist. He read the French with ease, and although his excellent accent astounded her, it was the clarity of his perception that engaged her and caused her to forget her embarrassment.

"According to the author," he said, "a new art form will evolve when new social concepts are foisted on society. It happened that way in France after the revolution, with the beginning of egalitarianism. Once there were portraits only of royalty and aristocrats. Then artists saw peasants and workers with new eyes, and a new school of painting developed."

"Exactly," she said excitedly, "and that is what will happen here—in Jewish Palestine. The taboos against the creation of graven images will be removed, and the creative spirit of Jewish artists will be released. It is already happening with Schatz's students at Bezalel. Jewish painters will paint their own people and their own landscapes."

"I have often wished that I could paint," he said, turning the pages of the book. "During my stay in New York, I went to the museums and saw the paintings of farms in the American Middle West. Ah, I thought, if only I had a painting of

Sadot Shalom, my farm in the Galilee. There is no landscape more beautiful. But surely Amos has told you about it.''

"Yes. Yes, he has. Amos has spoken of it," she said and averted her eyes from his. The mention of Amos's name briefly deadened the conversation that had sparked with life. "You know, of course, that Bezalel students are beginning to travel around the country. They paint the farmers on kibbutzim, the Jewish workers who are building the Haifa road, the children of moshavim." She spoke breathlessly, banishing the painful pause.

"Have you done such painting?" he asked.

"I am not a painter," she replied. "I draw only for pleasure. It is design that interests me. Handicraft and design. I love to work with my hands."

"I am kindly disposed to those who work with their hands," Ezra said, and he turned his own palms upward. She saw that they were smooth, yet thick as leather and pale as contrasted to the bronze color of his skin.

She reached out suddenly, surprising herself, surprising him, and touched his outstretched palm with her finger, tracing the hardened networks of heart lines and life lines. She had known a woman at Saana who read palms. A forked lifeline, according to the soothsayer—a toothless woman who wore a weighted gargoosh of amulets—meant greatness, extraordinary fulfillment.

"Such a man waits for you," the old woman had crooned to Mazal, a small girl then.

The words ricocheted back to her across the years and she dropped his hand as though scalded by the heat of his skin. She exposed her own palm, and her finger rested on the spot where she had gashed herself with a palette knife. A small white scar smiled out of the honeyed cushion of her hand. He resisted an impulse to touch his lips to that scar and asked her about her work.

"Embroidery," she said, "and metalcraft."

She pointed to the embroidery on her turquoise blouse.

"I designed the pattern and stitched it myself," she said, and in her own voice she heard echoes of her mother's tone as she boasted to one or another of the stream of improbable Yemenite suitors: "Mazal designed this work herself and sewed it as well. God's gift is in her fingers, blessed be His name." But Amos's father was not a suitor. He was a man with an eye for beauty and a gift for abstractions, a farmer who read French and discussed complex concepts with ease; a soldier who had traveled the world and returned to his farm; a man who carried documents of significant importance to frighten a Mandate police officer. Perhaps the twin forks in his life line were a confluence of paradoxes. He bent toward her now to examine the handiwork on her blouse. He held the fabric between his fingers, which brushed carelessly against her throat. Her skin tingled and grew unnaturally hot; her throat rattled with dryness.

"If you love landscapes," he said, "you must visit my farm."

"I should like that." Her voice was very faint but still his fingers did not release the fabric. He traced a moon, a silver sun.

"Wonderful," he said. "Like a painting."

Her face was on fire. She bent her head, and he lowered his in turn. He looked at her through eyes the same color as Amos's but softer; their brightness had been faded by grief and loss and had the look of wintry sea. Her heart turned. She had pitied the son for the loneliness that burned in his eyes, and now she pitied the father for the sorrow of his gaze.

A key turned in the latch and she sprang to her feet but Ezra Maimon did not move. He only turned his head and saw that Amos stood in the doorway, breathless because he had run part of the way home as he always did, propelled to urgency by the golden light in the arched window. He carried his green canvas book bag and a bouquet of pale white Sharon roses.

"Abba," he said, and his face turned crimson with surprise and unease. He dropped the book bag and moved across the room, still holding the flowers. Small white petals drifted to the floor and floated onto the woven rug.

"Amos." Ezra embraced his son and felt the unrelenting stiffness of his back. "I was in Jerusalem to report on my mission. I wanted to see you, and so I waited the few days for your return."

"That was good of you," Amos said, cringing from the formality of his own reply. "So you have met Mazal?"

"Yes, we have met."

"I hope your father will stay and have dinner with us," Mazal said. She took the white roses from Amos's hand.

"They are beautiful, Amos." She pressed them to her cheek as though the snow-white petals might cool her burning face.

Amos stared at her. He had never seen her color so high.

"I am sure my father is very busy," he said.

"No," Ezra said, "actually I am not. My work in Jerusalem, for what it was worth, is ended. Tomorrow I return to Sadot Shalom and become a farmer again. I can stay if it is no great inconvenience to you."

"As you wish," Amos said harshly.

He turned from the reproving frown in Mazal's eyes. No Yemenite would talk to a father in such a manner. He knew how they prized respect to one's parents. She had structured her life so that her independence was not forged out of her parents' pain. What must she think of a lover who could not even offer his father courtesy, hospitality? But neither did most Yemenite women sleep with men who were not their husbands in rented student quarters with whitewashed walls, he added mentally, catapulting his anger against her. Instantly the cruelty and treachery of his thought shamed him, and to make amends he smiled at his father.

"Please stay," he said. "We will be glad to have you."

But Mazal turned away, her eyes downcast, as though she had discerned his thoughts. He felt a searing anger at Ezra, who had always come between him and the things he loved.

"Excuse me," he said, and went into the bathroom to wash the Jerusalem dust from his hands and face. Through the closed door, above the splash of the water, he heard his father and Mazal talking softly. Surely he had lived this moment before—the rise and fall of his father's voice and that of a woman, heard through a partition. He recognized the timbre of their tone, but as before the words were lost to him. Slowly, he dried his face with a linen towel to which the lemon scent of Mazal's shampoo adhered—a sad and lingering fragrance.

They did not eat on the balcony that night. There was not enough room for three. Instead they gathered about the small table and ate the lamb dish in the light of the brass lamp which the metalsmith had polished for his daughter's friend. Ezra commented on the workmanship, and Mazal told him about her father who prayed twice daily at the Western Wall.

"And on the ninth day of Av, the anniversary of the temple's destruction, he goes there and reads the book of

Lamentations all through the night—reads and weeps,'' she added musingly.

"They say that during the night moisture drops from the stones. I remember my grandfather in Kharkov telling me that—he said that the Wall wept with all the tears of the Jews who yearned for the Messiah," Ezra reminisced.

"The stone is porous. The night air creates a condensation. There is no sentiment involved. It is a very real worry for archaeologists. Too much moisture may damage the stones." Amos's voice was curt, didactic, and again Mazal looked at him reprovingly. He was like a petulant child. It was not like him to behave this way.

"I would not worry," Ezra replied calmly. "The Wall has so long endured, and it will endure yet longer. Which reminds me, Amos. I have a gift for you—something I found in the Cairo bazaar where antiquities are sold."

"A gift?" Amos was surprised. His father had returned from his sojourn in America and Europe, from the desert wars, without the smallest souvenir. ("There was a war on. Your father was a soldier. He could not concern himself with buying mementos for children," his Uncle Saul had told Amos. But Ezra Maimon had found the time to buy a doll with real hair for small Elana. The doll had rolled out of his rucksack shrouded in a khaki undershirt. Ezra had carried it with him from New York to Egypt and then to the battlefields of Gaza and Jerusalem, of the Galilee and Damascus. Surely there had been room in the same rucksack for a small curio, an envelope of stamps—anything that might have assured Amos that Ezra Maimon remembered that he had a son as well as a daughter in Palestine.)

"Yes. A gift for you."

His father handed him a long vertical object shrouded in Egyptian newspaper, and a clumsily wrapped package.

"Thank you. Thank you very much." The words of childish gratitude fell shyly from his lips.

He peeled the newspaper off and felt the long hard object beneath it. The wrapping was almost gone. He saw a bit of black metal.

"Careful," Ezra said warningly but his words were too late. Amos had grazed the metal blade of the dagger and a jagged thread of blood trailed angry scarlet across his palm.

"Amos! Let me," Mazal cried and hurried to his side, holding a cloth.

"No. It's nothing," he said angrily.

He was not a small boy to be fussed over. He seized the cloth and wound it around his hand until the blood was stanched. Then he studied his father's gift. He admired the curved hilt of the handle, the heaviness of the blade. It was decidedly authentic. He had seen one like it in the Archaeological Institute's collection of ancient weapons. He held it up, felt its weight. Blood was no stranger to this blade. Men's hearts had been pierced by the sharp death-colored point. In fierce and distant times a man's head might have been balanced on the dagger and carried aloft by a Saracen warrior, a crusading knight.

"It's an amazing find," he said appreciatively. "It is pre-Christian, I am sure. I must show it to Professor Amitai."

"It pleases you then?" Ezra asked, and Amos heard the note of relief in his voice.

"Yes. Very much. I am grateful to you." His gratitude was sincere now, his voice appreciative. The gift was his father's long-withheld recognition of his calling, his vocation.

Mazal made strong Turkish coffee and they sipped it slowly from tiny golden cups. These too she had unearthed in the Arab market.

"It is getting late," she said when their cups were empty, and the flame beneath the petiliya glowed blue. "I must go home."

Amos stared at her in surprise. She seldom left so early. But then of course she would not want Ezra to realize that she was in the habit of staying. It was wise of her. The cut on his hand smarted and he regretted now that he had not allowed her to dress it with antiseptic.

"Then I must see you home," Ezra said, rising also.

"Thank you." She did not protest his kindness; she made no objection to his offer.

"I will go too," Amos said.

"Don't be foolish, Amos," Mazal interposed. "You know you are tired after your field trip and you must see to your hand. It must not get infected."

"And I am leaving in any case," Ezra added.

Amos did not protest further.

"Will I see you again, Abba?" he asked. "I know that you must be in a great hurry to return to Sadot Shalom."

"I think perhaps I will stay in Jerusalem a bit longer," Ezra replied. "Your sister will be glad of a few more days on the kibbutz, and I was thinking tonight as I walked here that it has been many years since I had a holiday. I will give myself one now and stay on for a few days. I have not yet seen the new site for the Hebrew University on Mount Scopus. And there are other places I want to visit. I know that you are very busy, but perhaps Mazal can spare me some time."

"I have planned some sketching trips this week." Her voice was very soft, breathless and shy. "If Ezra Maimon wishes to join me I should be pleased."

"Wonderful. We will make arrangements. Take care of your hand, Amos. Your Uncle Langerfeld expects you for Sabbath dinner tomorrow night. I will see you then." He was in command, making arrangements, giving directions. Amos's face grew set, his body became rigid.

Mazal's hand flew up to touch his cheek in farewell. It rested there for a moment, her fingers splayed, like the wing of a frightened bird.

"Good night, Amos."

They were gone. The heavy door slammed behind them; he heard the sound of their voices as they walked together down the stone steps past the cactus plant. He had forgotten to look inside the planter for messages. It did not matter. Mazal laughed. His father's voice was a soft rumble.

Amos rinsed the coffee cups and bent to pluck up the scattered rose petals. They were brown about the edges and lay limp in his hand. The cut throbbed and he washed it carefully, glad that he had the excuse of the pain for the tears that suddenly and inexplicably burned his eyes. It was only the next day that he unwrapped the second package and found the winged cup from Gallipoli.

Chapter 27

Ezra and Mazal met early the next morning. They were both possessed of a holiday mood, a determined gaiety which gave a spring to their step and an ease to their talk. She wore a long black abayah which she had embroidered with her own designs—silver and gold rickrack edges through which scarlet birds cavorted amid green satin grass. Long silver filigreed earrings which matched her heavy necklace dangled from delicate lobes, and her dark hair was coiled about her head in a single braid. She carried her sketchbook and her pencils in a burlap bag, as well as a straw basket laden with carefully wrapped food.

"Your necklace is beautiful," he said as he relieved her of the basket. He himself carried nothing but two canteens, his map case, and his compass. They had decided, the night before, to hike through the Valley of Kidron, and he noted with approval that the tips of sturdy hiking boots peeped out from beneath her long gauzy dark skirt.

"I made the necklace and the earrings myself," she said.

"Remarkable."

"No. I have watched my father work since I was a small girl in Saana. I learned from him. And you know, Jews are coming into Palestine from all the countries of the world. They bring their crafts with them. I think we must organize such skills and talents. We have weavers, metalsmiths, wood carvers. The Bukharians loom the most beautiful rugs. Just last week I met a ceramacist from Aleppo. He showed me the wonderful work he does in Damascene glazes. All this must not be lost."

"But how is it to be preserved?" Ezra asked. He had recognized the passion in her voice but knew that the children of new immigrants were often more interested in building new lives on the land than in perpetuating the ancient crafts of their people.

"We can set up workshops where the old teach the young. We can market the work and sell it all over the world. I listen to Amos and his friends discuss the economic future of the Jewish community of Palestine. They speak of agriculture, of import and export, of citrus and copper. They are clever men, academicians. They understand economics. But they do not understand that handiwork can be an important export—that batik wall hangings made in Jerusalem can hang in dining rooms in New York and Paris and that these French and American collectors will pay us in dollars and francs." There was quiet authority in her voice. She had thought everything through. "Our social thinkers speak of agricultural and industrial collectives. Why not an artistic collective? If craftsmen and artists all over the country worked together we could form an industry that would sustain us and bring foreign currency into the country."

"I think you are right," he said. "But how can it be accomplished?"

"Oh, I have already begun," she replied. "I work with some friends, and my friends have friends. Soon we will open a small gallery in Jerusalem and then another in Tel Aviv. I want to visit the Arab villages in the Galilee. The Arabs too will belong to our collective. They work in metal and clay; they do wonderful embroidery. Why shouldn't the world know about their skill, and why shouldn't their skill earn them some money?"

"You are so small and your dreams are so large," he said, smiling down at her.

"They are not merely dreams."

"I know."

He, after all, had also been a dreamer, and Sadot Shalom had emerged from his reverie. He for one did not doubt the efficacy of fantasy. They walked on in silence, relishing the stillness of the day, the muted calls of the low-flying birds winging southward to the undulating desert and the sudden piercing sweetness of an Arab shepherd boy's reed pipe filling the air with melancholy melody.

They passed the corner of the city wall called the Tower of the Storks. He looked up but there was no sign of the graceful long-legged birds who sometimes rested there on the trek to the sea.

"Storks often fly over Sadot Shalom," he told her. "When Amos was a boy, he and his friend Achmed found a stork fledgling with a broken wing. Nechama, my wife, helped them to care for it till the wing mended."

"And then it flew away?" she asked and wondered why she felt wounded because he had mentioned his wife, the pale woman who stared out at her from the framed photo on Amos's desk.

"We released it, and it flew away. A wild bird cannot be kept on a farm. It would be cruel. Each animal has its own natural habitat."

"Yes. Just as each man has his own course, his own inclination," she said. "But each man must find it for himself."

He looked at her and wondered if there was a veiled accusation in her words. Was she speaking on Amos's behalf? Was she saying, 'Farmer, let your son be a scholar'? But her gaze was guileless and untroubled, and she leaned lightly on him for support as they crossed the bridge that spanned the valley.

"My family," she said, "think that my natural habitat must not be dissimilar from their own. They want me to live as they do. They should like me to marry and settle near them in Jerusalem and hurry to my mother's house each Friday to help prepare the Sabbath meal."

She was thinking of herself then, he realized with relief.

"It is a weakness of parents," he said. "My father's dearest wish was that I should obtain the university degree he was denied. But ever since we came to the land I had wanted to farm. I love the Galilee."

"Where storks fly free," she said and smiled.

"Yes. Where storks fly free."

She stumbled then, and he reached out again to steady her, taking her arm. Again, he felt the wondrous fragility of her tiny bones and the softness of her flesh between his fingers. A smile played at her lips.

"I have formed the habit of relying on you to steady me," she said.

"It is a pleasant habit," he replied and took her hand in his own. "The road is rocky here." He held her fingers lightly, as he often held Elana's small hand when they walked through the hills near Sadot Shalom in search of wild flowers and berries. But Elana's fingers did not tremble as Mazal's did now, nor did their tips burn with a sweet and mysterious heat.

They continued on past Mary's Tomb to the foot of the Mount of Olives where they rested beneath the intricately twisted branches of a dwarfed olive tree that guarded the entrance to the Garden of Gethsemane. A group of Franciscan friars drifted by in melancholy procession, making their way barefoot through the rock-strewn fields to the small church of Dominus Flevit. Their leader carried a silver monstrance, and the robed friars chanted softly as they followed him. Their soutanes trailed the ground and created clouds of dust that settled on the pale verdure of the cactus spikes.

"It must be wonderful," Ezra said, "to be able to believe so deeply."

She heard again the strain of sadness in his voice and sensed anew the shadow of loss that trailed him.

"There are many different ways of believing," she replied softly. "My father believes in the power of God. He has told me that he feels that power when he touches the stones of the Wall as he prays. I too believe that there is a source for all the beauty that is ours and that when we work to protect and produce that beauty, we are, in our own way, doing God's work. Sometimes when I draw and see a new design emerge or form a new pattern with thread or metal, I feel as my father must feel when he prays or, perhaps, as you must feel when your grain field is ready for harvest."

"Yes." Her insight took him unawares. "I believe. I believe in the land. I believe in Sadot Shalom."

"I think Amos must feel that way about his work," she added.

"Yes. I should not be surprised if Amos shares that feeling," he agreed.

She bent then to shift her bag from one hand to the other, gently releasing her fingers from his grasp as though she had remembered suddenly who she was and where she was going.

They continued on through the Arab village of Silwan, where barefoot urchins darted out of the crouching mud huts and thrust outstretched hands at them. The children plucked at Mazal's skirt and tugged at the basket of food.

"I carry. Give me the basket. I strong. I help."

A small girl, Elana's age perhaps, carried an infant in her arms. Mazal took a coin from her pocket and gave it to the girl, who hurried away, staggering in her haste beneath the weight of the infant.

"*Yaala* geveret, *Yaala* adon," the other children screamed indignantly, and Ezra distributed a handful of coins to them.

"The adon is kind. Allah will bless the adon. He will live and prosper," they shouted. "We will take the adon to the graves of our ancestors."

The children danced before them in wild procession and led them to the necropolis of David's city. Mazal and Ezra stared up at the graves carved into the face of the cliff. Sheep and goats bleated loudly, mournfully, within the rock enclosures which the villagers used now as cattle pens.

"See. That is the tomb of the pharaoh's daughter," the tallest boy said and pointed to an elaborate stone monolith.

"She was one of Solomon's wives," Mazal added.

"Interesting. How did you know that?" Ezra asked.

"Amos told me."

"You have been here with him?"

"Yes. I have been here with him."

She determined then to answer truthfully any question he might ask. She would tell him (if he asked) that she was his son's friend, that she had cared for him deeply and had slept with him on the narrow bed in the whitewashed room that looked out on the walls of the Old City. She would tell him how it was for her with Amos, how loneliness and friendship and sweet tenderness had braided themselves into a single bond that tied her to the golden-haired young man who sometimes wept in his sleep. She would explain but she would not apologize. But Ezra Maimon asked no questions, and they continued on their way wrapped in the easy silence of those who do not fear their thoughts.

They ate their lunch at Absalom's Tower, leaning back

against the pocked and pitted column. The sculpted stone was
cool against their backs, and they rested their feet on the
loose boulders that littered the ground beneath the cone-topped
pillar which David's son had built for himself in the dale that
belonged to the king. A herd of sheep, their wool thick and
matted upon their clumsy fattened bodies, grazed leisurely
beneath the column. Across the glen their Arab shepherds,
wearing brightly striped robes, their heads covered with
kaffiyehs that fell to their waists, sat languidly in the shade of
a small stone enclave.

Ezra's own hunger surprised him. He remembered suddenly how after a long hike with Avremel he had popped a
hard-boiled egg whole into his mouth. There was a special
taste to food eaten out of doors after a long walk. She
watched with pleasure as he ate the cold ground lamb wrapped
in grape leaves, the pale green wands of thinly sliced cucum-
ber, the tomatoes and radishes she had cut into the shape of
petaled flowers. She would turn anything she touched into a
work of art, he thought, and smiled approvingly at her. She
lowered her eyes with the swift shyness of a child caught out
in a secret act of whimsey.

"May I have some water, please," she asked.

He drank first and passed the canteen to her. She did not
wipe the rim but drank directly and handed it back to him. He
drank yet again, imagining he could taste her mouth, sweet
against the metal. She peeled the cactus fruit, and they shared
the pink flesh that hid delicately beneath the spiked skin.
Juice trailed from her lips in thread-thin rivulets, and he
resisted the impulse to wipe them away.

She stood and studied the tower, eyes narrowed, pencil
poised above her pad. She noted that the columns that supported its rectangular base were cracked and scarred with
jagged crevices.

"They say that in ancient days travelers would stone the
tower to show their contempt for faithless sons," Ezra said.

"Foolish people," she observed. "They should have realized that men must be faithful only to themselves. Not to their
fathers."

"Nor to their sons," he added.

"Nor to their sons," she echoed, and the seriousness of her
voice matched his own.

She began to draw, moving her pencil slowly. The tower

rose to a decorative escarpment and then assumed a rounded shape, peaking to a concave cone top. At each level, thinly leafed bushes thrust their way through the boulders, and the sunlight pierced the translucent greenery with splinters of light. A young tree grew near the tower's peak, oddly rooted in the sparse soil wedged between tiers of masonry. Birds had nested in the outflung branches on which young leaves trembled. Ezra and Mazal watched the winged families circle their arboreal home, their dark wings flashing through the clear blue Judean sky. Could they be hummingbirds, he wondered, and strained to see them more clearly but, as though conscious of his gaze, they hid themselves amid the rock.

"It is strange how things grow in the most unlikely places," she said. "How can trees and grass take root in stone?"

"We cannot always predict how and why things grow," he replied. He was a farmer but he could not explain all the mysteries of the earth. Grain did not grow as he had planned. Young trees planted in sun-streaked orchards were barren and the sweetest fruit on his land came from a dwarfed plum tree that clung to shadow.

"I know." Her acknowledgment was weighted with sadness. She grieved for tender bits of greenery that grew stubbornly in rockbound earth, for sons who betrayed their fathers and for fathers who betrayed their sons. Their lives were governed by uncertainty. They stood helpless, startled by sudden beauty, wounded by sudden loss.

She turned again to her drawing and he took off his jacket, bunched it into a pillow, and slept in the long velvet column of shade cast by Absalom's Tower. When he awakened she was sitting beside him, her pencil flying across the paper, and he saw that she had drawn him in profile. He recognized the slope of his cheek, the square notch of his chin, the sleepbound smile of his full lips.

"It's not fair to draw a sleeping man," he said, and she blushed and covered the drawing with her upturned palm on which the small white scar smiled. "Let me see." He reached for the pad.

"No!" she pulled away from him and leaped to her feet.

"But I have the right."

He too rose and moved toward her, his hand outstretched.

"No." Anger and laughter mingled in her voice. She ran away, dashing from one slab of columned shade to another.

He followed after her, and they circled the tower in a wild playful game of tag which the grazing sheep watched with mournful eyes. The Arab shepherds stared after them and raised their eyebrows. Crazy Jews, running after each other during these hours of harshest sunlight. What did they want in the land that was not theirs? *Insh'Allah*. Allah must know.

"Aha. I have you now." Ezra seized her wrist as they rounded a corner. Panting and laughing, she leaned against the stone balustrade, pinioned in his grasp. The pad fluttered to the ground but he did not bend to pluck it up nor did he release her. She did not struggle.

"Mazal." He breathed her name into her mouth.

"Ezra." She mouthed his name for the first time. He was not Amos's father now. He was Ezra. Strong powerful Ezra who held her captive but would let her run free. His fingers released her wrist, and his arms encircled her body. He kissed her and felt her tremble. He held her all the more tightly. He was the rock against which all the waves of her fear and longing would break.

"Don't be frightened," he whispered.

She recognized the authority in his voice and relaxed in his arms, her lips parted and her face wet with tears.

"We do not know each other," she said helplessly. "We have only just met."

"We have always known each other."

"Yes. Always."

She surrendered then to the truth, surrendered to the tenderness of his touch, the sheltering warmth of his body pressed against her own, the sweeping engulfing embrace she had sought for so long.

"There is Amos," she said, and her voice broke with pity for the son and love for the father. She would always stand between them.

"I know about Amos." His voice was husky with sorrow yet firm. He had the strength to accept that which he could not change.

He took her face into his hands, her small flower face brushed golden by the harsh heat of the desert sun.

"You are so beautiful," he said.

They stood so close that their bodies formed a single shadow that fell between the sunlit columns built by David's favorite, the restless prince who had feared that he would have no son to keep his memory alive and so had named a monument for himself.

Amos dressed carefully for the Friday night dinner with his Langerfeld relatives. It had been a long week and he was glad that it was over, glad that the Sabbath was slowly descending across Jerusalem. The delicious odors of baking *challot*, egg breads, and slowly roasting chickens drifted through Geveret Amitai's kitchen window, and he knew that similar fragrances suffused his aunt's flat. Even now, his Langerfeld grandmother would be sprinkling the braided loaves with poppy seeds, humming as she worked.

Through the arched windows of his room, he could see the men of the Yemin Moshe quarter strolling home from the bathhouse. Each man carried a bouquet of flowers wrapped in yellowing newspaper, and some balanced baskets laden with last-minute purchases for the Sabbath. Yet they did not hurry. The rush of the work week was ended and already, during these last hours of Friday afternoon, they felt the ease of the beginning of the day of rest. Even the donkey that pulled the vegetable seller's cart moved at a slow pace. The city was winding down and within hours all activity would cease. Jerusalem would be immersed in wondrous healing stillness.

Amos too moved more slowly than usual, willing himself into an unnatural calm, a determined relaxation. It would be a good evening, he assured himself, made even better because Mazal would be there. She would meet his family for the first time although he had often invited her to join him for the Friday night dinner at his uncle's apartment.

"My parents would be very upset if I were not at home on Friday night," she had always told him, and he had accepted that explanation as he accepted everything she told him. He knew of her deep attachment to her family and he envied it.

"Difficulties come with closeness," Mazal had told him once, but he had brushed her comment aside. He would not be divested of his fantasies.

Still, he was very pleased that she had accepted his invitation for this evening. He had not seen her at all during the week simply because there had been no time. It had often happened, during the many months of their friendship, that the pressures of his work or hers kept them apart. And this last week had been an extraordinarily busy one for him. A Jewish bibliophile in Russia had managed to smuggle a remarkable collection of incunabula out of Saint Petersburg, and Amos had worked late into the night with Professor Amitai, cataloguing the precious books and manuscripts.

"I was certain these manuscripts were lost to us," the professor had said more than once as they removed the carefully wrapped treasures from the huge wooden cases. The Russian revolution had virtually slammed shut the doors between Russian Jewish scholars and collectors and their colleagues in other countries. Valuable private collections had suddenly been "nationalized" and just as suddenly had inexplicably vanished. Letters of query went unanswered or were returned with incomprehensible forms.

"You see why we must have a Jewish national library—a university." Professor Amitai insisted, his hands trembling as he caressed an original tractate by Maimonides. "There must be a central repository for Jewish scholarship, Jewish learning."

"Soon," Amos said. "Soon." He had the optimism of those who had been born in the country, and besides, he had passed Mount Scopus that very morning and paused long enough to view the progress of the Hebrew University and library under construction there. Only four short years had passed since General Allenby had sat on the slopes of the gentle mount and listened to the speeches of dedication. What was it Bialik had said—a hillside sanctified by learning? Within that short period, buildings had taken shape—an amphitheater, a hospital, a library. Amos, working beside the professor in the dank basement of Terra Sancta, where they had been lucky enough to find room for the Russian collection, thought that the next generation of scholars would select their books from the carefully built shelves and do their research in the wide-windowed room now being built high above the ancient city. But he did not envy them. His own work exhilarated him, filled him with a mute excitement.

"I did not disturb your plans for the week?" the professor had asked.

"No. I made arrangements," Amos assured him.

He had left a message for Mazal in the stone urn explaining that he would be working late into the night and asking her, yet again, if she would join him at his uncle's home for the Sabbath meal. They had often used the stone cactus planter as a mailbox, concealing their messages beneath the plant's thorny arms. Thus they arranged to meet at a cafe or at a concert or explained to each other why they could not meet at all. Mazal had received his message and answered with a note of her own accepting his invitation to the Friday night dinner. But that had been at the very beginning of the week of his father's visit, perhaps the very day she had invited Ezra Maimon to join her on her sketching trip. Where had they gone that day, Amos wondered. Perhaps to Ein Karem. Perhaps to Abu Tor. It did not matter. It was over—past and done with. Courtesy exchanged, duty fulfilled.

He had sent a similar message of explanation to his father, but he admitted to himself that he felt a subtle satisfaction that his father's rare visit to Jerusalem occurred during a week when Amos had not a minute to spare. It had, after all, been years since Ezra Maimon had found a minute to spare for his son.

Amos, during the week, had rebuked himself for the strange reaction he had had upon seeing Mazal and his father together that first evening. He had ridiculed himself for imagining, even for a moment, that there could be any feeling between them. His father was almost twice Mazal's age. They came from different worlds. What did Ezra Maimon know of the life of Jerusalem's student community? He was a middle-aged farmer who had been briefly swept up by the rush of history. Mazal was young, seething with energy and dreams. She had volunteered to spend time with Ezra because she was faithful to the patterns of her culture. She respected her elders. She would be kind to Ezra Maimon because he was Amos's father.

All this Amos had repeated to himself yet again as he had walked toward his room through the stillness of the Jerusalem streets. Briefly now, he stood naked in the half-darkness of the shuttered windows and felt the lithe strength of his slender body. He remembered then the revulsion he had felt when he first saw the scar on his father's knee, left by the frantic British medic on Gallipoli who had so hastily removed the Turkish shrapnel. Suddenly pity for his father washed over him, cleansing him of unarticulated resentment. The time had come to set grievances aside. Ezra Maimon was a man who had passed his youth and carried the scars of war. He, Amos, was young. His body pulsated with energy and expectation, and his life stretched before him, promising excitement and discovery.

"You have the seeds of greatness, Amos," Professor Amitai had told him, and the words had not embarrassed either the student or the teacher. They acknowledged the mystery of Amos's gifts and the great responsibility that came with them. "You will study abroad," the professor continued. "We will arrange scholarships, travel grants. And then you will return here to work for the Hebrew University, for the Jewish National Library."

Amos accepted his mentor's blueprint for his life. He knew that he had all but exhausted the academic resources of Jerusalem and that soon he would have to make a decision about continuing his studies abroad. He weighed the advantages of Göttingen against those of Oxford and Columbia. He compared libraries and doctoral programs. He examined catalogues and publications. Yet ultimately, the decision would rest with Mazal. Where was there a school of design which would give her the unique training she needed? Where could she get the kind of help she would need to organize the network of craft workshops she envisaged? They had never talked about it but she knew that he would have to leave the country, and he assumed that she also knew he would not leave without her.

He had known Mazal for only a few months yet she had left her mark everywhere on his life. Her touch was in every corner of this room, in the woven fabrics and the dull gleam of metal objects. Her scent clung to his linens. He stood on his narrow balcony and watched the sun drown in rushing waves of mauves and pinks; he imagined Mazal's gold-flecked eyes glinting with wonder as she watched the liquid rainbow-colored sky. He stretched toward her in the night and spoke softly to her although he knew she could not hear him. He loved her. He could not leave her. It had been difficult enough to be away from her during the long work-filled week. Still, the week was over and soon, very soon he would see her.

It would be a festive evening, he thought excitedly. He would introduce Mazal not only to his mother's family but to his Uncle David and his Aunt Chania, who were in Jerusalem on kibbutz business. They too would be guests at the Langerfelds' this Sabbath eve. His family would like her, he knew. It would not matter to them that Mazal was a few years older than he was or that she came from a Yemenite family. Only his Grandmother Rivka harbored any prejudice against the dark-skinned Oriental Jews, and no one paid any attention to his poor grandmother these days. Much of the time she imagined herself the hostess of a Kharkov salon. She spoke in a breathless amalgam of French and literary Hebrew, alternately quoting obscure poets and reciting from her own incomprehensible verses.

"My mother's tragedy is a simple one," Ezra had once observed wryly. "She came to Palestine to watch oranges grow golden in the sunlight but no one ever told her that it was necessary to spread manure on the earth beneath them."

Amos himself had great patience with his grandmother, and he listened for hours to her rambling while his grandfather watched them with a benevolent eye and pressed him for information about his studies. Had Amos considered doing his graduate work at the Sorbonne? Did he know that Ezra Maimon had been accepted as a student at the Sorbonne? He had not known.

"You are everything we expected your father to be," Yehuda Maimon had added sadly, and Amos thought bitterly that he was everything his father had not expected him to be. His grandparents offered him the approval and encouragement which his father had always denied him. Yes, for Amos's sake, for the scholar grandson who would realize her dreams, his grandmother would approve of Mazal.

He hurried now, swiftly buttoning the light blue cotton shirt which Mazal insisted became him better than the plain white shirts he had once worn. The blue looked well with the khaki trousers she had bought him in the supply store patronized by the British soldiers.

"Just because you are a scholar you needn't dress like an old man," she said severely.

He had been pleased to allow her to select his clothing. It had, after all, been years since anyone had picked out a singlet or a pair of trousers for him. Not since Nechama had died and his childhood had ended in suddeness and sorrow. Sadness jabbed him then and briefly, as he ran a wet comb through his thick golden hair, he allowed himself to feel pity for the orphaned and abandoned boy he had been. But all that was changed now and Mazal, lovely, tiny Mazal, had changed it. He was seized by a sudden urgency. She was perhaps already waiting for him in his aunt's living room, alone, shy, and vulnerable. He imagined her listening for his step. He must not be late. He plucked up the bunch of lilacs he had brought as his Sabbath gift and hurried out, slamming the door behind him and racing down the steps, past the small landing where the stone planter stood. He remembered, when he reached the next road, that he had not checked behind the cactus plant for a message. But there would be no message. There was no need for one. He was on his way to meet her—his lovely love, his Sabbath queen.

Chapter 28

Mazal had made a new dress especially for that evening, using the golden cloth woven in Saana which she had saved for so many years. It had a metallic sheen that matched her eyes and coaxed forth the secret hint of amber in her dusky skin. She stayed up late into the night to finish it, and she had no regrets as she studied herself in the long mirror. The neckline rose in a rounded curve from her breasts and softly encircled her graceful neck. The skirt was full and loosely pleated, hugging her waist and billowing about her legs. She had saved a strand of fabric for a band that crowned her hair, which she wore loose tonight, so that it fell like a dark velvet cape across her golden shoulders.

She had not planned to wear any jewelry but before she left her parents' house her mother had motioned her to wait and had given her the small pendant, a golden filigreed hand in which a smoky topaz teardrop glinted. Her father had crafted it on the day of her birth. It was an amulet, a hand to ward off the evil eye, and only now did they offer it to her and watch approvingly as it rested at last on her rose-gold skin.

"You look beautiful, my daughter," the metalsmith said.

He did not ask her why she did not remain at home to share

the Sabbath meal with her own family. She had never before left them on this night, and so he knew that her reason must be a powerful one which she would share with them in time. The metalsmith had faith. The Lord had blessed him with good children, blessed be the name of the Lord. And she, Mazal, their firstborn, named for beneficence, was the best and the most beautiful of his children. God would forgive him for favoring her as He had forgiven Jacob for loving Joseph the best. She kissed them before she left, an odd gesture because they were a family who took their love for granted and seldom demonstrated it. Her father lifted his fingers above her head and offered her the Sabbath blessing.

"Go in peace, my daughter," he said.

She walked slowly through the quiet streets, relishing the silence that had overtaken the city. Men on their way to evening prayers passed her and murmured gentle greetings. In her golden dress, she seemed to them an apparition of Sabbath royalty, the Sabbath queen herself, dark and comely, aglow against the muted twilight. One man looked furtively back, as though to assure himself that he had not imagined the tiny dark-haired woman who glided down the dusk-veiled street.

As she walked, Mazal glimpsed the quivering flames of newly lit candles through windows. Women stood on their balconies at this hour, silhouetted against the growing darkness. They were, for a brief moment, wondrously suspended in time. The worries and work of the week had passed and they surrendered themselves to peace and rest. The quarrels of children were stilled, and in dimly lit kitchens fragrant soups simmered and loaves of braided bread cooled. The women watched Mazal and smiled in recognition, as though they had suddenly remembered a wonderful dream, long since forgotten, its brightness obscured through passing years by crying children and dirt-streaked kitchen floors.

She hurried now as she approached the streets of the newly built section of the city where the European Jews had built their spacious stone houses with high ceilings and many-windowed rooms. She smiled at the thought that each group who came to Palestine struggled to rebuild the world left behind in a distant land. Her family lived among their Yemenite kinfolk in a warren of lanes and alleyways not unlike the dwelling place they had left behind in Saana. And here, in this newly built quarter which they called Rehavia, the Jews of Germany and Poland were building homes which would accommodate their crystal chandeliers, their heavy mahogany dining tables and damask-covered sofas.

Daniel Langerfeld and his family lived in such a flat. She sniffed the newness of the building as she mounted the stairs. Her heart beat rapidly. She hoped that Ezra had arrived before her. She hoped that Amos would arrive after her. She would need Ezra's strength, she knew, when she saw Amos's eyes. He would, of course, have read her letter, and he would have had time to consider it, to build toward an understanding of all that she had tried to explain to him on the closely covered pages. Her fingers had grown cramped with writing. There had been so much to say and so much that she could not say. There was that which he had the right to know and that which would remain her secret forever. More than once she had ripped a covered page in half and begun again. Dear Amos. Poor Amos. Beloved friend. Dear poor Amos.

"Wouldn't it be better to talk to him?" Ezra had asked.

It would have been better, she agreed, but it had not been possible. There had been no time. She had found Amos's note about the Russian collection the evening she returned from her walk with Ezra to Absalom's Tower. The relief she had felt when she read that he would not be able to see her all that week shamed her, but still it was there. A reprieve had been granted. Time. Freedom. Hours with Ezra and hours alone. She wrote Amos in reply that she would see him Friday night. She began work on her golden dress. The week belonged to her, to them.

She walked with Ezra through the bazaars of Jerusalem, down the street of the smiths and past the weavers' stalls.

"My father does such work," she told him as they watched a Bukharian craftsman in a bright green gown solder a gold chain.

They sat beneath the olive trees in the Valley of the Cross and watched the sun disappear behind the red roof of the Greek church. She walked with him through Meah Shaarim, the district of a hundred gates where the orthodox lived out their meager earthly lives as they waited for the Messiah. They stared into the courtyards where bewigged women draped lines with laundry and small girls in thick stockings and dark dresses crooned to infants. The air reverberated with the voices of men and boys chanting talmudic passages.

"My grandfather taught in such a yeshiva," he told her, "and I studied there."

They shared their worlds, crossed mysterious borders into each other's pasts.

He told her of his grandfather's parting gift and how he had purchased Sadot Shalom with the legacy of dollars concealed between the pages of the learned text. She told him of the suitors her parents had invited to meals served on the low table covered with the embroidered cloth of her own sewing. They acknowledged that all that had gone before had been prologue. Their future stretched before them.

They ate skewered kabobs at rough-hewn tables in the shadow of the Mount of Olives and drank arak from tiny red glasses that glowed like coals. The strong liquor burned their throats and they coughed and reddened and laughed. Their hearts pounded, and they hurried from the open-air restaurant to the shade of a cypress grove where they clung together, their lips hungrily meeting, his hands flying across her body, caressing its smallness, its softness. She breathed into the amber shell of his ear. She kissed the pulsating muscle of his arm. She was damp with desire, love-moistened. He was strong with yearning, love-taut. Yet she went home each night to her parents' house, and he slept in the narrow bed that had belonged to his murdered Langerfeld niece. They had the patience of promised lovers. They would be together and never parted. They would wait.

"When will we marry?" he asked.

"Soon."

It was spring now. Before the summer she would wear his marriage ring on her finger. She saw herself walking beside him through the tall wheat of Sadot Shalom, sitting with him beneath the plum trees. He would build a small room so that she would have her own studio. She could do her own work and would travel to the workshops she would establish in Tel Aviv and Jaffa, in the Druse villages and the tiny Arab hamlets.

"Very soon." They had known each other a week but they had known each other a lifetime.

"But I must tell Amos. I must write to him."

She sat at her father's work table and wrote by the liquid

radiance of a single candle. The flame that cast its light across the paper quivered in the slight breeze as she wrote.

"Amos, my friend, my dear . . . I love your father . . ."

She ripped the sheet of paper in half and began again.

"Amos, my dear, I hope you will understand when I tell you . . ."

"Amos, my dear Amos—this is the most difficult letter I have ever written . . ."

But at last the letter was written, her explanations made, her grief unraveled to form sentences. The blue ink was streaked where she had wept as she wrote. She cared so deeply for him. She had, from the first, read the need and unhappiness in his eyes, and because she cared for him she had been moved to comfort him, to offer herself to him, to cover him with her warmth. She had assuaged his loneliness and soothed her own. They had shared so much. They would always be friends. Their friendship was special, bonded as it was in such sweet knowledge of each other. She did not regret anything that had happened between them. She would remember always their moonlit hours in the whitewashed room. But it was his father she loved. She loved Ezra Maimon with the fullness of the love that a woman offers a man whose life she would share, whose children she would mother. Amos, one day, would understand this love she and his father had found. She knew that eventually he would understand. She prayed for that understanding. Sadot Shalom was his home. Now it would be her home. "Let us all be happy together, Amos," she wrote and felt the sad futility of her words.

By now he would have read the letter, waiting for him behind the cactus plant since dawn. He would know. If he came to his Uncle Langerfeld's tonight it would be because even if he could not accept her explanations, even if he could not yet forgive her, he accepted the reality of her love for Ezra, the inevitability of their marriage, and he was prepared to live within that reality.

The Langerfelds lived on the third floor of the tall stone building. The heavy oak door was slightly ajar and voices trailed down the stairwell. She recognized Daniel Langerfeld's deep baritone. Although she had never met Amos's family, she had heard his uncle speak. His voice was trained for speaking in resonant tones before Zionist congresses, and above the shouts of diverse opinions at the Jewish Agency.

"Weizmann and Ben Gurion must make peace with each other if the Jewish community is to be united," he said.

Ezra's voice rose in answer and she listened to it with pleasure. Her lover spoke with deliberation of tone, with the careful cadence of a man who chooses his words carefully, with the conscious economy of one who has lived for lengths of days within the confines of his own thoughts. She throbbed with pride.

"We may pay a heavy price for peace. Do we want unity at the expense of loss and impossible compromise? And we have no way of knowing whether the League of Nations will validate the British Mandate and the Balfour Declaration."

"Come. No more politics. It's Shabbat."

The voices of the women were soft. They appeased harsh words with the clink of china, the clatter of silver.

"Chania, please try my eggplant salad."

"Thank you."

They spoke the slightly guttural Hebrew of the European-born, still confusing their tenses after so many years in the country. They could not accustom themselves to a language that has no subjunctive. They came from a world where past and future had always been clearly delineated. They were not like the desert Semites whose yesterdays and tomorrows were curiously intermingled, blended perhaps by the undulating endless stretches of their land. She had babbled in Arabic from childhood yet she would marry a man whose first language had been that of the Jewish enclaves of Eastern Europe. That, she supposed, was the miracle of the idea of Zion, the ingathering and the commingling of the exiles.

"I'll have some eggplant salad, Aunt." Amos's voice. She trembled.

She had been listening for it, there in the shadow of the stairwell. Her heart soared. He had come. He had accepted everything. His presence proved that. She knocked at the half-open door. Daniel Langerfeld opened it, bid her welcome. She looked across the room to the sofa where Ezra and Amos sat side by side, father and son, at peace together this Sabbath eve. It was all right then. It would be all right. There would be friendship between them. Tears of relief burned her eyes, blurred her vision.

Father and son rose together as she entered. Each stared at her through eyes the color of a sun-kissed sea. Ezra's lips curved into a smile of pleasure, of pride. Amos's lips parted in gladness, in unarticulated welcome. But it was Ezra who moved to her side first, who drew her into the room, his large hand encircling her narrow waist, his touch melting her into familiar submission.

"My friends and family." He waved his hand, and the assembled group paused in their exchanges and arguments. Fragments of laughter froze into silence. "I want all of you to meet Mazal Bat Chaim. Mazal and I wish you to know that in a month's time we shall be married, and we will welcome all of you to Sadot Shalom on our wedding day."

There was a swift rush of voices, murmurs of surprise, exclamations of joy. Chania rushed to her brother-in-law's side and kissed him and then kissed the lovely diminutive Yemenite woman who stood beside him. She was so unlike the tall, pale Nechama yet there was something of Nechama about her—in her calm, her poise, her careful measured gaze as she accepted the congratulations of those who had been strangers to her only minutes before. And now at last Elana would have a mother. The vacuum at Sadot Shalom would be filled. The silence of the farmhouse would be shattered.

"Ezra, we are glad for you. We prayed for your happiness." Daniel Langerfeld had loved his sister, and he was glad that her husband and her children would at last have a home again. The Jerusalem gossips had been wrong, then, to have said that the beautiful Yemenite designer was his nephew Amos's mistress. She was, after all, several years older than Amos. And yet their friendship had been fortunate because surely it had been through Amos that Ezra and Mazal had met.

"We are so glad for you." Nechama's gentle mother kissed the tiny woman who would take her daughter's place in Ezra's bed. She noted, with obscure satisfaction, that Nechama's hair had been thicker, her breasts fuller, her gaze more serene. Ezra would not find this young woman as pliant and protective as her lovely, peaceful daughter had been.

"So this is how you proceed with a diplomatic mission," David said, embracing his brother, pummeling Ezra's back. "I admit she is much prettier than that bulldog, Winston Churchill." He lifted Mazal and kissed her on each cheek.

"You must come to Gan Noar. We will have a family reunion—all of us—eh, Amos?"

But Amos did not answer. He remained standing at the edge of the couch, frozen into the posture he had assumed when Mazal entered. Surely he was trapped within the flow of a dream, a mysterious nightmare like the recurring one in which he stood alone, abandoned at the edge of a forbidding waterway. He was abandoned now in this crowded room. Waves of joyous laughter rushed toward him but he was frightened of drowning in a joy that was not his. True, his Uncle David spoke to him but the avuncular question belonged to the dream and thus required no answer. There were no responsibilities in dreams. In nepenthean innocence, dreamers roamed through field and meadow, free of the obligations of fathers and sons. Surely he was dreaming, because it was not possible that his father had told this gathering of relations that he, Ezra Maimon, was to marry Mazal Bat Chaim. It was not possible that she (whose golden body, ribbed with shards of silver moonlight, Amos had watched through hours of darkness) had not protested, had not shouted her denial of Ezra's words. She was his own love, Amos's darling. He had trumpeted his manhood within her body and wept his boyhood against her breasts. Together they had kindled brass lamps in a twilit room and watched the walls of their ancient city vanish into darkness. She could not leave him in such a manner at such a time. She could not leave him for his own father. She could not leave him at all. He would drown within that phantasmal stream of loneliness. Even now the nightmare waters clogged his lungs so that his breath came in tortuous gasps.

His heart tapped out an arrhthymic message of despair. He stared at the lit candles in his aunt's menorah, heard his uncle's voice again.

"Amos, are you all right? Amos, you must congratulate your father."

He looked at her across the room. She stood at his father's side, her eyes liquid with pity, with regret. She held her arms out to him. The golden sleeves fluttered like wings that would enfold him, soothe his sorrow, still his pain.

"Amos," she said softly, pleadingly, and he moved across the room, walking through the waves of laughter, of excited chatter. He was an automaton, numbed and bereft of feeling.

"I congratulate you, Abba," he said and shook Ezra's hand.

How cold the boy's fingers are, Ezra thought, but he could not warm them. Not he. Least of all he.

"I wish you well, Mazal," he added, but he did not move toward her.

It was his Uncle Daniel Langerfeld who moved into her outstretched arms.

"And I know you will be happy," Daniel said.

Yes, they will be happy, Amos thought, and the words seared him. They were already happy. He stared at them as they stood framed in the doorway, his tall bronzed father and tiny honey-skinned Mazal. They would whisper together in the darkness and he would hear their voices through thin-walled rooms. Their laughter would haunt his dreams. Once again his father had snatched away that which was his. He was doubly orphaned. His mother was dead and his father had scorned his life and stolen his love.

"I must go now," he said.

He moved with the trancelike gait of a sleepwalker and was gone from the brightly lit room before they could stop him or shout after him.

"He did not find my letter," Mazal said.

"It would have made no difference."

Ezra's heart quivered with sorrow but nothing could ever make him surrender Mazal. She was his—his life, his love, his bride.

"He will accept it in time," he said.

But his words sounded hollow to his own ears and, although the evening was warm, he felt a slight chill as he and Mazal moved on into the dining room where the family was assembled about the festive table, their glasses raised as Daniel Langerfeld intoned the Sabbath blessing in tremulous voice.

They were married one month later when the sharav wind from the southland breathed heavily on Sadot Shalom. The grape arbor was their marriage canopy and the bright July sunlight danced between the latticed leaves and dappled their upturned faces with circlets of shifting light. Mazal wore the traditional pantaloons and the black and golden gown of the Yemenite bride. Layers of cloth had been wrapped about her slender neck so that it would not be chafed by the masses of necklaces and chains that adorned her. Some were laced with golden filigree and others were simple strands of silver. Some were inset with the dead-eyed precious stones of the desert, smoothly polished, impervious to light. They had been lent to her by friends and relations in keeping with the tradition that every bride must be as beautifully adorned as a queen.

Rings sparkled on her fingers and her head was covered with a pointed hood, woven of the same material as her dress. When Ezra lifted her hand to place the plain gold wedding band on her middle finger, he saw traces of the *hinna*, the henna paste which the Yemenites place on the palms of their bridal couples. The unguent had covered his own hands at the special ceremony two nights before the wedding, when the Yemenites of Jerusalem had gathered to beat their leather drums with joy and to honor the metalsmith's daughter and her farmer husband.

Ezra stood beside his bride wearing an open-necked white shirt and khaki pants, his head covered with the simple knitted skullcap his sister Sara (who knelt now on the cold floors of Polish churches) had fashioned for his bar mitzvah.

He repeated the words of the marriage vow, and Mazal's finger trembled as he slipped the ring on.

"Behold, with this ring thou art consecrated unto me according to the laws of Moses and of Israel."

He folded her hand into his own. The laws of Moses and of Israel had brought them together from distant worlds, here to the bright heat of the Galilee where their lives were linked forevermore.

The Mori, the spiritual leader of the Yemenite community, wrapped in his peacock-blue prayer shawl, intoned the first of the marriage blessings. Reb Langerfeld, in black caftan, chanted the second. The cadences varied, the accents differed, but one by one the seven marriage blessings were offered, now to the melody of the wooden synagogues of Eastern Europe, now to the lilting chant of the houses of prayer of the desert kingdom. But the words were the same, linking the guests, enchanting them with the miracle of their own history. They had been dispersed and they had come together. They had lived disparate lives in scattered lands but now they were one in Zion.

The marriage glass was broken. Ezra's booted foot came down hard on the linen-covered crystal.

"Mazal tov! Mazal tov!"

The shouts of joy rose in fierce crescendo. Rivka Maimon wept. The bride's mother uttered a piercing ululation. The sound ripped from the back of her throat. The Yemenite women beat their leather-covered drums. The guests from Gan Noar played their recorders and accordions. The son of Gedalia the wagoner played on his reed pipe, and the silver-haired wife of the Rishon pharmacist strummed her balalaika.

Mazal's cousins grouped to perform the intricate ancient wedding dance. Saul and David Maimon led a wild hora, Achmed and Saleem danced a debka, and a contingent of Druse villagers did a sword dance. Small Elana was placed on a chair that was lifted high by the cousins and friends who danced about her in a whirling circle. Mazal's uncles linked hands and circled her with rhythmic beat, burning candles balanced on their heads. They careened like spinning tops, and the glowing tapers became flashes of light upon their colorfully embroidered skullcaps.

Long tables had been set out in the orchards and beneath the arbors which Nechama had planted so long ago. They were laden with stuffed fish and roasted chickens, with platters of *humus* and *tehinna*, with stewed meat to be eaten with harsh red horseradish, and servings of lamb and pine nuts wrapped in glistening grape leaves. Glasses overflowed with arak and others were filled with schnapps and with the white wine of Rishon LeZion vintage. Songs were sung in Yiddish and tales were told in Arabic. The small metalsmith who had crossed the desert embraced Yehuda Maimon, the citrus farmer who had crossed the ocean. Mazal's mother, clad in glittering silver smock and embroidered pantaloons, embraced Rivka Maimon, elegant in pale blue silk that matched her faded eyes. They were linked now by ties of marriage. Their generations would be linked by ties of blood.

Amos Maimon alone was a silent guest. He had arrived at his childhood home too late to witness the marriage ceremony and he hovered at the edge of the gaiety. He danced with his small sister and with his uncles and then he whirled in a wild dance of his own, sinking closer and closer to the ground, his knees thrusting his legs forward so that he was almost level with the earth. Still, he circled, dancing faster and faster, madly kicking to the singing and clapping of the encircling celebrants. Sweat poured in rivulets down his face and his heart beat with frightening wildness.

"*Yechi* Amos," his uncles called in delight, but Ezra and
Mazal watched him with a grave-eyed gaze. They were not
deceived. Still, he had come, and they took mute comfort
from his presence. Bridges might yet be built between them;
given time, the emotional wasteland might be cleared. They
were heartened when he sat beside them with Elana on his lap
for the grace after the meal. They were a family, sitting
together in prayer as the long mauve evening shadows slatted
the sunlight and the wedding day came to an end. Slowly, the
guests departed, entering wagons and diligences for the journeys
to Tel Aviv and Jerusalem, to Gan Noar and Rishon LeZion.

Elana went with Chania and David to Gan Noar. She
would be gone for only a few days but small urgencies
delayed her departure. She said a tremulous farewell to each
of her three goats, and twice she checked the chicken run to
make sure that enough food was scattered. She hugged Ezra
and Amos tightly and planted a shy kiss on Mazal's cheek.
Her father's new wife smelled of lemon and lilac and of the
dusky scent that emanated from the small bushes which the
Yemenite women had carried up to Sadot Shalom. The flowers of the bushes were used for the making of incense and
unguents, she knew, and she understood that the scent belonged
to the magic and mystery that had drawn her father to Mazal.
One day she too would possess such secrets.

"Goodbye, Achmed," she called. "Do not stake the tomatoes until I return."

She threw her arms about the Arab youth's neck, ignoring
her aunt who plucked nervously at her sleeve.

"Everyone is waiting, Elana. We must go," Chania said
insistently.

Then they were off, and although Ezra watched the kibbutz
wagon disappear, Elana did not turn around. He walked
slowly back to the house.

Mazal turned to Amos, vague worry shadowing her golden
eyes.

"Is there always such intimacy between her and Achmed?"
she asked.

"Achmed is like a member of our family," Amos replied.
"We grew up as brothers. He thinks of Elana as a small
sister."

"Yes. I remember. You told me," she said.

"*Do* you remember?"

His voice was thin. He had told her about Achmed on a
night when watchtowers burned on the walls of the Old City.
They had stood naked together at the arched window of his
room and watched the flames. She had told him then about
the low-burning desert fires of her childhood, and he had told
her how he and Achmed burned the hay ricks at harvest's
end. But that night was consigned to forbidden memory. She
was his father's wife now, his mistress become his mother.

"Amos, I am glad you stayed."

Ezra approached them, carrying a small tray on which three
tiny crystal glasses filled with amber liquor were balanced.
(In his dream, Amos remembered, his father offered him
water from a crystal pitcher. He longed for that water now but
would sip liquor that would burn his throat.)

They carried their drinks to the low bench that Ezra had
placed beneath the avocado tree. Mazal, freed of her bridal
finery, perched on the stump of the fig tree. She wore a loose
gown of the gauzelike cotton which the Arabs used to make
their kaffiyehs. It occurred to both father and son that the
liquid in her glass matched the sheen of her skin.

"What kind of tree was this?" she asked, passing her hand
across the stump to which a fruity fragrance clung.

"It was a fig tree," Amos replied. "But it did not give
enough shade."

He did not look at his father, who drained his glass but
made no reply. Ezra knew that his son would keep a solemn
accounting of all the losses he had suffered at Ezra's hands—
of fallen trees and plundered love. There were indelible
etchmarks against debts which could never be cancelled.

"I want to tell you that I am going away," Amos said. "I
will be at Oxford for a year, and then I will go to New York
and complete my doctorate at Columbia."

"Amos, that is marvelous." Pride and relief mingled in
Mazal's voice. This was what they needed, the three of
them—time and distance.

"You will need money, Amos," Ezra said. *Please let me
help you*, he thought. *Please take what I can give*.

"No. Or at least not very much. I have been granted
generous fellowships and there is our family in New York."

"Yes, of course." Amos would, in turn, watch the dying
sun stain the Palisades and come to know his cousins, includ-

ing the son of Alex and Sonia, the small blond boy born while Ezra Maimon fought in the barren stretches of Gaza.

"When do you leave?" Ezra asked.

"Within a few days' time. I am on my way to Haifa to wait for my ship."

"Go in peace, then," Ezra said.

He longed to open his arms to his son, to press his head against his breast, but instead he extended his hand and was pleased that Amos took it and allowed his fingers to rest briefly on his father's palm. Mazal placed her hand across their own, and they looked down at her fingers stained ocher with the unguent of fertility.

One year later, on a day when the newly grown wheat covered the fields of Sadot Shalom in waves of gold and pearl-white grapes glowed against dark-leafed vines, Mazal Maimon was delivered of her first child. It was an easy birth, and the infant was a perfectly formed little girl. They named her Balfouria because she was born on the day the League of Nations confirmed the British Mandate and Lord Balfour's dream trembled on the edge of realization.

"Yes. Balfouria," Ezra said dreamily. "A new name for a new time."

He carried his newborn daughter to the window that overlooked sweep of meadow and hill, orchard and vineyard.

"Look," he said gently, "these are your fields of peace."

Bestsellers from Berkley
The books you've been hearing
about—and want to read